MISS PRIM'S GREEK ISLAND FLING

MICHELLE DOUGLAS

DOUBLE DUTY FOR THE COWBOY

BRENDA HARLEN

MILLS & BOON

First Published in Great Britain 2019
by Mills & Boon, an imprint of HarperCollinsPublishers,
1 London Bridge Street, London, SE1 9GF

Miss Prim's Greek Island Fling © 2019 Michelle Douglas
Double Duty for the Cowboy © 2019 Brenda Harlen

ISBN: 978-0-263-27238-3

0519

MIX
Paper from
responsible sources
FSC™ C007454

FSC
www.fsc.org

This book is produced from independently certified FSC™
paper to ensure responsible forest management.

For more information visit: www.harpercollins.co.uk/green

Printed and bound in Spain
by CPI, Barcelona

MISS PRIM'S GREEK ISLAND FLING

MICHELLE DOUGLAS

To Pam, who is always happy to share a bottle of red
and to talk into the wee small hours of the night.

CHAPTER ONE

IT WAS THE sound of shattering glass that woke her.

Audra shot bolt upright in bed, heart pounding, praying that the sound had been a part of one of her frequent nightmares, but knowing deep down in her bones—in all the places where she knew such things were real—that it wasn't.

A thump followed. Something heavy being dropped to the floor. And then a low, jeering voice. The sound of cupboard doors opening and closing.

She'd locked all the doors and windows downstairs! She'd been hyper-vigilant about such things ever since she'd arrived two days ago. She glanced at her bedroom window, at the curtain moving slowly on a draught of warm night air, and called herself a fool for leaving it open. Anyone could have climbed up onto the first-floor balcony and gained entry.

Slipping out of bed, she grabbed her phone and held it pressed hard against her chest as she crept out into the hallway. As the only person in residence in Rupert's Greek villa, she'd seen no reason to close her bedroom door, which at least meant she didn't have to contend with the sound of it creaking open now.

She'd chosen the bedroom at the top of the stairs and from this vantage point she could see a shadow bounce in and out of view from the downstairs living room. She heard Rupert's liquor cabinet being opened and the sound of a glass bottle being set down. Thieves were stealing her brother's much-loved single malt whisky?

Someone downstairs muttered something in…French? She didn't catch what was said.

Someone answered back in Greek.

She strained her ears, but could catch no other words. So…there were two of them? She refused to contemplate what would happen if they found her here—a lone woman. Swallowing down a hard knot of fear, she made her way silently down the hallway, away from the stairs, to the farthest room along—the master bedroom. The door made the softest of snicks as she eased it closed. In the moonlight she made out the walk-in wardrobe on the other side of the room and headed straight for it, closing that door behind her, fighting to breathe through the panic that weighed her chest down.

She dialled the emergency number. 'Please help me,' she whispered in Greek. 'Please. There are intruders in my house.' She gave her name. She gave the address. The operator promised that someone was on the way and would be there in minutes. She spoke in reassuringly calm tones. She asked Audra where in the house she was, and if there was anywhere she could hide. She told Audra to stay on the line and that helped too.

'I'm hiding in the walk-in wardrobe in the master bedroom.' And that was when it hit her. She was all but locked in a closet. *Again.* It made no difference that this time she'd locked herself in. Panic clawed at her throat as she recalled the suffocating darkness and the way her body had started to cramp after hours spent confined in her tiny hall closet. When Thomas had not only locked her in, but had left and she hadn't known if he would ever return to let her out again. And if he didn't return, how long would it take for anyone to find her? How long before someone raised the alarm? She'd spent hours in a terrified limbo—after screaming herself hoarse for help—where she'd had to fight for every breath. 'I can't stay here.'

'The police are almost there,' the operator assured her.

She closed her eyes. This wasn't her horridly cramped hall closet, but a spacious walk-in robe. It didn't smell of damp leather and fuggy cold. This smelled of…the sea.

And she could stretch out her full length and not touch the other wall if she wanted to. Anger, cold and comforting, streaked through her then. Her eyes flew open. She would *not* be a victim again. Oh, she wasn't going to march downstairs and confront those two villains ransacking her brother's house, but she wasn't going to stay here, a cornered quaking mess either.

Her free hand clenched to a fist. *Think!* If she were a thief, what would she steal?

Electrical equipment—televisions, stereos and computers. Which were all downstairs. She grimaced. Except for the television on the wall in the master bedroom.

She'd bet they'd look for jewellery too. And where was the most likely place to find that? The master bedroom.

She needed to find a better hiding place—one that had an escape route if needed.

And she needed a weapon. Just in case. She didn't rate her chances against two burly men, but she could leave some bruises if they did try to attack her. She reminded herself that the police would be here soon.

For the first time since arriving in this island idyll, Audra cursed the isolation of Rupert's villa. It was the last property on a peninsula surrounded by azure seas. The glorious sea views, the scent of the ocean and gardens, the sound of lapping water combined with the humming of bees and the chattering of the birds had started to ease the burning in her soul. No media, no one hassling her for an interview, no flashing cameras whenever she strode outside her front door. The privacy had seemed like a godsend.

Until now.

Using the torch app on her phone, she scanned the wardrobe for something she could use to defend herself. Her fingers closed about a lacrosse stick. It must've been years since Rupert had played, and she had no idea what he was still doing with a stick now, but at the moment she didn't care.

Cracking open the wardrobe door, she listened for a full minute before edging across the room to the glass sliding door of the balcony. She winced at the click that seemed to echo throughout the room with a *come-and-find-me* din when she unlocked it, but thanked Rupert's maintenance man when it slid open on its tracks as silent as the moon. She paused and listened again for another full minute before easing outside and closing the door behind her. Hugging the shadows of the wall, she moved to the end of the balcony and inserted herself between two giant pot plants. The only way anyone would see her was if they came right out onto the balcony and moved in this direction. She gripped the lacrosse stick so tightly her fingers started to ache.

She closed her eyes and tried to get her breathing under control. The thieves would have no reason to come out onto the balcony. There was nothing to steal out here. And she doubted they'd be interested in admiring the view, regardless of how spectacular it might be. The tight band around her chest eased a fraction.

The flashing lights from the police car that tore into the driveway a moment later eased the tightness even further. She counted as four armed men piled out of the vehicle and headed straight inside. She heard shouts downstairs.

But still she didn't move.

After a moment she lifted the phone to her ear. 'Is it… is it safe to come out yet?' she whispered.

'One of the men has been apprehended. The officers are searching for the second man.' There was a pause. 'The man they have in custody claims he's on his own.'

She'd definitely heard French *and* Greek.

'He also says he's known to your brother.'

'Known?' She choked back a snort. 'I can assure you that my brother doesn't associate with people who break into houses.'

'He says his name is Finn Sullivan.'

Audra closed her eyes. *Scrap that.* Her brother knew *one* person who broke into houses, and his name was Finn Sullivan.

Finn swore in French, and then in Greek for good measure, when he knocked the crystal tumbler from the bench to the kitchen tiles below, making a God-awful racket that reverberated through his head. It served him right for not switching on a light, but he knew Rupert's house as well as he knew his own, and he'd wanted to try to keep the headache stretching behind his eyes from building into a full-blown migraine.

Blowing out a breath, he dropped his rucksack to the floor and, muttering first in French and then in Greek, clicked on a light and retrieved the dustpan and brush to clean up the mess. For pity's sake. Not only hadn't Rupert's last house guest washed, dried and put away the tumbler—leaving it for him to break—but they hadn't taken out the garbage either! Whenever he stayed, Finn always made sure to leave the place exactly as he found it—spotlessly clean and tidy. He hated to think of his friend being taken advantage of.

Helping himself to a glass of Rupert's excellent whisky, Finn lowered himself into an armchair in the living room, more winded than he cared to admit. The cast had come off his arm yesterday and it ached like the blazes now. As did his entire left side and his left knee. Take it easy, the doctor had ordered. But he'd been taking it easy for eight long weeks. And Nice had started to feel like a prison.

Rupert had given him a key to this place a couple of years ago, and had told him to treat it as his own. He'd ring Rupert tomorrow to let him know he was here. He glanced at the clock on the wall. Two thirty-seven a.m. was too late…or early…to call anyone. He rested his head back and closed his eyes, and tried to will the pain coursing through his body away.

He woke with a start to flashing lights, and it took him a moment to realise they weren't due to a migraine. He blinked, but the armed policemen—two of them and each with a gun trained on him—didn't disappear. The clock said two forty-eight.

He raised his hands in the universal gesture of non-aggression. 'My name is Finn Sullivan,' he said in Greek. 'I am a friend of Rupert Russel, the owner of this villa.'

'Where is your accomplice?'

'Accomplice?' He stood then, stung by the fuss and suspicion. 'What accomplice?'

He wished he'd remained seated when he found himself tackled to the floor, pain bursting like red-hot needles all the way down his left side, magnifying the blue-black ache that made him want to roar.

He clamped the howls of pain behind his teeth and nodded towards his backpack as an officer rough-handled him to his feet after handcuffing him. 'My identification is in there.'

His words seemed to have no effect. One of the officers spoke into a phone. He was frogmarched into the grand foyer. Both policemen looked upwards expectantly, so he did too.

'Audra!'

Flanked by two more police officers, she pulled to a dead halt halfway down the stairs, her eyes widening—those too cool and very clear blue eyes. 'Finn?' Delicate nostrils flared. 'What on earth are you doing here?'

The glass on the sink, the litter in the kitchen bin made sudden sense. '*You* called the police?'

'Of course I called the police!'

'Of all the idiotic, overdramatic reactions! How daft can you get?' He all but yelled the words at her, his physical pain needing an outlet. 'Why the hell would you over-react like that?'

'Daft? Daft!' Her voice rose as she flew down the stairs.

'And what do you call breaking and entering my brother's villa at two thirty in the morning?'

It was probably closer to three by now. He didn't say that out loud. 'I didn't break in. I have a key.'

He saw then that she clutched a lacrosse stick. She looked as if she wouldn't mind cracking him over the head with it. With a force of effort he pulled in a breath. A woman alone in a deserted house...the sound of breaking glass... And after everything she'd been through recently...

He bit back a curse. He'd genuinely frightened her.

The pain in his head intensified. 'I'm sorry, Squirt.' The old nickname dropped from his lips. 'If I'd known you were here I'd have rung to let you know I was coming. In the meantime, can you tell these guys who I am and call them off?'

'Where's your friend?'

His shoulder ached like the blazes. He wanted to yell at her to get the police to release him. He bit the angry torrent back. Knowing Audra, she'd make him suffer as long as she could if he yelled at her again.

And he *was* genuinely sorry he'd frightened her.

'I came alone.'

'But I heard two voices—one French, one Greek.'

He shook his head. 'You heard one voice and two languages.' He demonstrated his earlier cussing fit, though he toned it down to make it more palatable for mixed company.

For a moment the knuckles on her right hand whitened where it gripped the lacrosse stick, and then relaxed. She told the police officers in perfect Greek how sorry she was to have raised a false alarm, promised to bake them home-made lemon drizzle cakes and begged them very nicely to let him go as he was an old friend of her brother's. He wasn't sure why, but it made him grind his teeth.

He groaned his relief when he was uncuffed, rubbing his wrists rather than his shoulder, though he was damned if he knew why. Except he didn't want any of them to know how much he hurt. He was sick to death of his injuries.

A part of him would be damned too before it let Audra see him as anything but hearty and hale. Her pity would…

He pressed his lips together. He didn't know. All he knew was that he didn't want to become an object of it.

Standing side by side in the circular drive, they waved the police off. He followed her inside, wincing when she slammed the door shut behind them. The fire in her eyes hadn't subsided. 'You want to yell at me some more?'

He'd love to. It was what he and Audra did—they sniped at each other. They had ever since she'd been a gangly pre-teen. But he hurt too much to snipe properly. It was taking all his strength to control the nausea curdling his stomach. He glanced at her from beneath his shaggy fringe. Besides, it was no fun sniping at someone with the kind of shadows under their eyes that Audra had.

He eased back to survey her properly. She was too pale and too thin. He wasn't used to seeing her vulnerable and frightened.

Frighteningly efficient? *Yes.*

Unsmiling? *Yes.*

Openly disapproving of his lifestyle choices? *Double yes.*

But pale, vulnerable and afraid? *No.*

'That bastard really did a number on you, didn't he, Squirt?'

Her head reared back and he could've bitten his tongue out. 'Not quite as big a number as that mountain did on you, from all reports.'

She glanced pointedly at his shoulder and with a start he realised he'd been massaging it. He waved her words away. 'A temporary setback.'

She pushed out her chin. 'Ditto.'

The fire had receded from her eyes and this time it was he who had to suffer beneath their merciless ice-blue scrutiny. And that was when he realised that all she wore was a pair of thin cotton pyjama bottoms and a singlet top that moulded itself to her form. His tongue stuck to the roof of his mouth.

The problem with Audra was that she was *exactly* the kind of woman he went after. If he had a type it was the buttoned-up, repressed librarian type, and normally Audra embodied that to a tee. But at the moment she was about as far from that as you could get. She was all blonde sleep-tousled temptation and his skin prickled with an awareness that was both familiar and unfamiliar.

He had to remind himself that a guy didn't mess with his best friend's sister.

'Did the police hurt you?'

'Absolutely not.' He was admitting nothing.

She cocked an eyebrow. 'Finn, it's obvious you're in pain.'

He shrugged and then wished he hadn't when pain blazed through his shoulder. 'The cast only came off yesterday.'

Her gaze moved to his left arm. 'And instead of resting it, no doubt as your doctors suggested, you jumped on the first plane for Athens, caught the last ferry to Kyanós, grabbed a late dinner in the village and trekked the eight kilometres to the villa.'

'Bingo.' He'd relished the fresh air and the freedom. For the first two kilometres.

'While carrying a rucksack.'

Eight weeks ago he'd have been able to carry twice the weight for ten kilometres without breaking a sweat.

She picked up his glass of half-finished Scotch and strode into the kitchen. As she reached up into a kitchen cupboard her singlet hiked up to expose a band of perfect pale skin that had his gut clenching. She pulled out a packet of aspirin and sent it flying in a perfect arc towards him—he barely needed to move to catch it. And then she lifted his glass to her lips and drained it and stars burst behind his eyelids. It was the sexiest thing he'd ever seen.

She filled it with tap water and set it in front of him. 'Take two.'

He did as she ordered because it was easier than arguing with her. And because he hurt all over and it seemed too much trouble to find the heavy-duty painkillers his doctor had prescribed for him and which were currently rolling around in the bottom of his backpack somewhere.

'Which room do you usually use?'

'The one at the top of the stairs.'

'You're out of luck, buddy.' She stuck out a hip, and he gulped down more water. 'That's the one I'm using.'

He feigned outrage. 'But that one has the best view!' Which was a lie. All the upstairs bedrooms had spectacular views.

She smirked. 'I know. First in and all that.'

He choked down a laugh. That was one of the things he'd always liked about Audra. She'd play along with him…all in the name of one-upmanship, of course.

'Right, which bedroom do you want? There are another three upstairs to choose from.' She strode around and lifted his bag. She grunted and had to use both hands. 'Yeah, right—light as a feather.'

He glanced at her arms. While the rucksack wasn't exactly light, it wasn't that heavy. She'd never been a weakling. She'd lost condition. He tried to recall the last time he'd seen her.

'Earth to Finn.'

He started. 'I'll take the one on the ground floor.' The one behind the kitchen. The only bedroom in the house that didn't have a sea view. The bedroom furthest away from Audra's. They wouldn't even have to share a bathroom if he stayed down here. Which would be for the best.

He glanced at that singlet top and nodded. *Definitely* for the best.

Especially when her eyes softened with spring-rain warmth. 'Damn, Finn. Do you still hurt that much?'

He realised then that she thought he didn't want to tackle the stairs.

'I—' He pulled in a breath. He *didn't* want to tackle the stairs. He'd overdone it today. He didn't want her to keep looking at him like that either, though. 'It's nothing a good night's sleep won't fix.'

Without another word, she strode to the room behind the kitchen and lifted his bag up onto the desk in there. So he wouldn't have to lift it himself later. Her thoughtfulness touched him. She could be prickly, and she could be mouthy, but she'd never been unkind.

Which was the reason, if he ever ran into Thomas Farquhar, he'd wring the mongrel's neck.

'Do you need anything else?'

The beds in Rupert's villa were always made up. He employed a cleaner to come in once a week so that the Russel siblings or any close friends could land here and fall into bed with a minimum of fuss. But even if the bed hadn't been made pride would've forbidden him from asking her to make it…or to help him make it.

He fell into a chair and slanted her a grin—cocky, assured and full of teasing to hide his pain as he pulled his hiking boots off. 'Well, now, Squirt…' He lifted a foot in her direction. 'I could use some help getting my socks off. And then maybe my jeans.'

As anticipated, her eyes went wide and her cheeks went pink. Without another word, she whirled around and strode from the room.

At that precise moment his phone started to ring. He glanced at the caller ID and grimaced. 'Rupert, mate. Sorry about—'

The phone was summarily taken from him and Finn blinked when Audra lifted it to her ear. Up this close she smelled of coconut and peaches. His mouth watered. Dinner suddenly seemed like hours ago.

'Rupe, Finn looks like death. He needs to rest. He'll call you in the morning and you can give him an ear-bashing then.' She turned the phone off before handing it back to him. 'Goodnight, Finn.'

She was halfway through the kitchen before he managed to call back a goodnight of his own. He stood in the doorway and waited until he heard her ascending the stairs before closing his door and dialling Rupert's number.

'Before you launch into a tirade and tell me what an idiot I am, let me apologise. I'm calling myself far worse names than you ever will. I'd have not scared Audra for the world. I was going to call you in the morning to let you know I was here.' He'd had no notion Audra would be here. It was a little early in the season for any of the Russels to head for the island.

Rupert's long sigh came down the phone, and it made Finn's gut churn. 'What are you doing in Kyanós?' his friend finally asked. 'I thought you were in Nice.'

'The, uh, cast came off yesterday.'

'And you couldn't blow off steam on the French Riviera?'

He scrubbed a hand down his face. 'There's a woman I'm trying to avoid and—'

'You don't need to say any more. I get the picture.'

Actually, Rupert was wrong. This time. It wasn't a romantic liaison he'd tired of and was fleeing. But he kept his mouth shut. He deserved Rupert's derision. 'If you want me to leave, I'll clear out at first light.'

His heart gave a sick kick at the long pause on the other end of the phone. Rupert was considering it! Rupert was the one person who'd shown faith in him when everyone else had written him off, and now—

'Of course I don't want you to leave.'

He closed his eyes and let out a long, slow breath.

'But…'

His eyes crashed open. His heart started to thud. 'But?'

'Don't go letting Audra fall in love with you. She's fragile at the moment, Finn...vulnerable.'

He stiffened. 'Whoa, Rupe! I've no designs on your little sister.'

'She's *exactly* your type.'

'Except she's your sister.' He made a decision then and there to leave in the morning. He didn't want Rupert worrying about this. It was completely unnecessary. He needed to lie low for a few weeks and Kyanós had seemed like the perfect solution, but not at the expense of either Rupert's or Audra's peace of mind.

'That said, I'm glad you're there.'

Finn stilled.

'I'm worried about her being on her own. I've been trying to juggle my timetable, but the earliest I can get away is in a fortnight.'

Finn pursed his lips. 'You want me to keep an eye on her?'

Again there was a long pause. 'She needs a bit of fun. She needs to let her hair down.'

'This *is* Audra we're talking about.' She was the most buttoned-up person he knew.

'You're good at fun.'

His lips twisted. He ought to be. He'd spent a lifetime perfecting it. 'You want me to make sure she has a proper holiday?'

'Minus the holiday romance. Women *like* you, Finn... they fall for you.'

'Pot and kettle,' he grunted back. 'But you're worrying for nothing. Audra has more sense than that.' She had *always* disapproved of him and what she saw as his irresponsible and daredevil lifestyle.

What had happened eight weeks ago proved her point. What if the next time he did kill himself? The thought made his mouth dry and his gut churn. His body was re-

covering but his mind… There were days when he was a
maelstrom of confusion, questioning the choices he was
making. He gritted his teeth. It'd pass. After such a close
brush with mortality it had to be normal to question one's
life. Needless to say, he wasn't bringing anyone into that
mess at the moment, especially not one who was his best
friend's little sister.

'If she had more sense she'd have not fallen for Farquhar.'

Finn's hands fisted. 'Tell me the guy is toast.'

'I'm working on it.'

Good.

'I've tried to shield her from the worst of the media
furore, but…'

'But she has eyes in her head. She can read the headlines for herself.' And those headlines had been everywhere. It'd been smart of Rupert to pack Audra off to
the island.

'Exactly.' Rupert paused again. 'None of the Russels
have any sense when it comes to love. If we did, Audra
wouldn't have been taken in like she was.'

And she was paying for it now. He recalled her pallor,
the dark circles beneath her eyes…the effort it'd taken her
to lift his backpack. He could help with some of that—get
her out into the sun, challenge her to swimming contests…
and maybe even get her to run with him. He could make
sure she ate three square meals a day.

'If I'd had more sense I'd have not fallen for Brooke
Manning.'

'Everyone makes a bad romantic decision at least once
in their lives, Rupe.'

He realised he sounded as if he were downplaying what
had happened to his friend, and he didn't want to do that.
Rupert hadn't looked at women in the same way after
Brooke. Finn wasn't sure what had happened between
them. He'd been certain they were heading for matrimony,

babies and white picket fences. But it had all imploded, and Rupert hadn't been the same since. 'But you're right—not everyone gets their heart shredded.' He rubbed a hand across his chest. 'Has Farquhar shredded her heart?'

'I don't know.'

Even if he hadn't, he'd stolen company secrets from the Russel Corporation while posing as her attentive and very loving boyfriend. That wasn't something a woman like Audra would be able to shrug off as just a bad experience.

Poor Squirt.

He only realised he'd said that out loud when Rupert said with a voice as dry as a good single malt, 'Take a look, Finn. I think you'll find Squirt is all grown up.'

He didn't need to look. The less looking he did, the better. A girl like Audra deserved more than what a guy like him could give her—things like stability, peace of mind, and someone she could depend on.

'It'd be great if you could take her mind off things—make her laugh and have some fun. I just don't want her falling for you. She's bruised and battered enough.'

'You've nothing to worry about on that score, Rupe, I promise you. I've no intention of hurting Audra. Ever.'

'She's special, Finn.'

That made him smile. 'All of the Russel siblings are special.'

'She's more selfless than the rest of us put together.'

Finn blinked. 'That's a big call.'

'It's the truth.'

He hauled in a breath and let it out slowly. 'I'll see what I can do.'

'Thanks, Finn, I knew I could count on you.'

Audra pressed her ringing phone to her ear at exactly eight twenty-three the next morning. She knew the exact time because she was wondering when Finn would emerge. She'd started clock-watching—a sure sign of worry. Not that she had any intention of letting Rupert know she was worried. 'Hey, Rupe.'

He called to check on her every couple of days, which only fed her guilt. Last night's false alarm sent an extra surge of guilt slugging through her now. 'Sorry about last night's fuss. I take it the police rang to let you know what happened.'

'They did. And you've nothing to apologise for. Wasn't your fault. In fact, I'm proud of the way you handled the situation.'

He was? Her shoulders went back.

'Not everyone would've thought that quickly on their feet. You did good.'

'Thanks, I… I'm relieved it was just Finn.' She flashed to the lines of strain that had bracketed Finn's mouth last night. 'Do you know how long he plans to stay?'

'No idea. Do you mind him being there? I can ask him to leave.'

'No, no—don't do that.' She already owed Rupert and the rest of her family too much. She didn't want to cause any further fuss. 'He wasn't looking too crash hot last night. I think he needs to take it easy for a bit.'

'You could be right, Squirt, and I hate to ask this of you…'

'Ask away.' She marvelled how her brother's *Squirt* could sound so different from Finn's. When Finn called her Squirt it made her tingle all over.

'No, forget about it. It doesn't matter. You've enough on your plate.'

She had nothing on her plate at the moment and they both knew it. 'Tell me what you were going to say,' she ordered in her best boardroom voice. 'I insist. You know you'll get no peace now until you do.'

His low chuckle was her reward. Good. She wanted him to stop worrying about her.

'Okay, it's just… I'm a bit worried about him.'

She sat back. 'About Finn?' It made a change from Rupert worrying about her.

'He's never had to take it easy in his life. Going slow is an alien concept to him.'

He could say that again.

'He nearly died up there on that mountain.'

Her heart clenched. 'Died? I mean, I knew he'd banged himself up pretty bad, but…I had no idea.'

'Typical Finn, he's tried to downplay it. While the medical team could patch the broken arm and ribs easily enough, along with the dislocated shoulder and wrenched knee, his ruptured spleen and the internal bleeding nearly did him in.'

She closed her eyes and swallowed. 'You want me to make sure he takes it easy while he's here?'

'That's probably an impossible task.'

'Nothing's impossible,' she said with a confidence she had no right to. After all her brother's support these last few weeks—his lack of blame—she could certainly do this one thing for him. 'Consider it done.'

'And, Audra…?'

'Yes?'

'Don't go falling in love with him.'

She shot to her feet, her back ramrod straight. 'I make one mistake and—'

'This has nothing to do with what happened with Farquhar. It's just that women seem to like Finn. *A lot.* They fall at his feet in embarrassing numbers.'

She snorted and took her seat again. 'That's because he's pretty.' She preferred a man with a bit more substance.

You thought Thomas had substance.

She pushed the thought away.

'He's in Kyanós partly because he's trying to avoid some woman in Nice.'

Good to know.

'If he hurts you, Squirt, I'll no longer consider him a friend.'

She straightened from her slouch, air whistling between her teeth. Rupert and Finn were best friends, and had been ever since they'd attended their international boarding school in Geneva as fresh-faced twelve-year-olds.

She made herself swallow. 'I've no intention of doing anything so daft.' She'd never do anything to ruin her brother's most important friendship.

'Finn has a brilliant mind, he's built a successful company and is an amazing guy, but...'

'But what?' She frowned, when her brother remained silent. 'What are you worried about?'

'His past holds him back.'

By *his past* she guessed he meant Finn's parents' high-octane lifestyle, followed by their untimely deaths. It had to have had an impact on Finn, had to have left scars and wounds that would never heal.

'I worry he could end up like his father.'

She had to swallow the bile that rose through her.

'I'm not sure he'll ever settle down.'

She'd worked that much out for herself. And she wasn't a masochist. Men like Finn were pretty to look at, but you didn't build a life around them.

Women had flings with men like Finn...and she suspected they enjoyed every moment of them. A squirrel of curiosity wriggled through her, but she ruthlessly cut it off. One disastrous romantic liaison was enough for the year. She wasn't adding another one to the tally. She suppressed a shudder. The very thought made her want to crawl back into bed and pull the covers over her head.

She forced her spine to straighten. She had no intention of falling for Finn, but she could get him to slow down for a bit—just for a week or two, right?

CHAPTER TWO

'YOU HAD BREAKFAST YET, Squirt?'

Audra almost jumped out of her skin at the deep male voice and the hard-muscled body that materialised directly in front of her. She bit back a yelp and pressed a hand to her heart. After sitting here waiting for him to emerge, she couldn't believe she'd been taken off guard.

He chuckled. 'You never used to be jumpy.'

Yeah, well, that was before Thomas Farquhar had locked her in a cupboard. The laughter in his warm brown eyes faded as they narrowed. Not that she had any intention of telling him that. She didn't want his pity. 'Broken sleep never leaves me at my best,' she said in as tart a voice as she could muster. Which was, admittedly, pretty tart.

He just grinned. 'I find it depends on the reasons for the broken sleep.' And then he sent her a broad wink.

She rolled her eyes. 'Glass shattering and having to call the police doesn't fall into the fun category, Finn.'

'Do you want me to apologise again? Do the full grovel?' He waggled his eyebrows. 'I'm very good at a comprehensive grovel.'

'No, thank you.' She pressed her lips together. She bet he was good at a lot of things.

She realised she still held her phone. She recalled the conversation she'd just had with Rupert and set it to the table, heat flushing through her cheeks.

Finn glanced at her and at the phone before cracking eggs into the waiting frying pan. 'So... Rupe rang to warn you off, huh?'

Her jaw dropped. How on earth...? *Ah.* 'He rang you too.'

'You want a couple of these?' He lifted an egg in her direction.

'No…thank you,' she added as a belated afterthought. It struck her that she always found it hard to remember her manners around Finn.

'Technically, I called him.' The frying pan spat and sizzled. 'But he seems to think I have some magic ability to make women swoon at my feet, whereby I pick them off at my leisure and have my wicked way with them before discarding them as is my wont.'

She frowned. Had she imagined the bitterness behind the lightness?

'He read me the Riot Act where you're concerned.' He sent her a mock serious look. 'So, Squirt, while I know it'll be hard for you to contain your disappointment, I'm afraid I'm not allowed to let a single one of my love rays loose in your direction.'

She couldn't help it, his nonsense made her laugh.

With an answering grin, he set a plate of eggs and toast in front of her and slid into the seat opposite.

'But I said I didn't want any.'

Her stomach rumbled, making a liar of her. Rather than tease her, though, he shrugged. 'Sorry, I must've misheard.'

Finn never misheard anything, but the smell of butter on toast made her mouth water. She picked up her knife and fork. It'd be wasteful not to eat it. 'Did Rupert order you to feed me up?' she grumbled.

He shook his head, and shaggy hair—damp from the shower—fell into his eyes and curled about his neck and some pulse inside her flared to life before she brutally strangled it.

'Nope. Rupe's only dictum was to keep my love rays well and truly away from his little sister. All uttered in his most stern of tones.'

She did her best not to choke on her toast and eggs. 'Doesn't Rupert know me at all?' She tossed the words back at him with what she hoped was a matching carelessness.

'See? That's what I told him. I said, Audra's too smart to fall for a guy like me.'

Fall for? Absolutely not. Sleep with…?

What on earth…? She frowned and forced the thought away. She didn't think of Finn in those terms.

Really?

She rolled her shoulders. So what if she'd always thought him too good-looking for his own good? That didn't mean anything. In idle moments she might find herself thinking he'd be an exciting lover. If she were the kind of person who did flings with devil-may-care men. But she wasn't. And *that* didn't mean anything either.

'So…?'

She glanced up at the question in his voice.

'How long have you been down here?'

'Two days.'

'And how long are you here for?'

She didn't really know. 'A fortnight, maybe. I've taken some annual leave.'

He sent her a sharp glance from beneath brows so perfectly shaped they made her the tiniest bit jealous. 'If you took all the leave accrued by you, I bet you could stay here until the middle of next year.'

Which would be heaven—absolute heaven.

'What about you? How long are you staying?'

'I was thinking a week or two. Do some training…get some condition back.'

He was going to overdo it. Well, not on her watch!

'But if my being here is intruding on your privacy, I can shoot off to my uncle's place.'

'No need for that. It'll be nice to have some company.'

His eyes narrowed and she realised she'd overplayed her hand. It wasn't her usual sentiment where Finn was concerned. Normally she acted utterly disdainful and scornful. They sparred. They didn't buddy up.

She lifted her fork and pointed it at him. 'As long as you stop calling me Squirt, stop blathering nonsense about love rays…and cook me breakfast every day.'

He laughed and she let out a slow breath.

'You've got yourself a deal…*Audra*.'

Her name slid off his tongue like warm honey and it was all she could do not to groan. She set her knife and fork down and pushed her plate away.

'I had no idea you didn't like being called Squirt.'

She didn't. Not really.

He stared at her for a moment. 'Don't hold Rupert's protectiveness against him.'

She blinked. 'I don't.' And then grimaced. 'Well, not much. I know I'm lucky to have him…and Cora and Justin.' It was a shame that Finn didn't have a brother or sister. He did have Rupert, though, and the two men were as close as brothers.

'He's a romantic.'

That made her glance up. 'Rupert?'

'Absolutely.'

He nodded and it made his hair do that fall-in-his-eyes thing again and she didn't know why, but it made her stomach clench.

'On the outside he acts as hard as nails, but on the inside…'

'He's a big marshmallow,' she finished.

'He'd go to the ends of the earth for someone he loved.'

That was true. She nodded.

'See? A romantic.'

She'd never thought about it in those terms.

His phone on the table buzzed. She didn't mean to look, but she saw the name Trixie flash up on the screen before Finn reached over and switched it off. *Okay.*

'So…' He dusted off his hands as if ready to take on

the world. 'What were you planning to do while you were here?'

Dear God. *Think of nice, easy, relaxing things.* 'Um… I was going to lie on the beach and catch some rays—' *not love rays* '—float about in the sea for a bit.'

'Sounds good.'

Except he wouldn't be content with lying around and floating, would he? He'd probably challenge himself to fifty laps out to the buoy and back every day. 'Read a book.'

His lip curled. 'Read a book?'

She tried not to wince at the scorn that threaded through his voice.

'You come to one of the most beautiful places on earth to *read a book*?'

She tried to stop her shoulders from inching up to her ears. 'I like reading, and do you know how long it's been since I read a book for pleasure?'

'How long?'

'Over a year,' she mumbled.

He spread his hands. 'If you like to read, why don't you do more of it?'

Because she'd been working too hard. Because she'd let Thomas distract and manipulate her.

'And what else?'

She searched her mind. 'I don't cook.'

He glanced at their now empty plates and one corner of his mouth hooked up. 'So I've noticed.'

'But I want to learn to cook…um…croissants.'

His brow furrowed. 'Why?'

Because they took a long time to make, didn't they? The pastry needed lots of rolling out, didn't it? Which meant, if she could trick him into helping her, he'd be safe from harm while he was rolling out pastry. 'Because I love them.' That was true enough. 'But I've had to be strict with myself.'

'Strict, how?'

'I've made a decision—in the interests of both my waistline and my heart health—that I'm only allowed to eat croissants that I make myself.'

He leaned back and let loose with a long low whistle. 'Wow, Squ— Audra! You really know how to let your hair down and party, huh?'

No one in all her life had ever accused her of being a party animal.

'A holiday with reading and baking at the top of your list.'

His expression left her in no doubt what he thought about that. 'This is supposed to be a holiday—some R & R,' she shot back, stung. 'I'm all go, go, go at work, but here I want time out.'

'Boring,' he sing-songed.

'Relaxing,' she countered.

'You've left the recreation part out of your R & R equation. I mean, look at you. You even look…'

She had to clamp her hands around the seat of her chair to stop from leaping out of it. 'Boring?' she said through gritted teeth.

'Buttoned-up. Tense. The opposite of relaxed.'

'It's the effect you and your love rays always seem to have on me.'

He tsk-tsked and shook his head. 'We're not supposed to mention the love rays, remember?'

Could she scream yet?

'I mean, look at your hair. You have it pulled back *in a bun*.'

She touched a hand to her hair. 'What's wrong with that?'

'A bun is for the boardroom, not the beach.'

She hated wearing her hair down and have it tickle her face.

'Well, speaking of hair, you might want to visit a

hairdresser yourself when you're next in the village,' she shot back.

'But I visited my hairdresser only last week.' He sent her a grin full of wickedness and sin. 'The delectable Monique assured me this look is all the rage at the moment.'

He had a hairdresser called Monique…who was delectable? She managed to roll her eyes. 'The *too-long-for-the-boardroom-just-right-for-the-beach* look?'

'Precisely. She said the same about the stubble.'

She'd been doing her best not to notice that stubble. She was trying to keep the words *dead sexy* from forming in her brain.

'What do you think?' He ran a hand across his jawline, preening. It should've made him look ridiculous. Especially as he was hamming it up and trying to look ridiculous. But she found herself having to jam down on the temptation to reach across and brush her palm across it to see if it was as soft and springy as it looked.

She mentally slapped herself. 'I think it looks…scruffy.' In the best possible way. 'But it probably provides good protection against the sun, which is wise in these climes.'

He simply threw his head back and laughed, not taking the slightest offence. The strain that had deepened the lines around his eyes last night had eased. And when he rose to take their dishes to the sink he moved with an easy fluidity that belied his recent injuries.

He almost died up there on that mountain.

She went cold all over.

'Audra?'

She glanced up to find him staring at her, concern in his eyes. She shook herself. 'What's your definition of a good holiday, then?'

'Here on the island?'

He'd started to wash the dishes so she rose to dry them. 'Uh-huh, here on the island.'

'Water sports,' he said with relish.

'What kind of water sports?' Swimming and kayaking were gentle enough, but—

'On the other side of the island is the most perfect cove for windsurfing and sailing.'

But…but he could hurt himself.

'Throw in some water-skiing and hang-gliding and I'd call that just about the perfect holiday.'

He could kill himself! Lord, try explaining *that* to Rupert. 'No way.'

He glanced at her. 'When did you become such a scaredy-cat, Audra Russel?'

She realised he thought her 'No way' had been in relation to herself, which was just as well because if he realised she'd meant it for him he'd immediately go out and throw himself off the first cliff he came across simply to spite her.

And while it might be satisfying to say I told you so if he did come to grief, she had a feeling that satisfaction would be severely tempered if the words were uttered in a hospital ward…or worse.

'Why don't you let your hair down for once, take a risk? You might even find it's fun.'

She bit back a sigh. Maybe that was what she was afraid of. One risk could lead to another, and before she knew it she could've turned her whole life upside down. And she wasn't talking sex with her brother's best friend here either. Which—*obviously*—wasn't going to happen. She was talking about her job and her whole life. It seemed smarter to keep a tight rein on all her risk-taking impulses. She was sensible, stable and a rock to all her family. That was *who* she was. She repeated the words over and over like a mantra until she'd fixed them firmly in her mind again.

She racked her brain to think of a way to control Finn's risk-taking impulses too. 'There's absolutely nothing wrong with some lazy R & R, Finn Sullivan.' She used his full name in the same way he'd used hers. 'You should try it some time.'

His eyes suddenly gleamed. 'I'll make a deal with you. I'll try your kind of holiday R & R if you'll try mine?'

She bit her lip, her pulse quickening. This could be the perfect solution. 'So you'd be prepared to laze around here with a book if I...if I try windsurfing and stuff?'

'Yep. Quid pro quo.'

'Meaning?'

'One day we do whatever you choose. The next day we do whatever I choose.'

She turned to hang up the tea towel so he couldn't see the self-satisfied smile that stretched across her face. For at least half of his stay she'd be able to keep him out of trouble. As for the other half...she could temper his pace— be so inept he'd have to slow down to let her keep up or have to spend so much time teaching her that there'd been no time for him to be off risking his own neck. *Perfect.*

She swung back. 'Despite what you say, I'm not a scaredy-cat.'

'And despite what you think, I'm not hyperactive.'

Finn held his breath as he watched Audra weigh up his suggestion. She was actually considering it. Which was surprising. He'd expected her to tell him to take a flying leap and stalk off to read her book.

But she was actually considering his suggestion and he didn't know why. He thought he'd need to tease and rile her more, bring her latent competitive streak to the fore, where she'd accept his challenge simply to save face. Still, he *had* tossed out the bait of her proving that her way was better than his. Women were always trying to change him. Maybe Audra found that idea attractive too?

In the next moment he shook his head. That'd only be the case if she were interested in him as a romantic prospect. And she'd made it clear that wasn't the case.

Thank God.

He eyed that tight little bun and swallowed.

'I'll agree to your challenge...'

He tried to hide his surprise. She would? He hadn't even needed to press her.

'On two conditions.'

Ha! He knew it couldn't be that easy. 'Which are?'

'I get to go first.'

He made a low sweeping bow. 'Of course—ladies first, that always went without saying.' It was a minor concession and, given how much he still hurt, one he didn't mind making. They could pick up the pace tomorrow.

'And the challenge doesn't start until tomorrow.'

He opened his mouth to protest, but she forged on. 'We need to go shopping. There's hardly any food in the place. And I'm not wasting my choice of activities on practicalities like grocery shopping, thank you very much.'

'We could get groceries delivered.'

'But it'd be nice to check out the produce at the local market. Rupert likes to support the local businesses.'

And while she was here she'd consider herself Rupert's representative. And it was true—what she did here would reflect on her brother. The Russels had become a bit of a fixture in Kyanós life over the last few years.

'I also want to have a deliciously long browse in the bookstore. And you'll need to select a book too, you know?'

Oh, joy of joys. He was going to make her run two miles for that.

'And...' she shrugged '...consider it a fact-finding mission—we can research what the island has to offer and put an itinerary together.'

Was she really going to let him choose half of her holiday activities for the next week or two? *Excellent.* By the time he was through with her, she'd have colour in her cheeks, skin on her bones—not to mention some muscle tone and a spring in her step. 'You've got yourself a deal… on one condition.'

Her eyebrows lifted.

'That you lose the bun.' He couldn't think straight around that bun. Whenever he glanced at it, he was seized by an unholy impulse to release it. It distracted him beyond anything.

Without another word, she reached up to pull the pins from her bun, and a soft cloud of fair hair fell down around her shoulders. Her eyes narrowed and she thrust out her chin. 'Better?'

It took an effort of will to keep a frown from his face. A tight band clamped around his chest.

'Is it *beachy* enough for you?'

'A hundred per cent better,' he managed, fighting the urge to reach out and touch a strand, just to see if it was as silky and soft as it looked.

She smirked and pulled it back into a ponytail. 'There, the bun is gone.'

But the ponytail didn't ease the tightness growing in his chest, not to mention other places either. It bounced with a perky insolence that had him aching to reach out and give it a gentle tug. For pity's sake, it was just hair!

She stilled, and then her hands went to her hips. 'Are you feeling okay, Finn?'

He shook himself. 'Of course I am. Why?'

'You gave in to my conditions without a fight. That's not like you. Normally you'd bicker with me and angle for more.'

Damn! He had to remember how quick she was, and keep his wits about him.

'If you want a few more days before embarking on our challenge, that's fine with me. I mean, you only just got the cast off your arm.'

He clenched his jaw so hard it started to ache.

'I understand you beat yourself up pretty bad on that mountain.'

She paused as if waiting for him to confirm that, but he had no intention of talking about his accident.

She shrugged. 'And you looked pretty rough last night so…'

'So…what?'

'So if you needed a couple of days to regroup…'

Anger directed solely at himself pooled in his stomach. 'The accident was two month ago, *Squirt*.' He called her Squirt deliberately, to set her teeth on edge. 'I'm perfectly fine.'

She shrugged. 'Whatever you say.' But she didn't look convinced. 'I'm leaving for the village in half an hour if you want to come along. But if you want to stay here and do push-ups and run ten miles on the beach then I'm more than happy to select a book for you.'

'Not a chance.' He shuddered to think what she would make him read as a penance. 'I'll be ready in twenty.'

'Suit yourself.' She moved towards the foyer and the stairs. And the whole time her ponytail swayed in jaunty mockery. She turned when she reached the foyer's archway. 'Finn?'

He hoped to God she hadn't caught him staring. 'What?'

'The name's Audra, not Squirt. That was the deal. Three strikes and you're out. That's Strike One.'

She'd kick him out if he… He stared after her and found himself grinning. She wasn't going to let him push her around and he admired her for it.

'I'll drive,' Finn said, thirty minutes later.

'I have the car keys,' Audra countered, sliding into the driver's seat of the hybrid Rupert kept on the island for running back and forth to the village.

To be perfectly honest, he didn't care who drove. He

just didn't want Audra to think him frail or in need of ba-
bying. Besides, it was only ten minutes into the village.

One advantage of being passenger, though, was the
unencumbered opportunity to admire the views, and out
here on the peninsula the views were spectacular. Olive
trees interspersed with the odd cypress and ironwood tree
ranged down the slopes, along with small scrubby shrubs
bursting with flowers—some white and some pink. And
beyond it all was the unbelievable, almost magical blue of
the Aegean Sea. The air from the open windows was warm
and dry, fragrant with salt and rosemary, and something
inside him started to unhitch. He rested his head back and
breathed it all in.

'Glorious, isn't it?'

He glanced across at her profile. She didn't drive as if
she needed to be anywhere in a hurry. Her fingers held the
steering wheel in a loose, relaxed grip, and the skin around
her eyes and mouth was smooth and unblemished. The last
time he'd seen her she'd been in a rush, her knuckles white
around her briefcase and her eyes narrowed—no doubt
her mind focussed on the million things on her to-do list.

She glanced across. 'What?'

'I was just thinking how island life suits you.'

Her brows shot up, and she fixed her attention on the
road in front again, her lips twitching. 'Wow, you must
really hate my bun.'

No, he loved that bun.

Not that he had any intention of telling her that.

She flicked him with another of her cool glances. 'Do
you know anyone that this island life wouldn't suit?'

'Me…in the long term. I'd go stir-crazy after a while.'
He wasn't interested in holidaying his whole life away.

*What are you interested in doing with the rest of your
life, then?*

He swallowed and shoved the question away, not ready

to face the turmoil it induced, focussed his attention back on Audra.

'And probably you too,' he continued. 'Seems to me you don't like being away from the office for too long.'

Something in her tensed, though her fingers still remained loose and easy on the wheel. He wanted to turn more fully towards her and study her to find out exactly what had changed, but she'd challenge such a stare, and he couldn't think of an excuse that wouldn't put her on the defensive. Getting her to relax and have fun was the remit, not making her tense and edgy. His mention of work had probably just been an unwelcome reminder of Farquhar.

And it was clear she wanted to talk about Farquhar as much as he wanted to talk about his accident.

He cleared his throat. 'But in terms of a short break, I don't think anything can beat this island.'

'Funnily enough, that's one argument you won't get from me.'

He didn't know why, but her words made him laugh.

They descended into the village and her sigh of appreciation burrowed into his chest. 'It's such a pretty harbour.'

She steered the car down the narrow street to the parking area in front of the harbour wall. They sat for a moment to admire the scene spread before them. An old-fashioned ferry chugged out of the cove, taking passengers on the two-hour ride to the mainland. Yachts with brightly coloured sails bobbed on their moorings. The local golden stone of the harbour wall provided the perfect foil for the deep blue of the water. To their left houses in the same golden stone, some of them plastered brilliant white, marched up the hillside, the bright blue of their doors and shutters making the place look deliciously Mediterranean.

Audra finally pushed out of the car and he followed. She pulled her hair free of its band simply to capture it again, including the strand that had worked its way loose, and retied it. 'I was just going to amble along the main shopping strip for a bit.'

She gestured towards the cheerful curve of shops that lined the harbour, the bunting from their awnings fluttering in the breeze. Barrels of gaily coloured flowers stood along the strip at intervals. If there was a more idyllic place on earth, he was yet to find it.

'Sounds good to me.' While she was ambling she'd be getting a dose of sun and fresh air. 'Do you mind if I tag along?' He asked because he'd called her Squirt earlier to deliberately rub her up the wrong way and he regretted it now.

Cool blue eyes surveyed him and he couldn't read them at all. 'I mean to take my time. I won't be rushed. I do enough rushing in my real life and...'

Her words trailed off and he realised she thought he meant to whisk her through the shopping at speed and... and what? Get to the things he wanted to do? What kind of selfish brute did she think he was? 'I'm in no rush.'

'I was going to browse the markets and shops...maybe get some lunch, before buying whatever groceries we needed before heading back.'

'Sounds like an excellent plan.'

The faintest of frowns marred the perfect skin of her forehead. 'It does?'

Something vulnerable passed across her features, but it was gone in a flash. From out of nowhere Rupert's words came back to him: *'She's more selfless than the rest of us put together.'* The Russel family came from a privileged background, but they took the associated social responsibility of that position seriously. Each of them had highly honed social consciences. But it struck him then that Audra put her family's needs before her own. Who put her needs first?

'Audra, a lazy amble along the harbour, while feeling

the sun on my face and breathing in the sea air, sounds pretty darn perfect to me.'

She smiled then—a real smile—and it kicked him in the gut because it was so beautiful. And because he realised he'd so very rarely seen her smile like that.

Why?

He took her arm and led her across the street, releasing her the moment they reached the other side. She still smelled of coconut and peaches, and it made him want to lick her.

Dangerous.

Not to mention totally inappropriate.

He tried to find his equilibrium again, and for once wished he could blame his sense of vertigo, the feeling of the ground shifting beneath his feet, on his recent injuries. Audra had always been able to needle him and then make him laugh, but he had no intention of letting her get under his skin. Not in *that* way. He'd been out of circulation too long, that was all. He'd be fine again once he'd regained his strength and put the accident behind him.

'It's always so cheerful down here,' she said, pausing beside one of the flower-filled barrels, and dragging a deep breath into her lungs.

He glanced down at the flowers to avoid noticing the way her chest lifted, and touched his fingers to a bright pink petal. 'These are…nice.'

'I love petunias,' she said. She touched a scarlet blossom. 'And these geraniums and begonias look beautiful.'

He reached for a delicate spray of tiny white flowers at the same time that she did, and their fingers brushed against each other. It was the briefest of contacts, but it sent electricity charging up his arm and had him sucking in a breath. For one utterly unbalancing moment he thought she meant to repeat the gesture.

'That's alyssum,' she said, pulling her hand away.

He moistened his lips. 'I had no idea you liked gardening.'

She stared at him for a moment and he watched her snap back into herself like a rubber band that had been stretched and then released. But opposite to that because the stretching had seemed to relax her while the snapping back had her all tense again.

'Don't worry, Finn. I'm not going to make you garden while you're here.'

Something sad and hungry, though, lurked in the backs of her eyes, and he didn't understand it at all. He opened his mouth to ask her about it, but closed it again. He didn't get involved with complicated emotions or sensitive issues. He avoided them like the plague. Get her to laugh, get her to loosen up. That was his remit. Nothing more. But that didn't stop the memory of that sad and hungry expression from playing over and over in his mind.

CHAPTER THREE

AUDRA WHEELED AWAY from Finn and the barrel of flowers to survey the length of the village street, and tried to slow the racing of her pulse…to quell the temptation that swept through her like the breeze tugging at her hair. But the sound of the waves splashing against the seawall and the sparkles of light on the water as the sun danced off its surface only fed the yearning and the restlessness.

She couldn't believe that the idea—the temptation—had even occurred to her. She and Finn? The idea was laughable.

For pity's sake, she'd had one romantic disaster this year. Did she really want to follow that up with another?

Absolutely not.

She dragged a trembling hand across her eyes. She must be more shaken by Thomas and his betrayal than she'd realised. She needed to focus on herself and her family, and to make things right again. That was what this break here on Kyanós was all about—that and avoiding the media storm that had surrounded her in Geneva. The one thing she didn't want to do was to make things worse.

The building at the end of the row of shops drew her gaze. Its white walls and blue shutters gleamed in the sun like the quintessential advertisement for a Greek holiday. The For Sale sign made her swallow. She resolutely dragged her gaze away, but the gaily coloured planter pots dotted along the thoroughfare caught her gaze again and that didn't help either. But…

A sigh welled inside her. But if she ever owned a shop, she'd have a tub—or maybe two tubs—of flowers like these outside its door.

You're never going to own a shop.

She made herself straighten. No, she was never going to own a shop. And the sooner she got over it, the better.

The lengthening silence between her and Finn grew more and more fraught.

See what happens when you don't keep a lid on the nonsense? You become tempted to do ridiculous things.

Well, she could annihilate that in one fell swoop.

'If I ever owned a shop, I'd want flowers outside its door too, just like these ones.' And she waited for the raucous laughter to scald her dream with the scorn it deserved.

Rather than laughter a warm chuckle greeted her, a chuckle filled with...affection? 'You used to talk about opening a shop when you were a little girl.'

And everyone had laughed at her—teased her for not wanting to be something more glamorous like an astronaut or ballerina.

Poor poppet, she mocked herself.

'What did you want to be when you were little?'

'A fireman...a knife-thrower at the circus...an explorer...and I went through a phase of wanting to be in a glam-rock band. It was the costumes,' he added when she swung to stare at him. 'I loved the costumes.'

She couldn't help but laugh. 'I'm sure you'd look fetching in purple satin, platform boots and silver glitter.'

He snorted.

'You know what the next challenge is going to be, don't you? The very next fancy dress party you attend, you have to go as a glam rocker.'

'You know there'll be a counter challenge to that?'

'There always is.' And whatever it was, she wouldn't mind honouring it. She'd pay good money to see Finn dressed up like that.

One corner of his mouth had hooked up in a cocky grin, his eyes danced with devilment, and his hair did that 'slide across his forehead perilously close to his eyes' thing and her stomach clenched. Hard. She forced her gaze away, reminded herself who he was. And what he was. 'Well, it might not come with fancy costumes, but playboy adventurer captures the spirit of your childhood aspirations.'

He slanted a glance down at her, the laughter in his eyes turning dark and mocking, though she didn't know if it was directed at her or himself. 'Wow,' he drawled. 'Written off in one simple phrase. You've become a master of the backhanded compliment. Though some might call it character assassination.'

It was her turn to snort. 'While you've perfected drama queen.' But she found herself biting her lip as she stared unseeing at the nearby shop fronts as they walked along. Had she been too hard, too…*dismissive* just then? 'I'm not discounting the fact that you make a lot of money for charity.'

The car races, the mountaineering expeditions, the base jumps were all for terribly worthy causes.

'And yet she can't hide her disapproval at my reckless and irresponsible lifestyle,' he told the sky.

It wasn't disapproval, but envy. Not that she had any intention of telling him so. All right, there was some disapproval too. She didn't understand why he had to risk his neck for charity. There were other ways to fundraise, right? Risking his neck just seemed…stupid.

But whatever else Finn was, she'd never accuse him of being stupid.

She was also officially tired of this conversation. She halted outside the bookshop. 'Our first stop.'

She waited for him to protest but all he did was gesture for her to precede him. 'After you.'

With a big breath she entered, and crossed her fingers and hoped none of the shopkeepers or villagers would mention her recent troubles when they saw her today. She just wanted to forget all about that for a while.

They moved to different sections of the store—him to Non-Fiction, while she started towards Popular Fiction, stopping along the way to pore over the quaint merchandise that lined the front of the shop—cards and pens, bookmarks in every shape and size, some made from paper while others were made from bits of crocheted string with coloured beads dangling from their tails. A large selection of journals and notebooks greeted her too, followed by bookends and paperweights—everything a booklover could need. How she loved this stuff! On her way out she'd buy a gorgeous notebook. Oh, and bookmarks—one for each book she bought.

She lost herself to browsing the row upon row of books then; most were in Greek but some were in English too. She didn't know for how long she scanned titles, admired covers and read back-cover blurbs, but she slowly became aware of Finn watching her from where he sat on one of the low stools that were placed intermittently about the shop for customers' convenience. She surprised a look of affection on his face, and it made her feel bad for sniping at him earlier and dismissing him as a playboy adventurer.

He grinned. 'You look like you're having fun.'

'I am.' This slow browsing, the measured contemplation of the delights offered up on these shelves—the sheer *unrushedness* of it all—filled something inside her. She glanced at his hands, his lap, the floor at his feet. 'You don't have a book yet.'

He nodded at the stack she held. 'Are you getting all of those?'

'I'm getting the French cookbook.' She'd need a recipe for croissants. 'And three of these.'

He took the cookbook from her, and then she handed him two women's fiction titles and a cosy mystery, before putting the others back where they belonged.

'What would you choose for me?' His lip curled as he reached forward to flick a disparaging finger at a blockbuster novel from a big-name writer. 'Something like that?'

'That's a historical saga with lots of period detail. I'd have not thought it was your cup of tea at all.' She suspected the pace would be a bit slow for his taste. 'The object of the exercise isn't to make you suffer.'

Amber eyes darker than the whisky he liked but just as intoxicating swung to her and she saw the surprise in their depths. She recalled the affection she'd surprised in his face a moment ago and swallowed. Had she become a complete and utter shrew somewhere over the last year or two? 'I know that our modus operandi is to tease each other and…and to try to best each other—all in fun, of course.'

He inclined his head. 'Of course.'

'But I want to show you that quieter pursuits can be pleasurable too. If I were choosing a book for you I'd get you—' she strode along to the humour section '—this.' She pulled out a book by a popular comedian that she knew he liked.

He blinked and took it.

She set off down the next row of shelves. 'And to be on the safe side I'd get you this as well…or this.' She pulled out two recent non-fiction releases. One a biography of a well-known sportsman, and the other on World War Two.

He nodded towards the second one and she added it to the growing pile of books in his arms.

She started back the way they'd come. 'If I were on my own I'd get you this one as a joke.' She held up a self-help book with the title *Twelve Rules for Life: An Antidote to Chaos*.

'Put it back.'

The laughter in his voice added a spring to her step. She slotted it back into place. 'I'd get you a wildcard too.'

'A wildcard?'

'A book on spec—something you might not like, but could prove to be something you'd love.'

He pursed his lips for a moment and then nodded. 'I want a wildcard.'

Excellent. But what? She thought back over what he'd said earlier—about wanting to be a fireman, a knife-thrower, an explorer. She returned to the fiction shelves. She'd bet her house on the fact he'd love tales featuring heroic underdogs. She pulled a novel from the shelf—the first book in a fantasy trilogy from an acclaimed writer.

'That's…that's a doorstop!'

'Yes or no?'

He blew out a breath. 'What the hell, add it to the pile.'

She did, and then retrieved her own books from his arms. 'I'm not letting you buy my books.'

'Why not?'

'I like to buy my own books. And I've thrust three books onto you that you may never open.'

He stretched his neck, first one way and then the other. 'Can I buy you lunch?'

'As a thank you for being your bookstore personal shopper? Absolutely. But let's make it a late lunch. I'm still full from breakfast.'

She stopped to select her bookmarks, and added two notebooks to her purchases. Finn chose a bookmark of his own, and then seized a satchel in butter-soft black leather. 'Perfect.'

Perfect for what? She glanced at the selection of leather satchels and calico book bags and bit her lip. Maybe—

With a laugh, Finn propelled her towards the counter. 'Save them for your next visit.'

They paid and while Audra exchanged greetings with Sibyl, the bookshop proprietor, he put all their purchases into the satchel and slung it over his shoulder. 'Where to next?'

She stared at that bag. It'd make his shoulder ache if he wasn't careful. But then she realised it was on his right shoulder, not his left, and let out a breath. 'Wherever the mood takes us,' she said as they moved towards the door.

She paused to read the community announcement board and an advertisement for art classes jumped out at her. Oh, that'd be fun and…

She shook her head. R & R was all very well, but she had to keep herself contained to the beach and her books. Anything else… Well, anything else was just too hard. And she was too tired.

Finn trailed a finger across the flyer. 'Interested?'

She shook her head and led him outside.

He frowned at her. 'But—'

'Ooh, these look like fun.' She shot across to the boutique next door and was grateful when he let himself be distracted.

They flicked through a rack of discounted clothing that stood in blatant invitation out the front. Finn bought a pair of swimming trunks, so she added a sarong to her growing list of purchases. They browsed the markets. Finn bought a pair of silver cufflinks in the shape of fat little aeroplanes. 'My uncle will love these.' He pointed to an oddly shaped silver pendant on a string of black leather. 'That'd look great on you.' So she bought that too. They helped each other choose sunhats.

It felt decadent to be spending like this, not that any of her purchases were particularly pricey. But she so rarely let herself off the leash that she blithely ignored the voice of puritan sternness that tried to reel her in. What was more, it gave her the chance to exchange proper greetings with the villagers she'd known for years now.

Her worries she'd be grilled about Thomas and her reputed broken heart and the upcoming court case dissolved within ten minutes. As always, the people of Kyanós embraced her as if she were one of their own. And she loved them for it. The Russel family had been coming for holidays here for nearly ten years now. Kyanós felt like a home away from home.

'Hungry yet?'

'Famished!' She glanced at her watch and did a double take when she saw it was nearly two o'clock. 'We haven't done the bakery, the butcher, the delicatessen or the wine merchant yet.'

'We have time.'

She lifted her face to the sun and closed her eyes to relish it even more. 'We do.'

They chose a restaurant that had a terrace overlooking the harbour and ordered a shared platter of warm olives, cured meats and local cheeses accompanied with bread warm from the oven and a cold crisp carafe of *retsina*. While they ate they browsed their book purchases.

Audra surreptitiously watched Finn as he sampled the opening page of the fantasy novel…and then the next page…and the one after that.

He glanced up and caught her staring. He hesitated and then shrugged. 'You know, this might be halfway decent.'

She refrained from saying I told you so. 'Good.'

'If I hadn't seen you choose me those first two books I'd have not given this one a chance. I'd have written it off as a joke like the self-help book. And as I suspect I'll enjoy both these other books…'

If he stayed still long enough to read them.

He frowned.

She folded her arms. 'Why does that make you frown?'

'I'm wishing I'd known about this book when I was laid up in hospital with nothing to do.'

The shadows in his eyes told her how stir-crazy he'd gone. 'What did you do to pass the time?'

'Crosswords. And I watched lots of movies.'

'And chafed.'

'Pretty much.'

'I almost sent you a book, but I thought…'

'You thought I'd misinterpret the gesture? Think you were rubbing salt into the wound?'

Something like that.

He smiled. 'I appreciated the puzzle books.' And then he scowled. 'I didn't appreciate the grapes, though. Grapes are for invalids.'

She stiffened. 'It was supposed to be an entire basket of fruit!' Not just grapes.

'Whatever. I'd have preferred a bottle of tequila. I gave the fruit to the nurses.'

But his eyes danced as he feigned indignation and it was hard to contain a grin. 'I'll keep that in mind for next time.'

He gave a visible shudder and she grimaced in sympathy. 'Don't have a next time.' She raised her glass. 'To no more accidents and a full and speedy recovery.'

'I'll drink to that.'

He lifted his glass to hers and then sipped it with an abandoned enjoyment she envied. 'Who knew you'd be such fun to shop with?'

The words shot out of her impulsively, and she found herself speared on the end of a keen-edged glance. 'You thought I'd chafe?'

'A bit,' she conceded. 'I mean, Rupert and Justin will put up with it when Cora or I want to window-shop, but they don't enjoy it.'

'I wouldn't want to do it every day.'

Neither would she.

'But today has been fun.' He stared at her for a beat too long. 'It was a revelation watching you in the bookstore.'

She swallowed. Revelation, how?

'It's been a long time since I saw you enjoy yourself so much, Squirt, and—' He shot back in his seat. 'Audra! I meant to say Audra. Don't make that Strike Two. I…'

He gazed at her helplessly and she forgave him instantly. He hadn't said it to needle her the way he had with his earlier *Squirt*. She shook herself. 'Sorry, what were you saying? I was miles away.'

He smiled his thanks, but then leaned across the table towards her, and that smile and his closeness made her breath catch. 'You should do things you enjoy more often, Miss Conscientiousness.'

Hmm, she'd preferred Squirt.

'There's more to life than boardrooms and spreadsheets.'

'That's what holidays are for,' she agreed. The boardrooms and spreadsheets would be waiting for her at the end of it, though, and the thought made her feel tired to the soles of her feet.

CHAPTER FOUR

AUDRA GLANCED ACROSS at Finn, who looked utterly content lying on his towel on the sand of this ridiculously beautiful curve of beach, reading his book. It seemed ironic, then, that she couldn't lose herself in her own book.

She blamed it on the half-remembered dreams that'd given her a restless night. Scraps had been playing through her mind all morning—sexy times moving to the surreal and the scary; Finn's and Thomas's faces merging and then separating—leaving her feeling restless and strung tight.

One of those sexy-time moments played through her mind again now and she bit her lip against the warmth that wanted to spread through her. The fact that this beach was so ridiculously private didn't help. She didn't want the words *private* and *Finn*—or *sexy times*—to appear in the same thought with such tempting symmetry. It was *crazy*. She'd always done her best to not look at Finn in *that* way. And she had no intention of letting her guard down now.

This whole preoccupation was just a…a way for her subconscious to avoid focussing on what needed to be dealt with. Which was to regather her resources and refocus her determination to be of service at the Russel Corporation, to be a valuable team member rather than a liability.

'What was that sigh for?'

She blinked to find Finn's beautiful brown eyes surveying her. And they were beautiful—the colour of cinnamon and golden syrup and ginger beer, and fringed with long dark lashes. She didn't know how lashes could look decadent and sinful, but Finn's did.

'You're supposed to be relaxing—enjoying the sun and the sea…your book.'

'I am.'

'Liar.'

He rolled to his side to face her more fully, and she shrugged. 'I had a restless night.' She stifled a yawn. 'That's all.'

'When one works as hard as you do, it can be difficult to switch off.'

'Old habits,' she murmured, reaching for her T-shirt and pulling it over her head and then tying her sarong about her waist, feeling ridiculously naked in her modest one-piece.

Which was crazy because she and Finn and the rest of her family had been on this beach countless times together, and in briefer swimsuits than what either of them were wearing now. 'I don't want to get too much sun all at once,' she said by way of explanation, although Finn hadn't indicated by so much as a blink of his gorgeous eyelashes that he'd wanted or needed one. She glanced at him. 'You've been incapacitated for a couple of months and yet I'm paler than you.'

'Yeah, but my incapacitation meant spending a lot of time on the rooftop terrace of my apartment on the French Riviera, so…not exactly doing it tough.'

Fair point.

'You ever tried meditation?'

'You're talking to me, Audra, remember?'

His slow grin raised all the tiny hairs on her arms. 'Lie on your back in a comfortable position and close your eyes.'

'Finn…' She could barely keep the whine out of her voice. 'Meditation makes me feel like a failure.' And there was more than enough of that in her life at the moment as it was, thank you very much. 'I know you're supposed to *clear your mind*, but…it's impossible!'

'Would you be so critical and hard on someone else? Cut yourself some slack.' He rolled onto his back. 'Work on quietening your mind rather than clearing it. When a thought appears, as it will, simply acknowledge it before focussing on your breathing again.'

He closed his eyes and waited. With another sigh, Audra rolled onto her back and settled her hat over her face. It was spring and the sun wasn't fierce, but she wasn't taking any chances. 'Okay,' she grumbled. 'I'm ready. What am I supposed to do?'

Finn led her through a guided meditation where she counted breaths, where she tensed and then relaxed different muscle groups. The deep timbre of his voice, unhurried and undemanding, soothed her in a way she'd have never guessed possible. Her mind wandered, as he'd said it would, but she brought her attention back to his voice and her breathing each time, and by the time he finished she felt weightless and light.

She heard no movement from him, so she stayed exactly where she was—on a cloud of euphoric relaxation.

And promptly fell asleep.

Finn didn't move until Audra's deep rhythmic breaths informed him that she was asleep. Not a light and sweet little nap, but fully and deeply asleep.

He rolled onto his tummy and rested his chin on his arms. When had she forgotten how to relax? He'd spent a large portion of every Christmas vacation from the age of twelve onwards with the Russel family.

She'd been a sweet, sparky little kid, fiercely determined to keep up with her older siblings and not be left behind. As a teenager she'd been curious, engaged…and a bit more of a dreamer than the others, not as driven in a particular direction as they'd been either. But then he'd figured that'd made her more of an all-rounder.

When had she lost her zest, her joy for life? During her final years of school? At university? He swallowed. When her mother had died?

Karen Russel had died suddenly of a cerebral aneurysm

ten years ago. It'd shattered the entire family. Audra had only been seventeen.

Was it then that Audra had exchanged her joy in life for…? For what? To become a workaholic managing the charitable arm of her family's corporation? In her grief, had she turned away from the things that had given her joy? Had it become a habit?

He recalled the odd defiance in her eyes when she'd spoken about owning a shop—the way she'd mocked the idea…and the way the mockery and defiance had been at odds. He turned to stare at her. 'Hell, sweetheart,' he whispered. 'What are you doing to yourself?'

She slept for an hour, and Finn was careful to pretend not to notice when she woke, even though his every sense was honed to her every movement. He kept his nose buried in his book and feigned oblivion, which wasn't that hard because the book was pretty gripping.

'Hey,' she said in sleepy greeting.

'Hey, yourself, you lazy slob.' Only then did he allow himself to turn towards her. 'I didn't know napping was included on the agenda today.'

'If I remember correctly, the order for the day was lazing about in the sun on the beach, reading books and a bit of swimming.' She flicked out a finger. 'My nap included lying on the beach *and*—' she flicked out a second finger '—lazing in the sun. So I'm following the remit to the letter, thank you very much.'

The rest had brightened her eyes. And when she stretched her arms back over her head, he noted that her shoulders had lost their hard edge. He noted other things—things that would have Rupert taking a swing at him if he knew—so he did his best to remove those from his mind.

In one fluid motion, she rose. 'I'm going in for a dip.'

That sounded like an excellent plan. He definitely needed to cool off. Her glance flicked to the scar of his splenectomy when he rose too, and it took an effort to not turn away and hide it from her gaze.

And then she untied her sarong and pulled her T-shirt over her head and it was all he could do to think straight at all.

She nodded at the scar. 'Does it still hurt?'

He touched the indentations and shook his head. 'It didn't really hurt much after it was done either.' At her raised eyebrows he winked. 'Wish I could say the same about the broken ribs.'

She huffed out a laugh, and he was grateful when she moved towards the water's edge without asking any further questions about his accident. Its aftershocks continued to reverberate through him, leaving him at a loss. He didn't know how much longer he'd have to put up with it. He didn't know how much longer he *could* put up with it.

The cold dread that had invaded the pit of his stomach in the moments after his fall invaded him again now, and he broke out in an icy sweat. He'd known in that moment—his skis flying one way and the rest of him going another—that he'd hurt himself badly. He'd understood in a way he never had before that he could die; he had realised he might not make it off the mountain alive.

And every instinct he'd had had screamed a protest against that fate. He hadn't wanted to die, not yet. There were things he wanted—*yearned*—to do. If he'd had breath to spare he'd have begged the medical team to save him. But there'd been no breath to spare, and he'd started spiralling in and out of consciousness.

When he'd awoken from surgery…the relief and gratitude…there were no words to describe it. But for the life of him, now that he was all but recovered, he couldn't remember the things he'd so yearned to do—the reasons why staying alive had seemed so urgent.

All of it had left him with an utter lack of enthusiasm for any of the previous high-octane sports that had once sung to his soul. Had he lost his nerve? He didn't think so. He didn't feel afraid. He just—

A jet of water hit him full in the face and shook him immediately out of his thoughts. 'Lighten up, Finn. I'd have not mentioned the scar if I'd known it'd make you so grim. Don't worry. I'm sure the girls will still fall at your feet with the same old regularity. The odd scar will probably add to your mystique.'

She thought he was brooding for reasons of...*vanity*?

She laughed outright at whatever she saw in his face. 'You're going to pay for that,' he promised, scooping water up in his hands.

They were both soaked at the end of their water fight. Audra simply laughed and called him a bully when he picked her up and threw her into the sea.

He let go of her quick smart, though, because she was an armful of delicious woman...and he couldn't go there. Not with her. 'Race you out to the buoy.'

'Not a chance.' She caressed the surface of the water with an unconscious sensuality that had his gut clenching. 'I'm feeling too Zen after that meditation. And, if you'll kindly remember, there's no racing on today's agenda, thank you very much.'

'Wait until tomorrow.'

She stuck her nose in the air. 'Please don't disturb me while I'm living in the moment.'

With a laugh, he turned and swam out to the buoy. He didn't rush, but simply relished the way his body slid through the water, relished how good it felt to be rid of the cast. He did five laps there and back before his left arm started up a dull ache...and before he could resist finding out what Audra was up to.

He glanced across at where she floated on her back, her face lifted to the sky. He couldn't tell from here whether she had her eyes open or closed. She looked relaxed—now. And while *now* she might also be all grown up, during their water fight she'd laughed and squealed as she had when a girl.

He had a feeling, though, that when her short holiday was over all that tension would descend on her again, pulling her tight. Because…?

Because she wasn't doing the things that gave her joy, wasn't living the life that she should be living. And he had a growing conviction that this wasn't a new development, but an old one he'd never picked up on before. He had no idea how to broach the topic either. She could be undeniably prickly, and she valued her privacy. *Just like you do.* She'd tell him to take a flying leap and mind his own business. And that'd be that.

Walk away. He didn't do encouraging confidences. He didn't do complicated. And it didn't matter which way he looked at it—Audra had always been complicated. Fun and laughter, those were his forte.

He glided through the water towards her until he was just a couple of feet away. 'Boo.'

He didn't shout the word, just said it in a normal tone, but she started so violently he immediately felt sick to his gut. She spun around, the colour leaching from her face, and he wanted to kick himself—hard. 'Damn, Audra, I didn't mean to scare the living daylights out of you.'

She never used to startle this easily. What the hell had happened to change that?

None of the scenarios that played in his mind gave him the slightest bit of comfort.

'Glad I didn't grab you round the waist to tug you under, which had been my first thought.' He said it to try to lighten the moment. When they were kids they all used to dunk each other mercilessly.

If possible she went even paler. And then she ducked under the water, resurfacing a moment later to slick her hair back from her face. 'Note to self,' she said with remarkable self-possession, though he noted the way her hands shook. 'Don't practise meditation in the sea when Finn is around.'

He wanted to apologise again, but it'd be making too big a deal out of it and he instinctively knew that would make her defensive.

'I might head in.' She started a lazy breaststroke back towards the shore. 'How many laps did you do?'

'Just a couple.' Had she been watching him?

'How does the arm feel?'

He bit back a snap response. *It's fine. And can we just forget about my accident already?* She didn't deserve that. She had to know he didn't like talking about his injuries, but if this was the punishment she'd chosen for his ill-timed *Boo* then he'd take it like a man. 'Dishearteningly weak.'

Her gaze softened. 'You'll get your fitness back, Finn. Just don't push it too hard in these early days.'

He'd had every intention of getting to Kyanós and then swimming and running every day without mercy until he'd proven to himself that he was as fit as he'd been prior to his accident. And yet he found himself more than content at the moment to keep pace beside her. He rolled his shoulders. He'd only been here a couple of days. That old fire would return to his belly soon enough.

He pounced on the cooler bag as soon as he'd towelled off. 'I'm famished.'

He tossed her a peach, which she juggled, nearly dropped and finally caught. He grinned and bit into a second peach. The fragrant flesh and sweet juice hitting the back of his throat tasted better than anything he'd eaten in the last eight weeks. He groaned his pleasure, closing his eyes to savour it all the more. When he opened his eyes again, he found her staring at him as if she'd never seen him before.

Hell, no! Don't look at me like that, Audra.

Like a woman who looked at a man and considered his…um…finer points. It made his skin go hot and tight.

It made him want to reach out, slide a hand behind the back of her head and pull her close and—

He glanced out to sea, his pulse racing. He wanted to put colour back into her cheeks, but not like that. The two of them were like oil and water. If he did something stupid now, it'd impact on his relationship with her entire family, and the Russels and his uncle Ned were the only family he had.

He dragged in a gulp of air. Given his current state of mind, he had to be hyper-vigilant that he didn't mess all this up. He had a history of bringing trouble to the doors of those he cared about—Rupert all those years ago, and now Joachim. Rupert was right—Audra had been through enough. He had no intention of bringing more trouble down on her head.

He forced his stance to remain relaxed. 'Wanna go for a run?'

'A run?' She snapped away and then stared at him as if he'd lost his mind. Which was better. Much *much* better. 'Do you not know me at all?'

He shrugged. 'It was worth a shot.'

'No running, no rushing, no racing.' She ticked the items off her fingers. 'Those are the rules for today. I'm going to explore the rock pools.'

He followed because he couldn't help it. Because a question burned through him and he knew he'd explode if he didn't ask it.

They explored in silence for ten or fifteen minutes. 'Audra?' He worked hard to keep his voice casual.

'Hmm?'

'What the hell did that bastard Farquhar do to you?'

She froze, and then very slowly turned. 'Wow, excellent tactic, Sullivan. Don't get your way over going for a run so hit a girl with an awkward question instead.'

A question he noted she hadn't answered. He rolled with it. 'I work with what I've got.'

Her hands went to her waist. She wore her T-shirt again but not her sarong, and her legs… Her legs went on and on…and on. Where had she been hiding them? 'Who's this woman in Nice you're trying to avoid?'

Oho! So Rupert had told her about that. 'You answer my question, and I'll answer any question you want.'

Her brows rose. '*Any* question?'

'Any time you want to ask it.'

CHAPTER FIVE

ANY TIME SHE wanted to ask it?

That meant… Audra's mind raced. That meant if Finn were running hell for leather, doing laps as if training for a triathlon, risking his neck as if there were no tomorrow, then…then she could ask a question and he'd have to stop and answer her?

Oh, she'd try other stalling tactics first. She wasn't wasting a perfectly good question if she could get him to slow down in other ways, but…

She tried to stop her internal glee from showing. 'You have yourself a deal.'

Finn readjusted his stance. 'So what's the story with Farquhar? The bit that didn't make the papers.'

She hiked herself up to sit on a large rock, its top worn smooth, but its sides pitted with the effects of wind and sand. It was warm beneath her hands and thighs.

He settled himself beside her. 'Is it hard to talk about?'

She sent him what she hoped was a wry glance. 'It's never fun to own up to being a fool…or to having made such a big mistake.'

'Audra—'

She waved him silent. 'I'm surprised you don't know the story.' She'd have thought Rupert would've filled him in.

'I know what was in the paper but not, I suspect, the whole story.'

Dear Rupert. He'd kept his word.

Oddly, though, she didn't mind Finn knowing the story in its entirety. While they might've been friendly adversaries all these years, he was practically family. He'd have her best interests at heart, just as she did his.

'Right.' She slapped her hands to her thighs and he glanced down at them. His face went oddly tight and he immediately stared out to sea. A pulse started up in her throat and her heart danced an irregular pattern in her chest.

Stop it. Don't think of Finn in that way.

But...he's hot.

And he thinks you're hot.

Nonsense! He's just... He just found it hard to not flirt with every woman in his orbit.

She forced herself to bring Thomas's face to mind and the pulse-jerking and heart-hammering came to a screeching halt. 'So the part that everyone knows—' the part that had made the papers '—is that Thomas Farquhar and I had been dating for over seven months.'

Wary brown eyes met hers and he gave a nod. 'What made you fall for him?'

She shrugged. 'He seemed so...*nice*. He went out of his way to spend time with me, and do nice things for me. It was just...nice,' she finished lamely. He'd been so earnest about all the things she was earnest about. He'd made her feel as if she were doing exactly what she ought to be doing with her life. She'd fallen for all of that intoxicating attention and validation hook, line and sinker.

'But it's clear now that he was only dating me to steal company secrets.' A fact the entire world now knew thanks to the tabloids. She shrivelled up a little more inside every time she thought about it.

The Russel Corporation, established by her Swiss grandfather sixty years ago, had originally been founded on a watchmaking dynasty but was now made up of a variety of concerns, including a large charitable arm. Her father was the CEO, though Rupert had been groomed to take over and, to all intents and purposes, was running the day-to-day operations of the corporation.

Her siblings were champions of social justice, each in

their own way, just as her parents and grandparents had been in their younger days. Their humanitarian activities were administered by the Russel Corporation, and, as one of the corporation's chief operation managers, Audra had the role of overseeing a variety of projects—from hiring the expertise needed on different jobs and organising the delivery of necessary equipment and goods, to wrangling with various licences and permissions that needed to be secured, and filling in endless government grant forms. And in her spare time she fundraised. It was hectic, high-powered and high-stakes.

For the last five years her sister, Cora, a scientist, had been working on developing a new breakthrough vaccine for the Ebola virus. While such a vaccine would help untold sufferers of the illness, it also had the potential to make pharmaceutical companies vast sums of money.

She tried to slow the churning of her stomach. 'Thomas was after Cora's formulae and research. We know now that he was working for a rival pharmaceutical company. We suspect he deliberately targeted me, and that our meeting at a fundraising dinner wasn't accidental.'

From the corner of her eye she saw Finn nod. She couldn't look at him. Instead she twisted her hands together in her lap and watched the progress of a small crab as it moved from one rock pool to another. 'He obviously worked out my computer password. There were times when we were in bed, when I thought he was asleep, and I'd grab my laptop to log in quickly just to check on something.'

She watched in fascination as his hand clenched and then unclenched. 'You'd have had to have more than one password to get anywhere near Cora's data.'

'Oh, I have multiple passwords. I have one for my laptop, different ones for my desktop computers at home and work. There's the password for my Russel Corporation account. And each of the projects has its own password.'

There'd been industrial espionage attempts before. She'd been briefed on internet and computer security. 'But it appears he'd had covert cameras placed around my apartment.'

'How…?'

How did he get access? 'I gave him a key.' She kept her voice flat and unemotional. She'd given an industrial spy unhampered access to her flat—what an idiot! 'I can tell you now, though, that all those romantic dinners he made for us—' his pretext for needing a key '—have taken on an entirely different complexion.' It'd seemed mean-spirited not to give him a key at the time, especially as he'd given her one to his flat.

He swore. 'Did he have cameras in the bedroom?'

'No.' He'd not sunk that low. But it didn't leave her feeling any less violated. 'But…but he must've seen me do some stupid, ugly, unfeminine things on those cameras. And I know it's nothing on the grand scale, but… it *irks* me!'

'What kind of things?'

She slashed a hand through the air. 'Oh, I don't know. Like picking my teeth or hiking my knickers out from uncomfortable places, or… Have you ever seen a woman put on a pair of brand-new sixty-denier opaque tights?'

He shook his head.

'Well, it's not sexy. It looks ludicrous and contortionist and it probably looks hilarious and… And I feel like enough of a laughing stock without him having footage of that too.'

A strong arm came about her shoulder and pulled her in close. Just for a moment she let herself sink against him to soak up the warmth and the comfort. 'He played me to perfection,' she whispered. 'I didn't suspect a damn thing. I thought—' She faltered. 'I thought he liked me.'

His arm tightened about her. 'He was a damn fool. The

man has to be a certifiable idiot to choose money over you, sweetheart.'

He pressed his lips to her hair and she felt an unaccountable urge to cry.

She didn't want to cry!

'Stop it.' She pushed him away and leapt down from the rock. 'Don't be nice to me. My stupidity nearly cost Cora all of the hard work she's put in for the last five years.'

'But it didn't.'

No, it hadn't. And it was hard to work up an outraged stomp in flip-flops, and with the Aegean spread before her in twinkling blue perfection and the sun shining down as if the world was full of good things. The files Thomas had stolen were old, and, while to an outsider the formulae and hypotheses looked impressive, the work was neither new nor ground-breaking. Audra didn't have access to the information Thomas had been so anxious to get his hands on for the simple fact that she didn't need it. The results of Cora's research had nothing to do with Audra's role at work.

But Thomas didn't know that yet. And there was a court case pending. 'So…' She squinted into the sun at him. 'Rupert told you that much, huh?'

'I didn't know about the hidden cameras, but as for the rest…' He nodded.

'You know that's all classified, right?'

He nodded again. 'What hasn't Rupert told me?' He dragged in a breath, his hands clenching. 'Did Farquhar break your heart?'

She huffed out a laugh. 'Which of those questions do you want me to answer first?' When he didn't answer, she moved back to lean against the rock. 'I'll answer the second first because that'll move us on nicely to the first.' She winced at the bitterness that laced her *nicely*. 'No, he didn't break my heart. In fact I was starting to feel smothered by him so I…uh…'

'You...?'

'I told him I wanted to break up.'

He stared at her for a long moment. The muscles in his jaw tensed. 'What did he do?'

She swallowed. 'He pushed me into the hall closet and locked me in.'

He swore and the ferocity of his curse made her blink. He landed beside her, his expression black.

'I...I think he panicked when I demanded my key back. So he locked me in, stole my computer and high-tailed it out of there.'

'How long were you in there?'

'All night.' And it'd been the longest night of her life.

'How...?'

He clenched his fists so hard he started to shake. In a weird way his outrage helped.

'How did you get out?'

'He made the mistake of using my access code to get into the office early the next morning. Very early when he didn't think anyone else would be around. But Rupert, who had jet lag, had decided to put in a few hours. He saw the light on in my office, and came to drag me off to breakfast.' She shrugged. 'He found Thomas rifling through my filing cabinets instead. The first thing he did was to call Security. The second was to call my home phone and then my mobile. Neither of which I could answer. He has a key to my flat, so...'

'So he raced over and let you out.'

'Yep.'

She'd never been happier to see her older brother in her life. Her lips twisted. 'It was only then, though, that I learned of the extent of Thomas's double-dealing. And all I wanted to do was crawl back in the closet and hide from the world.'

'Sweetheart—'

She waved him quiet again. 'I know all the things you're

going to say, Finn, but don't. Rupert's already said them. *None of this is my fault. Anyone can be taken in by a con-man... Blah-blah-blah.*'

She moved to the edge of the rock shelf and stared out at the sea, but its beauty couldn't soothe her. She'd been taken in by a man whose interest and undivided attention had turned her head—a man who'd seemed not only interested but invested in hearing about her hopes and dreams...and supporting her in those dreams. She hadn't felt the focus of somebody's world like that since her mother had died.

She folded her arms, gripped her elbows tight. But it'd all been a lie, and in her hunger for that attention she'd let her guard down. It'd had the potential to cause untold damage to Cora's career, not to mention the Russel Corporation's reputation. She'd been such an idiot!

And to add insult to injury she'd spent the best part of six weeks trying to talk herself out of breaking up with him because he'd seemed so darn perfect.

Idiot! Idiot! Idiot!

'So now you feel like a gullible fool who's let the family down, and you look at every new person you meet through the tainted lens of suspicion—wondering if they can be trusted or if they're just out for whatever they can get.'

Exactly. She wanted to dive into the sea and power through the water until she was too tired to think about any of this any more. It was a decent swim from here back to the beach, but one that was within her powers. Only... if she did that Finn would follow and five laps out to the buoy and back was enough for him for one day.

She swung around to meet his gaze. 'That sounds like the voice of experience.'

He shrugged and moved to stand beside her, his lips tightening as he viewed the horizon. 'It's how I'd feel in your shoes.'

'Except you'd never be so stupid.' She turned and

started to pick her way back along the rock pools towards the beach.

'I've done stupider things with far less cause.'

He had? She turned to find him staring at her with eyes as turbulent as the Aegean in a storm. She didn't press him, but filed the information away. She might ask him about that some day.

'And even Rupert isn't mistake free. Getting his heart broken by Brooke Manning didn't show a great deal of foresight.'

'He was young,' she immediately defended. 'And we all thought she was as into him as he was into her.'

He raised an eyebrow, and she lifted her hands. 'Okay, okay. I know. It's just… Rupert's mistake didn't hurt anyone but himself. My mistake had the potential to ruin Cora's life's work to date and impact on the entire Russel Corporation, and—'

Warm hands descended to her shoulders. 'But it didn't. Stop focussing on what could have happened and deal with what actually did happen. And the positives that can be found there.'

'Positives?' she spluttered.

'Sure.'

'Oh, I can't wait to hear this. C'mon, wise guy, name me one positive.'

He rubbed his chin. 'Well, for starters, you'd worked out Farquhar was a jerk and had kicked his sorry butt to the kerb.'

Not exactly true. She'd just been feeling suffocated, and hadn't been able to hide from that fact any more.

'And don't forget that's been caught on camera too.'

She stared up at him. And a slow smile built through her. 'Oh, my God.'

He cocked an eyebrow.

'He argued about us breaking up. He wanted me to re-consider and give him another chance.'

'Not an unusual reaction.'

'I told him we could still see each other as friends.'

Finn clutched his chest as if he'd been shot through the heart. 'Ouch!'

'And then he ranted and paced for a bit, and when he had his back to me a few times I, uh, rolled my eyes and...'

'And?'

'Checked my watch because there was a programme on television I was hoping to catch.'

He barked out a laugh.

'And this is embarrassing, for him, so I shouldn't tell it.'

'Yes, you should. You *really* should.'

'Well, he cried. Obviously they were crocodile tears, but I wasn't to know that at the time. I went to fetch the box of tissues, and while my back was to him I pulled this horrible kind of "God help me" face at the wall.'

She gave him a demonstration and he bent at the waist and roared. 'Crocodile tears or not, that's going to leave his ego in shreds. I'm sorry, sweetheart, but getting caught picking your nose suddenly doesn't seem like such a bad thing.'

'I do *not* pick my nose.' She stuck that particular appendage in the air. But Finn was right. She found she didn't care quite so much if Thomas had seen her pigging out on chocolate or dancing to pop music in her knickers. Now whenever she thought about any of those things she'd recall her hilarious grimace—probably straight at some hidden camera—and would feel partially vindicated.

She swung to Finn. 'Thank you.'

'You're welcome.'

They reached the beach and shook sand off their towels, started the five-minute climb back up the hill to the villa. 'Audra?'

'Hmm?'

'I'm sorry I scared you when I arrived the other night.

I'm sorry I scared you with my *boo* out there.' He waved towards the water.

She shrugged. 'You didn't mean to.'

'No, I didn't mean to.'

And his voice told her he'd be careful it wouldn't happen again. Rather than being irked at being treated with kid gloves, she felt strangely cared for.

'I guess I owe you an answer now to your question about the woman in Nice who I'm avoiding.'

'No, thank you very much. I mean, you *do* owe me an answer to a question—that was the deal. But I'm not wasting it getting the skinny on some love affair gone wrong.'

He didn't say anything for a long moment. 'What's your question, then?'

'I don't know yet. When I do know I'll ask it.' And then he'd have to stop whatever he was doing and take a timeout to answer it. *Perfect.*

Finn studied Audra across the breakfast table the next morning. Actually, their breakfast table had become the picnic table that sat on the stone terrace outside, where they could drink in the glorious view. She'd turned down the bacon and eggs, choosing cereal instead. He made a mental note to buy croissants the next time they were in the village.

'What are you staring at, Finn?'

He wanted to make sure she was eating enough. But he knew exactly how well that'd go down if he admitted as much. 'I'm just trying to decide if that puny body of yours is up to today's challenge, Russel.'

A spark lit the ice-blue depths of her eyes, but then she shook her head as if realising he was trying to goad her into some kind of reaction. 'This puny body is up for a whole lot more lazing on a beach and a little bobbing about in the sea.'

'Nice try, sweetheart.'

She rolled her eyes. 'What horrors do you have planned?'

'You'll see.' He was determined that by the time she left the island she'd feel fitter, healthier and more empowered than she had when she'd arrived.

She harrumphed and slouched over her muesli, but her gaze wandered out towards the light gleaming on the water and it made her lips lift and her eyes dance. Being here— taking a break—had already been good for her.

But he wanted her to have fun too. A workout this morning followed by play this afternoon. That seemed like a decent balance.

'You want us to what?'

An hour later Audra stared at him with such undisguised horror it was all he could do not to laugh. If he laughed, though, it'd rile her and he didn't want her riled. Unless it was the only way to win her cooperation.

'I want us to jog the length of the beach.'

Her mouth opened and closed. 'But…why? How can this be fun?'

'Exercise improves my mood.' It always had. As a teenager it'd also been a way to exorcise his demons. Now it just helped to keep him fit and strong. He *liked* feeling fit and strong.

He waited for her to make some crack about being in favour of anything that improved his mood. Instead she planted her hands on her hips and stared at him. She wore a silky caftan thing over her swimsuit and the action made it ride higher on her thighs. He tried not to notice.

'Your mood has been fine since you've been here. Apart from your foul temper when you first arrived.'

'You mean when the police had me in handcuffs?'

She nodded.

'I'd like to see how silver-tongued you'd be in that situation!'

She smirked and he realised she'd got the rise out of

him that she'd wanted, and he silently cursed himself. He fell for it every single time.

'But apart from that blip your mood has been fine.'

She was right. It had been. Which was strange because he'd been an absolute bear in Nice. He'd been a bear since the accident.

He shook that thought off. 'And we want to keep it that way.'

'But—' she gestured '—that has to be nearly a mile.'

'Yep.' He stared at her downturned mouth, imagined *again* that mongrel Farquhar shoving her in a cupboard, and wanted to smash something. He didn't want to bully her. If she really hated the idea… 'Is there any medical reason why you shouldn't run?'

She eyed him over the top of her sunglasses. 'No. You?'

'None. Running ten miles is out of the question, but one mile at a gentle pace will be fine.' He'd checked with his doctors.

'I haven't run since I was a kid. I work in an office… sit behind a desk all day. I'm not sure I can run that far.'

He realised then that her resistance came from a sense of inadequacy.

'I mean, even banged up you're probably super fit and—'

'We'll take it slow. And if you can't jog all the way, we'll walk the last part of it.'

'And you won't get grumpy at me for holding you back?'

'I promise.'

'No snark?'

He snorted. 'I'm not promising that.'

That spark flashed in her eyes again. 'Slow, you said?'

'Slow,' he promised.

She hauled in a breath. 'Well, here goes nothing…'

He started them slowly as promised. It felt good to be running again, even if it was at half his usual pace. Audra started a bit awkwardly, a trifle stiffly, as if the action were unfamiliar, but within two minutes she'd found a steady rhythm and he couldn't help but admire her poise and balance.

That damn ponytail, though, threatened his balance every time he glanced her way, bobbing with a cheeky nonchalance that made things inside him clench up…made him lose his tempo and stray from his course and have to check himself and readjust his line.

At the five-minute mark she was covered in a fine sheen of perspiration, and he suddenly flashed to a forbidden image of what she might look like during an athletic session of lovemaking. He stumbled and broke out into a cold sweat.

Audra seemed to lose her rhythm then too. Her elbows came in tight at her sides…she started to grimace…

And then her hands lifted to her breasts and he nearly fell over. She pulled to a halt and he did too. He glanced at her hands. She reefed them back to her sides and shot him a dark glare. 'Look, you didn't warn me that this is what we'd be doing before we hit the beach.'

Because he hadn't wanted her sniping at him the entire time they descended the hill.

'But they created exercise gear for a reason, you know? If I'm going to jog I need to wear a sports bra.'

He stared at her, not comprehending.

'It hurts to run without one,' she said through gritted teeth.

He blinked. *Hell.* He hadn't thought about that. She wasn't exactly big-breasted, but she was curvy where it mattered and…

'And while we're at it,' she ground out, 'I'd prefer to wear jogging shoes than run barefoot. This is darn hard on the ankles.' Her hands went to her hips. 'For heaven's sake, Finn, you have to give a girl some warning so she can prepare the appropriate outfit.'

He felt like an idiot. 'Well, let's just walk the rest of the way.'

It was hell walking beside her. Every breath he took was scented with peaches and coconut. And from the corner of his eye he couldn't help but track the perky progress of her ponytail. In his mind's eye all he could see was the way she'd cupped her breasts, to help take their weight while running, and things inside him twisted and grew hot.

When they reached the tall cliff at the beach's far end, Audra slapped a hand to it in a 'we made it' gesture. 'My mood doesn't feel improved.'

She sounded peeved, which made him want to laugh. But those lips...that ponytail... He needed a timeout, a little distance. *Now.*

She straightened and gave him the once-over. 'You're not even sweating the tiniest little bit!'

Not where she could see, at least. For which he gave thanks. But he needed to get waist-deep in water soon before she saw the effect she was having on him.

He gestured back the way they'd come. 'We're going to swim back.' Cold water suddenly seemed like an excellent plan.

Her face fell. 'Why didn't you say so before? I don't want to get my caftan wet. I could've left it behind.'

He was glad she hadn't. The less on show where she was concerned, the better.

'It'll take no time at all to dry off at the other end.'

'It's not designed to be swum in. It'll fall off my shoulder and probably get tangled in my legs.'

He clenched his jaw tight. *Not* an image he needed in his mind.

'I won't be able to swim properly.'

He couldn't utter a damn word.

Her chin shot up. 'You think I'm trying to wriggle my way out, don't you? You think I'm just making up excuses.'

It was probably wiser to let her misinterpret his silence than tell her the truth.

'Well, fine, I'll show you!'

She pulled the caftan over her head and tossed it to him. He did his best not to notice the flare of her hips, the long length of her legs, or the gentle swell of her breasts.

'I'll swim while you keep my caftan dry, cabana boy.'

Her, in the water way over there? Him, on the beach way over here? Worked for him.

'But when we reach the other end it's nothing but lazing on the beach and reading books till lunchtime.'

'Deal.' He was looking forward to another session with his book.

He kept pace with her on the shore, just in case she got a cramp or into some kind of trouble. She alternated freestyle with breaststroke and backstroke. And the slow easy pace suited him. It helped him find his equilibrium again. It gave him the time to remind himself in detail of all the ways he owed Rupert.

He nodded. He owed Rupert big-time—and that meant Audra was off limits and out of bounds. It might be different if Finn were looking to settle down, but settling down and Finn were barely on terms of acquaintance. And while he might feel as if he were at a crossroads in his life, that didn't mean anything. The after-effects of his accident would disappear soon enough. When they did, life would return to normal. He'd be looking for his next adrenaline rush and…and he'd be content again.

'Jetskiing?'

Audra stared at him with… Well, it wasn't horror at least. Consternation maybe? 'We had a laze on the beach, read our books, had a slow leisurely lunch…and now it's time for some fun.'

She rolled her bottom lip between her teeth. 'But aren't jetskis like motorbikes? And motorbikes are dangerous.'

He shook his head. 'Unlike a motorbike, it doesn't hurt if you fall off a jetski.' At least, not at the speeds they'd be going. 'They're only dangerous if we don't use them right…if we're stupid.'

'But we're going to be smart and use them right?'

He nodded. 'We're even going to have a lesson first.' He could teach her all she needed to know, but he'd come to the conclusion it might be *wiser* to not be so hands-on where Audra was concerned.

She stared at the jetskiers who were currently buzzing about on the bay. 'A lesson?' She pursed her lips. 'And…and it doesn't look as if it involves an awful lot of strength or stamina,' she said, almost to herself. And then she started and jutted her chin. 'Call me a wimp if you want, but I have a feeling I'm going to be sore enough tomorrow as it is.'

'If you are, the best remedy will be a run along the beach followed by another swim.'

She tossed her head. 'In your dreams, cabana boy.'

He grinned. It was good to see her old spark return. 'This is for fun, Audra, and no other reason. Just fun.'

He saw something in her mind still and then click. 'I guess I haven't been doing a whole lot of that recently.'

She could say that again.

'Okay, well…where do we sign up?'

There were seven of them who took the lesson, and while Finn expected to chafe during the hour-long session, he didn't. It was too much fun watching Audra and her cheeky ponytail as she concentrated on learning how to manoeuvre her jetski. They had a further hour to putter around the bay afterwards to test out her new-found skills. He didn't go racing off on his own. He didn't want her trying to copy him and coming to grief. They'd practised what to do in case of capsizing, but he didn't want them to have to put it into practice. Besides, her laughter and the way her eyes sparkled were too much fun to miss out on.

'Oh, my God!' She practically danced on the dock when they returned their jetskis. 'That was the best fun ever. I'm definitely doing that again. Soon!'

He tried to stop staring at her, tried to drag his gaze from admiring the shape of her lips, the length of her legs, the bounce of her hair. An evening spent alone with her in Rupert's enormous villa rose in his mind, making him sweat. 'Beer?' Hanging out in a crowd for as long as they could suddenly struck him as a sound strategy.

'Yes, please.'

They strode along the wooden dock and he glanced at her from the corner of his eye. The transformation from two days ago was amazing. She looked full of energy and so…*alive*.

He scrubbed both hands back through his hair. Why *was* she hell-bent on keeping herself on such a tight leash? Why didn't she let her hair down once in a while? Why…?

The questions pounded at him. He pressed both hands to the crown of his head in an effort to tamp them down, to counter the impulse to ask her outright. The thing was, even if he did break his protocol on asking personal questions and getting dragged into complicated emotional dilemmas, there was no guarantee Audra would confide in him. She'd never seen him as that kind of guy.

What if she needs to talk? What if she has no one else to confide in?

He wanted to swear.

He wanted to run.

He also wanted to see her filled with vitality and enthusiasm and joy, as she was now.

They ordered beers from a beachside bar and sat at a table in the shade of a jasmine vine to drink them.

'Today has been a really good day, Finn. Thank you.'

Audra wasn't like the women he dated. If she needed someone to confide in, he could be there for her, couldn't he? He took a long pull on his beer. 'Even the running?'

'Ugh, no, the running was awful.' She sipped her drink. 'I can't see I'm ever going to enjoy that, even with the right gear. Though I didn't mind the swimming. There's bound to be a local gym at home that has a pool.'

She was going to keep up the exercise when she returned home? Excellent.

He leaned back, a plan solidifying in his gut. 'You haven't asked your question yet.'

'I already told you—I don't want to hear about your woman in Nice. If you want to brag or grumble about her go right ahead. But I'm not wasting a perfectly good question on it.'

He wondered if he should just tell her about Trixie, but dismissed the idea. Trixie had no idea where he was. She wouldn't be able to cause any trouble here for him, for Joachim or for Audra. And he wanted to keep the smile, the sense of exhilaration, on Audra's face.

He stretched back, practically daring Audra to ask him a question. 'Isn't there anything personal you want to ask me?'

CHAPTER SIX

DID FINN HAVE any clue how utterly mouth-wateringly gorgeous he looked stretched out like that, as if for her express delectation? Audra knew he didn't mean anything by it. Flirting was as natural to him as breathing. If he thought for a moment she'd taken him seriously, he'd backtrack so fast it'd almost be funny.

Almost.

And she wasn't an idiot. Yet she couldn't get out of her mind the idea of striding around the table and—

No, not striding, *sashaying* around the table to plant herself in his lap, gently because she couldn't forget his injuries, and running her hand across the stubble of his jaw before drawing his lips down to hers.

Her mouth went dry and her heart pounded so hard she felt winded…dizzy. Maybe she was an idiot after all.

It was the romance of this idyllic Greek island combined with the euphoria of having whizzed across the water on a jetski. It'd left her feeling wild and reckless. She folded her hands together in her lap. She didn't do wild and reckless. If she went down that path it'd lead to things she couldn't undo. She'd let her family down enough as it was.

Finn folded himself up to hunch over his beer. 'Scrap that. Don't ask your question. I don't like the look on your face. You went from curiously speculative to prim and disapproving.'

She stiffened. 'Prim?'

'Prim,' he repeated, not budging.

'I am *not* prim.'

'Sweetheart, nobody does prim like you.'

His laugh set her teeth on edge. She forced herself to

settle back in her chair and to at least appear relaxed. 'I see what you're doing.'

'What am I doing?'

'Reverse psychology. Tell me not to ask a question in the hope I'll do the exact opposite.'

'Is it working?'

'Why are you so fixated on me asking you my owed question?'

A slow grin hooked up one side of his mouth and looking at it was like staring into the sun. She couldn't look away.

'Is that your question?'

Strive for casual.

'Don't be ridiculous.' If Rupert hadn't put the darn notion in her head—*Don't fall for Finn*—she wouldn't be wondering what it'd be like to kiss him.

She sipped her beer. As long as speculation didn't become anything more. She did what she could to ignore the ache that rose through her; to ignore the way her mouth dried and her stomach lurched.

She wasn't starting something with Finn. Even if he proved willing—which he wouldn't in a million years—there was too much at stake to risk it, and not enough to be won. She was *determined* there wouldn't be any more black marks against her name this year. There wouldn't be any more *ever* if she could help it.

If only she could stop thinking about him…*inappropriately*!

For heaven's sake, she was the one in her family who kept things steady, regulated, trouble-free. If there were choppy waters, she was the one who smoothed them. She didn't go rocking the boat and causing drama. That wasn't who she was. She ground her teeth together. And she wasn't going to change now.

She stared out at the harbour and gulped her beer. This was what happened when she let her hair down and indulged in a bit of impulsive wildness. It was so hard to get her wayward self back under wraps.

Finn might call her prim, but she preferred the terms self-controlled and disciplined. She needed to get things back on a normal grounding with him again, but when she went to open her mouth, he spoke first. 'I guess it's a throwback to the old game of Truth or Dare. I'm not up for too much daredevilry at the moment, but your question—the truth part of the game—is a different form of dangerousness.'

He stared up at the sky, lips pursed, and just like that he was familiar Finn again—family friend. Their session of jetskiing must've seemed pretty tame to him. He'd kept himself reined in for her sake, had focussed on her enjoyment rather than his own. Which meant that dark thread of restlessness would be pulsing through him now, goading him into taking unnecessary risks. She needed to dispel it if she could, to prevent him from doing something daft and dangerous.

'The truth can be ugly, Finn. Admitting the truth can be unwelcome and...' she settled for the word he'd used '...dangerous.'

Liquid brown eyes locked with hers as he drank his beer. He set his glass down on the table and wiped the back of his hand across his mouth. 'I know.'

'And yet you still want me to ask you a possibly dangerous question?'

'I'm game if you are.'

Was there a particular question he wanted her to ask? He stared at her and waited. She moistened her lips again and asked the question that had been rattling around in her mind ever since Rupert's phone call. 'Why do you avoid long-term romantic commitment?'

He blinked. '*That's* what you want to know?'

She shrugged. 'I'm curious. You've never once brought a date to a Russel family dinner. The rest of us have, multiple times. I want to know how you got to avoid the youthful mistakes the rest of us made. Besides…'

'What?'

'When Rupe was warning me off, he made some comment about you not being long-term material. Now we're going to ignore the fact that Rupert obviously thinks women only want long-term relationships when we all know that's simply not true. He obviously doesn't want to think of his little sister in those terms, bless him. But it made me think there's a story there. Hence, my question.'

He nodded, but he didn't speak.

She glanced at his now empty glass. 'If you want another beer, I'm happy to drive us home.'

He called the waiter over and ordered a lime and soda. She did the same. He speared her with a glare. 'I don't need Dutch courage to tell you the truth.'

'And yet that doesn't hide the fact that you don't want to talk about it.' Whatever *it* was. She shrugged and drained the rest of her beer too. 'That's okay, you can simply fob me off with an "I just haven't met the right girl yet" and be done with it.'

'But that would be lying, and lying is against the rules.'

'Ah, so you have met the right girl?' Was it Trixie who'd texted him?

He wagged a finger at her, and just for a moment his eyes danced, shifting the darkness her question had triggered. 'That's an altogether different question. If you'd rather I answer that one…?'

It made her laugh. 'I'll stick with my original question, thank you very much.'

The waiter brought their drinks and Finn took the straw from his glass and set it on the table. His eyes turned sombre again. 'You know the circumstances surrounding my father's death?'

'He died in a caving accident when you were eight.'

'He liked extreme sports. He was an adrenaline junkie. I seem to have inherited that trait.'

She frowned and sat back.

His eyes narrowed. 'What?'

She took a sip of her drink, wondering at his sharp tone. 'Can one inherit risk-taking the same way they can brown eyes and tawny hair?'

'Intelligence is inherited, isn't it? And a bad temper and... Why?'

He glared and she wished she'd kept her mouth shut. 'Just wondering,' she murmured.

'No, you weren't.'

Fine. She huffed out a breath. 'I always thought your adventuring was a way of keeping your father's memory alive, a way to pay homage to him.'

He blinked.

She tried to gauge the impact her words had on him. 'There isn't any judgement attached to that statement, Finn. I'm not suggesting it's either good or bad.'

He shook himself, but she noted the belligerent thrust to his jaw. 'Does it matter whether my risk-taking is inherited or not?'

'Of course it does. If it's some gene you inherently possess then that means it's always going to be a part of you, a...a natural urge like eating and sleeping. If it's the latter then one day you can simply decide you've paid enough homage. One means you can't change, the other means you can.'

He shoved his chair back, physically moving further away from her, his eyes flashing. She raised her hands. 'But that's not for me to decide. Your call. Like I said, no judgement here. It was just, umm...idle speculation.' She tried not to wince as she said it.

The space between them pulsed with Finn's...outrage? Shock? Disorientation? Audra wasn't sure, but she wanted to get them back on an even keel again. 'What does this have to do with avoiding romantic commitment?'

He gave a low laugh and stretched his legs out in front of him. 'You warned me this could be dangerous.'

It had certainly sent a sick wave of adrenaline coursing through her. 'We don't have to continue with this conversation if you don't want to.'

He skewered her with a glance. 'You don't want to know?'

She ran a finger through the condensation on her glass. He was being honest with her. He deserved the same in return. 'I want to know.'

'Then the rules demand that you get your answer.'

Was he laughing at her?

He grew serious again. 'My father's death was very difficult for my mother.'

Jeremy Sullivan had been an Australian sportsman who for a brief moment had held the world record for the men's four-hundred-metre butterfly. Claudette Dupont, Finn's mother, had been working at the French embassy in Canberra. They'd met, fallen in love and had moved to Europe where Jeremy had pursued a life of adventure and daring. Both of Finn's grandfathers came from old money. They, along with the lucrative sponsorship deals Jeremy received, had funded his and Claudette's lifestyle.

And from the outside it had been an enviable lifestyle—jetting around the world from one extreme sporting event to another—Jeremy taking part in whatever event was on offer while Claudette cheered him from the sidelines. And there'd apparently been everything from cliff diving to ice climbing, bobsledding to waterfall kayaking, and more.

But it had ended in tragedy with the caving accident that had claimed Jeremy's life. Audra dragged in a breath. 'She was too young to be a widow.' And Finn had been too young to be left fatherless.

'She gave up everything to follow him on his adventures—her job, a stable network of friends…a home. She was an only child and there weren't many close relatives apart from her parents.'

Audra wondered how she'd cope in that same situation. 'She had you.'

He shook his head. 'I wasn't enough.'

The pain in his eyes raked through her chest, thickened her throat. 'What happened?' She knew his mother had died, but nobody ever spoke of it.

'She just…faded away. She developed a lot of mystery illnesses—spent a lot of time in hospital. When she was home she spent a lot of time in bed.'

'That's when your uncle Ned came to look after you?' His father's brother was still a big part of Finn's life. He'd relocated to Europe to be with Finn and Claudette.

'He moved in and looked after the both of us. I was eleven when my mother died, and the official verdict was an accidental overdose of painkillers.' He met her gaze. 'Nobody thought she did it deliberately.'

That was something at least. But it was so sad. Such a waste.

'My uncle's verdict was that she'd died of a broken heart.'

Audra's verdict was that Claudette Sullivan had let her son down. Badly. But she kept that to herself. Her heart ached for the little boy she'd left behind and for all the loss he'd suffered.

'Ned blamed my father.'

Wow. 'It must've been hard for Ned,' she offered. 'I don't know what I'd do if I lost one of my siblings. And to then watch as your mother became sicker… He must've felt helpless.'

'He claimed my father should never have married if he wasn't going to settle down to raise a family properly.'

Finn's face had become wooden and she tried not to

wince. 'Families aren't one-size-fits-all entities. They don't come in pretty cookie-cutter shapes.'

He remained silent. She moistened her lips. 'What happened after your mother died?'

He straightened in his chair and took a long gulp of lime and soda. 'That's when Ned boarded me at the international school in Geneva. It was full of noisy, rowdy boys and activities specifically designed to keep us busy and out of mischief.'

It was an effort, but she laughed as he'd meant her to. 'I've heard stories about some of the mischief you got up to. I think they need to redesign some of those activities.'

He grinned. 'It was full of life. Ned came to every open day, took me somewhere every weekend we had leave. I didn't feel abandoned.'

Not by Ned, no. But what about his mother? She swallowed. 'And you met Rupert there.'

His grin widened. 'And soon after found myself adopted by the entire Russel clan.'

'For your sins.' She smiled back, but none of it eased the throb in her heart.

'I always found myself drawn to the riskier pastimes the school offered…and that only grew as I got older. There's nothing like the thrill of paragliding down a mountain or surfing thirty-foot waves.'

'Or throwing oneself off a ski jump with gay abandon,' she added wryly, referencing his recent accident.

'Accidents happen.'

But in the pastimes Finn pursued, such accidents could have fatal consequences. Didn't that bother him? 'Did Ned never try and clip your wings or divert your interests elsewhere?' He'd lost a brother. He wouldn't have wanted to lose a nephew as well.

'He's too smart for that. He knew it wouldn't work, not once he realised how determined I was. Before I was of age, when I still needed a guardian's signature, he just made sure I had the very best training available in whatever activity had taken my fancy before he'd sign the permission forms.'

'It must've taken an enormous amount of courage on his behalf.'

'Perhaps. But he'd seen the effect my grandfather's refusals and vetoes had had on my father. He said it resulted in my father taking too many unnecessary chances. In his own way, Ned did his best to keep me safe.'

She nodded.

'The way I live my life, the risks I take, they're not conducive to family life, Audra. When I turned eighteen I promised my uncle to never take an unnecessary risk—to make sure I was always fully trained to perform whatever task I was attempting.'

Thinking about the risks he took made her temples ache.

'I made a promise to myself at the same time.' His eyes burned into hers. 'I swore I'd never become involved in a long-term relationship until I'd given up extreme sports. It's not fair to put any woman through what my father put my mother through.'

It was evident he thought hell had a better chance of freezing over than him ever giving up extreme sports. She eyed him for a moment. 'Have you ever been tempted to break that contract with yourself?'

'I don't break my promises.'

It wasn't an answer. It was also an oblique reminder of the promise he'd made to Rupert. As if that were something she was likely to forget.

'But wouldn't you like a long-term relationship some day? Can't you ever see a time when you'd give up extreme sports?'

His eyes suddenly gleamed. 'Those are altogether separate questions. I believe I've answered your original one.'

Dammit! He had to know that only whetted her appetite for more.

None of your business.

It really wasn't, but then wasn't that the beauty, the temptation, of this game of 'truth or dare' questions—the danger?

Finn wanted to laugh at the quickened curiosity, the look of pique, in Audra's face. He shouldn't play this game. He should leave it all well enough alone, but...

He leaned towards her. 'I'll make a tit-for-tat deal with you.'

Ice-blue eyes shouldn't leave a path of fire on his skin, but beneath her gaze he started to burn. She cocked her head to one side. 'You mean a question-for-question, quid pro quo bargain?'

'Yep.'

She leaned in and searched his face as if trying to decipher his agenda. He did his best to keep his face clear. Finally she eased back and he could breathe again.

'You must be *really* bored.'

He wasn't bored. Her company didn't bore him. It never had. He didn't want to examine that thought too closely, though. He didn't want to admit it out loud either. 'Life has been...quieter of late than usual.'

'And you're finding that a challenge?'

He had in Nice, but now...not really. Which didn't make sense.

Can you inherit a risk-taking gene? He shied away from that question, from the deeper implications that lay beneath its surface. So what if some of his former pursuits had lost their glitter? That didn't mean anything.

He set his jaw. 'Let's call it a new experience.'

Her lips pressed together into a prim line he wanted to mess up. He'd like to kiss those lips until they were plump and swollen and— *Hell!*

'Are you up for my question challenge?' He made his voice deliberately mocking in a way he knew would gall her.

'I don't know. I'll think about it.'

He kinked an eyebrow, deliberately trying to inflame her competitive spirit. 'What are you afraid of?'

She pushed her sunglasses further up her nose and re-adjusted her sunhat. 'Funny, isn't it, how every question now seems to take on a double edge?'

He didn't pursue it. In all honesty letting sleeping dogs lie would probably be for the best.

Really?

He thrust out his jaw. And if not, then there was more than one way to find out what was troubling her. He just needed to turn his mind to it. Find another way.

Finn laughed when Audra pulled the two trays of crois-sants from the oven. Those tiny hard-looking lumps were supposed to be croissants? Her face, comical in its indig-nation, made him laugh harder.

'How can you laugh about this? We spent hours on these and…and *this* is our reward?'

'French pastry has a reputation for being notoriously difficult, hasn't it?' He poked a finger at the nearest hard lump and it disintegrated to ash beneath his touch. 'Wow, I think we just took French cooking to a new all-time low.'

'But…but you're half French! That should've given us a head start.'

'And you're half Australian but I don't see any particu-lar evidence of that making you handy with either a cricket bat or a barbecue.'

Like Finn's father, Audra's mother had been Austra-lian. Audra merely glowered at him, slammed the cook-book back to the bench top and studied its instructions once again. He hoped she wasn't going to put him through the torture of working so closely beside her in the kitchen again. There'd been too much accidental brushing of arms, too much…heat. Try as he might, he couldn't blame it all on the oven. Even over the smell of flour, yeast and milk, the scent of peaches and coconut had pounded at him, making him hungry.

But not for food.

He opened a cupboard and took out a plate, unwrapped the bakery bag he'd stowed in the pantry earlier and placed half a dozen croissants onto it. He slid the plate towards Audra.

She took a croissant without looking, bit into it and then pointed at the cookbook. 'Here's where we went wrong. We—'

She broke off to stare at the croissant in her hand, and then at the plate. 'If you dare tell me here are some croissants you prepared earlier, I'll—'

'Here are some croissants I *bought* at the village bakery earlier.'

'When earlier?'

'Dawn. Before you were up.'

The croissant hurtled back to the plate and her hands slammed to her hips. He backed up a step. 'I wasn't casting aspersions on your croissant-making abilities. But I wanted a back-up plan because…because I wanted to eat croissants.' Because she'd seemed so set on them.

Her glare didn't abate. 'What else have you been doing at the crack of dawn each morning?'

He shook his head, at a loss. 'Nothing, why?'

'Have you been running into the village and back every morning?'

He frowned. 'I took the car.' Anyway, he wasn't up to running that distance yet. And he hadn't felt like walking. Every day he felt a little stronger, but… It hadn't occurred to him to run into the village. Or to run anywhere for that matter. Except with her on the beach, when it was his turn to choose their daily activities. Only then he didn't make her jog anyway. They usually walked the length of the beach and then swam back.

'Or…or throwing yourself off cliffs or…or kite surfing or—'

He crowded in close then, his own temper rising, and it made her eyes widen…and darken. 'That wouldn't be in the spirit of the deal we made, would it?'

She visibly swallowed. 'Absolutely not.'

'And I'm a man of my word.'

Her gaze momentarily lowered to his lips before lifting again. 'You're also a self-professed adrenaline junkie.'

Except the adrenaline flooding his body at the moment had nothing to do with extreme sports. It had to do with the perfect shape of Audra's mouth and the burning need to know what she'd taste like. Would she taste of peaches and coconut? Coffee and croissant? Salty or sweet? His skin tightened, stretching itself across his frame in torturous tautness.

Her breathing grew shallow and a light flared to life in her eyes and he knew she'd recognised his hunger, his need, but she didn't move away, didn't retreat. Instead her gaze roved across his face and lingered for a beat too long on his mouth, and her lips parted with an answering hunger.

'A man of his word?' she murmured, swaying towards him.

Her words penetrated the fog surrounding his brain. *What are you doing? You can't kiss her!*

He snapped away, his breathing harsh. Silence echoed off the walls for three heart-rending beats and then he heard her fussing around behind him…dumping the failed croissants in the bin, rinsing the oven trays. 'Thank you for buying backup croissants, Finn.'

He closed his eyes and counted to three, before turning around. He found her surveying him, her tone nonchalant and untroubled—as if she hadn't been about to reach up on her tiptoes and kiss him. He'd seen the temptation in her eyes, but somehow she'd bundled up her needs and desires and hidden them behind a prim wall of control and restraint. It had his back molars grinding together.

He didn't know how he knew, but this was all related— her tight rein on her desires and needs, her refusal to let her hair down and have fun, the dogged determination to repress it all because…?

He had no idea! He had no answer for why she didn't simply reach out and take what she wanted from life.

She bit into her croissant and it was all he could do then not to groan.

'I have a "truth or dare" question for you, Finn.'

He tried to match her coolness and composure. 'So you've decided to take me up on the quid pro quo bargain?'

She nodded and stuck out a hip. If he'd been wearing a tie he'd have had to loosen it. 'If you're still game,' she purred.

In normal circumstances her snark would've had him fighting a grin. But nothing about today and this kitchen and Audra felt the least bit normal. Or the least bit familiar. 'Ask your question.'

She eyed him for a moment, her eyes stormy. 'Don't you want something more out of life?'

'More?' He felt his eyes narrow. 'Like what?'

'I mean, you flit from adventure to adventure, but…' That beautiful brow of hers creased. 'Don't you want something more worthwhile, more…*lasting*?'

His lips twisted. A man showed no interest in settling down—

'I'm not talking about marriage and babies!' she snapped as if reading his mind. 'I'm talking about doing something good with your life, making a mark, leaving a legacy.'

Her innate and too familiar disapproval stung him in

ways it never had before. Normally he'd have laughed it off, but...

He found himself leaning towards her. He had to fight the urge to loom. He wasn't Thomas-blasted-Farquhar. He didn't go in for physical intimidation. 'Do you seriously think I *just* live off my trust fund while I go trekking through the Amazon and train for the London marathon, and—'

'Look, I know you raise a lot of money for charity, but there doesn't seem to be any rhyme or reason to your methods—no proper organisation. You simply bounce from one thing to the next.'

'And what about my design company?'

Her hands went to her hips. 'You don't seem to spend a lot of time in the office.'

His mouth worked. 'You think I treat my company like a...a toy?'

'Well, don't you? I mean, you never talk about it!'

'You never ask me about it!'

She blinked. 'From where I'm standing—'

'With all the other workaholics,' he shot back.

'It simply looks as if you're skiving off from the day job to have exciting adventures. Obviously that's your prerogative, as you're the boss, but—'

He raised his arms. 'Okay, we're going to play a game.'

She stared at him. Her eyes throbbed, and he knew that some of this anger came from what had almost happened between them—the physical frustration and emotional confusion. He wanted to lean across and pull her into his arms and hug her until they both felt better. But he had a feeling that solution would simply lead to more danger.

Her chin lifted. 'And what about my question?'

'By the end of the game you'll have your answer. I promise.' And in the process he meant to challenge her to explore the dreams she seemed so doggedly determined to bury.

Her eyes narrowed and she folded her arms. 'What does this game involve?'

'Sitting in the garden with a plate of croissants and my computer.'

She raised her eyebrows. 'Sitting?'

'And eating…and talking.'

She unfolded her arms. 'Fine. That I can do.'

What was it his uncle used to say? *There's more than one way to crack an egg.* He might never discover the reasons Audra held herself back, but the one thing he could do was whet her appetite for the options life held, give her the push she perhaps needed to reach for her dreams. After all, temptation and adventure were his forte. He frowned as he went to retrieve his laptop. At least, they had been once. And he'd find his fire for them again soon enough.

And he couldn't forget that once he'd answered her question, he'd have one of his own in the kitty. He might never use it—she was right, these questions could be dangerous—but it'd be there waiting just in case.

CHAPTER SEVEN

AUDRA BLINKED WHEN Finn handed her a large notepad and a set of pencils. She opened her mouth to ask what they were for, but when he sat opposite and opened his laptop she figured she'd find out soon enough.

For the moment she was simply content to stare at him and wonder what that stubble would feel like against her palms and admire the breadth of his shoulders and—

No, no. *No!*

For the moment she was content to…to congratulate herself for keeping Finn quiet for another day. And she'd… *admire the view*. The brilliant blue of the sea contrasted with the soft blue of the sky, making her appreciate all the different hues on display. A yacht with a pink and blue sail had anchored just offshore and she imagined a honeymooning couple rowing into one of the many deserted coves that lay along this side of the island, and enjoying…

Her mind flashed with forbidden images, and she shook herself. *Enjoying a picnic.*

'Audra?'

She glanced up to find Finn staring at her, one eyebrow raised. She envied that. She'd always wanted to do it. She tried it now, and he laughed. 'What are you doing?'

'I love the "one eyebrow raised" thing. It looks great and you do it really well. I've always wanted to do it, but…' She tried again and he convulsed. Laughter was good. She needed to dispel the fraught atmosphere that had developed between them in the kitchen. She needed to forget about kissing him. He'd been looking grim and serious in odd moments these last few days too…sad, after telling her about the promise he'd made to himself when he'd turned eighteen.

She didn't want him sad. In the past she'd often wanted to get the better of him, but she didn't want that now either. She just wanted to see him fit and healthy. Happy. And she wanted to see him the way she used to see him— as Rupert's best friend. If she focussed hard enough, she could get that back, right?

She gave a mock sigh. 'That's not the effect I was aiming for.'

'There's a trick.'

She leaned towards him. 'Really?'

He nodded.

'Will you tell it to me?'

'If you'll tell me what you were thinking about when you were staring out to sea.' He gestured behind him at the view. 'You were a million miles away.'

Heat flushed her cheeks. She wasn't going to tell him about her imaginary honeymoon couple, but... 'It's so beautiful here. *So* beautiful. It does something to me— fills me up...makes me feel more...'

He frowned. 'More what?'

She lifted her hands only to let them drop again. 'I'm not sure how to explain it. It just makes me feel more... myself.'

He sat back as if her words had punched the air from his lungs. 'If that's true then you should move here.'

'Impossible.' Her laugh, even to her own ears, sounded strained.

'Nothing's impossible.'

She couldn't transplant her work here. She didn't even want to try. It'd simply suck the colour and life from this place for her anyway, so she shook her head. 'It's just a timely reminder that I should be taking my holidays more often.' She had a ridiculous amount of leave accrued. She had a ridiculous amount of money saved too. Maybe even enough for a deposit on a little cottage in the village? And then, maybe, she could own her own bit of paradise—a bit that was just hers.

And maybe having that would help counter the grey monotony her life in Geneva held for her.

Finn stared at her as if he wanted to argue the point further. No more. Some pipe dreams made her chest ache, and not in a good way. 'Fair's fair. Share your eyebrow-raising tip.'

So he walked her through it. 'But you'll need to practise. You can do an internet search if you want to.'

Really? Who'd have thought?

He rubbed his hands together. 'Now we're going to play my game.'

'And the name of the game…?'

'Designing Audra's favourite…'

'Holiday cottage?' she supplied helpfully.

His grin widened and he clapped his hands. 'Designing Audra's favourite shop.'

Her heart started to pound.

'How old were you when you decided shopkeeping sang to your soul?'

She made herself laugh because it was quite clearly what he intended. 'I don't know. I guess I must've been about six.' And then eleven…fifteen…seventeen. But her owning a shop—it was a crazy idea. It was so *indulgent*.

But this was just a game. Her heart thumped. It wouldn't hurt to play along for an hour or so. Finn obviously wanted to show off some hidden talent he had and who was she to rain on his parade? The lines of strain around his eyes had eased and the grooves bracketing his mouth no longer bit into his flesh so deeply. Each day had him moving more easily and fluidly. Coming here had been good for him. Taking it easy was good for him. She wanted all that goodness to continue in the same vein.

She made herself sit up straighter. 'Right, the name of the game is Designing Audra's Dream Shop.'

He grinned and it sent a breathless kind of energy zinging through her.

'We're going to let our minds go wild. The sky's the limit. Got it?'

'Got it.'

He held her gaze. 'I mean it. The point of the game is to not be held back by practicalities or mundane humdrummery. That comes later. For this specific point in time we're aiming for best of the best, top of the pops, no compromises, just pure unadulterated dream vision.'

She had a feeling she should make some sort of effort to check the enthusiasm suddenly firing through her veins, but Finn's enthusiasm was infectious. And she was in the Greek islands on holiday. She was allowed to play. She nodded once, hard. 'Right.'

'First question…' his fingers were poised over the keyboard of his computer '…and experience tells me that the first answer that pops into your mind is usually the right one.'

'Okay, hit me with Question One.'

'Where is your ideal location for your shop?'

'Here on Kyanós…in the village's main street, overlooking the harbour. There's a place down there that's for sale and…' she hesitated '…it has a nice view.'

His fingers flew over the keyboard. 'What does your ideal shop sell?'

'Beautiful things,' she answered without hesitation.

'Specifics, please.'

So she described in detail the beautiful things she'd love to sell in her dream shop. 'Handicrafts made by local artisans—things like jade pendants and elegant bracelets, beautiful scented candles and colourful scarves.' She pulled in a breath. 'Wooden boxes ornamented with beaten silver, silver boxes ornamented with coloured beads.' She described gorgeous leather handbags, scented soaps and journals made from handcrafted paper.

She rested her chin on her hands and let her mind drift into her dream shop—a pastime she'd refused to indulge in for…well, years now. 'There'd be beautiful prints for sale on the walls. There'd be wind chimes and pretty vases… glassware.'

She pulled back, suddenly self-conscious, heat bursting across her cheeks. 'Is that…uh…specific enough?'

'It's perfect.'

He kept tap-tapping away, staring at the computer screen rather than at her, and the heat slowly faded from her face. He looked utterly engrossed and she wondered if he'd worn the same expression when he'd set off on his ill-fated ski jump.

He glanced at her and she could feel herself colour again at being caught out staring. Luckily, he didn't seem to notice. He just started shooting questions at her again. How big was her shop? Was it square or rectangle? Where did she want to locate the point of sale? What colour scheme would she choose? What shelving arrangements and display options did she have in mind?

Her head started to whirl at the sheer number of questions, but she found she could answer them all without dithering or wavering, even when she didn't have the correct terminology for what she was trying to describe. Finn had a knack for asking her things and then reframing her answers in a way that captured exactly what she meant. She wasn't sure how he did it.

'Okay, you need to give me about fifteen minutes.'

'I'll get us some drinks.' She made up a fruit and cheese platter to supplement their lunch of croissants, added some dried fruits and nuts before taking the tray outside.

Finn rose and took the tray from her. 'Sit. I'll show you what I've done.'

She did as he bid. He turned the computer to face her.

She gasped. She couldn't help it. She pulled the computer towards her. She couldn't help that either. If she could've she'd have stepped right inside his computer because staring out at her from the screen was the interior of the shop she'd dreamed about ever since she was a little girl—a dream she'd perfected as she'd grown older and her tastes had changed. 'How…?' She could barely push the word past the lump in her throat. 'How did you do this?'

'Design software.'

He went to press a button, but she batted his hand away. 'Don't touch a thing! This is *perfect*.' It was amazing. The interior of her fantasy shop lived and breathed there on the screen like a dream come true and it made everything inside her throb and come alive.

'Not perfect.' He placed a slice of feta on a cracker and passed it across to her. 'It'd take me another couple of days to refine it for true perfection. But it gives a pretty good indication of your vision.'

It did. And she wanted this vision. She wanted it so bad it tasted like raspberries on her tongue. Instead of raspberries she bit into feta, which was pretty delicious too.

'If you push the arrow key there're another two pictures of your shop's interior from different angles.'

She popped the rest of the cracker into her mouth and pressed the arrow key…and marvelled anew at the additional two pictures that appeared—one from the back of the shop, and one from behind the sales counter, both of which afforded a glorious view of a harbour. There was a tub of colourful flowers just outside the door and her eyes filled. She reached out and touched them. 'You remembered.'

'I did.'

She pored over every single detail in the pictures. She could barely look away from the screen, but she had to. This dream could never be hers. She dragged in a breath, gathered her resources to meet Finn's gaze and to pretend that this hadn't been anything more than a game, an interesting exercise, when her gaze caught on the logo in the bottom right corner of the screen. The breath left her lungs in a rush. She knew that logo!

Her gaze speared to his. '*You're* Aspiration Designs?'

'Along with my two partners.'

He nodded a confirmation and she couldn't read the expression in his eyes. 'How did I not know about this?'

He shrugged. 'It's not a secret.'

'But…your company was called Sullivan Brand Consultants.'

'Until I merged with my partners.'

She forced her mind back to the family dinners and the few other times in recent years that she'd seen Finn, and tried to recall a conversation—any conversation—about him expanding his company or going into partnership. There'd been some vague rumblings about some changes, but…she'd not paid a whole lot of attention. She wanted to hide her face in her hands. Had she really been so uninterested…so set in her picture of who Finn was?

She moistened her lips. Aspiration Designs was a boutique design business in high demand. 'You created the foyer designs for the new global business centre in Geneva.'

He lifted a shoulder in a silent shrug.

Those designs had won awards.

She closed the lid of the laptop, sagging in her seat. 'I've had you pegged all wrong. For all these years you haven't been flitting from one daredevil adventure to another. You've been—' she gestured to the computer '—making people's dreams come true.'

'I don't make people's dreams come true. They make their own dreams come true through sheer hard work and dedication. I just show them what their dream can look like.'

In the same way he'd burned the vision of her dream shop onto her brain.

'And another thing—' he handed her another cracker

laden with cheese '—Aspirations isn't a one-man band. My partners are in charge of the day-to-day running. Also, I've built an amazing design team and one of my super-powers is delegation. Which means I can go flitting off on any adventure that takes my fancy, almost at a moment's notice.'

She didn't believe that for a moment. She bet he timed his adventures to fit in with his work demands.

'And in hindsight it's probably not all that surprising that you don't know about my company. How often have we seen each other in the last four or five years? Just a handful of times.'

He had a point. 'Christmas…and occasionally when you're in Geneva I'll catch you when you're seeing Rupert.' But that was often for just a quick drink. They were on the periphery of each other's lives, not inside them.

'And when you do see me you always ask me what my latest adventure has been and where I'm off to next.'

Her stomach churned. Never once had she asked him about his work. She hadn't thought he did much. Instead, she'd vicariously lived adventure and excitement through him. But the same disapproval she directed at herself— to keep herself in check—she'd also aimed at him. How unfair was that!

She'd taken a secret delight in his exploits while maintaining a sense of moral superiority by dismissing them as trivial. She swallowed. 'I owe you an apology. I'm really sorry, Finn. I've been a pompous ass.'

He blinked. 'Garbage. You just didn't know.'

She hadn't wanted to know. She'd wanted to dismiss him as an irresponsible lightweight. Her mouth dried. And in thinking of him as a self-indulgent pleasure-seeker it had been easier to battle the attraction she'd always felt simmering beneath the surface of her consciousness for him.

God! That couldn't be true.

Couldn't it?

She didn't know what to do with such an epiphany, so she forced a smile to uncooperative lips. 'You have your adventures *and* you do good and interesting work. Finn...' she spread her hands '...you're living the dream.'

He laughed but it didn't reach his eyes. She recalled what he'd told her—about the promise he'd made to himself when he'd come of age—and a protest rose through her. 'I think you're wrong, Finn—both you and Ned. I think you *can* have a long-term relationship *and* still enjoy the extreme sports you love.' The words blurted out of her with no rhyme or reason. Finn's head snapped back. She winced and gulped and wished she could call them back.

'Talk about a change of topic.' He eased away, eyed her for a moment. 'Wrong how?'

She shouldn't have started this. But now that she had... She forced herself to straighten. 'I just don't think you can define your own circumstances based on what happened to your parents. And I'm far from convinced Ned should blame your father for everything that happened afterwards.' She raised her hands in a conciliatory gesture. 'I know! I know! He has your best interests at heart. And, look, I love your uncle Ned.' He came to their Christmas dinners and had become as much a part of the extended family as Finn had. 'But surely it's up to you and your prospective life partner to decide what kind of marriage will work for you.'

'But my mother—'

Frustration shot through her. 'Not every woman deals with tragedy in the same way your mother did!'

'Whoa!' He stared at her.

Heck!

'Sorry. Gosh, I...' She bit her lip.

What had she been thinking?

'Sorry,' she said again, swallowing. 'That came out harsher than I meant it to—*way* harsher. I just meant, people react to tragedy in different ways. People react to broken hearts in different ways. I'm not trying to trivialise it; I'm not saying it's easy. It's just…not everyone falls into a decline. If you live by those kinds of rules then—'

He leaned towards her and she almost lost her train of thought. 'Um, then…it follows that *you'd* better never marry a woman who's into extreme sports or…or has a dangerous job because if she dies then you wouldn't be able to survive it.'

His jaw dropped.

'And from the look on your face, it's clear you don't think of yourself as that kind of person.'

He didn't.

Finn stared at Audra, not sure why his heart pounded so hard, or why something chained inside him wanted to suddenly break free.

She retied her ponytail, not quite meeting his eyes. 'I mean, not everyone wants to marry and that's fine. Not everyone wants to have kids, and that's fine too. Maybe you're one of those people.'

'But?'

She bit her bottom lip and when she finally released it, it was plump from where she'd worried at it. She shrugged. 'But maybe you're not.'

'You think I want to marry and have kids?'

Blue eyes met his, and they had him clenching up in strange ways. 'I have no idea.' She leaned towards him the tiniest fraction. 'Wouldn't you eventually like to have children?'

'I don't know.' He'd never allowed himself to think about it before. 'You?'

'I'd love to be a mother one day.'

'Would you marry someone obsessed with extreme sports?'

'I wouldn't marry someone obsessed with anything,

thank you very much. I don't want my life partner spending all his leisure time away from me—whether it's for rock climbing, stamp collecting or golf. I'd want him to want to spend time with me.'

Any guy lucky enough to catch Audra's eye would be a fool not to spend time with her. *Lots* of time. As much as he could.

'I don't want *all* of his leisure time, though.' She glared as if Finn had accused her of exactly that. 'There are girl-friends to catch up with over coffee and cake…or cocktails. And books to read.'

Speaking of books, he hoped she had reading down on today's agenda. He wouldn't mind getting back to his book. 'But you'd be okay with him doing some rock climbing, hang-gliding or golf?'

'As long as he doesn't expect me to take up the sport too. I mean, me dangling from a thin rope off a sheer cliff or hurtling off a sheer cliff in a glorified paper plane—what could possibly go wrong?'

A bark of laughter shot out of him. 'We're going to assume that this hypothetical life partner of yours would insist on you getting full training before attempting anything dangerous.'

She wrinkled her nose. 'Doesn't change the fact I'm not the slightest bit interested in rock climbing, hang-gliding or golf. I wouldn't want to go out with someone who wanted to change me.'

He sagged back on the wooden bench, air leaving his lungs. 'Which is why you wouldn't change him.' It didn't mean she wouldn't worry when her partner embarked on some risky activity, but she'd accept them for who they were. She'd want them to be happy.

Things inside him clenched up again. So what if laps around a racetrack had started to feel just plain boring—round and round in endless monotonous laps? *Yawn.* And so what if he couldn't remember why he'd thought hurtling off that ski jump had been a good idea. It didn't mean he wanted to change his entire lifestyle. It didn't mean anything. Yet...

He'd never let himself think about the possibility of having children before. He moistened suddenly dry lips. He wasn't sure he should start now either.

And yet he couldn't let the matter drop. 'Do you think about having children a lot?'

Her brow wrinkled. 'Where are you going with this? It's not like I'm obsessed or anything. It's not like it's constantly on my mind. But I am twenty-seven. Ideally, if I were going to start a family, I'd want that to happen in the next ten years. And I wouldn't want to get married and launch immediately into parenthood. I'd want to enjoy married life for a bit first.'

She frowned then. 'What?' he demanded, curious to see inside this world of hers—unsure if it attracted or repelled him.

'I was just thinking about this hypothetical partner you've landed me with. I hope he understands that things change when babies come along.'

Obviously, but...um. 'How?'

She selected a brazil nut before holding the bowl out to him. 'Suddenly you have way less time for yourself. Cocktail nights with the girls become fewer and farther between.'

He took a handful of nuts. 'As do opportunities to throw yourself off a cliff, I suppose?'

'Exactly.'

Except having Finn hadn't slowed his father down. And his mother certainly hadn't insisted on having a stable home base. She'd simply towed Finn and his nanny along with them wherever they went. And when he was old enough, she hired tutors to homeschool him.

And everything inside him rebelled at blaming his parents for that.

'A baby's needs have to be taken into consideration and—'

She broke off when she glanced into his face. 'I'm not criticising your parents, Finn. I'm not saying they did it wrong or anything. I'm describing how *I'd* want to do it. Each couple works out what's best for them.'

'But you'd want to be hands-on. I have a feeling that nannies and boarding schools and in-home tutors aren't your idea of good parenting. You'd want a house in the suburbs, to host Christmas dinner—'

'It doesn't have to be in the burbs. It could be an apartment in the city or a house overlooking a Greek beach. And if I can afford a nanny I'll have one of those too, thank you very much. I'd want to keep working.'

His parents had chosen to not work. At all.

'But when I get home from work, I'd want to have my family around me. That's all.' Their eyes locked. 'It's not how my parents did it…and I'm not saying I hated boarding school, because I didn't. I know how lucky I've been. I'm not saying my way is better than anybody else's. I'm just saying that's the way that'd make *me* happy.'

She'd just described everything he'd wanted when he was a child, and it made the secret places inside him ache. It also brought something into stark relief. She knew what would make her happy in her personal life—she knew the kind of home life and family that she wanted, and it was clear she wasn't going to settle for less. So why was she settling for less in her work life?

The question hovered on his tongue. He had a 'truth or dare' question owing to him, but something held him back, warned him the time wasn't right. Audra was looking more relaxed with each day they spent here. Her appetite had returned, as had the colour in her cheeks. But he recalled the expression in her eyes when he'd first turned his computer around to show her that shop, and things inside him knotted up. It was too new, and too fragile. She needed more time to pore over those pictures…to dream.

He wanted her hunger to build until she could deny it no longer.

He loaded two crackers with cheese and handed her one, before lifting the lid of his computer. 'I'll email those designs through to you.'

'Oh, um…thank you. That'll be fun.'

Fun? Those walls had just gone back up in her eyes. That strange restraint pulled back into place around her. He didn't understand it, but he wasn't going to let her file those pictures away in a place where she could forget about them. He'd use Rupert's office later to print hard copies off as well. She might ignore her email, but she'd find the physical copies much harder to ignore.

'What's on the agenda for the rest of the day?'

She sent him a cat-that-got-the-cream grin. 'Nothing. Absolutely nothing.'

Excellent. 'Books on the beach?'

'You're getting the hang of this, Sullivan.' She rose and collected what was left of the food, and started back towards the house. 'Careful,' she shot over her shoulder, 'you might just find yourself enjoying it.'

He was enjoying it. He just wasn't sure what that meant.

He shook himself. It didn't mean anything, other than relief at being out of hospital and not being confined to quarters. He'd be an ingrate—not to mention made of marble—not to enjoy all this glorious Greek sun and scenery.

And whatever else he was, he wasn't made of marble. With Audra proving so intriguing, this enforced slower pace suited him fine for the moment. Once he got to the bottom of her strange restraint his restlessness would return. And then he'd be eager to embark on his next adventure—in need of a shot of pure adrenaline.

His hunger for adventure would return and consume him, and all strange conversations about children would be forgotten. He rose; his hands clenched. This was about Audra, not him.

Audra stared at the ticket Finn had handed her and then at the large barn-like structure in front of them. She stared down at the paper in her hand again. 'You…you enrolled us in an art class?'

If Finn had been waiting for her to jump up and down in excitement and delight, he'd have been disappointed.

Which meant… Yeah, he was disappointed.

How had he got this wrong? 'When you saw the flyer in the bookshop window you looked…'

'I looked what?'

Her eyes turned wary with that same damn restraint that was there when she talked about her shop. Frustration rattled through him. Why did she do that?

'Looked what?' she demanded.

'Interested,' he shot back.

Wistful, full of yearning…hungry.

'I can't draw.'

'Which is why it says *"Beginners"*—' he pointed '—right here.'

She blew out a breath.

'What's more I think you were interested, but for some reason it intimidated you, so you chickened out.'

Her chin shot up, but her cheeks had reddened. 'I just didn't think it'd be your cup of tea.'

'You didn't think lying on a beach reading a book would float my boat either, but that didn't stop you. And I've submitted with grace. I haven't made a single complaint about your agendas. Unlike you with mine.'

'Oh!' She took a step back. 'You make me sound mean-spirited.'

She *wasn't* mean-spirited. But she *was* the most frustrating woman on earth!

'I'm sorry, Finn. Truly.' She seemed to gird her loins.

'You've chosen this specifically with me in mind. And I'm touched. Especially as I know you'd rather be off paragliding or aqua boarding or something.'

He ran a finger around the collar of his T-shirt. That wasn't one hundred per cent true. It wasn't even ten per cent true. Not that he had any intention of saying so. 'But?' he countered, refusing to let her off the hook. 'You don't want to do it?'

'It's not that.'

He folded his arms. 'Then what is it?'

'Forget it. You just took me by surprise, is all.' She snapped away from him. 'Let's just go in and enjoy the class and—'

He reached out and curled his hand around hers and her words stuttered to a halt. 'Audra?' He raised an eyebrow and waited.

Her chin shot up again. 'You won't understand.'

'Try me.'

A storm raged in her eyes. He watched it in fascination. 'Do you ever have rebellious impulses, Finn?'

He raised both eyebrows. 'My entire life is one big rebellion, surely?'

'Nonsense! You're living your life exactly as you think your parents would want you to.'

She snatched her hand back and he felt suddenly cast adrift.

'You've not rebelled any more than I have.'

That wasn't true, but… He glanced at the studio behind her. 'Art class is a rebellion?'

'In a way.'

'How?'

She folded her arms and stared up at the sky. He had a feeling she was counting to ten. 'Look, I can see the sense in taking a break, in having a holiday. Lying on a beach and soaking up some Vitamin D, getting some gentle exercise via a little swimming and walking, reading a book—I see the sense in those things. They lead to a rested body and mind.'

'How is an art class different from any of those things?'

'It just is! It feels…self-indulgent. It's doing something for the sake of doing it, rather than because it's good for you or…or…'

'What about fun?'

She stared at him. 'What's *fun* got to do with it?'

He couldn't believe what he was hearing. 'Evidently nothing.' Was she really that afraid of letting her hair down?

'When I start doing one thing just for the sake of it— *for fun*,' she spat, 'I'll start doing others.'

He lifted his arms and let them drop. 'And the problem with that would be…?'

Her eyes widened as if he were talking crazy talk and a hard, heavy ball dropped into the pit of his stomach. It was all he could do not to bare his teeth and growl.

'I knew you wouldn't understand.'

'I'll tell you what I understand. That you're the most uptight, repressed person I have *ever* met.'

'Repressed?' Her mouth opened and closed. 'I— What are you doing?'

He'd seized her hand again and was towing her towards a copse of Aleppo pine and carob trees. 'What's that?' He flung an arm out at the vista spread below them.

She glared. 'The Aegean. It's beautiful.'

'And that?' He pointed upwards.

She followed his gaze. Frowned and shrugged, evidently not following where he was going with this. 'The… sky?'

'The sun,' he snapped out. 'And it's shining in full force in case you hadn't noticed. And where are we?'

She swallowed. 'On a Greek island.'

He crowded her in against a tree, his arms going either side of her to block her in. 'If there was ever a time to let your hair down and rebel against your prim and proper strictures, Audra, now's the time to do it.'

She stared up at him with wide eyes, and he relished the moment—her stupefaction…her bewilderment…her undeniable hunger when her gaze lowered to his lips. This moment had seemed inevitable from when she'd appeared on the stairs a week ago to peer at him with those icy blue eyes, surveyed him in handcuffs, and told him it served him right.

His heart thudded against his ribs, he relished the adrenaline that surged through his body, before he swooped down to capture her lips in a kiss designed to shake up her safe little world. And he poured all his wildness and adventurous temptation into it in a devil-may-care invitation to dance.

CHAPTER EIGHT

THE ASSAULT ON Audra's senses the moment Finn's lips touched hers was devastating. She hadn't realised she could feel a kiss in so many ways, that its impact would spread through her in ever-widening circles that went deeper and deeper.

Finn's warmth beat at her like the warmth of the sun after a dip in the sea. It melted things that had been frozen for a very long time.

His scent mingled with the warm tang of the trees and sun-kissed grasses, and with just the tiniest hint of salt on the air it was exactly what a holiday should smell like. It dared her to play, it tempted her to reckless fun… and…and to a youthful joy she'd never allowed herself to feel before.

And she was powerless to resist. She had no defences against a kiss like this. It didn't feel as if defences were necessary. A kiss like this…it should be embraced and relished…welcomed.

Finn had been angry with her, but he didn't kiss angry. He kissed her as though he couldn't help it—as though he'd been fighting a losing battle and had finally flung himself wholeheartedly into surrender. It was *intoxicating*.

Totally heady and wholly seductive.

She lifted her hands, but didn't know what to do with them so rested them on his shoulders, but they moved, restless, to the heated skin of his neck, and the skin-on-skin contact sent electricity coursing through both of them. He shuddered, she gasped…tongues tangled.

And then his arms were around her, hauling her against his body, her arms were around his neck as she plastered herself to him, and she stopped thinking as desire and the moment consumed her.

It was the raucous cry of a rose-ringed parakeet that penetrated her senses—and the need for air that had them easing apart. She stared into his face and wondered if her lips looked as well kissed as his, and if her eyes were just as dazed.

And then he swore, and a sick feeling crawled through the pit of her stomach. He let her go so fast she had to brace herself against the trunk of the tree behind her. She ached in places both familiar and unfamiliar and…and despite the myriad emotions chasing across his face—and none of them were positive—she wished with all her might that they were somewhere private, and that she were back in his arms so those aches could be assuaged.

And to hell with the consequences.

'I shouldn't have done that,' he bit out. 'I'm sorry.'

'I don't want an apology.'

The words left her without forethought, and with a brutal honesty that made her cringe. But they both knew what she *did* want couldn't happen. Every instinct she had told her he was hanging by a thread. His chest rose and fell as if he'd been running. The pulse at the base of his throat pounded like a mad thing. He wanted her with the same savage fury that she wanted him. And everything inside her urged her to snap his thread of control, and the consequences be damned.

It was *crazy*! Her hands clenched. She couldn't go on making romantic mistakes like this. Oh, he was nothing like Thomas. He'd never lie to her or betray her, but…but if she had an affair with Finn, it'd hurt her family. They'd see her as just another in a long line of Finn's *women*. It wasn't fair, but it was the reality all the same. She wouldn't hurt her family for the world; especially after all they'd been through with Thomas. She couldn't let them down so badly.

If she and Finn started something, when it ended—and that was the inevitable trajectory to all of Finn's relationships—he'd have lost her family's good opinion. They'd shun him. She knew how much that'd hurt him, and she'd do anything to prevent that from happening too.

And yet if he kissed her again she'd be lost.

'I'm not the person I thought I was,' she blurted out.

He frowned. 'What do you mean?'

Anger came to her rescue then. 'You wanted me to lose control. You succeeded in making that happen.' She moved in close until the heat from their bodies mingled again. 'And now you want me to just what…? Put it all back under wraps? To forget about it? What kind of game are you playing, Finn?'

The pulse in his jaw jumped and jerked. 'I just wanted you to loosen up a bit. Live in the moment instead of over-thinking and over-analysing everything and…'

She slammed her hands to her hips. 'And?' She wasn't sure what she wanted from him—what she wanted him to admit—but it was more than this. That kiss had changed *everything*. But she wasn't even sure what that meant. Or what to do about it.

'And I'm an idiot! It was a stupid thing to do.' His eyes snapped fire as if *he* were angry with *her*. 'I do flings, Audra. Nothing more.' Panic lit his face. 'But I don't do them with Rupert's little sister.'

The car keys sailed through the air. She caught them automatically.

'I'll see you back at the villa.'

She watched as he stormed down the hill. He was running scared. From her? From fear of destroying his friendship with Rupert? Or was it something else…like thoughts of babies and marriage?

Was that what he thought she wanted from him?

Her stomach did a crazy twirl and she had to sit on a

nearby rock to catch her breath. She'd be crazy to pin those kinds of hopes on him. And while she might be crazy with lust, she hadn't lost her mind completely.

She touched her fingers to her lips. *Oh, my, but the man could kiss.*

Audra glanced up from her spot on the sofa when Finn finally came in. She'd had dinner a couple of hours ago. She'd started to wonder if Finn meant to stay out all night.

And then she hadn't wanted to follow that thought any further, hadn't wanted to know where he might be and with whom…and what they might be doing.

He halted when he saw her. The light from the doorway framed him in exquisite detail—outlining the broad width of his shoulders and the lean strength of his thighs. Every lusty, heady impulse that had fired through her body when they'd kissed earlier fired back to life now, making her itch and yearn.

'I want to tell you something.'

He moved into the room, his face set and the lines bracketing his mouth deep. She searched him for signs of exhaustion, over-exertion, a limp, as he moved towards an armchair, but his body, while held tight, seemed hale and whole. Whatever else he'd done—or hadn't done—today, he clearly hadn't aggravated his recent injuries.

She let out a breath she hadn't even known she'd been holding. 'Okay.' She closed her book and set her feet to the floor. Here it came—the 'it's not you it's me' speech, the 'I care about you, but…' justifications. She tried to stop her lips from twisting. She'd toyed with a lot of scenarios since their kiss…and this was one of them. She had no enthusiasm for it. Perhaps it served her right for losing her head so completely earlier. A penance. She bit back a sigh. 'What do you want to tell me?'

'I want to explain why it's so important to me that I don't break Rupert's trust.'

That was easy. 'He's your best friend.' He cared more for Rupert than he did for her. It made perfect sense, so she couldn't explain why the knowledge chafed at her.

'I want you to understand how much I actually owe him.'

'How you *owe* him?' Would it be rude to get up, wish him goodnight and go to bed?

Of course it'd be rude.

Not as rude as sashaying over to where he sat, planting herself in his lap, and kissing him.

She tried to close her mind to the pictures that exploded behind her eyelids. How many times did she have to tell herself that he was off limits?

'I haven't told another living soul about this and I suspect Rupert hasn't either.'

Her eyes sprang open. 'Okay. I'm listening.'

His eyes throbbed, but he stared at the wall behind her rather than at her directly. It made her chest clench. 'Finn?'

His nostrils flared. 'I went off the rails for a while when we were at school. I don't know if you know that or not.'

She shook her head.

'I was seventeen—full of hormones and angry at the world. I took to drinking and smoking and…and partying hard.'

With girls? She said nothing.

'I was caught breaking curfew twice…and one of those times I was drunk.'

She winced. 'That wouldn't have gone down well. Your boarding school was pretty strict.'

'With an excellent reputation to uphold. I was told in no uncertain terms that one more strike and I was out.'

She waited. 'So…? Rupert helped you clean up your act?'

'Audra, Audra, Audra.' His lips twisted into a mockery of a smile. 'You should know better than that.'

Her stomach started to churn, though she wasn't sure why. 'You kept pushing against the boundaries and testing the limits.'

He nodded.

'And were you caught?'

'Contraband was found in my possession.'

'What kind of contraband?'

'The type that should've had me automatically expelled.'

She opened her mouth and then closed it. It might be better not to know. 'But you weren't expelled.' Or had he been and somehow it'd all been kept a secret?

'No.'

The word dropped from him, heavy and dull, and all of the fine hairs on her arms lifted. 'How...?'

'Remember the Fallonfield Prize?'

She snorted. 'How could I not? Rupert was supposed to have been the third generation of Russel men to win that prize. I swear to God it was the gravest disappointment of both my father's and grandfather's lives when he didn't.'

Nobody had been able to understand it, because Rupert had been top of his class, and that, combined with his extra-curricular community service activities and demonstrated leadership skills...

Her throat suddenly felt dry. 'He was on track to win it.'

Finn nodded.

Audra couldn't look away. The Fallonfield Prize was a prestigious award that opened doors. It practically guaranteed the winner a place at their university of choice, and it included a year-long mentorship with a business leader and feted humanitarian. As a result of winning the prize, her grandfather had gone to Chile for a year. Her father had gone to South Africa, which was where he'd met Audra's mother, who'd been doing aid work there.

The Russel family's legacy of social justice and responsibility continued to this very day. Rupert had planned to go to Nicaragua.

'What happened?' she whispered, even though she could see the answer clear and plain for herself.

'Rupert took the blame. He said the stuff belonged to him, and that he'd stowed it among my things for safe-keeping—so his parents wouldn't see it when they'd come for a recent visit.'

She moistened her lips. 'He had to know it'd cost him the scholarship.'

Finn nodded. He'd turned pale in the telling of the story and her heart burned for him. He'd lost his father when he was far too young, and then he'd watched his mother die. Who could blame him for being angry?

But... 'I'm amazed you—' She snapped her mouth closed. *Shut up!*

His lips twisted. 'You're amazed I let him take the rap?'

She swallowed and didn't say a word.

'I wasn't going to. When I'd found out what he'd done I started for the head's office to set him straight.'

'What happened?'

'Your brother punched me.'

'Rupert...' Her jaw dropped. Rupert had punched Finn?

'We had a set-to like I've never had before or since.'

She wanted to close her eyes.

'We were both bloody and bruised by the end of it, and when I was finally in a state to listen he grabbed me by the throat and told me I couldn't disappoint my uncle or your parents by getting myself kicked out of school—that I owed it to everyone and that I'd be a hundred different kinds of a weasel if I let you all down. He told me I wasn't leaving him there to cope with the fallout on his own. He told me I wasn't abandoning him to a life of stolid respectability. And...'

'And?' she whispered.

'And I started to cry like a goddamn baby.'

Her heart thumped and her chest ached.

'I'd felt so alone until that moment, and Rupert hugged me and called me his brother.'

Audra tried to check the tears that burned her eyes.

'He gave me a second chance. And make no mistake, if he hadn't won me that second chance I'd probably be dead now.'

Even through the haze of her tears, the ferocity of his gaze pierced her.

'He made me feel a part of something—a family, a community—where what I did mattered. And that made me turn my life around, made me realise that what I did had an impact on the people around me, that it mattered to somebody…that what I did with my life mattered.'

'Of course it matters.' He just hadn't been able to see that then.

'So I let him take the rap for me, knowing what it would cost him.'

She nodded, swiped her fingers beneath her eyes. 'I'm glad he did what he did. I'm glad you let him do it.' She understood now how much he must feel he owed Rupert.

'So when Rupert asks me to…to take care with his little sister, I listen.'

She stilled. Her heart gave a sick thump.

'I promised him that I wouldn't mess with you and your emotions. And I mean to keep my word.'

She stiffened. Nobody—not Rupert, not Finn—had any right to make such decisions on her behalf.

His eyes flashed. 'You owe me a "truth or dare" question.'

She blinked, taken off guard by the snap and crackle of his voice, by the way his lips had thinned. 'Fine. Ask your question.'

'Knowing what you know now, would you choose to destroy my friendship with Rupert for a quick roll in the hay, Squirt?'

He knew he was being deliberately crude and deliberately brutal, but he had to create some serious distance between him and Audra before he did something he'd regret for the rest of his life.

She rose, as regal as a queen, her face cold and her eyes chips of ice. 'I'd never do anything to hurt your friendship with Rupert. Whether I'd heard that story or not.'

And yet they'd both been tempted to earlier.

'So, Finn, you don't need to worry your pretty little head over that any longer.'

He had to grind his teeth together at her deliberately patronising tone.

She spun away. 'I'm going to bed.'

She turned in the doorway. 'Also, the name is Audra— not Squirt. Strike Two.'

With that she swept from the room. Finn fell back into his chair and dragged both hands through his hair. He should never have kissed her. He hadn't known that a kiss could rock the very foundations of his world in the way his kiss with Audra had. Talk about pride coming before a fall. The gods punished hubris, didn't they? He'd really thought he could kiss her and remain unmarked… unmoved…untouched.

The idea seemed laughable now.

He'd wanted to fling her out of herself and force her to act on impulse. He hadn't known he'd lose control. He hadn't known that kiss would fling him out of himself… and then return him as a virtual stranger.

If it'd been any other woman, he'd have not been able to resist following that kiss through to its natural conclusion, the consequences be damned. His mouth dried. Whatever else they were, he knew those consequences would've been significant. Maybe he and Audra had dodged a bullet.

Or maybe they'd—

Maybe nothing! He didn't do long term. He didn't do family and babies. He did fun and adventure and he kept things uncomplicated and simple. Because that was the foundation his life had been built on. It was innate, in-born…intrinsic to who he was. There were some things in this world you couldn't change. Leopards couldn't change their spots and Finn Sullivan couldn't change his free-wheeling ways.

Finn heard Audra moving about in the kitchen the next morning, but he couldn't look up from the final pages of his book.

He read the final page…closed the cover.

Damn!

He stormed out into the kitchen and slammed the book to the counter. The split second after he'd done it, he winced and waited for her to jump out of her skin—waited for his stomach to curdle with self-loathing. He was such an idiot. He should've taken more care, but she simply looked at him, one eyebrow almost raised.

He nodded. 'Keep practising, it's almost there.'

She ignored that to glance at the book. 'Finished?'

He pointed at her and then slammed his finger to the book. 'That was a dirty, rotten, low-down trick. It's not finished!'

'My understanding is that particular story arc con-cludes.'

'Yeah, but I don't know if he gets his kingdom back. I don't know if she saves the world and defeats the bad guy. And…and I don't know if they end up together!'

Both her eyebrows rose.

'You…you tricked me!'

She leaned across and pointed. 'It says it's a trilogy here… And it says that it's Book One here. I wasn't keeping anything from you.'

Hot damn. So it did. He just… He hadn't paid any attention to the stuff on the cover. He rocked back on his heels, hands on hips. 'Didn't see that,' he murmured. 'And I really want to know how it ends.'

'And you feel cheated because you have to read another two books to find that out?'

Actually, the idea should appal him. But… 'I, uh…just guess I'm impatient to know how it all works out.'

'That's easily fixed. The bookshop in the village has the other two books in stock.'

He shoved his hands into his back pockets. 'Sorry, I shouldn't have gone off like that. Just didn't know what I was signing up for when I started the book.'

'God, Finn!' She took a plate of sliced fruit to the table and sat. 'That's taking commitment phobia to a whole new level.'

He indicated her plate. 'I'm supposed to do breakfast. That was part of the deal.'

'Part of the deal was calling me Audra too.'

She lifted a piece of melon to her lips. He tried to keep his face smooth, tried to keep his pulse under control as her mouth closed about the succulent fruit. 'So…what's on the agenda today?'

She ate another slice of melon before meeting his gaze. 'I want a Finn-free day.'

He fought the automatic urge to protest. An urge he knew was crazy because a day spent not in each other's company would probably be a wise move. 'Okay.'

'I bags the beach this morning.'

It took all his strength to stop from pointing out it was a long beach with room enough for both of them.

'Why don't you take the car and go buy your books, and then go do something you'd consider fun?'

Lying on a beach, swimming and reading a book, those things were fun. He rolled his shoulders. So were jetskiing and waterskiing and stuff. 'Okay.' He thrust out his jaw. 'Sounds great.'

She rose and rinsed her plate. 'And you'll have the house to yourself this evening.'

Her words jolted him up to his full height. 'Why?'

'Because I'm going into the village for a meal, and maybe some dancing. *Not* that it's any of your business.'

She wanted to go dancing? 'I'll take you out if that's what you want.'

'No, thank you, Finn.'

'But—'

Her eyes sparked. 'I don't want to go out to dinner or dancing with you.'

'Why not?' The words shot out of him and he immediately wished them back.

She folded her arms and peered down her nose at him. 'Do you really want me to answer that?'

He raised his hands and shook his head, but the anger in her eyes had his mind racing. 'You're annoyed with me. Because I kissed you?' Or because he wouldn't kiss her again?

Stop thinking about kissing her.

'Oh, I'm livid with you.'

He swallowed.

'And with Rupert.'

He stiffened. 'What's Rupert done? He's not even here.'

'And with myself.' She folded her arms, her expression more bewildered than angry now. 'You really don't see it, do you?'

See what?

'Between you, you and Rupert decided what was in my best interests. And—' the furrow in her brow deepened '—I let you. I went along with it instead of pointing out how patronising and controlling it was.' She lifted her chin. 'I'm a grown-up who has the right to make her own choices and decisions, be they wise or unwise. I'm not a child. I don't need looking after, and I do *not* have to consult with either of you if I want to kiss someone or… or start a relationship. And that's why I'm going into the village this evening on my own without an escort—to remind myself that I'm an adult.'

She swept up her beach bag and her sunhat and stalked out of the door.

I do not have to consult…if I want to kiss someone…

Was she planning on kissing someone tonight? But… but she couldn't.

Why not?

Scowling, he slammed the frying pan on a hot plate, turned it up to high before throwing in a couple of rashers of bacon. He cracked in two eggs as well. Oops—fine, he'd have scrambled eggs. He ground his teeth together. He *loved* scrambled eggs.

He gathered up the litter to throw into the bin, pushed open the lid…and then stilled. Setting the litter down on the counter again, he pulled out three A4 sheets of paper from the bottom of the bin, wiped off the fruit skins and let forth a very rude word. These were his designs for Audra's shop. He glared out of the glass sliding doors, but Audra had disappeared from view. 'That's not going to work, Princess.'

He pulled the frying pan from the heat, went to his room to grab his laptop and then strode into Rupert's office, heading straight for the printer.

He placed one set of printouts on the coffee table. The next set he placed on the tiny hall table outside her bedroom door. The third set he put in a kitchen drawer. The next time she reached for the plastic wrap, they'd greet her. The rest he kept in a pile in his bedroom to replace any of the ones she threw away.

* * *

'You're not taking the car?'

Audra didn't deign to answer him.

He glanced at his watch. 'Six thirty is a bit early for dinner, isn't it?'

She still didn't answer him. She simply peered at her reflection in the foyer mirror, and slicked on another coat of ruby-red lipstick. Utter perfection. She wore a sundress that made his mouth water too—the bodice hugged her curves, showing off a delectable expanse of golden skin at her shoulders and throat while the skirt fell in a floaty swirl of aqua and scarlet to swish about her calves. His heart pounded.

Don't think about messing up that lipstick.

He shoved his hands into his pockets. 'Why aren't you taking the car?'

She finally turned. 'Because I plan to have a couple of drinks. And I don't drink and drive.'

'But how will you get home?'

She raised an eyebrow.

He raised one back at her. 'You've almost got that down pat.'

She waved a hand in front of her face. 'Stop it, Finn.'

'What? It was a compliment and—'

'Stop it with the twenty questions. I know what time I want to eat. I know how to get home at the end of an evening out. Or—' she smiled, but it didn't reach eyes that flashed and sparked '—how to get home the morning after an evening out if that's the way the evening rocks.'

She…she might not be coming home? But—

And then she was gone in a swirl of perfume and red and aqua skirt as the village taxi pulled up in the driveway and tooted its horn.

Finn spent the evening pacing. Audra might be a grown woman, but she'd had fire in her eyes as she'd left. He knew she was angry with him and Rupert, but what if that anger led her to do something stupid…something she'd later regret? What the hell would he tell Rupert if something happened to her?

He lasted until nine p.m. Jumping in the car, it felt like a relief to finally be doing something, to be setting off after her. Not that he knew what he was going to do once he did find her.

She was in the first place he looked—Petra's Taverna. The music pouring from its open windows and doors was lively and cheerful. Tables spilled onto the courtyard outside and down to a tiny beach. Finn chose a table on the edge of the scene in the shadows of a cypress with an excellent view, via two enormous windows, inside the taverna.

Audra drew his eyes like a magnet. She sat on a stool framed in one of the windows and threw her head back at something her companion said, though Finn's view of her companion was blocked. She nodded and her companion came into view—a handsome young local—as they moved to the dance floor.

Beneath the table, Finn's hands clenched. When a waiter came he ordered a lemon squash. Someone had to keep their wits about them this evening! As the night wore on, Finn's scowl only grew and it deterred anyone who might've been tempted from coming across and trying to engage him in conversation.

And the more morose he grew, the merrier the tabloid inside became. As if those two things were related.

Audra was the life of the party. He lost track of the number of dance partners she had. She laughed and talked with just about every person in the taverna. She alternated glasses of white wine with big glasses of soda water. She snacked on olives and crisps and even played a hand of cards. She charmed everyone. And everything charmed her. He frowned. He'd not realised before how popular she was here in Kyanós. His frown deepened. It struck him that she was more alive here than he could ever remember seeing her.

And at a little after midnight, and after many pecks on cheeks were exchanged, she caught the taxi—presumably back to the villa—on her own.

He sat there feeling like an idiot. She'd had an evening out—had let her hair down and had some fun. She hadn't drunk too much. She hadn't flirted outrageously and hadn't needed to fight off inappropriate advances. She hadn't done anything foolish or reckless or ill-considered. She hadn't needed him to come to her rescue.

I'm a grown-up who has the right to make her own choices.

And what was he? Not just a fool, but some kind of creep—a sneak spying on a woman because he'd been feeling left out and unnecessary. And as far as Audra was concerned, he *was* unnecessary. *Completely* unnecessary. She didn't need him.

He could try to dress it up any way he liked—that he'd been worried about her, that he wanted to make sure she stayed safe—but what he'd done was spy on her and invade her privacy.

Why the hell had he done that? What right did he think he had?

Earlier she'd accused him and Rupert of being patronising and controlling, and she was right.

She deserved better from him. Much better.

CHAPTER NINE

WHEN AUDRA REACHED in the fridge for the milk for her morning coffee and found yet another set of printouts—in a plastic sleeve, no less, that would presumably protect them from moisture and condensation—it was all she could do not to scream.

She and Finn had spent the last three days avoiding each other. She'd tried telling herself that suited her just fine, but...

It *should* suit her just fine. She had the beach to herself in the mornings, while Finn took the car and presumably headed into the village. And then he had the beach in the afternoons while she commandeered the car. In terms of avoiding each other, it worked *perfectly*. It was just...

She blew out a breath. She wished avoidance tactics weren't necessary. She wished they could go back to laughing and having fun and teasing each other as they had before that stupid kiss.

And before she'd got all indignant about Rupert's overprotectiveness, and galled that Finn had unquestioningly fallen into line with it...and angry with herself for not having challenged it earlier. Where once her brother's protectiveness had made her feel cared for, now it left her feeling as if she was a family liability who needed safeguarding against her own foolishness.

Because of Thomas?

Or because if she could no longer hold tight to the label of being responsible and stable then...then what could she hold onto?

Stop it! Of course she was still responsible and stable. Thomas had been a mistake, and everyone was entitled to one mistake, right? Just as long as she didn't compound that by doing something stupid with Finn; just as long as she maintained a sense of responsibility and calm and balance, and remembered who *he* was and remembered who *she* was.

Sloshing milk into her coffee, she went to throw the printouts in the bin when her gaze snagged on some subtle changes to the pictures. Curiosity warred with self-denial. Curiosity won. Grabbing a croissant—Finn always made sure there was a fresh supply—she slipped outside to the picnic table to pore over the designs of this achingly and heart-wrenchingly beautiful shop.

Letting her hair down and doing things she wanted to do just for the sake of it—for fun—hadn't helped the burning in her soul whenever she was confronted with these pictures. They were snapshots of a life she could never have. And with each fresh reminder—and for some reason Finn seemed hell-bent on reminding her—that burn scorched itself into her deeper and deeper.

She bit into the croissant, she sipped coffee, but she tasted nothing.

Ever since Finn had kissed her she'd…*wanted*.

She'd *wanted* to kiss him again. She wanted *more*. She'd not known that a kiss could fill you with such a physical need. That it could make you crave so hard. She was twenty-seven years old. She'd thought she knew about attraction. She'd had good sex before. But that kiss had blown her preconceptions out of the stratosphere. And it had left her floundering. Because there was no way on God's green earth that she and Finn could go *there*. She didn't doubt that in the short term it'd be incredible, but ultimately it'd be destructive. She wasn't going to be responsible for that kind of pain—for wounding friendships and devastating family ties and connections.

She couldn't do that to Rupert.

She wouldn't do that to Finn.

But the kiss had left her wanting *more* from life too.

And she didn't know how to make that restlessness and sense of dissatisfaction go away.

So she'd tried a different strategy in the hope it would help. Instead of reining in all her emotions and desires, she'd let a few of them loose. Finn was right: if there was ever a time to rebel it was now when she was on holiday. She'd hoped a mini-rebellion would help her deal with her attraction for Finn. She'd hoped it would help her deal with the dreary thought of returning home to her job.

She'd gone dancing. It'd been fun.

She'd taken an art class and had learned about form and perspective. Her drawing had been terrible, but moving a pencil across paper had soothed her. The focus of next week's class was going to be composition. Her shoulders sagged. Except she wouldn't be here next week.

She'd even gone jetskiing again. It'd felt great to be zipping across the water. But no sooner had she returned the jetski than her restlessness had returned.

She pressed her hands to her face and then pulled them back through her hair. She'd hoped those things would help ease the ache in her soul, but they hadn't. They'd only fed it. It had been a mistake to come here.

And she wished to God Finn had never kissed her!

'Morning, Audra.'

As if her thoughts had conjured him, Finn appeared. His wide grin and the loose easy way he settled on the seat opposite with a bowl of cereal balanced in one hand inflamed her, though she couldn't have said why. She flicked the offending printouts towards him. 'Why are you leaving these all over the house?'

He ate a spoonful of cereal before gesturing to them. 'Do you like the changes I've made?'

'I—'

'Market research suggests that locating the point of sale over here provides for "a more comfortable retail experience"—' he made quotation marks in the air with one hand '—for the customer.'

She had to physically refrain from reaching across and shaking him. Drawing in a breath, she tried to channel responsible, calm balance. 'Why does any of this matter?'

'Because it needs to be perfect.'

Her chest clenched. Her eyes burned. Balance fled. 'Why?'

He shrugged and ate more cereal. 'Because that's what I do. I create designs as near perfect as possible.'

Didn't he know what these pictures and the constant reminders were doing to her?

He pulled the sheets from their plastic sleeve. 'What do you think about this shelving arrangement? It's neither better nor more functional than the ones you've already chosen, but apparently this design is all the range in Scandinavia at the moment, so I thought I'd throw it into the mix just to see what you thought?'

She couldn't help it; she had to look. The sleek lines were lovely, but these didn't fit in with the overall feel she was trying to achieve at all.

You're not trying to achieve an overall feel, remember? Pipe dream!

With a growl she slapped the picture facedown.

'No?' He raised one eyebrow—perfectly—which set her teeth even further on edge. 'Fair enough.'

'Enough already,' she countered through gritted teeth. 'Stop plastering these designs all over the house. I've had enough. I can see you do good work—excellent work. I'm sorry I misjudged you, but I believe I've already apologised. I'll apologise again if you need me to. But stop with the pictures. *Please.*'

He abandoned his breakfast to lean back and stare at her. She couldn't help wondering what he saw—a repressed woman he'd like to muss up?

It was what she wanted to believe. If it were true it'd

provide her with a form of protection. But it wasn't true. She knew that kiss had shaken him as much as it'd shaken her. It was why he'd avoided her for these last few days as assiduously as she had him.

'I'll stop with the pictures of the shop if you answer one question for me.'

'Oh, here we go again.' She glared. She didn't raise an eyebrow. She needed more practice before she tried that again. She folded her arms instead. 'Ask your question.'

He leaned towards her. The perfect shape of his mouth had a sigh rising up through her. 'Why are you working as an operations manager instead of opening up your dream shop here on this island and living a life that makes you happy?'

She flinched. His words were like an axe to her soul. How did he know? When Rupert, Cora and Justin had no idea? When she'd been so careful that none of them should know?

He held up the printouts and shook them at her. 'Your face when you described this shop, Audra... You came alive. It was...'

Her heart thumped so hard she could barely breathe.

'Magnificent,' he finally decided. 'And catching.'

She blinked. 'Catching...how?'

'Contagious! Your enthusiasm was contagious. I've not felt that enthusiastic about anything—'

He broke off with a frown. '—for a long time,' he finished. He stared at each of the three pictures. 'I want you to have this shop. I want you to have this life. I don't understand why you're punishing yourself.'

Her head reared back. 'I'm not punishing myself.'

'I'm sorry, Princess, but that's not what it looks like from where I'm sitting.'

'I do worthy work!' She shot to her feet, unable to sit for the agitation roiling through her. 'The work the Russel Corporation does is important.' She strode across to the bluff to stare out at the turquoise water spread below.

'I'm not disputing that.' His voice came from just behind her. 'But…so what?'

She spun to face him. 'How can you say that? Look at the amazing things Rupert, Cora and Justin are doing.'

His jaw dropped. 'This is about sibling rivalry? Come on, Audra, you're twenty-seven years old. I know you always wanted to keep up with the others when you were younger, but—' He scanned her face, rocked back on his heels. 'It's not about sibling rivalry.'

'No,' she said. It was about sibling loyalty. *Family* loyalty.

He remained silent, just…waiting.

She pressed her fingers to her temples for a moment before letting her arms drop back to her sides. 'When our mother died it felt like the end of the world.'

He reached out and closed his hand around hers and she suddenly felt less alone, less…diminished. She gripped his hand and stared doggedly out to sea. She couldn't look at him. If she looked at him she might cry. 'She was the lynchpin that kept all our worlds turning. The crazy thing was I never realised that until she was gone.' She hauled in a breath. 'And the work she did at the Russel Corporation was crucial.'

Karen Russel had been the administrator of the Russel Corporation's charity arm, and Audra's father had valued her in that role without reservation. Humanitarian endeavours formed a key component of the corporation's mission statement and it wasn't one he was comfortable trusting to anyone outside the family.

'But her influence was so much wider than that.' She blinked against the sting in her eyes. 'She worked out a strategy for Rupert to evolve into the role of CEO; she researched laboratories that would attract the most funding and would therefore provide Cora with the most promising opportunities. If she'd lived long enough she'd have found excellent funding for Justin's efforts in South-East Asia.' Justin was implementing a dental-health programme to the impoverished populations in Cambodia. He had ambitions to take his programme to all communities in need throughout South-East Asia.

She felt him turn towards her. 'Instead you found those funding opportunities for him. You should be proud of yourself.'

No sooner were the words out of his mouth than he stilled. She couldn't look at him. He swore softly. 'Audra—'

'When our mother died, I'd never seen the rest of my family so devastated.' She shook her hand free. 'I wanted to make things better for them. You should've seen my father's relief when I said I'd take over my mother's role in the corporation after I'd finished university. Justin floundered towards the end of his last year of study. He had exams coming up but started panicking about the licences and paperwork he needed to file to work in Cambodia, and finding contacts there. The laboratory Cora worked for wanted sponsorship from business and expected her to approach the family corporation. And Rupert… well, he missed the others so having me around to boss helped.'

She'd stepped into the breach because Karen was no longer there to do it. And someone had to. It'd broken her heart to see her siblings hurting so badly.

Finn had turned grey. He braced his hands on his knees, and she couldn't explain why, but she had to swallow the lump that did everything it could to lodge in her throat. 'You've been what they've all needed you to be.'

'I'm not a martyr, Finn. I *love* my family. I'm proud I've been able to help.' Helping them had helped her to heal. It'd given her a focus, when her world had felt as if it were spinning out of control.

He straightened, his eyes dark. 'She wouldn't want this for you.'

'You don't know that.' She lifted her chin. 'I think she'd be proud of me.'

He chewed on his bottom lip, his brows lowering over his eyes. 'Have you noticed how each of you have coped with your mother's death in different ways?'

She blinked.

'Rupert became super-protective of you all.'

Rupert had always been protective, but… She nodded. He'd become excessively so since their mother's death.

'Cora threw herself into study. She wanted to top every class she took.'

Cora had found solace in her science textbooks.

'Justin started living more in the moment.'

She hadn't thought about it in those terms, but she supposed he had.

One corner of Finn's mouth lifted. 'Which means he leaves things to the last minute and relies on his little sister to help make them right.'

Her lips lifted too.

'While you, Princess…' He sobered. 'You've tried to fill the hole your mother has left behind.'

She shook her head. 'Only the practical day-to-day stuff.' Nobody could fill the emotional hole she'd left behind.

'Your siblings have a genuine passion for what they do, though. They're following their dreams.'

And in a small way she'd been able to facilitate that. She didn't regret that for a moment.

'You won't be letting your mother down if you follow your own dreams and open a shop here on Kyanós.'

'That's not what it feels like.' She watched a seabird circle and then dive into the water below. 'If I leave the Russel Corporation it'll feel as if I'm betraying them all.'

'You'll be the only who feels that way.'

The certainty in his tone had her swinging to him.

He lifted his hands to his head, before dropping them back to his sides. 'Audra, they're all doing work they love!'

'Good!' She stared at his fists and then into his face. He was getting really het-up about this. 'I want them to love what they do.'

'Then why don't you extend yourself that same courtesy?'

He bellowed the words, and her mouth opened and closed but no sound came out. He made it sound so easy. But it wasn't! She loved being there for her brothers and sister. She loved that she could help them.

'How would you feel if you discovered Rupert or Cora or Justin were doing their jobs just to keep you feeling comfortable and emotionally secure?'

Oh, that'd be awful! It'd—

She took a step away from him, swallowed. Her every muscle scrunched up tight. That scenario, it wasn't synonymous with hers.

Why not?

She pressed her hands to her cheeks, trying to cool them. Her siblings were each brilliant in their own way—fiercely intelligent, politically savvy and driven. She wasn't. Her dreams were so ordinary in comparison, so lacking in ambition. A part of her had always been afraid that her family would think she wasn't measuring up to her potential.

Her heart started to pound. Had she been using her role in the family corporation as an excuse to hide behind? Stretching her own wings required taking risks, and those risks frightened her.

'I hate to say this, Princess, but when you get right down to brass tacks you're just a glorified administrator, a pen-pusher, and anyone can do the job that you do.'

* * *

'Why don't you tell me what you really think, Finn?'

The stricken expression in Audra's eyes pierced straight through the centre of him. He didn't want to hurt her. But telling her what he really thought was wiser than doing what he really wanted to do, which was kiss her.

He had to remind himself again of all the reasons kissing her was a bad idea.

He pulled in a breath. He didn't want to hurt her. He wanted to see her happy. He wanted to see her happy the way she'd been happy when describing her shop…when she'd been learning to ride a jetski…and when she'd been dancing. Did she truly think those things were frivolous and self-indulgent?

He tapped a fist against his lips as he stared out at the glorious view spread in front of them. The morning sun tinged everything gold, not so much as a breeze ruffled the air and it made the water look otherworldly still, and soft, like silk and mercury.

He pulled his hand back to his side. *Right.* 'It's my day.'

From the corner of his eye he saw her turn towards him. 'Pardon?'

'To choose our activities. It's my day.'

She folded her arms and stuck out a hip. She was going to tell him to go to blazes—that she was spending the day *on her own*. She opened her mouth, but he rushed on before she could speak. 'There's something I want to show you.'

She snapped her mouth shut, but her gaze slid over him as if it couldn't help it, and the way she swallowed and spun seawards again, her lips parted as if to draw much-needed air into her lungs, had his skin drawing tight. She was right. It'd be much wiser to continue to avoid each other.

But…

But he might never get this opportunity again. He

wanted to prove to her that she had a right to be happy, to urge her to take that chance.

'The yacht with the pink and blue sail is back.'

She pointed but he didn't bother looking. 'Please,' he said quietly.

She met his gaze, her eyes searching his, before she blew out a breath and shrugged. 'Okay. Fine.'

'Dress code is casual and comfortable. We're not hiking for miles or doing anything gruelling. I just… I've been exploring and I think I've found some things that will interest you.'

'Sunhat and sandals…?'

'Perfect. How soon can you be ready?'

One slim shoulder lifted. 'Half an hour.'

'Excellent.' He gathered up his breakfast things and headed back towards the house before he did something stupid like kiss her.

Their first port of call was Angelo's workshop. Angelo was a carpenter who lived on the far side of the village. He made and sold furniture from his renovated garage. Most of the pieces he made were too large for Audra's hypothetical shop—chest of drawers, tables and chairs, bedheads and bookcases—but there were some smaller items Finn knew she'd like, like the pretty trinket boxes and old-fashioned writing desks that were designed to sit on one's lap.

As he'd guessed, Audra was enchanted. She ran a finger along a pair of bookends. 'The workmanship is exquisite.'

Finn nodded. 'He says that each individual piece of wood that he works with tells him what it wants to be.'

'You've spoken to him?'

'Finn!' Angelo rushed into the garage. 'I thought that was your car out front. Come, you and Audra must have coffee with the family. Maria has just made *baklava*.'

'Angelo!' Audra gestured around the room. 'I didn't know you made such beautiful things.'

Finn stared at her. 'You know Angelo?'

'Of course! His brother Petros is Rupert's gardener. And Maria used to work in the bakery.'

They stayed an hour.

Next Finn took Audra to Anastasia's studio, which sat solitary on a windswept hill. He rolled his eyes. 'Now you're going to tell me you know Anastasia.'

She shook her head. 'I've not had that pleasure.'

Anastasia took Audra for a tour of her photography studio while Finn trailed along behind. If the expression on Audra's face was anything to go by, Anastasia's photographs transfixed her. They'd transfixed him too. It was all he could do to drag her back to the car when the tour was finished.

Then it was back into the village to visit Eleni's workshop, where she demonstrated how she made not only scented soap from products sourced locally, but a range of skincare and cosmetic products as well. Audra lifted a set of soaps in a tulle drawstring bag, the satin ribbon entwined with lavender and some other herbs Finn couldn't identify. 'These are packaged so prettily I can't resist.' She bought some candles too.

They visited a further two tradespeople—a leather worker who made wallets and purses, belts and ornately worked book jackets, and a jeweller. Audra came away with gifts for her entire family.

'Hungry?' he asked as he started the car. He'd walked this hill over the last three days, searching for distraction, but today, for the sake of efficiency, he'd driven.

'Starved.'

They headed back down the hill to the harbour, and ate a late lunch of *marida* and *spanakorizo* at a taverna that had become a favourite. They dined beneath a bougainvillea-covered pergola and watched as the water lapped onto the pebbled beach just a few metres away.

Audra broke the silence first. 'Anastasia's work should hang in galleries. It's amazing. Her photographs reveal a Greece so different from the tourist brochures.'

'She's seventy. She does everything the old way. She doesn't even have the internet.'

She nodded and sipped her wine, before setting her wine glass down with a click. 'I'd love for Isolde, one of my friends from school—she's an interior decorator and stager, furnishes houses and apartments so they look their absolute best for selling—to see some of Angelo's bigger pieces. She'd go into raptures over them.' She started to rise. 'We need to go back and take some photos so I can send her—'

'My *loukoumades* haven't come yet.' He waved her back to her seat. 'There's time. We can go back tomorrow.' He topped up her wine. 'What about Eleni's pretty smelly things? They'd look great in a shop.'

Audra shook her head and then nodded, as if holding a conversation with herself. 'I should put her in touch with Cora's old lab partner, Elise. Remember her? She moved into the cosmetic industry. Last I heard she was making a big push for eco-friendly products. I bet she'd love Eleni's recipes.'

She was still putting everyone else's needs before her own. The *loukoumades* came and a preoccupied Audra helped him eat them. While her attention was elsewhere, he couldn't help but feast his eyes on her. She'd put on a little weight over the last eleven days. She had colour in her cheeks and her eyes sparked with interest and vitality. An ache grew inside him until he could barely breathe.

He tried to shake it off. Under his breath he called himself every bad name he could think of. Did he really find the allure of the forbidden so hard to resist?

He clenched his jaw. He *would* resist. He'd cut off his

right hand rather than let Rupert down. He'd cut off his entire arm rather than ever hurt Audra.

But when she came alive like this, he couldn't look away.

She slapped her hands lightly to the table. 'I wonder how the villagers would feel about an annual festival.'

'What kind of festival?'

'One that showcases the local arts and crafts scene, plus all the fresh produce available here—the cured meats, the cheeses, the olive oils and…and…'

'The *loukoumades*?'

'Definitely the *loukoumades*!'

She laughed. She hadn't laughed, not with him, since he'd kissed her…and the loss of that earlier intimacy had been an ache in his soul.

The thought that he might be able to recapture their earlier ease made his heart beat faster.

'What?' she said, touching her face, and he realised he was staring.

He forced himself backwards in his seat. 'You're amazing, you know that?'

Her eyes widened. 'Me?'

'Absolutely. Can't you see how well you'd fit in here, and what a difference you could make? You've connections, energy and vision…passion.'

She visibly swallowed at that last word, and he had to force his gaze from the line of her throat. He couldn't let it linger there or he'd be lost.

Her face clouded over. 'I can't just walk away from the Russel Corporation.'

'Why not?' He paused and then nodded. 'Okay, you can't leave *just like that*.' He snapped his fingers. 'You'd have to hang around long enough to train up your replacement…or recruit a replacement.'

He could see her overdeveloped sense of duty begin to overshadow her excitement at the possibilities life held for her. He refused to let it win. 'Can you imagine how much your mother would've enjoyed the festival you just described?'

Her eyes filled.

'I remember how much she used to enjoy the local market days on Corfu, back when the family used to holiday there…when we were all children,' he said. Karen Russel had been driven and focussed, but she'd relished her downtime too.

'I know. I just…' Audra glanced skywards and blinked hard. 'I'd just want her to be proud of me.'

Something twisted in Finn's chest. Karen had died at a crucial stage in Audra's life—when Audra had been on the brink of adulthood. She'd been tentatively working her way towards a path that would give her life purpose and meaning, and searching for approval and support from the woman she'd looked up to. Her siblings had all had that encouragement and validation, but it'd been cruelly taken from Audra. No wonder she'd lost her way. 'Princess, I can't see how she could be anything else.'

Blue eyes, swimming with uncertainty and remembered grief, met his.

'Audra, you're kind and you work hard. You love your family and are there for them whenever they need you. She valued those things. And I think she'd thank you from the bottom of her heart for stepping into the breach when she was gone and doing all the things that needed doing.'

A single tear spilled onto her cheek, and he had to blink hard himself.

'The thing is,' he forced himself to continue, 'nobody needs you to do those things any more. And I'd lay everything on the bet that your mother would have loved the shop you described to me. Look at the way she lived her life—with passion and with zeal. She'd want you to do the same.'

Audra swiped her fingers beneath her eyes and pulled in a giant breath. 'Can…can we walk for a bit?'

They walked along the harbour and Audra hooked her arm through his. The accidental brushing of their bodies as they walked was a sweet torture that made him prickle and itch and want, but she'd done it without thinking or forethought—as if she needed to be somehow grounded while her mind galloped at a million miles an hour. So he left it there and didn't pull away, and fought against the growing need that pounded through him.

She eventually released him to sit on the low harbour wall, and he immediately wanted to drag her hand back into the crook of his arm and press his hand over it to keep it there.

'So,' she started. 'You're saying it wouldn't be selfish of me to move here and open my shop?'

'That's exactly what I'm saying. I know you can't see it, but you don't have a selfish bone in your body.'

Sceptical eyes lifted to meet his. 'You really don't think I'd be letting my family down if I did that?'

'Absolutely not. I think they'd be delighted for you.' He fell down beside her. 'But don't take my word for it. Ask them.'

She pondered his words and then frowned. 'Do you honestly think I could fit in and become a permanent part of the community here on Kyanós?'

He did, but… 'Don't you?' Because at the end of the day it wasn't about what he thought. It was what she thought and believed that mattered.

'I want to believe it,' she whispered, 'because I want so badly for it to be true. I'm afraid that's colouring my judgement.'

He remained silent.

'I don't have half the talents of the artisans we visited today.' She drummed her fingers against her thigh. 'But

I do have pretty good admin and organisational skills. I know how to run a business. I have my savings.'

She pressed her hands to her stomach. 'And it'd be so exciting to showcase local arts and crafts in my shop—nobody else is doing that so I'd not be going into competition with another business on the island. I'd be careful not to stock anything that was in direct competition with the bookshop or the clothing boutiques. And I could bring in some gorgeous bits and bobs that aren't available here.'

Her face started to glow. 'And if everyone else here thought it was a good idea, it'd be really fun to help organise a festival. All my friends would come. And maybe my family could take time off from their busy schedules.'

She leapt to her feet, paced up and down in front of him. 'I could do this.'

'You could. But the question is…'

She halted and leaned towards him. 'What's the question?'

He rested back on his hands. 'The question is, are you going to?'

Fire streaked through her eyes, making them sparkle more brilliantly than the water in the harbour. 'Uh-huh.' She thrust out her chin, and then a grin as wide as the sky itself spread across her face. And Finn felt as if he were scudding along on an air current, sailing through the sky on some euphoric cloud of warmth and possibility.

'I'm going to do it.'

She did a little dance on the spot. She grinned at him as if she didn't know what else to do. And then she leaned forward and, resting her hands on his shoulders, kissed him. Her lips touched his, just for a moment. It was a kiss of elation and excitement—a kiss of thanks, a kiss between friends. And it was pure and magical, and it shifted the axis of Finn's world.

She eased away, her lips parted, her breath coming fast and her eyes dazed, the shock in her face no doubt reflecting the shock in his. She snatched her hands away, smoothed them down the sides of her skirt and it was as if the moment had never been.

Except he had a feeling it was branded on his brain for all time. Such a small contact shouldn't leave such an indelible impression.

'Thank you, Finn.'

He shook himself. 'I didn't do anything.'

She raised an eyebrow and then shook her head and collapsed back down beside him on the sea wall. 'Don't say anything. I know it needs more practice. And you did do something—something big. You helped me see things differently. You gave me the nudge I needed and...' She turned and met his gaze, her smile full of excitement. 'I'm going to change my life. I'm going to turn it upside down. And I can't wait.'

Something strange and at odds like satisfaction and loss settled in the pit of his stomach, warring with each other for pre-eminence. He stoutly ignored it to grin back and clap his hands. 'Right! This calls for champagne.'

CHAPTER TEN

AUDRA WOKE EARLY, and the moment her eyes opened she found herself grinning. She drummed her heels against the mattress with a silent squeal as her mind sparked and shimmered with plans and purpose.

She threw on some clothes and her running shoes, before picking her way down to the beach and starting to run.

To run.

Unlike the previous three mornings—when she and Finn had been avoiding each other—she didn't time herself. She ran because she had an excess of energy and it seemed a good idea to get rid of some of it. The decisions she was about to make would impact the rest of her life and, while joy and excitement might be driving her, she needed to make decisions based on sound business logic. She wanted this dream to last forever—not just until her money ran out and she'd bankrupted herself.

She reached the sheer wall of cliff at the beach's far end and leaned against it, bracing her hands on her knees, her breath coming hard and fast. Who'd have thought she could run all this way? She let out a whoop. Who knew running could feel so *freeing*?

She pulled off her shoes and socks and ambled back along the shoreline, relishing the wash of cool water against her toes as she made her way back towards the villa.

When she walked in, Finn glanced up from where he slouched against the breakfast bar, mug of coffee clasped in one hand. His eyes widened as they roved over her. He straightened. 'Have you been for a run?'

Heat mounted her cheeks. 'I, uh…'

One side of his mouth hooked up in that grin, and her

blood started to pound harder than when she'd been running. 'That's not a "truth or dare" question, Audra. A simple yes or no will suffice.'

She dropped her shoes to the floor and helped herself to coffee. 'You got me kind of curious when you wanted us to run that day.' He'd made her feel like a lazy slob, but she didn't say that out loud because she didn't want him to feel bad about that. Not after everything he'd done for her yesterday. 'Made me wonder if I *could* run the length of the beach.'

'I bet you rocked it in.'

His faith warmed her. 'Not *rocked* it in,' she confessed, planting herself at the table. 'But I did it. And it gets a bit easier every day.'

He moved to sit opposite. 'You've been for more than one run? How many?'

She rolled her shoulders. 'Only four.'

'And you don't hate it?'

'It's not like my new favourite thing or anything.' But she didn't *hate* it. Sometimes it felt good to be pounding along the sand. It made her feel…powerful. 'I like having done it. It makes me feel suitably virtuous.'

He laughed and pointed to a spot above her head. 'That's one very shiny halo.'

He leaned back and drained his coffee. 'Who'd have thought it? You find you don't hate running, and I find I don't hate lying on a beach reading a book.'

He hadn't seemed restless for any of his usual hard and fast sports. She opened her mouth to ask him about it, but closed it again. She didn't want to put ideas into his head.

He rose. 'I had a couple of new thoughts about some designs for your shop. Wanna see them after breakfast?'

That caught her attention. 'Yes, please!'

An hour later she sat at the outdoor picnic table with Finn, soaking up the sun, the views and the incredible designs he kept creating. 'These are amazing.' She pulled his laptop closer towards her. 'You've gone into so much detail.'

'You gave me good material to work with.'

She flicked through the images he'd created, loving everything that she saw. 'You said—that first day when you showed me what you did—that the first step was the "dreaming big with no holds barred" step.'

He nodded.

She pulled in a breath. 'What's the next step?'

'Ah.' His lips twisted. 'The next step consists of the far less sexy concept of compromise.'

'Compromise?'

He pointed towards his computer. 'These are the dream, but what are the exact physical dimensions of your shop going to be? We won't know that until you find premises and either buy them or sign a lease. So these designs would have to be modified to fit in with that.'

Right.

'You'll also need to take into account any building works that may need doing on these new premises. And if so, what kind of council approvals you might need. Does the building have any covenants in place prohibiting certain work?'

Okay.

'What's your budget for kitting out your shop? See this shelving system here? It costs twice as much as that one. Is it worth twice as much to you? If it's not, which other shelving system do you settle on?'

'So…fitting the dream to the reality?'

'Exactly. Deciding on the nitty-gritty detail.'

He swung the computer back his way, his fingers flying across the keyboard, his brow furrowed in concentration and his lips pursed. As she stared at him something inside Audra's chest cracked open and she felt herself falling and falling and falling. Not 'scream and grab onto something' falling, but flying falling.

Like anything was possible falling.

Like falling in love falling.

Her heart stopped. The air in front of her eyes shimmered. Finn? She'd…she'd fallen in love with Finn? Her heart gave a giant kick and started beating in triple time. She swallowed. No, no, that was nonsense. She wasn't stupid enough to fall for Finn. He didn't do serious. He treated women as toys. He was a playboy!

And yet… He *did* do serious because they'd had several very serious discussions while they'd been here. She'd discovered depths to him she'd never known. He wasn't just an adrenaline junkie, but a talented designer and canny businessman. The playboy thing… Well, he hadn't been out carousing every night. And he hadn't treated her like a toy. Even when she'd wanted him to. So it was more than possible that she had him pegged all wrong about that too.

In the next moment she shook her head. Rupert had warned her against Finn, and Rupert would know.

But…

She didn't want to kill the hope trickling through her. Was it really so stupid?

'Okay, here's a budget version of your shop.'

Finn turned the laptop back towards her. She forced herself to focus on his designs rather than the chaos of her mind. And immediately lost herself in the world he'd created.

'What do you think?'

'This is still beautiful.'

He grinned and her heart kicked against the walls of her chest. She brushed her fingers across the picture of the barrel of flowers standing by the front door. 'You have such a talent for this. Don't you miss it when you're off adventuring?'

Very slowly he reached across and closed the lid of his laptop. 'That's a "truth or dare" question, Audra. And the answer is yes.'

Her heart stuttered. So did her breath.

'I've been fighting it. Not wanting to acknowledge it.'

'Why not?'

'Because I want to be more than a boring, driven businessman.'

'That's not boring!' She pointed to his computer. 'That…it shows what an artist you are.'

Hooded eyes met hers. 'I lead this exciting life—living the dream. It should be enough.'

But she could see that it wasn't. 'Dreams can change,' she whispered.

He stared down at his hands. 'I've had a lot of time to think over the last fortnight…and our discussions have made me realise a few things.'

Her mouth went dry. In a part of her that she refused to acknowledge, she wanted him to tell her that he loved her and wanted to build a life and family with her. 'Like?' she whispered.

'Like how much the way I live my life has to do with my parents.'

'In what way?' She held her breath and waited to see if he would answer.

He shrugged, but she sensed the emotion beneath the casual gesture. 'I hated not having a home base when I was growing up. I hated the way we were constantly on the move. I hated that I didn't have any friends my own age. But when my parents died…' He dragged a hand down his face. 'I'd have done anything to have them back. But at the same time—' the breath he drew in was ragged '—I didn't want to give up the life Uncle Ned had created for me. I liked that life a hundred times better.'

Her heart squeezed at the darkness swirling in his eyes—the remembered grief and pain, the confusion and strange sense of relief. She understood how all those things could bewilder and baffle a person, making it impossible to see things clearly.

'And that made me feel guilty. So I've tried to mould my life on a balance between the kind of life they lived and the kind of life Ned lived. I wanted to make them all proud. Similar to the way you wanted to make your mother proud, I guess. I thought I could have the best of both worlds and be happy.'

'But you're not happy.'

He wanted it to be enough. She could see that. But the simple fact was it wasn't. And him wishing otherwise wouldn't change that fact.

She swallowed. 'Have you ever loved a song so much that you played it over and over and over, but eventually you play it too much and you wreck it somehow? And then you don't want to listen to it any more, and when you do unexpectedly hear it somewhere it doesn't give you the same thrill it once did?'

Hooded eyes lifted. 'I know what you mean.'

'Well, maybe that's what you've done with all of your adrenaline-junkie sports. Maybe you're all adrenalined out and now you need to find a new song that sings to your soul.'

He stared at her, scepticism alive in his eyes. 'This is more than that. This is the entire way I live my life. Walking away from it feels as if I'm criticising the choices my parents made.'

'I don't see it as a criticism. You're just…just forging your own path.'

He shrugged, but the darkness in his eyes belied the casual gesture. 'The thing is I can no longer hide from the fact that racing down a black ski run no longer gives me the thrill it once did, or that performing endless laps in a sports car is anything other than monotonous, and that trekking to base camp at Everest is just damned cold and uncomfortable.'

But she could see it left him feeling like a bad person—an ingrate.

He speared her with a glance. 'I can't hassle and lecture you about living your dreams and then hide from it when it applies to my own life. That'd make me a hypocrite on top of everything else.'

Her heart burned. She wanted to help him the way he'd helped her—give him the same clarity. 'How old was your father when he died?'

'Thirty-five.'

'So only a couple of years older than you are now?' She gave what she hoped was an expressive shrug. 'Who knows what he might've chosen to do if he'd lived longer?'

'Give up extreme sports, my father?' Finn snorted. 'You can't be serious.'

'Is it any crazier than me opening a shop?'

He smiled. 'That's not crazy. It's what you have a passion for. It's *exciting*.'

Her heart chugged with so much love she had to lower her gaze in case he saw it shining there. 'We can never know what the future might've held for your father, but he could've had a mid-life crisis and decided to go back to Australia and…and start a hobby farm.'

A bark of laughter shot out of him.

'I know a lot of people have criticised the way your parents lived, wrote them off as irresponsible and frivolous.' And she guessed she was one of them. 'But they didn't hurt anyone living like they did; they paid their bills. They were…free spirits. And free spirits, Finn, would tell you to follow your heart and do the things that make you happy. And to not care what other people think.'

His head snapped up.

'If they were true free spirits they'd include themselves amongst those whose opinions didn't matter.'

She watched his mind race. 'What are you going to do?' she asked when she couldn't hold the question back any longer.

He shook his head. 'I've no idea.'

She swallowed. He needed time to work it out.

When his gaze returned to hers, though, it was full of warmth and…and something she couldn't quite define. Affection…laughter…wonder? 'It's been a hell of a holiday, Audra.'

Her name sounded like gold on his tongue. All she could do was nod.

A warm breeze ruffled her hair, loose tendrils tickling her cheek. She pulled it back into a tighter ponytail, trying to gather up all the loose strands. For some reason her actions made Finn smile. 'I'm going to get it cut,' she announced, not realising her intention until the words had left her.

His eyebrows shot up.

'Short. *Really* short. A pixie cut, perhaps. I hate it dangling about my face. I always have.'

'So how come you haven't cut it before now?'

She had no idea. 'Just stuck in the old ways of doing things, I guess. Walking a line I thought I should and presenting the image I thought I should, and not deviating from it. But now…'

'Now?'

'Now anything seems possible.' Even her and Finn didn't seem outside the realms of possibility. He cared for her, she knew that much. And look at everything they'd shared this last fortnight. Look how much he'd done for her. Look how much of an impact they'd had on each other. It had to mean something, right?

'I'm going to ask Anna in the village if she'll cut it for me.'

'When?'

'Maybe…maybe this afternoon.' If she could get an appointment.

He stared at her for a long moment and she had to fight the urge to fidget. 'What?'

'I did something.'

There was something in his tone—something uncertain, and a little defiant, and…a bit embarrassed, maybe? She didn't know what it meant. 'What did you do?'

He scratched a hand through his hair, his gaze skidding away. 'It might be best if I simply show you.'

'Okay. Now?'

He nodded.

'Where are we going? What's the dress code?'

'Into the village.' His gaze wandered over her and it left her burning and achy, prickly and full of need. 'And what you're wearing is just fine.'

They stopped at the hairdresser's first, because Finn insisted. When Anna said she could cut Audra's hair immediately Finn accepted the appointment on her behalf before she could say anything. Audra surveyed him, bemused and not a little curious.

'It'll give me some time to get set up properly,' he explained when he caught her stare.

She shook her head. 'I've no idea what you're talking about.'

'I know.' He leaned forward and pressed a kiss to her brow. 'All will be revealed soon. I'll be back in an hour.'

He was gone before the fresh, heady scent of him had invaded her senses, before she could grab him by the collar of his shirt and kiss him properly. Dear God, what did she do with her feelings for him? She had no idea! Should she try to bury them…or did she dare hope that, given time, he could return them?

Don't do anything rash.

She swallowed and nodded. She couldn't afford to make another mistake. She and Thomas had only broken up six weeks ago. This could be a rebound thing. Except… She'd not been in love with Thomas. She'd wanted to be, but she could see now it'd been nothing but a pale imitation—a combination of loneliness and feeling flattered by his attentions. She pressed her hands to her stomach as it started to churn.

Don't forget Rupert warned you against falling in love with Finn.

Yeah, but Rupert was overprotective and—

'Audra, would you like to take a seat?'

Audra shook herself, and tried to quiet her mind as she gave herself over to Anna's ministrations.

As promised, Finn returned an hour later. Audra's hair had been cut, shampooed and blow-dried and it felt…*wonderful*! She loved what Anna had done—short at the back and sides but still thick and tousled on top. She ran her fingers through it, and the excitement she'd woken with this morning vibrated through her again now.

She and Anna were sharing a cup of tea and gossip when Finn returned, and the way his eyes widened when he saw her, the light that flared in his eyes, and the low whistle that left his lips, did the strangest things to her insides.

'It looks…' He gestured. 'I mean, you look…' He swallowed. 'It's great. You look great.'

Something inside her started to soar. He wanted her. He tried to hide it, but he wanted her in the same way she wanted him. It wasn't enough. But it was something, right? She could build on that, and… Her heart dipped. Except their holiday was almost over and there was so little time left—

He frowned. 'You're not regretting it, are you?'

She tried to clear her face. 'No! I love it.' She touched a self-conscious hand to her new do. 'It feels so liberating.' She did what she could to put her disturbing thoughts from her mind. 'Now put me out of my misery and show me whatever it is you've done. I'm dying here, Finn!'

'Come on, then.' He grinned and took her arm, but

dropped it the moment they were outside. She knew why—because the pull between them was so intense.

What if she were to seduce him? Maybe...

That could be a really bad idea.

Or an inspired one.

Her heart picked up speed. She had to force herself to focus on where they were going.

Finn led her along the village's main street. She made herself glance into the windows of the fashion boutiques with their colourful displays, dragged in an appreciative breath as they passed the bakery that sold those decadent croissants. She slowed when they reached the bookshop, but with a low laugh Finn urged her past it.

At the end of the row stood the beautiful whitewashed building with freshly painted shutters the colour of a blue summer day that had silently sat at the centre of herÁ dreams. The moment she'd seen the For Sale sign when she'd clambered off the ferry a fortnight ago, she'd wanted to buy it. Her heart pounded. This place was...*perfect*.

'I remember you saying there was a place for sale in the village that would be the ideal location for your shop, and I guessed this was the place you meant.'

She spun to him, her eyes wide.

'So I asked around and found it belongs to the Veros family.'

'The Veros family who own the deli?'

'One and the same. I asked if we could have a look inside.' He brandished a key. 'And they said yes.'

Excitement gathered beneath her breastbone until she thought she might burst.

'Shall we?'

'Yes, please!'

He unlocked the door. 'Do you want the shutters open?' He gestured to the shutters at the front window. She could barely speak so she simply nodded. She wanted to see the interior bathed in the blues and golds of the late morning light. 'You go on ahead, then, while I open them.'

Pressing one hand to her chest, she reached out with the other to push the door open. Her heart beat hard against her palm. Could this be the place where she could make her dreams come true? Was this the place where she could start the rest of her life? She tried to rein in her excitement. This was the next step—making the dream fit the reality. She needed to keep her feet on the ground.

Inside it was dim and shadowy. She closed her eyes and made a wish, and when she opened her eyes again, light burst through the spotlessly clear front window as Finn flung the shutters back. Her heart stuttered. The world tilted on its axis. She had to reach out and brace herself against a wall to stop from falling.

Her heart soared…stopped…pounded.

She couldn't make sense of what she was seeing, but in front of her the designs Finn had created for her shop had taken shape and form in this magical place. She squished her eyes shut, but when she opened them again nothing had changed.

She spun around to find Finn wrestling a tub of colourful flowers into place just outside the front door. Her eyes filled. He'd done all of this for her?

He came inside then and grinned, but she saw the uncertainty behind the smile. 'What do you think?'

'I think this is amazing! How on earth did you manage to do this in such a short space of time?'

One shoulder lifted. 'I asked Angelo to whip up a couple of simple display arrangements—don't look too closely because they're not finished.'

'But…but there's stock on the shelves!'

'I borrowed some bits and pieces from Angelo, Eleni, Kostas and Christina. They were more than happy to help me out when I told them what it was for. You're very well thought of in these parts. They consider you one of their own, you know?'

It was how she'd always felt here.

'So you'll see it gets a little more rough and ready the further inside we go.'

He took her arm and led her deeper into the shop and she saw that he'd tacked pictures of all the things she meant to sell on temporary shelves. It brought her dream to magical life, however—helped her see how it could all look in reality. The layout and design, the colours and the light flooding in, the view of the harbour, it was all so very, *very* perfect. 'I love it.'

'Wait until you see upstairs.' Reaching for her hand, he towed her to the back of the shop. 'There's a kitchenette and bathroom through here and storeroom there.' He swung a door open and clicked on the light, barely giving her time to glance inside before leading her up a narrow set of stairs to a lovely apartment with a cosy living room, compact but adequate kitchen, and two bedrooms. The living room and the master bedroom, which was tucked beneath the eaves on the third floor, had exceptional views of the harbour. It was all *utterly* perfect.

'I can't believe you did this!'

'So you like it?'

'I couldn't love it any better.'

His grin was full of delight and...affection.

Her mind raced. He was attracted to her, and he cared for her. He'd done all of this for her. It had to *mean* something.

'I made enquiries and the price they're asking seems reasonable.'

He named a price that made her gulp, but was within her means. She pulled in a breath. 'I'm going to get a building inspection done and...and then put in an offer.'

He spun back to her. 'You mean it?'

She nodded. She wanted to throw herself at him and hug him. But if she did that it'd make his guard go back up. And before that happened she needed to work through the mass of confusion and turbulence racing through her mind.

She followed him back down the stairs silently. His gaze narrowed when they reached the ground floor. 'Is everything okay?'

'My mind is racing at a hundred miles a minute. I'm feeling a little overwhelmed.'

His eyes gentled. 'That's understandable.'

She gestured around. 'Why did you do this for me, Finn? I'm not complaining. I love it. But…it must've taken a lot of effort on your part.'

'I just want you to have your dream, Princess. You deserve it.'

She stared at him, wishing she could read his mind. 'You've spent a lot of time thinking about my future, and I'm grateful. But don't you think you should've been spending that time focussing on some new directions for yourself?'

His gaze dropped. He straightened a nearby shelf, wiped dust from another. 'I've been giving some thought to that too.'

The admission made her blink. He had?

'Kyanós, it seems, encourages soul-searching.' He shoved his hands into the back pockets of his cargo shorts and eyed her for a long moment. 'I've been toying with a plan. I don't know. It could be a stupid idea.' He pulled his hands free, his fingers opening and closing at his sides. 'Do you want to see?'

Fear and hope warred in her chest. All she could do was nod.

'Come on, then. We'll return the key and then I'll show you.'

The car bounced along an unsealed road that was little more than a gravel track. Audra glanced at the forest of olive and pine trees that lined both sides. She'd thought he'd meant to take them back to the villa. 'I've not been on this road before.'

'I've spent some time exploring the island's hidden places these last few days.'

Along with exploring all the ways she could make her dream a reality. He'd been busy.

'It brings us out on the bluff at the other end of the beach from Rupert's place.'

The view when they emerged into a clearing five minutes later stole her breath. Finn parked and cut the engine. She pushed out of the car and just stared.

He shoved his hands into his pockets, keeping the car between them. 'It's a pretty amazing view.'

Understatement much? 'I'm not sure I've ever seen a more spectacular view. This is…*amazing*.' Water surrounded the headland on three sides. From this height she could only make out a tiny strip of beach to her left and then Rupert's villa gleaming in amongst its pines in the distance.

Directly out in front was the Aegean reflecting the most glorious shade of blue that beguiled like a siren's call, the horizon tinted a fiery gold, the outlines of other islands in the distance adding depth and interest. It'd be a spectacular sight when the sun set.

To her right the land fell in gentle undulations, golden grasses rippling down to a small but perfectly formed beach. A third of the way down was a collection of run-down outbuildings.

'This plot—thirty acres in total—is for sale.' He pointed to the outbuildings. 'The farmer who owns it used those to store olives from his groves…and goats, among other things apparently. They haven't been used for almost fifteen years. The moment I clapped eyes on them I knew exactly how to go about transforming them into an amazing house.'

It was the perfect site for a home—sheltered and sunny, and with that beautiful view. Audra swallowed. 'That sounds lovely.'

'I even came up with a name for the house—the Villa Óneira.'

Óneira was the Greek word for dreams. The House of Dreams. He…he wanted to live here on Kyanós? Her heart leapt. *That* had to mean something.

She tried to keep her voice casual. 'What would you do with the rest of the plot?' Because no matter how hard she tried, she couldn't see Finn as an olive farmer or a goat herder.

He gestured to the crest of the headland. 'Do you remember once asking me what activities I couldn't live without?'

She'd been thinking of the rally-car racing, the rock climbing, the skydiving. 'What's the answer?'

'Hang-gliding.'

She blinked. 'Hang-gliding?'

'It's the best feeling in the world. Sailing above it all on air currents—weightless, free…exhilarating.'

Her heart burned as she stared at him. He looked so *alive*.

'That was a great question to ask, Audra, because it made me think hard about my life.'

It had?

'And when I stumbled upon this plot of land and saw that headland, I knew what I could do here.'

She found it suddenly hard to breathe.

'I've been fighting it and telling myself it's a stupid pipe dream.' He swung to her, his face more animated than she'd ever seen it. 'But after our talk this morning, maybe it's not so daft after all.'

'What do you want to do?'

'I want to open a hang-gliding school. I'm a fully qualified instructor.'

He was?

'And I've had a lot of experience.'

He had?

'The school would only run in the summer.' He shrugged. 'For the rest of the time I'd like to focus on the work I do for Aspiration Designs. But I want to work off the grid.' He flung out an arm. 'And here seems as good a place to do it as any. Kyanós has a great community vibe, and I'd love to become a part of it.'

He stopped then as if embarrassed, shoved his hands in his pockets and scuffed a tussock of grass with the toe of his sneaker.

She stared at him. His dream… It was lovely. Beautiful. 'Your plan sounds glorious, Finn.'

He glanced up. 'But?'

She shook her head. 'No buts. It's just… I remember you saying island life wouldn't suit you.'

'I was wrong. Being on a permanent holiday wouldn't suit me. But being in an office all day wouldn't suit me either. I'd want to leave the day-to-day running of Aspirations to my partners—they're better at that than me. Design is my forte. But the thought of sharing my love of hang-gliding with others and teaching them how to do it safely in this amazing place answers a different need.'

'Wow.' She couldn't contain a grin. 'Looks like we're going to be neighbours.'

He grinned back and it nearly dazzled her. 'Looks like it. Who'd have thought?'

This had to mean something—something big! Even if he wasn't aware of it yet.

He tossed the car keys in the air and caught them. 'Hungry?'

'Starved.'

CHAPTER ELEVEN

'LOOKS LIKE YOUR sailboat is coming in again, Audra.'

They were eating a late lunch of crusty bread, cheese and olives, and Audra's mind was buzzing with Finn's plans for the future. If they were both going to be living on Kyanós, then...

Her heart pounded. It was possible that things could happen. Romantic things. She knew he hadn't considered settling down, falling in love—marrying and babies. Not yet. But who knew how that might change once he settled into a new life here? Given time, who knew what he might choose to do?

She tried to control the racing of her pulse. She had no intention of rushing him. *She* was in no rush. She meant to enjoy their friendship, and to relish the changes she was making in her life. And—she swallowed—they would wait and see what happened.

He'd risen to survey the beach below. She moved to stand beside him, and was greeted with the now familiar pink and blue sail. 'It looks like they're coming ashore.'

Heat burned her cheeks when she recalled her earlier musings about the honeymooners who might be on board. She hoped they weren't planning to have hot sex on her beach. Not that it was *hers* per se, but... She turned her back on the view, careful not to look at Finn. 'Do you want any more of these olives or cheese?'

He swung back and planted himself at the table again. 'Don't take the olives! They're the best I've ever eaten.'

She tried to laugh, rather than sigh, at the way he savoured one.

He helped himself to another slice of a Greek hard

cheese called *kefalotiri*. 'Whose turn is it to choose the activities for the day?'

She helped herself to a tiny bunch of grapes. 'I've no idea.' She'd lost count. Besides, the day was half over.

'Then I vote that a long lazy lunch is the order of the day.'

She laughed for real this time. 'It's already been long and lazy.'

'We could make it longer and lazier.'

Sounded good to her.

'We could open a bottle of wine...grab our books...'

Okay, it sounded perfect. 'Count me in.'

'We could head down to the beach if you want...'

She shook her head. 'Let the visitors enjoy it in privacy. I'm stuffed too full of good food to swim.'

He grinned. 'I'll grab the wine.'

'I'll grab our books.'

But before either of them could move, the sound of voices and crackling undergrowth had them looking towards the track. Audra blinked when Rupert, accompanied by a woman she didn't know, emerged.

A smile swept through her—he should've let them know he was coming! Before she could leap up, however, Finn's low, savage curse had her senses immediately going on high alert. She glanced at him, and her stomach nosedived at the expression on his face.

Finn rose.

Rupert and the woman halted when they saw him. The air grew thick with a tension Audra didn't understand. Nobody spoke.

She forced herself to stand too. 'What's going on, Finn?'

He glanced down at her and she recognised regret and guilt swirling in his eyes, and something else she couldn't decipher. 'I really should've told you about that woman in Nice I'd been trying to avoid. I'm sorry, Princess.'

Audra stared at the woman standing beside Rupert— a tall, leggy brunette whose eyes were hidden behind a large pair of sunglasses—and her mouth went dry. That gorgeous woman was Finn's latest girlfriend? Her stomach shrivelled to the size of a small hard pebble. *Why* had Rupert brought her to the island? She recalled his warnings about Finn and closed her eyes.

'Trust me!'

Her eyes flew open at Finn's words. She wasn't sure if they were a command or a plea.

His eyes burned into hers. 'I promise I will not allow anything she does to hurt you.'

What on earth…?

'You're going to make damn sure of it,' Rupert snarled, striding forwards. He kissed her cheek with a clipped, 'Squirt.' But the glare he shot Finn filled her stomach with foreboding. And it turned Finn grey. 'Audra, this is Trixie McGraw.'

The woman held out her hand. Audra shook it. Trixie? She *hated* that name. It took all her strength to stop her lips from twisting.

'What Rupert has left out of his introduction,' Finn drawled, 'is that Ms McGraw here is an investigative journalist. *Not* an ex-girlfriend, *not* an ex-lover.'

She wasn't…

She was a journalist!

Audra swung to Rupert, aghast. 'You've brought the press to the island?'

Rupert opened his mouth, but Finn cut in. 'She's not here for you, Audra. She wants to interview me.'

'Why?'

If possible, Finn turned even greyer and she wanted to take his hand and offer him whatever silent support she could, but Rupert watched them both with such intensity she didn't want to do anything he could misinterpret. She didn't want to do anything that would damage their friendship.

'My recent accident—the ski-jump disaster—it happened on a resort owned by a friend, Joachim Firrelli. Trixie here was Joachim's girlfriend before they had an ugly bust-up. She's now trying to prove that his facilities are substandard—that he's to blame for my accident. Except I'm not interested in being a pawn in her little game of revenge.'

'It doesn't sound *little* to me. It sounds bitter and a lot twisted.'

Trixie didn't bat so much as an eyelid. Rupert's mouth tightened.

'As I've repeatedly told Ms McGraw, the accident was nobody's fault but my own. I lost concentration. End of story. And I'm not going to let a friend of mine pay the price for my own recklessness.'

His guilt made sudden and sickening sense. He felt guilty that his actions could cause trouble for his friend. And he felt guilty that he'd unwittingly attracted a member of the press to the island when she was doing all that she could to avoid them. *Oh, Finn.*

Finn had crossed his arms and his mouth was set. Her heart pounded, torn between two competing impulses. One was the nausea-inducing reminder that Finn wasn't the kind of man to settle down with just one woman and that to love him would leave her with nothing but a broken heart.

The other…well, it continued to hope. After all, he'd wasted no time in telling her who this Trixie McGraw was, and what she wanted from him. He hadn't wanted her to think this woman was a girlfriend or lover, and that had to mean something, right?

She glared at Rupert. 'Why on earth…? Did you *know* this woman was on a witch hunt?'

Rupert's hands fisted. He turned to Trixie. 'Is what Finn said true?'

One shoulder lifted. 'Pretty much. Except for the "witch hunt" part.'

The woman had the most beautiful speaking voice Audra had ever heard.

'Your sister seems to think I'm motivated by revenge, though I can assure you that is not the case. I believe it's in the public interest to know when the safety standards on a prominent ski resort have deteriorated.'

It was all Audra could do not to snort. 'I can't believe you've brought the media to the island.' Not when he'd done everything he could to protect her from the attention of the press before she'd arrived here.

'I didn't *bring* her. She was already here. I received an email from her yesterday. That's why I'm here now. I left Geneva this morning. I'm not this woman's friend.'

She took a moment to digest that.

So... None of them wanted to talk to this woman?

The press had made her life hell back in Geneva. She wasn't going to let that happen again here on the island. She wasn't going to let them turn Finn and his friend Joachim into their next victims either. She folded her arms. 'Rupert, you have a choice to make.'

He blinked. 'What choice?'

She met his gaze. It was sombre and focussed. 'This is your house. You can invite whomever you want. But you either choose me or you choose her, because one of us has to leave. And if you do choose her, there will be repercussions. There won't be any family dinners in the foreseeable future, and you can kiss a family Christmas goodbye.'

Rupert's nostrils flared.

'Audra,' Finn started, but she waved him quiet.

'I don't trust her, Rupe, but I do trust Finn.' Something in Rupert's eyes darkened and it made her blink. *Wow.* He didn't? When had that happened? She swallowed. 'And you trust me, so—'

'Forgive me, Ms Russel,' the beautiful voice inserted. 'I understand your current aversion to the press given the circus surrounding your relationship with Thomas Farquhar but I'm not here to discuss that. Your privacy is assured.'

Maybe, but Finn's wasn't. She ignored her. 'I want her off this property. Choose, Rupert.'

'It's no competition, Squirt. You'd win in a heartbeat. But I need your help with something first. We won't go inside the house, I promise. But bear with me here. This will take ten minutes. Less. If you still want Trixie to leave after that, I'll escort her off the premises.'

It didn't seem too much to ask. And in the face of Rupert's sheer reasonableness she found her outrage diminishing. 'Ten minutes.' She pulled out her phone and set a timer.

Rupert motioned to Trixie and she pulled a large A4 manila envelope from her backpack and placed it on the table. Rupert gestured for her and Finn to take a look at the contents. His glance, when it clashed with Finn's, was full of barely contained violence that made Finn's gaze narrow and his shoulders stiffen. Wasting no further time, she reached inside the envelope and pulled out...photographs.

She inhaled sharply, and her heart plummeted. Pictures of her and Finn.

The first captured the moment yesterday when she'd leant forward and in the excitement of the moment had kissed Finn. The next showed the moment after when they'd stared at each other—yearning and heat palpable in both their faces. She could feel the heat of need rising through her again now. She flipped to the next one. It was of her and Finn drinking champagne in a harbourside tavern afterwards. They were both smiling and laughing. And she couldn't help it, her lips curved upwards again now. This dreadful woman had captured one of the happiest moments of Audra's life.

'This is what you do?' she asked the other woman. 'You spy on people?'

Trixie, probably wisely, remained silent.

She glanced at Rupert. 'You're upset about this? I know you warned Finn off, but *I* kissed *him*, not the other way around. I took him off guard. He didn't stand a chance.' Behind her Finn snorted. 'Besides, it was a friendly kiss… a thank-you kiss. And it lasted for less than two seconds.'

Without a word, Rupert leaned across and pulled that photo away to reveal the one beneath. She stared at it and everything inside her clenched up tight. It was of her and Finn outside the art studio that day, and they were… She fought the urge to fan her face. They were oblivious to everything. They were wrapped so tightly in each other's arms it was impossible to tell where one began and the other ended. It had, quite simply, been the best kiss of her life.

She lifted her head and shrugged. 'I'm not sure she got my best side.'

Nobody laughed.

'Trixie has informed me that unless she gets an interview with Finn, she'll sell these photos to the tabloids.' Rupert speared Finn with a glare that made all the hairs on her arms lift. 'Finn *will* give her that interview and make sure *you* aren't subjected to any more grubby media attention.'

A fortnight ago she might've agreed with Rupert, but now… She drew in a breath, then lifted her chin. 'I'm not ashamed of these photos.'

'It's okay, Princess. I don't mind. I don't have anything incriminating to tell our fair crusader here, so an interview won't take long at all.'

She wanted to stamp her feet in her sudden frustration. 'No, you're not hearing me. *I'm not ashamed of these photographs.*'

He met her gaze, stilled, and then rocked back on his heels. 'I—'

She held up a hand and shook her head. Pursing his lips, he stared at her for what seemed like forever, and then eventually nodded, and she knew he was allowing her to choose how they'd progress from here. She swung back to Rupert and Trixie. 'In fact, I'm so *not* ashamed of these photographs, if Ms McGraw doesn't mind, I'm going to keep them.'

'I have the digital files saved in several different locations. Your keeping that set won't prevent them from being made public.'

'I didn't doubt that for a moment.' Audra's phone buzzed. 'Time's up, Rupert.'

'You still want her to leave?'

'Absolutely! I'd much rather these pictures appear in the papers than any more gratuitous speculation about me and Thomas.' The situation with Thomas had left her feeling like a fool, not to mention helpless and a victim. The pictures of her and Finn, however... Well, they didn't.

'Besides, we all know how the press can twist innocent words to suit their own purposes. It sounds to me as if Joachim doesn't deserve to become the next target in a media scandal that has no substance.'

'You're mistaken. There's substance,' Trixie said.

'Then go find your evidence elsewhere, because you're not going to hit the jackpot here,' Audra shot back.

Rupert's eyes flashed as he turned to Finn. 'So you refuse to do the honourable thing?'

Rupert's words felt like a knife to his chest. Finn refused to let his head drop. 'I'm going to do whatever Audra wants us to do.' He'd known how disempowered Farquhar had left her feeling. He wasn't going to let Trixie McGraw make her feel the exact same way. *He* wasn't going to make her feel that same way.

He'd sensed that the photographs had both amused and empowered her, though he wasn't sure why. She'd been amazing to watch as she'd dealt with the situation—strong and capable, invulnerable. He wasn't raining on her parade now.

Rupert's hands clenched. 'You promised you wouldn't mess with her!'

Finn braced himself for the impact of Rupert's fist against his jaw, but Audra inserted herself between them. 'Not in front of Lois Lane here, please, Rupe.' She pointed back down the path. 'I believe you mentioned something about escorting her from the premises.'

A muscle in Rupert's jaw worked. 'You sure about this?'

'Positive.'

Trixie shook her head. 'You're making a mistake.'

'And you're scum,' Audra shot back.

Amazingly, Trixie laughed. As Rupert led her to the top of the path, she said, 'I like your sister.'

'I'm afraid she doesn't return the favour. I'll meet you back on the boat later.'

Without another word, Trixie started back down to the beach. She waved to them all when she reached the bottom.

'I think we should take this inside,' Audra said, when Rupert turned to stare at Finn.

Finn's heart slugged like a sick thing in his chest. He'd kissed Audra, and Rupert's sense of betrayal speared into him in a thousand points of pain.

Rupert hadn't been joking when he'd said he'd no longer consider Finn a friend if Finn messed about with Audra. Finn had to brace his hands against his knees at the sense of loss that pounded through him. He'd destroyed the most important friendship of his life. This was his fault, no one else's. The blame was all his. He forced himself to straighten. 'I think we'll do less damage out here, Audra.'

'The two of you are *not* fighting.'

He met the other man's gaze head-on. 'I'm not going to fight, Princess.' But if Rupert wanted to pound him into the middle of next week, he'd let him. Rupert's eyes narrowed and Finn saw that he'd taken his meaning.

'*Rupe,*' Audra warned.

Rupert made for the house. 'You're not worth the bruised knuckles.'

The barb hit every dark place in Finn's soul. He'd never been worth the sacrifice Rupert had made for him. He'd never been worth the sacrifices he'd always wanted his parents to make for him.

Hell! A fortnight on this island with Audra and he'd laid his soul bare. He lifted his arms and let them drop. He didn't know what any of it meant. What he did know was that this Greek island idyll was well and truly over. He wanted to roar and rage at that, but he had no right.

No right at all. So he followed Rupert and Audra into the house, and it was all he could do to walk upright rather than crawl.

They went into the living room. Audra glanced from Rupert to Finn and back again. 'I think we need to talk about that kiss.'

Finn fell into an armchair. Was it too early for a whisky? 'It won't help.' He'd broken his word and that was that. He'd blown it.

Rupert settled on the sofa, stretched his legs out. 'I'm interested in what you have to say, Squirt.' He ignored Finn.

'The kiss—the steamy one—it wasn't calculated, you know?'

She twisted her hands together and more than anything Finn wanted to take them and kiss every finger. He hated the thought of anything he'd done causing her distress. *You should've thought about that before kissing her!*

For a moment he felt the weight of Rupert's stare, but he didn't meet it. The thought of confronting the other man's disgust left him exhausted.

'It was Finn who ended the kiss. I wanted to take it to its natural conclusion, but Finn held back because of how much he feels he owes you.'

He sensed the subtle shift in Rupert's posture. 'You know about that?'

She nodded. 'I'm glad you did what you did when you were sixteen, Rupe. It was a good thing to do.' She folded her arms. 'But it doesn't change the fact that I'm furious with you at the moment.'

Rupert stiffened. 'With me?'

She leaned forward and poked a finger at him. 'You have no right to interfere in my love life. I can kiss whoever I want, and you don't get to have any say in that.'

Finn dragged a hand down his face, trying to stop her words from burrowing in beneath his flesh. Rupert knew Finn wasn't good enough for his sister. Finn knew it too.

'I understand the kiss,' Rupert growled. 'I get the spur-of-the-moment nature of being overwhelmed before coming to your senses. I understand attraction and desire. None of those things worry me, Squirt.' He reached for the photos she'd set on the coffee table, rifled through them and then held one up. '*This* is what worries me.'

Audra stilled, and then glanced away, rubbing a hand across her chest.

Finn glanced at it. What the hell…? It was the second photo—the one after the kiss. Okay, there was some heat in the way they looked at each other, but that picture was innocent. 'What the hell is wrong with that?'

Rupert threw him a withering glare before turning his attention back to his sister. 'Have you fallen in love with him?'

Every cell in Finn's body stiffened. His breathing grew ragged and uneven. What the hell was Rupert talking about?

'Princess?' He barely recognised the croak that was his voice.

Her face fell as if something inside her had crumbled. 'Your timing sucks, big brother.'

'You're family. You matter to me. I don't want to see you hurt. Have you fallen in love with Finn?'

Her chin lifted and her eyes sparked. 'Yes, I have. What's more I don't regret it. I think you're wrong about him.'

Finn shot to his feet. 'You can't have! That's not possible!' He pointed a finger at her. 'We talked about this.'

Audra's chin remained defiant. 'We talked about a lot of things.'

They had and—

He shook himself. 'None of what I said means I'm ready to settle down.'

Her hands went to her hips, but the shadows in her eyes made his throat burn. 'I think that's *exactly* what it means. I just think you're too afraid to admit it to yourself.'

He might be ready to put his freewheeling, adrenaline-loving days behind him, but it didn't mean he'd ever be ready for a white picket fence.

Even as he thought it, though, a deep yearning welled inside him.

He ignored it. Happy families weren't for him. They hadn't worked out when he was a child and he had no faith they'd work out for him as a man. 'Look, Audra, what you're feeling at the moment is just a by-product of your excitement…for all the changes you're going to make in your life, and—'

From the corner of his eyes he saw Rupert lean forward.

'And the romance of the Greek islands.' If he called her Squirt now, she'd tell him that was Strike Three and… and it'd all be over. He opened his mouth, but the word refused to come.

Audra drew herself up to her full height, her eyes snapping blue fire. 'Don't you dare presume to tell me what I'm feeling. I know exactly what I'm feeling. *I love you, Finn.*' She dragged in a shaky breath. 'And I know this feels too soon for you to admit, but you either love me too.

Or you don't. But I'm not letting you off the hook with platitudes like that.'

He flinched.

Her eyes filled and he hated himself. He glanced at Rupert. The other man stared back, his gaze inscrutable. Finn wished he'd shoot off that sofa and beat him to a pulp. Rupert turned back to Audra. 'When did he start calling you Princess?'

He could see her mentally go back over their previous conversations. 'After that kiss—the steamy one.'

Rupert pursed his lips. 'He doesn't do endearments. He never has.'

What the hell...? That didn't mean anything!

Audra moved a step closer then as if Rupert's observation had given her heart. 'You might want to look a little more closely, a little more deeply, at the reasons it's been so important to you to look after me this last fortnight.'

'I haven't looked after you!' He didn't do nurturing.

'What do you call it, then?' She started counting things off on her fingers. 'You've fed me up. You forced me to exercise. And you made sure I got plenty of sun and R & R.'

He rolled his shoulders. 'You were too skinny.' And she'd needed to get moving—stop moping. Exercise was a proven mood enhancer. As for the sun and the R & R... 'We're on a Greek island!' He lifted his hands. 'When in Rome...'

Her eyes narrowed. 'You read a book on the beach, Finn. If that's not going above and beyond...'

Rupert's head snapped up. 'He read a book? *Finn* read a book?' Audra glared at him and he held his hands out. 'Sorry, staying quiet again now.'

So what? He'd read a book. He'd *liked* the book.

'And that's before we get to the really important stuff like you challenging me to follow a path that will make me happy—truly happy.' She swallowed. 'And don't you think it's revealing that you sensed that dream when no one else ever has?'

His mouth went dry. 'That's…that's just because of how much time we've been spending together recently—a by-product of forced proximity.'

She snorted. 'There was nothing forced about it. We spent three days avoiding each other, Finn. We never had to spend as much time together as we did.' She folded her arms and held his gaze. 'And I know you spent those three days thinking about me.'

His head reared back.

'You spent that time bringing my dream to full Technicolor life.'

He scowled. 'Nonsense. I just showed you what it could look like.' He'd wanted to convince her she could do it.

'And while you're analysing your motives for why you did all those things for me, you might also want to consider why it is you've enjoyed being looked after by me so much too.'

She hadn't—

He stared at her. 'That ridiculous nonsense of yours when we went running… And then making sure I didn't overdo it when we went jetskiing.' Enticing him to read not just a book, but a trilogy that had hooked him totally. 'You wanted me to take it easy after my accident.'

She'd been clever and fun, and she'd made him laugh. He hadn't realised what she'd been up to. She'd challenged him in ways that had kept his mind, not just active, but doing loop-the-loops, while his body had been recuperating and recovering its strength. *Clever.*

'You haven't chafed the slightest little bit at the slower pace.'

Because it hadn't felt slow. It'd felt perfect. Everything inside him stilled. *Perfect?* Being here with Audra…? She made him feel… He swallowed. She made him feel as if he were hang-gliding.

She was perfect.

Things inside him clenched up. She said that she loved him.

'You're planning to move to the island too. Don't you think that means something?'

It felt as if a giant fist had punched him in the stomach. He saw now exactly what it did mean. He loved her. He wasn't sure at what point in the last fortnight that'd happened, but it had. *She said she loved him.* His heart pounded. With everything he had he wanted to reach out and take it, but...

He glanced at Rupert. Rupert stared back, his dark eyes inscrutable, and a cold, dank truth swamped Finn in darkness. Acid burned hot in his gut. Rupert *knew* Finn wasn't good enough for his sister. Rupert knew Finn couldn't make Audra happy...he knew Finn would let her down.

A dull roar sounded in his ears; a throbbing pounded at his temples.

'I have a "truth or dare" question for you, Finn.'

He forced himself to meet her gaze.

'Do you or don't you love me?'

The question should've made him flinch, but it didn't. He loved her more than life itself. And if he denied it, he knew exactly how much pain that'd inflict on her. He knew exactly how it'd devastate her.

He glanced at Rupert. He glanced back at her. She filled his vision. He'd helped her find her dream, had helped her find the courage to pursue it. That was no small thing. She would lead a happier life because of it. And he—

He swung to Rupert, his hands forming fists. 'Look, I know you don't think I'm good enough for your little sister, and you're probably right! But you don't know how amazing she is. If I have to fight you over this I will, but—'

Rupert launched himself out of his seat. 'What the hell! I *never* said you weren't good enough for Audra. When have I ever given you the impression that you weren't good enough?'

Finn's mouth opened and closed, but no sound came out.

'When have I ever belittled you, made light of your achievements, or treated you like you weren't my equal?'

Rupert's fists lifted and Finn kept a careful eye on them, ready to dodge if the need arose. He'd rarely seen Rupert so riled.

'That's just garbage!' Rupert slashed a hand through the air. 'Garbage talk from your own mind, because you still feel so damn guilty about me giving up that stupid prize all those years ago.'

Rupert glared at him, daring him to deny it. Finn's mind whirled. He'd carried the guilt of what Rupe had sacrificed for him for seventeen years. He'd used that guilt to keep him on the straight and narrow, but in the process had it skewed his thinking?

'But you ordered me to keep my distance from Audra. *Why?*'

'Because I always sensed you could break her heart. And with you so hell-bent on avoiding commitment I—'

'Because of the promise he made to himself when he was eighteen,' Audra inserted.

'What promise?' Rupert stared from one to the other. He shook himself. 'It doesn't matter. The thing is, I never realised Audra had the potential to break your heart too.'

Finn couldn't say anything. He could feel the weight of Audra's stare, but he wasn't ready to turn and meet it. 'You saved my life, Rupe.' Rupert went to wave it away, but Finn held a hand up to forestall him. 'But Audra is the one who's made me realise I need to live that life properly.'

Rupert dragged a hand down his face. 'I should never have interfered. It wasn't fair. I should've kept my nose well and truly out, and I hope the two of you can forgive me.' He looked at Audra. 'You're right to be furious with me. It's just…'

'You've got used to looking out for me. I know that. But, Rupe, I've got this.'

He nodded. 'I'm going to make myself scarce.'

She nodded. 'That would be appreciated.'

He leaned forward to kiss the top of her head. 'I love you, Squirt.' And then he reached forward and clapped Finn on the shoulder. 'I'll be back tomorrow.' And then he was gone.

Finn turned towards Audra. She stared at him, her eyes huge in her face. 'You haven't answered my question yet,' she whispered.

He nodded. 'All my life I've thought I've not been worthy of family…or commitment. I never once thought I was worth the sacrifice Rupert made for me seventeen years ago.'

'Finn.'

She moved towards him, but he held up a hand. 'I can see now that my parents left me with a hell of a chip on my shoulder, and a mountain-sized inferiority complex. All of my racing around choosing one extreme sport after another was just a way to try to feel good about myself.'

She nodded.

'It even worked for a while. Until I started wanting more.'

Her gaze held his. 'How much more?'

He moved across to cup her face. 'Princess, you've made me realise that I can have it *all*.'

A tear slipped down her cheek. She sent him a watery smile. 'Of course you can.'

A smile built through him. 'I want the whole dream, Audra. Here on Kyanós with you.'

Her chin wobbled. 'The whole dream?'

She gasped when he went down on one knee in front of her. 'At the heart of all this is you, Princess. It's you and your love that makes me complete. I love you.' He willed her to believe every word, willed her to feel how intensely he meant them. 'I didn't know I could ever love anyone the way I love you. The rest of it doesn't matter. If you hate the idea of me opening up a hang-gliding school I'll do something different. If you'd prefer to live in the village rather than on the plot of land I'm going to buy, then that's fine with me too. I'll make any sacrifice necessary to make you happy.'

Her eyes shimmered and he could feel his throat thicken.

He took her hands in his and kissed them. 'I'm sorry it took me so long to work it out. But I realise now that I'm not my father...and I'm not my mother. I'm in charge of my own life, and I mean to make it a good life. And it's a life I want to share with you, if you'll let me.'

Tears spilled down her cheeks.

'Audra Russel, will you do me the very great honour of marrying me and becoming my wife?'

And then he held his breath and waited. She'd said she loved him. But had he just screwed up here? Had he rushed her before she was ready? Had—?

She dropped to her knees in front of him, took his face in her hands and pulled his head down to hers. Heat and hunger swept through him at the first contact, spreading like an inferno until he found himself sprawled on the floor with her, both of them straining to get closer and closer to each other. Eventually she pulled back, pushed upwards and rolled until she straddled him. 'That was a yes, by the way.' She traced her fingers across his broad chest. 'I love your dream, Finn. I love you.'

He stroked her cheek, his heart filled with warmth and wonder. 'I don't know how I got so lucky. I'm going to make sure you never regret this decision. I'm going to spend the rest of my life making you happy.'

She bit her lip. 'Can...can you take me back to your plot of land?'

'What, now?' Right this minute?

She nodded, but looked as if she was afraid he'd say no.

He pulled his baser instincts back into line and hauled them both upright. Without another word, he moved her in the direction of the car. From now on he had every intention of making her every wish come true.

Audra stared at the amazing view and then at the man who stood beside her. She pointed towards the little bay. 'Do you think we could have a jetski?'

'Will that make you happy?'

'Yes.'

'Then we can have two.'

She turned and wrapped her arms around his neck. He pulled her in close; the possessiveness of the gesture and the way his eyes darkened thrilled her to the soles of her feet. 'I want you to teach me to hang-glide.'

His eyes widened. Very slowly he nodded. 'I can do that.'

She stared deep into his eyes and all the love she felt for him welled inside her. She felt euphoric that she no longer had to hide it. 'Do you know why I wanted to come here this afternoon?'

'Why?'

'Because I want *this* to be the place where we start our life together.' She swallowed. 'I love your vision of our future. And this…'

He raised an eyebrow. 'This…?'

She raised an eyebrow too and he laughed. 'Spot on,' he told her. 'The practice has paid off.'

Heat streaked through her cheeks then. His eyebrow lifted a little higher. 'Is that a blush, Princess?' His grin was as warm as a summer breeze. 'I'm intrigued.'

Suddenly embarrassed, she tried to ease away from him, but his hands trailed down her back to her hips, moulding her to him and making her gasp and ache and move against him restlessly instead. 'Tell me what you want, Audra.'

'You,' she whispered, meeting his gaze. He was right. There was no need for secrets or coyness or awkwardness. Not now. She loved him. And the fact that he loved her gave her wings. 'I wanted to come here because this is where I want our first time to be.' She lifted her chin. 'And I want that first time to happen this afternoon.'

His eyes darkened even further. His nostrils flared, and he lifted a hand to toy with a button on her blouse, a question in his eyes.

She shook her head, her breath coming a little too fast. 'No more kisses out in the open, thank you very much. I bet Lois Lane is still lurking around here somewhere. And one set of photographs in circulation is more than enough.'

He laughed.

She glanced down the hill at the outbuildings. 'Why don't you walk me through your plans for our home?'

He grinned a slow grin that sent her pulse skyrocketing, before sliding an arm about her waist and drawing her close as they walked down the slope. 'What an excellent plan. I hope you don't have anywhere you need to be for the next few hours, Princess. My plans are…big.' He waggled his eyebrows. 'And it'd be remiss of me to not show them to you in comprehensive detail.'

'That,' she agreed, barely able to contain her laughter and her joy, 'would be *very* remiss of you.'

When they reached the threshold of what looked as if it were once a barn, he swung her up into his arms. 'Welcome home, Princess.'

She wrapped her arms about his neck. *He* was her home. Gazing into his eyes, she whispered, 'It's a beautiful home, Finn. The best. I love it.'

His head blocked out the setting sun as it descended towards her, and she welcomed his kiss with everything inside her as they both started living the rest of their lives *right now*.

EPILOGUE

'Go! Go, *PAIDI MOU*!'

Audra laughed as Maria shooed her in the direction of Finn, who was waiting beside a nearby barrel of flowers in full bloom. The town square was still full of happy holidaymakers and *very* satisfied vendors.

'You listen to my wife, Audra,' Angelo said with a wide grin. 'Your husband wants to spend some time with his beautiful wife. Go and drink some wine and eat some olives, and bask in the satisfaction of what you've achieved over the last three days.'

'What *we've* achieved,' she corrected. 'And there's still things to—'

'We have it under control,' Maria told her with a firm nod. 'You work too hard. Go play now.'

Audra submitted with a laugh, and affectionate pecks to the cheeks of the older couple who'd become so very dear to both her and Finn during the last fourteen months since they'd moved to the island.

As if afraid she'd change her mind and head back to work, Finn sauntered across to take her hand. As always, it sent a thrill racing through her. *Her husband.* A sigh of pure appreciation rose through her.

'You make her put her feet up, Finn,' Maria ordered.

He saluted the older woman, and, sliding an arm around Audra's shoulders, led her down towards the harbour. Audra slipped her arm around his waist, leaning against him and relishing his strength. They'd been married for eight whole months, but she still had to pinch herself every day.

Standing on tiptoe, she kissed him. 'I think we can safely say the festival went well.'

'It didn't just *go well*, Princess.' He grinned down at her. 'It's been a resounding success. The festival committee has pulled off the event of the year.'

She stuck her nose in the air. 'The event of the year was our wedding, thank you very much.' They'd been married here on the island in the tiny church, and it had been perfect.

His grin widened. 'Okay, it was the second biggest event of the year. And there are plans afoot for next year already.'

He found a vacant table at Thea Laskari's harbourside taverna. 'I promised Thea you'd be across for her *kataifi*.'

They'd no sooner sat than a plate of the sweet nutty pastry was placed in front of them, along with a carafe of sparkling water. 'Yum!' She'd become addicted to these in recent weeks.

'On the house,' Ami, the waitress, said with a smile. 'Thea insists. If we weren't so busy she'd be out here herself telling everyone how fabulous the festival has been for business.' Ami glanced around the crowded seating area with a grin. 'I think we can safely predict that the festival cheer will continue well into the night. Thea sends her love and her gratitude.'

'And give her mine,' Audra said.

She did a happy dance when Ami left to wait on another table. 'Everyone has worked so hard. And it's all paid off.' She gestured at the main street and the town square, all festooned in gaily coloured bunting and stall upon stall of wares and produce. Satisfaction rolled through her. It'd been a lot of work and it'd taken a lot of vision, but they'd created something here they could all be proud of.

'*You've* worked so hard.' Finn lifted her hand to his mouth and kissed it, and just like that the blood heated up in her veins.

'I heard Giorgos tell Spiros that next year the committee needs to market Kyanós as an authentic Greek getaway.

With so many of the young people leaving the island, most families have a spare room they can rent out—so people can come here to get a bona fide taste of genuine Greek island life.'

She laughed. 'Everyone has been so enthusiastic.'

'This is all your doing, you know?'

'Nonsense!'

'You were the one that suggested the idea and had everyone rallying behind it. You've been the driving force.'

'*Everyone* has worked hard.'

He stared at her for a long moment. 'You're amazing, you know that? I don't know how I got to be so lucky. I love you, Audra Sullivan.'

Her throat thickened at the love in his eyes. She blinked hard. 'And I love you, Finn Sullivan.' This was the perfect time to tell him her news—with the sun setting behind them, and the air warm and fragrant with the scent of jasmine.

She opened her mouth but he spoke first. 'I had a word with Rupert earlier.'

She could tell from the careful way he spoke that Rupert had told him the outcome of the court case against Thomas Farquhar. She nodded. 'I had a quiet word with Trixie.'

Finn shook his head. 'I can't believe you're becoming best friends with a reporter.'

'I believe it might be Rupert who's her best friend.' Something was going on with her brother and the beautiful journalist, but neither of them was currently giving anything away. 'She told me the pharmaceutical company Thomas was working for have paid an exorbitant amount of money to settle out of court.'

'Are you disappointed?'

'Not at all. Especially as I have it on rather good authority that Rupert means for me to administer those funds in any way I see fit.'

He started to laugh. 'And you're going to give it all to charity?'

'Of course I am. I want that money to do some good. I suspect Thomas and his cronies will think twice before they try something like that again.'

They ate and drank in silence for a bit. 'Everyone is meeting at Rupert's for a celebratory dinner tonight,' Finn finally said.

'Excellent. It's so nice to have the whole family together.' She'd like to share her news with all of them tonight. But she had to tell Finn first. 'Do you ever regret moving to Kyanós, Finn?'

His brow furrowed. 'Not once. Never. Why?'

She shrugged. 'I just wanted to make sure you weren't pining for a faster pace of life.'

'I don't miss it at all. I have you.' His grin took on a teasing edge. '*And* I get to hang-glide.' He raised an eyebrow. 'We could sneak off to continue your training right now if you wanted.'

She'd love to, but… Her pulse started to skip. 'I'm afraid my training is going to have to go on hold for a bit.'

He leaned towards her. 'Why? You've been doing so well and…and you love it.' Uncertainty flashed across his face. 'You do love it, don't you? You're not just saying that because it's what you think I want to hear?'

'I totally love it.' She reached out to grip his hand, a smile bursting through her. 'But I'm just not confident enough in my abilities to risk it for the next nine months.'

He stared at her. She saw the exact moment the meaning of her words hit him. His jaw dropped. 'We're…we're having a baby?'

She scanned his face for any signs of uncertainty… for any consternation or dismay. Instead what she found mirrored back at her were her own excitement and love. Her joy.

He reached out to touch her face. His hands gentle and full of reverence. 'We're having a baby, Princess?'

She nodded. He drew her out of her seat to pull her into his lap. 'I—'

She could feel her own tears spill onto her cheeks at the moisture shining in his eyes. 'Amazing, isn't it?'

He nodded, his arms tightening protectively around her.

'And exciting,' she whispered, her heart full.

He nodded again. 'I don't deserve—'

She reached up and pressed her fingers to his mouth. 'You deserve every good thing, Finn Sullivan, and don't you forget it.' She pulled his head down for a kiss and it was a long time before he lifted it again. 'And they lived happily ever after,' she whispered.

He smiled, and Audra swore she could stay here in his arms forever. 'Sounds perfect.'

She had to agree that it did.

* * * * *

DOUBLE DUTY
FOR THE
COWBOY

BRENDA HARLEN

For my readers—because I would never have
made it to this milestone book (#50) without you!

Prologue

It had been a fairly quiet week in Haven, and Connor Neal was grateful that trend seemed to be continuing on this Friday night of the last long weekend of summer. Sometimes the presence of law enforcement was enough to deter trouble, so the deputy had parked his patrol car in front of Diggers' Bar & Grill and strolled along Main Street.

There was a crowd gathered outside Mann's Theater, moviegoers waiting for the early show to let out so they could find their seats for the late viewing. Construction workers were sawing and hammering inside The Stagecoach Inn, preparing the old building for its grand reopening early in the New Year. Half a dozen vehicles were parked by The Trading Post; several people lingered over coffee and conversation at The Daily Grind.

He waved at Glenn Davis, as the owner of the hardware store locked up, then resumed his journey. Making his way back toward Diggers', he heard the unmistakable sound of retching. Apparently, patrol tonight was going to include chauffeur service for at least one inebriated resident, which was preferable to letting a drunk navigate the streets. He only hoped that whoever would be getting into the backseat of his car for the ride home had thoroughly emptied their stomach first.

He followed the sound around to the side of the building, where he discovered a nicely shaped derriere in a short navy skirt, beneath the hem of which stretched long, shapely legs. He felt a familiar tug low in his belly that immediately identified the owner of those sexy legs—it was the same reaction he had whenever he was in close proximity to Regan Channing.

She braced a hand on the brick and slowly straightened up, and he could see that she wore a tailored shirt in a lighter shade of blue with the skirt, and her long blond hair was tied back in a loose ponytail. She turned around then, and her eyes—an intriguing mix of green and gray—widened with surprise.

Her face was pale and drawn, her cheekbones sharply defined, her lips full and perfectly shaped. It didn't seem to matter that she'd been throwing up in the bushes, Regan Channing was still—to Connor's mind—the prettiest girl in all of Haven, Nevada.

She pulled a tissue out of her handbag and wiped her mouth.

He gave her a moment to compose herself before he said, "Are you okay?"

"No." She shook her head, those gorgeous eyes filling with tears. "But thanks for asking."

He waited a beat, but apparently she didn't intend to say anything more on the subject. He took the initiative again. "Can I give you a ride home?"

"No need," she said. "I've got my car."

"Maybe so, but I don't think you should be driving."

"I'm feeling a lot better now—really," she told him.

"I'm glad," he said. "But I can't let you get behind the wheel in your condition."

"My condition?" she echoed, visibly shaken by his remark. "How do you know—" she cut herself off, shaking her head again. "You don't know. You think I've been drinking."

"It's the usual reason for someone throwing up outside the town's favorite watering hole," he noted.

Regan nodded, acknowledging the validity of his point. "But I'm not drunk… I'm pregnant."

Chapter One

Six-and-a-half months later

Regan shifted carefully in the bed.

She felt as if every muscle in her body had been stretched and strained, but maybe that was normal after twenty-two hours of labor had finally resulted in the birth of her twin baby girls. Despite her aches, the new mom felt a smile tug at her lips when she looked at the bassinet beside her hospital bed and saw Piper and Poppy snuggled close together, as they'd been in her womb.

The nurse had advocated for "cobedding," suggesting that it might help the newborns sleep better and longer. Regan didn't know if the close proximity was responsible for their slumber now or if they were just exhausted from the whole birthing ordeal, but she was grateful that they were sleeping soundly.

And they weren't the only ones, she realized, when she saw a familiar figure slumped in a chair in the corner. "Connor?"

He was immediately awake, leaning forward to ask, "What do you need?"

She just shook her head. "What time is it?"

He glanced at his watch. "A few minutes after eleven."

Which meant that she'd been out for less than two hours. Still, she felt a little better now than when she'd closed her eyes. Not exactly rested and refreshed, but better.

Her husband hadn't left her side for a moment during her labor, which made her wonder, "Why are you still here?"

Thick, dark brows rose over warm brown eyes. "Where did you think I'd be?"

"Home," she suggested. "Where you could get some real sleep in a real bed."

He shrugged, his broad shoulders straining the seams of the Columbia Law sweatshirt—a Christmas gift from his brother—that he'd tugged over his head when she'd awakened him to say that her water had broken. "I didn't want to leave you."

Her throat tightened with emotion and she silently cursed the hormones that had kept her strapped into an emotional roller coaster for the past eight months. Since that long ago night when she'd first told Connor about her pregnancy, he'd been there for her, every step of the way. He'd held her hand at the first prenatal appointment—where they'd both been shocked to learn that she was going to have twins; he'd coached her through every contraction as she worked to bring their babies into the world; he'd even cut the umbilical cords—an act that somehow bonded them even more closely than the platinum bands they'd exchanged six months earlier.

"I think you couldn't stand to let the girls out of your sight," she teased now.

"That might be true, too." He covered her hand with his, squeezing gently. "Because they're every bit as beautiful as their mama."

She lifted her other hand to brush her hair away from her face. "I'd be afraid to even look in a mirror right now," she confided, all too aware that she hadn't washed her hair or even showered after sweating through the arduous labor.

"You're beautiful," Connor said again, and sounded as if he meant it.

She glanced away, uncertain how to respond. Over the past few months, there had been hints of something growing between them—aside from the girth of her belly—tempting Regan to hope that the marriage they'd entered into for the sake of their babies might someday become more.

Then a movement in the bassinet caught her eye. "It looks like Poppy's waking up."

He followed the direction of her gaze and smiled at the big yawn on the little girl's face. "Are you sure that's not Piper?"

"No," she admitted.

Although the twins weren't genetically identical, it wasn't easy to tell them apart. Poppy's hair was a shade darker than her sister's, and Piper had a half-moon-shaped birthmark beside her belly button, but of course, they were swaddled in blankets with caps on their heads, so neither telltale feature was visible right now.

He chuckled softly.

"Do you think she's hungry?" Regan asked worriedly.

The nurse had encouraged her to feed on demand, which meant putting the babies to her breast whenever they were awake and hungry. But her milk hadn't come in yet, so naturally Regan worried that her babies were always hungry because they weren't getting any sustenance.

"Let me change her diaper and then we'll see," Connor suggested.

She appreciated that he didn't balk at doing the messy jobs. Of course, parenthood was brand new to both of them, and changing diapers was still more of a novelty than a chore. With two infants, she suspected that would change quickly. The doting daddy might be ducking out of diaper changes before the week was out, but for now, she was grateful for the offer because it meant that her weary and aching body didn't have to get out of bed.

"She's so tiny," he said again, as he carefully lifted one of the pink-blanketed bundles out of the bassinet.

They were the first words he'd spoken when newborn Piper had been placed in his hands, his voice thick with a combination of reverence and fear.

"Not according to Dr. Amaro," she reminded him.

In fact, the doctor had remarked that the babies were good sizes for twins born two weeks early. Piper had weighed in at five pounds, eight ounces and measured eighteen and a half inches; Poppy had tipped the scale at five pounds, ten ounces and stretched out to an even eighteen inches. Still, she'd recommended that the new mom spend several days in the hospital with her babies to ensure they were feeding and growing before they went home.

But Regan agreed with Connor that the baby did look tiny, especially cradled as she was now in her daddy's big hands.

"And you were right," he said, as he unsnapped the baby's onesie to access her diaper. "This is Poppy."

Which only meant that the newborn didn't have a birthmark, not that her mother was particularly astute or intuitive.

Throughout her pregnancy, Regan had often felt out of her element and completely overwhelmed by the prospect of motherhood. When she was younger, several of her friends had earned money by babysitting, but Regan had never done so. She liked kids well enough; she just didn't have any experience with them.

She'd quickly taken to her niece—the daughter of her younger brother, Spencer. But Dani had been almost four years old the first time Regan met her, a little girl already walking and talking. A baby was a completely different puzzle—not just smaller but so much more fragile, unable to communicate except through cries that might mean she was hungry or wet or unhappy or any number of other things. And even after months spent preparing for the birth of her babies, Regan didn't feel prepared.

Thankfully, Connor didn't seem to suffer from the same worries and doubts. He warmed the wipe between his palms before folding back the wet diaper to gently clean the baby's skin.

"Did you borrow that plastic baby from our prenatal classes to practice on?" she wondered aloud.

He chuckled as he slid a clean diaper beneath Poppy's bottom. "No."

"Then how do you seem to know what you're doing already?"

"My brother's eight years younger than me," he reminded her. "And I changed enough of Deacon's diapers way back when to remember the basics of how it's done."

There was a photo in Brielle's baby album of Regan holding her infant sister in her lap and a bottle in the baby's mouth, but she didn't have any recollection of the event. She'd certainly never been responsible for taking care of her younger siblings. Instead, the routine child-care tasks had fallen to the family housekeeper, Celeste, because both Margaret and Ben Channing had spent most of their waking hours at Blake Mining.

But Connor's mom hadn't had the help of a live-in cook and housekeeper. If even half the stories that circulated around town were true, Faith Parrish worked three part-time jobs to pay the bills, often leaving her youngest son in the care of his big brother. Deacon's father had been in the picture for half a dozen years or so, but the general consensus in town was that he'd done nothing to help out at home and Faith was better off when he left. But everything Regan thought she knew about Connor's childhood was based on hearsay and innuendo, because even after six months of marriage, her husband remained tight-lipped about his family history.

Which didn't prevent her from asking: "Your father didn't help out much, did he?"

"Stepfather," he corrected automatically. "And no. He was always too busy."

"Doing what?" she asked, having heard that a serious fall had left the man with a back injury and unable to work.

"Watching TV and drinking beer," Connor said bluntly, as he slathered petroleum jelly on Poppy's bottom to protect her delicate skin before fastening the Velcro tabs on the new diaper.

"I guess you didn't miss him much when he left," she remarked.

He lifted the baby, cradling her gently against his chest as he carried her over to the bed. "I certainly didn't miss being knocked around."

She felt her skin go cold. "Your stepfather hit you?"

"Only when he was drinking."

Which he'd just admitted the man spent most of his time doing.

"How did I not know any of this?" she wondered aloud, as she unfastened her top to put the baby to her breast.

He shrugged again and turned away, as if to give her privacy.

If the topic of their conversation hadn't been so serious, Regan might have laughed at the idea of preserving even a shred of modesty with a man who'd watched the same baby now suckling at her breast come into the world between her widely spread legs.

"It's not something I like to talk about," he said, facing the closed blinds of the window.

"So why are you telling me now?" she asked curiously.

It was a good question, Connor acknowledged to himself.

He'd tried to bury that part of his past in the past. He didn't even like to think about those dark days when Dwayne Parrish had lived in the rented, ramshackle bungalow with him and his brother and their mother. To Dwayne, ruling with an iron fist wasn't just an expression but a point of pride most often made at his stepson's expense.

He turned back around, silently acknowledging that if he was going to have this conversation with his wife, they needed to have it face-to-face.

"Because part of me worries that, after living with him for seven years, I might have picked up his short fuse," he finally confided.

Regan immediately shook her head. "You didn't."

"We've only been married for six months. How can you know?"

"Because I know *you*," she said. "You are gentle and generous and giving."

"I hit him back once," he revealed.

She didn't seem bothered or even surprised by the admission. "Only once?"

"I never thought to fight back."

As a kid, he'd believed he was being disciplined for misbehavior. By the time he was old enough to question what was happening, he was so accustomed to being smacked around, it was no more or less than he expected.

"Not until he backhanded Deacon," he confided.

His little brother had been about seven years old when he'd accidentally kicked over a bottle of beer on the floor by Dwayne's recliner, spilling half its contents. Deacon's father had responded with a string of curses and a swift backhand that knocked the child off his feet.

"You wouldn't stand up for yourself, but you stood up for your brother," she mused.

"Someone had to," he pointed out. "He was just a kid."

"And how old were you?"

"Fifteen."

"Still a kid yourself," she remarked. "What did he... How did your stepfather respond?"

"He was furious with me—that I dared to interfere." And he'd expressed his anger with his fists and his feet, while Deacon cowered in the corner, sobbing. "But I guess one of our neighbors heard the ruckus and called the sheriff."

Faith had arrived home at almost the same time as the lawman. Connor didn't know if his mother would have found the strength to ask her husband to leave if Jed Traynor hadn't been there with his badge and gun. But he was and she did, and Dwayne opted to pack up and take off rather than spend the night—or maybe several years—in lockup.

"He left that night and never came back," Connor said.

"Is that when you decided that you wanted to wear a badge someday?" Regan asked.

"It was," he confirmed. "I know it sounds cheesy, but I wanted to help those who couldn't help themselves."

She shook her head. "I don't think it sounds cheesy. And that's how I know you're going to be an amazing dad."

"Because I finally stood up to my stepfather?"

"Because you didn't hesitate to do what was necessary to protect someone you care about," she clarified.

"There isn't anything I wouldn't do for my brother," Connor acknowledged.

And apparently, that included lying to his wife about the reasons he'd married her.

Chapter Two

As Regan climbed the steps toward the front door of the modest two-story on Larrea Drive that had been her home since she married the deputy, she knew that she should be accustomed to surprises by now. Over the past eight months, her life had been a seemingly endless parade of unexpected news and events.

It had all started with the plus sign in the little window on the home pregnancy test. The second—and even bigger surprise—had come in the form of not one but two heartbeats on the screen at her ultrasound appointment. The third—and perhaps the biggest shock of all—Connor Neal's unexpected marriage proposal, followed by her equally unexpected yes.

She hadn't known him very well when they exchanged vows, and if she hadn't been pregnant, she never would have said yes to his proposal. Of course, if she hadn't been pregnant, he never would have proposed. And though marriage had required a lot of adjustments from both of them, Connor had proven himself to be a devoted husband.

He'd been attentive to her wants and needs, considerate of her roller-coaster emotions and indulgent of her various pregnancy cravings. He'd attended childbirth classes, painted the babies' room, assembled their furniture and diligently researched car seat safety. And in the eight days that she'd spent in the hospital since their babies were born, he'd barely left her side.

But when she finally stepped inside the house, after fussing over the dog, whose whole back end was wagging with excitement as if she'd finally returned from eight weeks rather than only eight days away, she found another surprise.

The living room was filled with flowers and balloons and streamers. There was even a banner that read: *Welcome Home Mommy, Piper & Poppy!*

She looked at him, stunned. "When did you—"

"It wasn't my doing," he said, as he set the babies' car seats down inside the doorway.

Baxter immediately came to investigate, which meant sniffing the tiny humans all over, but he dutifully backed off when Connor held up a hand.

"Then who…" The rest of her question was forgotten as Regan looked past the bouquets of pink and white balloons to see a familiar figure standing there. "Ohmygod… *Brie.*"

Her sister smiled through watery eyes. "Surprise!"

Before Regan could say anything else, Brielle's arms were around her, hugging her tight. She held on, overwhelmed by so many emotions she didn't know whether to laugh or cry; she only knew that she was so glad and grateful her sister was home.

"Nobody told me you were coming," she said, when she'd managed to clear her throat enough to speak. She looked at Connor then. "Why didn't you tell me she was coming?" And back at Brielle again. "Why didn't *you* tell me you were coming?"

"When I spoke to you on the phone, I wasn't sure I'd be able to get any time off. But I needed to see you and your babies, so I decided that if I had to quit my job, I would."

Regan gasped, horrified, because she knew how much her sister loved working as a kindergarten teacher at a prestigious private school in Brooklyn. "Tell me you didn't quit your job."

Brie laughed. "No need to worry. I'm due back in the classroom Monday morning."

Which meant that they had less than four days together before her sister had to return to New York City. Four days was a short time, but it was more time than they'd had together in the seven years that had passed since Brielle moved away, and Regan would treasure every minute of it.

"Well, you're here now," she said.

"I'm here now," her sister agreed. "And I asked the rest of the family, who have already seen the babies, to give us some one-on-one time—with your husband and Piper and Poppy, of course." She moved closer to peek at the sleeping babies. "If they ever wake up."

"They'll be awake soon enough," Connor said. "And you'll have lots of time with them."

"Promise?" Brie asked.

He chuckled. "Considering that neither of them has slept for more than three consecutive hours since they were born, I feel confident making that promise. But for now, I'm going to take them upstairs so that you and your sister can relax and catch up."

Regan smiled her thanks as he exited the room with the babies, Baxter following closely on his heels, then she turned back to her sister. "When did you get in? Are you hungry? Thirsty?"

"I got in a few hours ago, I had a sandwich on the plane and, since you asked, I wouldn't mind a cup of tea to go with the cookies I picked up at The Daily Grind on the way from the airport, but I can make it."

"You stopped for cookies?"

"I made Spencer stop for cookies," Brie explained. "Because he picked me up from the airport. And because oatmeal chocolate chip are my favorite, too."

"Now I really want a cookie," Regan admitted. "But I no longer have the excuse of pregnancy cravings to indulge."

"Nursing moms need extra calories, too," her sister pointed out.

"In that case, what kind of tea do you want with your cookies?" she asked, already heading toward the kitchen.

Brie nudged her toward a chair at the table. "Your husband told you to relax."

"Making tea is hardly a strenuous task," Regan noted.

"Then it's one I should be able to handle." Her sister filled the electric kettle with water and plugged it in. "Where do you keep your mugs?"

"The cupboard beside the sink. Tea's on the shelf above the mugs."

Brie opened the cupboard and read the labels. "Spicy chai, pure peppermint, decaffeinated Earl Grey, honey lemon, country peach, blueberry burst, cranberry and orange, vanilla almond, apple and pear, and soothing chamomile." She glanced at her sister. "That's a lot of tea."

"I was a coffee addict," Regan confided. "The contents of that cupboard reflect my desperate effort to find something to take its place."

"Anything come close?" her sister wondered.

She shook her head. "But I'm thinking the vanilla almond would probably go well with the cookies."

"That works for me," Brie said, setting the box and two mugs on the counter.

Connor walked into the kitchen then, a baby monitor in hand. "Baxter missed his morning w-a-l-k so I'm going to take him out now, if you don't mind."

"Of course not," Regan assured him. "But why are you spelling?"

"Because you know how crazy he gets when I say the word."

Regan did know. In fact, Connor didn't even have to say the word; he only had to reach for the leash that hung on a hook by the door and Baxter went nuts—spinning in circles and yipping his excitement. But today the dog was nowhere to be found.

Brielle took a couple of steps back and peered up the staircase her brother-in-law had descended. "Is that first door the babies' room?"

"It's the master bedroom," Connor said, following her gaze. "But we've got the babies' bassinets set up in there for now."

"He's stretched out on the floor in front of the door," Brie said to Regan, so that her sister didn't have to get up to see what everyone else was seeing.

"And you were worried that he might be jealous of the babies," Regan remarked to her husband.

"He was abandoned when I found him," Connor explained. "So I had no idea if he'd ever been around kids or how he'd behaved with them if he had."

"What kind of dog is he?" Brie asked.

"A mutt," Connor said.

"A puggle," Regan clarified. "Though Connor refuses to acknowledge he has a designer dog."

"He has no papers, which makes him a mutt," her husband insisted.

"A puggle is part pug, part…beagle?" Brie guessed. Her sister nodded.

"That might explain why he's already so protective of the babies," Brie said. "Beagles are pack animals, and Piper and Poppy are now part of his pack."

"Say that five times fast," Regan teased. "And since when do you know so much about dogs?"

"I don't," her sister said. "But for a few months last year, I dated a vet who had a beagle. And a dachshund and a Great Dane."

"That's an eclectic assortment," Connor noted.

"He had three cats, too."

"Wait a minute," Regan said. "I'm still stuck on the fact that you dated this guy for a few months and I never heard anything about him until right now."

"Because there was nothing to tell," her sister said.

"Baxter," Connor called, obviously preferring to walk rather than hear about his sister-in-law's dating exploits.

The dog obediently trotted down the stairs, though he hesitated at the bottom. His tail wagged when Connor held up the leash, but he turned his head to glance back at where the babies were sleeping.

"Piper and Poppy will be fine," Connor promised. "Their mommy and Auntie Brie will be here if they need anything while we're out."

Of course, the dog probably didn't understand what his master was saying, but he seemed reassured enough to let Connor hook the leash onto his collar.

"I won't be too long," Connor said, then reached across the counter to flip the switch on the kettle.

Brie looked at her sister. "How long were you going to let me wait for the water to boil before telling me that there was a switch?"

"Only a little while longer."

Connor chuckled as he led Baxter to the door.

"So tell me when and how you met the hunky deputy," Brie said, as she poured the finally boiling water into the mugs.

"I've known Connor since high school. He was a year ahead of me, but we were in the same math class because I accelerated through some of my courses."

"I remember now," Brie said. "He was a scrawny guy with a surly attitude who you tutored in calculus."

She was grateful her sister didn't refer to him as the bastard kid of "Faithless Faith"—a cruel nickname that had followed Connor's mother to her grave. Regan had never met Faith Neal—later Faith Parrish—but she knew of her reputation.

In her later years, Faith had been a hardworking single mom devoted to her two sons, but people still remembered her as a wild teenager who'd snuck out after curfew, hung with a bad crowd and smoked cigarettes and more.

Some people believed she was desperately looking for the love she'd never known at home. Others were less charitable in their assessment and made her the punchline to a joke. If a man suffered any kind of setback, such as the loss of a job or the breakup of a relationship, others would encourage him to "Have Faith." That advice was usually followed by raucous laughter and the rejoinder: "Everyone else in town has had her."

"He sure did fill out nicely," Brie remarked now. "Was it those broad shoulders that caught your eye? Or the sexy dent in his square chin? Because I'm guessing it wasn't his kitchen decor."

Regan reached into the bakery box for a cookie. "This room is an eyesore, isn't it?"

"Or are white melamine cupboards with red plastic handles retro-chic?"

"Connor's saving up to renovate."

"Saving up?" Brie echoed, sounding amused. "I guess that means he didn't marry you for your money."

"He married me because I was pregnant," Regan told her. Because when a bride gave birth six months after the ring was put on her finger, what was the point in pretending otherwise?

"Well, if you had to get knocked up, at least it was by a guy who was willing to do the right thing."

"Hmm," Regan murmured in apparent agreement.

Brie broke off a piece of cookie. "I would have come home for your wedding, if you'd asked."

"We eloped in Reno," Regan told her.

"Doesn't that count as a wedding?"

She shook her head. "Weddings take time to plan, and I didn't want to be waddling down the aisle."

"I'm sure you didn't waddle," her sister said loyally.

"I showed you my belly when we Facetimed, so you know I was huge. I was waddling before the end of my fifth month."

"Well, you were carrying two babies," Brie acknowledged. She chewed on another bite of cookie before she asked, "What did the folks think about your elopement?"

"They were surprisingly supportive. Or maybe just grateful that their second and third grandchildren wouldn't be born out of wedlock."

Their first was Spencer's daughter, but he hadn't even known about Dani's existence until her mother was killed in an accident. He'd given up his career on the rodeo circuit to assume custody, then moved back to Haven with his little girl and fallen in love with Kenzie Atkins, who had been Brielle's BFF in high school.

"They were a lot less happy to learn that I was pregnant," Regan confided to her sister now. " Dad's exact words were, 'And you were supposed to be the smart one.'"

Brie winced. "That's harsh. Although it's true that you're the smart one."

"They don't let dummies into Columbia," Regan pointed out.

"True," her sister said again. "But no one I met at Columbia is as smart as you." She selected another cookie from the box. "What did Mom say?"

"You know Mom," Regan said. "Always practical and looking for the solution to a problem."

Brie's expression darkened. "Because a baby is a problem to be solved and not a miracle to be celebrated."

"I like to think they were happy about the babies but concerned about my status in town as an unwed mother," Regan said, though even she wasn't convinced it was true. "You know how people here like to gossip."

"And then Connor stepped up to ensure the legitimacy of his babies and all was right in the world?" Brie asked, her tone dubious.

"Well, Dad was happy that Connor had done the right thing—at least, from his perspective. Mom made no secret of the fact that she thinks Connor and I aren't well-suited."

"How about *you*?" Brie asked. "Are you happy with the way everything turned out?"

"I never thought I could be this happy," Regan responded sincerely. Not that her marriage was perfect, but she was confident that she'd made the right choice for her babies—and hopeful that it would prove to be the right choice for her and her husband, too.

"I'm glad."

It was the tone rather than the words that tripped Regan's radar. "So why don't you sound glad?" she asked her sister.

Brie shrugged. "I guess I'm just thinking about the fact that everyone around me seems to be having babies," she explained. "Two of my colleagues are off on mat leave right now, a third is due at the end of the summer and another just announced that she's expecting."

"That's a lot of babies. But still, you're a little young for your biological clock to be ticking already," Regan noted.

"I'm not in any rush," Brie said. "But I do hope that someday I'll have everything you've got—a husband who loves me and the babies we've made together. Although I'd be happier if they came one at a time."

Regan managed a smile, despite the tug of longing in her own heart—and the twinge of guilt that she wasn't being completely honest with her sister. "I have no doubt that your time will come."

"Maybe. But until then, I'll be happy to dote on your beautiful babies."

"You'd be able to dote a lot more if you didn't live twenty-five hundred miles away," she felt compelled to point out.

"I know," her sister acknowledged. "I love New York, my job, my coworkers and all the kids. And I have a great apartment that I share with wonderful friends. But there are times when I miss being here. When I miss you and Kenzie and—well, I miss you and Kenzie."

Regan's smile came more easily this time. "So come home," she urged.

Brie shook her head. "There's one elementary school in Haven and it already has a kindergarten teacher."

"That's what's holding you back?" Regan asked skeptically. "A lack of job opportunities?"

"It's a valid consideration," her sister said. Then, when she heard a sound emanate from the monitor, "Is that one of my nieces that I hear now?"

Regan chuckled, even as her breasts instinctively responded to the sound of the infant stirring. "You know, most people don't celebrate the sound of a baby crying," she remarked.

"But doting aunts are always happy to help with snuggles and cuddles."

"And diaper changes?"

"Whatever you need," Brie promised.

Chapter Three

As soon as Connor and Baxter stepped outside, the dog put his nose to the ground and set off, eager to explore all the sights and smells. They had a specific route that they walked in the mornings and a different, longer route they usually followed later in the day. At the end of the street, Baxter instinctively turned east, to follow the longer route.

"We're doing the short route this afternoon," he said. Although he enjoyed their twice-daily walks almost as much as the dog, he didn't want to leave Regan for too long on her first day back from the hospital.

He knew it was silly, especially considering that her sister was there to help with anything she might need help with. But Connor was the one who'd been with her through every minute of twenty-two hours of labor and for most of the eight days since, and he was feeling protective of the new mom and babies—and maybe a little proprietary.

Baxter gave him a look that, on a human, might have been disapproving, but the dog obediently turned in the opposite direction.

Connor started to jog, hoping to compensate for the abbreviated course with more intense exercise. Baxter trotted beside him, tongue hanging out of his mouth, tail wagging.

He lifted a hand in response to Cal Thompson's wave

and nodded to Sherry Witmer, who was carrying an armload of groceries into her house. It had taken some time, but he was finally beginning to feel as if he was part of the community he'd moved into three years earlier.

There were still some residents who pretended they didn't see him when he walked by. People like Joyce Cline, the retired music teacher whose disapproval of "that no-good Neal boy" went back to his days in high school. And Rick Beamer, whose daughter Connor had gone out with exactly twice, more than a dozen years earlier.

But he was pleased to note that the Joyce Clines and Rick Beamers were outnumbered in the neighborhood. The day that Connor moved in, he'd barely started to unpack when Darlene and Ron Grassley were at his door to introduce themselves—and to give him a tray of stuffed peppers. An hour later, Lois Barkowsky had stopped by with a plate of homemade brownies—assuring him that they weren't the "funny kind," even though recreational marijuana use was now legal in Nevada. He told her that he was aware of the law and thanked her for the goodies.

Over the next few weeks, he'd gotten to know most of the residents of Larrea Street. When he'd taken in Baxter and started walking on a regular basis, he'd met several more who lived in the surrounding area.

Estela Lopez was one of those people, and as he and Baxter turned onto Chaparral Street, they saw the older woman coming toward them. At seventy-nine years of age, she kept herself active, walking every morning before breakfast and every evening after supper—and apparently also at other times in between.

"Oh, this is a treat," she said, clearly delighted to see them.

In response to the word *treat*, Baxter immediately

assumed the "sit" position and waited expectantly. She chuckled and reached into the pocket of her coat for one of the many biscuits she always had on hand. Baxter gobbled up the offering.

An avid dog lover who'd had to say goodbye to her seventeen-year-old Jack Russell the previous winter, Estela worried that she wasn't able-bodied enough to take on the responsibility of another animal. Instead, she gave her love and doggy biscuits to the neighborhood canines who wandered by.

"How are you doing, Mrs. Lopez?" Connor asked her.

"I'm eager to see pictures of your girls," the old woman told him.

Connor dutifully pulled out his phone. "They came home today."

"Eight days later." She shook her head. "I remember when they kicked you out of the hospital after only a day or two. Of course, most people couldn't afford to stay any longer than that."

Which they both knew wasn't a concern for his wife, whose family had not only paid the hospital bill but made a significant donation to the maternity ward as a thank you to the staff for their care of Regan and the twins.

He opened the screen and scrolled through numerous images of Piper and Poppy—a few individual snaps of each girl, others of them together and a couple with their mom.

"Oh, my, they are so precious," Estela proclaimed. "And Regan doesn't look like she labored for twenty-something hours."

"Twenty-two," Connor said. "And she did. And she was a trouper."

"You're a lucky man, Deputy Neal."

"I know it," he assured her.

Baxter nudged her leg with his nose, as if to remind her of his presence. She obligingly reached down and scratched behind his ears.

"I heard your sister-in-law made a surprise visit from New York City."

"Well, there's obviously nothing wrong with your hearing," Connor teased.

"I was at The Daily Grind, having coffee with Dolores Lorenzo, when she stopped in to pick up a dozen oatmeal chocolate chip cookies," Estela confided.

"Regan's favorite."

"I almost didn't recognize her—Brielle, I mean," Estela clarified. "Of course, she's only been back a few times since she moved out East—it's gotta be about seven years ago, I'd guess. And even when she came back for Spencer and Kenzie's wedding, she only stayed a couple of days."

"She's only here for a few days now, too," Connor noted.

"Is she staying with you or at that fancy house up on the hill?"

That fancy house up on the hill was the description frequently ascribed to the three-story stone-and-brick mansion owned by his in-laws. The street was called Miners' Pass, and it was the most exclusive—and priciest—address in town.

"With us," he said. "She wants to spend as much time as possible with Regan and the twins."

"Of course she does," Estela agreed. "I can't wait to take a peek at the little darlings myself, but I'll give your wife some time to settle in first. Although my kids are all grown-up now—and most of my grandkids, too—I remember how stressful it was in those early days, trying to respond to all the new demands of motherhood—and I only had to deal with one baby at a time."

"Regan would love to see you," Connor said. "Especially after she's had a chance to catch up on her rest."

"Well, I'm not waiting until the twins' second birthday," she told him, sneaking another biscuit out of her pocket for Baxter.

"Please don't tell me it's going to be that long before Piper and Poppy sleep through the night."

"Probably not," she acknowledged. "But dealing with the needs of infants requires a special kind of endurance—which I don't have anymore, so I'm going to get these weary bones of mine inside where it's warm."

"You do that," he said.

She started up the drive toward her house, then paused to turn back. "But don't let those babies exhaust all your energy—" she cautioned, with a playful wink "—because new moms have needs that require attention, too."

"I'll keep that in mind," Connor promised, then he waited to ensure his old neighbor was safely inside before heading on his way again.

But the truth was, if his wife had any such needs, Connor would likely be the last to know. Although he and Regan presented themselves as happy newlyweds whenever they were in public together, they mostly lived separate lives behind closed doors. Sure, it was an unorthodox arrangement for expectant parents, but it had worked for them.

Until his brother came home for the Christmas holidays.

Because, of course, Deacon expected to sleep in his own room. He had no reason to suspect that his brother's marriage wasn't a love match—although he was undoubtedly smart enough to realize that his sister-in-law's rapidly expanding belly was the reason they'd married in such a hurry—and Connor didn't ever want him to know the truth.

So for the sixteen days—and fifteen nights—that his brother was home, Connor moved his belongings back into the master bedroom to maintain the charade that his and Regan's marriage was a normal one.

The days hadn't really been a problem—especially as Regan continued to work her usual long hours in the finance department at Blake Mining. But the nights, when Connor was forced to share a bed with his wife, were torture.

He made a valiant effort to stay on his side of the mattress, to ignore the fragrant scent of her hair spread out over the pillow next to his own, and the soft, even sound of breath moving in and out of her lungs, causing her breasts to rise and fall in a steady rhythm. But it was impossible to pretend she wasn't there, especially when she tossed and turned so frequently.

She apologized to him for her restlessness, acknowledging that it was becoming more and more difficult to find a comfortable position as her belly grew rounder. Connor knew she was self-conscious about her "babies bump," but he honestly thought she looked amazing. He knew it was a common belief that all pregnant women were beautiful, though he'd never paid much attention to expectant mothers before he married Regan. But he couldn't deny that his pregnant wife was stunning.

Of course, he'd always believed she was beautiful— and maybe a little intimidating in her perfection. In addition to the inches on her waistline, pregnancy had added a natural glow to her cheeks and warmth to her smile, making her look softer and more approachable. And as the weeks turned into months, Connor realized that he was in danger of falling for the woman he'd married.

During one of those endlessly long nights that his brother was home, Connor pretended to be asleep so that Regan would relax and sleep, too. But he froze when he heard her breath catch, then slowly release.

"Are you okay?" he asked, breaking the silence as he rolled over to face her.

"I'm fine," she said. Then she took his hand and pressed it against the curve of her belly.

He was so startled by the impulsive gesture, he nearly pulled his hand away. But then he felt it—a subtle nudge against his palm. Then another nudge.

His other hand automatically came up so that he had both on her belly as his heart filled with joy and wonder. "Is that...your babies?"

"Our babies," she correctly quickly. "Or at least one of them." Then she moved his second hand. "That's the other one."

"Oh, wow." He couldn't help but smile at this proof that there were tiny human beings growing inside her. Sure, he'd seen them on the ultrasound, but feeling tangible evidence of their movements was totally different than watching them on a screen. "Apparently, they've decided that Mommy's bedtime is their playtime," he noted.

"According to the baby books, it's not uncommon for an expectant mother to be more aware of her baby's movements at night," she told him.

"Or for babies to be more active at night, as their mother's movements during the day rock them to sleep," he remarked.

"You've been reading the books, too," she realized.

"I can't wait to meet your—our—" he corrected himself this time "—little ones."

"I'm not sure how little they are anymore," Regan said. "I know that I'm certainly not."

"You're beautiful," he said sincerely.

"You don't have to placate me. I know I look like I swallowed a beach ball."

"You look like you're pregnant—and you're beautiful."

She looked at him then, and their gazes held for a long, lingering moment in the darkness of the night.

Afterward, he couldn't have said who made the first move. He only knew that she was suddenly in his arms, and her lips were locked with his in a kiss that was so much hotter than he'd imagined.

Because yes, there had been occasions since they'd exchanged vows that he'd found himself wondering what it might be like if their marriage was more than a piece of paper. There had been times when their eyes had locked, and he'd thought that maybe she wouldn't mind if he breached the distance between them to kiss her, that maybe she even wished he would.

But he'd always held back, because he knew that if he was wrong and the attraction he felt was not recipro-cated, their living arrangement would become so much more awkward.

Neither of them was holding back now.

She wriggled closer—as close as her belly would allow. He cupped her breasts through the soft cotton nightshirt. His thumbs brushed over the peaks of her already taut nipples, and she gasped. "Oh, yes." She whispered the words of encouragement against his lips. "Touch me, please."

He couldn't respond, because she was kissing him again.

And he was touching her, tracing the luscious con-tours of her body, learning what she liked and what she really liked by the way she arched and sighed.

Their lips clung as their hands eagerly searched and explored. The encounter was as hot and passionate as it was surprising—and it might have led to more if he hadn't suddenly remembered that theirs wasn't a real marriage and recalled that all the baby books he'd been reading talked about how the hormonal changes a woman went through during pregnancy could increase or decrease her sexual appetites. Add to that the forced proximity of their sleeping arrangements and the excitement of the holidays, and he had to wonder how much those factors were influencing her reactions right now.

But did it matter what was motivating her sudden desire?

Or did it only matter that she wanted him—as he wanted her?

Unfortunately, his body and his brain were in disagreement on the answers to those questions.

And his conscience—reminding him of the deal he'd made with her father—won out.

Because even if making love was her *choice, it couldn't be an informed choice so long as there were secrets between them. And there was a very big secret between them.*

For the remainder of the holidays, he'd stayed up late every night to ensure Regan was asleep before he slid between the sheets of their shared bed. Thankfully, Deacon returned to Columbia early in the New Year, allowing his brother and sister-in-law to once again retreat to their respective corners. But there was no "back to normal" for Connor, because there was no way he could forget the passionate kiss they'd shared. Or stop wondering what their marriage might be like now if he hadn't put on the brakes that night.

And with her sister visiting, he would be forced to share his wife's bed again.

Of course, there was no question of anything happening between them only eight days after she'd given birth. But he suspected that knowledge wouldn't prevent his body from responding to her nearness, and he prepared himself for the sleepless nights ahead that had nothing to do with the demands of their newborn babies.

Regan and Brielle were on the sofa in the living room, each with a baby in her arms, when Connor and Baxter returned from their walk.

"You weren't gone very long," Regan remarked.

"We did the short route," Connor said, unhooking the dog's leash to hang it up again.

Baxter immediately ran to his bowl for a drink of water.

"Did you see Mrs. Lopez?" she asked.

He nodded. "And Baxter got two treats."

"Spoiled dog," she said affectionately. "What about you?" she asked her husband. "Did you get any treats?"

He shook his head.

"Well, then it's lucky you did the short route," she told him. "Because there are still a couple of cookies left in the bakery box on the counter."

"Only a couple out of the dozen that Brie picked up at The Daily Grind?" he teased.

"How did you know where I got the cookies? And how many?" Brie wondered.

"Mrs. Lopez was in the café when you stopped by," he admitted.

"You've been away so long you've forgotten the many joys of small-town living," Regan remarked sardonically.

"Because having everyone know your business is a joy?" her sister asked skeptically.

"Having a freezer full of casseroles courtesy of neighbors who want you to be able to focus on your babies is a joy."

"I'll reserve judgment on that—until after dinner," Brie said. "Just don't expect me to eat anything called tuna surprise, because I'm not a fan of tuna and I don't think anyone should ingest something with *surprise* in the name."

"No tuna surprise tonight," Connor promised. "Celeste dropped off a tray of lasagna, a loaf of garlic bread and a bowl of green salad."

Brie gave her sister a sidelong glance. "Now who's spoiled?"

Regan just grinned.

Over dinner Brielle entertained them with stories about her job and her life in New York. Though Regan was in regular contact with her sister via telephone and email, she'd missed this in-person connection. Connor seemed content to listen to their spirited conversation while he rubbed Baxter's belly with his foot beneath the table.

It seemed a strange coincidence to Regan that her sister and his brother were both currently living in the Big Apple. If their circumstances had been different—and they didn't have two newborn babies—she might have suggested that they take a trip to New York to visit their respective siblings. But their circumstances weren't different, and she didn't envision any joint travel plans anywhere in their immediate future.

"There's an Italian restaurant near our place—Nonna's Kitchen—that my roommate Grace would swear has the best lasagna she's ever tasted." Brie dug her fork into her pasta again. "I told her that she only thought it was the best because she's never had Celeste's lasagna, but even I'd forgotten how good this really is."

"Her chicken cacciatore is even better," Connor noted.

"Apples and oranges," Brie said. "Though I would say they're both equally delicious."

By the time they'd finished eating, Piper was awake and wanting her dinner, so Regan and Brie went to deal with the babies while Connor washed the dishes and tidied the kitchen. He walked into the living room as Regan lifted a hand to her mouth, attempting to stifle a yawn.

"I'm sorry," she said to her sister.

"I should be the one to apologize," Brielle said. "You just got home from the hospital after giving birth barely more than a week ago—it's a wonder you're still awake."

"And since the babies are sleeping…" Connor began.

"I should be, too," his wife said, finishing the recitation of the advice all the doctors and nurses had given to her. "And I will, as soon as I make up the bed in the spare room—"

"Already done," he said.

"You didn't have to go to any trouble," Brielle protested. "I would have been happy camping on the sofa with a blanket and pillow."

"It wasn't any trouble at all," Connor assured her.

She hugged him then. "You are, without a doubt, my absolute favorite brother-in-law."

"I'm your only brother-in-law," he remarked dryly.

Brielle grinned. "And that's why you're my favorite."

Regan couldn't help but smile, too, as she listened to the banter between them. She was pleased that Brie had so readily accepted Connor as part of the family, especially because she knew he hadn't been welcomed with open arms by her mom and dad.

But she wasn't worried about his relationship with her parents right now—a bigger and more immediate concern was the fact that she had to share a bed with her husband tonight.

Chapter Four

"Does your sister have everything she needs?" Connor asked, when Regan entered the master bedroom a few minutes later.

"I think so." She paused at the bassinet to check on the babies. "I still can't believe that she's here."

"You're surprised that your sister wanted to see you and meet her nieces?"

"No," she admitted. "But I am surprised that the wanting was stronger than her determination to stay away."

"I'm obviously missing something," he realized.

She nodded. "Brie moved to New York seven years ago and she's only been home twice since. The first was for my grandmother's funeral, the second—four years later—for Spencer and Kenzie's wedding."

"What's the story?" he wondered.

"I'm not sure I know all of it," his wife said. "But even if I did, it's not my story to tell."

"Well, whatever her reasons for staying away for so long, she's here now."

"And I'm grateful," Regan told him. "But I wouldn't have minded if she'd chosen to stay at our parents' place, where she would have had her pick of half a dozen empty guest rooms."

"Here she can maximize her time with you and Piper and Poppy."

"I know," she agreed, lowering her voice. "I just feel

bad, because I could hardly tell her that she's kicking you out of your room."

Actually, it was his brother's room, but Connor had been sleeping in it since his wife had moved in at the beginning of October—save for the two endlessly long weeks that Deacon was home over the Christmas holidays.

"It's only for a few nights," he said philosophically.

"You're right," she agreed, pulling open a dresser drawer to retrieve a nightgown.

But Regan knew that her brother-in-law would be home again at the beginning of May—and not just for a couple of weeks but the whole summer this time. And she had to wonder how long she and Connor would be able to maintain a physical distance while they were sharing a bed—or even if they'd want to.

Because even now, when her body was still aching and exhausted from the experience of childbirth, it was also hyper-aware of his nearness, stirring with desire.

In defense against this unexpected yearning, she went into the bathroom to change and brush her teeth, and when she came back, she saw that Connor had pulled on an old T-shirt and a pair of sleep pants. The clothes covered most of her husband's body but couldn't disguise his size or strength.

She estimated his height at six feet four inches, because even when she added heels to her five-foot-eight-inch frame, he stood several inches above her. His shoulders were broad, his pecs sculpted, his arms strong. He had a long-legged stride and moved with purpose—a man who knew where he was going and inevitably drew glances of female admiration along the way.

He had an attractive face on top of those broad shoulders. Lean and angular with a square jaw, straight brows and a slightly crooked nose. His lips, though exquisitely shaped, were usually compressed in a thin line. Many people attributed his serious demeanor to his serious job in law enforcement, but Regan had known him since high school, so she knew that his somber outlook predated his employment. The little he'd told her about his youth confirmed that he hadn't had much to smile about while he was growing up. Yet despite his often stern and imposing expression, his eyes—the color of dark, melted chocolate—were invariably kind.

Her husband was a good man. She had no doubts about that. It was their future together that was a whole series of questions without answers—none of which she was going to get tonight so she might as well climb into bed and get some sleep.

But first, she checked on the babies one more time. They were sleeping peacefully for the moment, each with one arm stretched out toward the other, so that their fingertips were touching.

"I want to believe that they'll be the best of friends someday, but I think they already are," she said quietly.

"Like you and your sister?"

"We weren't always so close," she admitted. "Of course, there are four years between us, and only fourteen minutes between Piper and Poppy."

He moved so that he was standing directly behind Regan to peer down at the sleeping babies. "Not to mention that they were roommates in your womb for thirty-six weeks."

"We probably didn't need two bassinets," she acknowledged. "By the time they're too big to share this one, they'll be ready for a crib."

"So we'll put the other one downstairs," he suggested.

"That's a good idea."

"I have one every once in a while."

She tipped her head back against his shoulder and looked up at him. "Was getting married a good idea?"

"One of my best," he assured her.

"We'll see if you still think so when they wake you up several times in the night."

"In order to be woken up, we first have to go to sleep."

She nodded and, with a last glance at her babies, tiptoed to "her" side of the bed. The queen-size mattress had been plenty big enough when she was the only one sleeping in it, but it seemed to have shrunk to less than half its usual size now that Connor would be sharing it.

For the past six and a half months, he'd been a strong and steady presence by her side—if not in her bed. And she was sincerely grateful for everything he'd done and continued to do.

She'd always prided herself on being a strong, independent woman. She'd never balked at a challenge or let any obstacles deter her; she didn't need anyone to hold her hand or bolster her courage. Not until that plus sign appeared in the little window of her home pregnancy test.

Somehow, that tiny symbol changed everything. She suddenly felt scared and vulnerable and alone, unprepared and ill-equipped for the future.

Then Connor had shown up at her ultrasound appointment and changed everything again—but in a good way this time.

She remembered taking a quick look around the waiting room of the maternal health clinic and noting that many of the seats were already taken by couples sitting with their heads close. No doubt they were whispering their thoughts about the journey into parenthood they were taking together. And that was great for them, she'd acknowledged. But she didn't need a husband or boy-friend or partner. She could do this on her own.

So she'd stepped up to the counter and given her name to the receptionist, then taken a seat as directed—a single woman in the midst of countless happy couples.

But that was okay because she was excited enough for two people, because this was her first ultrasound. A first look at her baby. There were still some days that she wondered if her pregnancy was real or just a dream. As shocked and scared as she'd felt when she'd seen the result of the home pregnancy test, her brain didn't seem able to connect that little plus sign with the concept of a baby.

Even after Dr. Amaro had confirmed the results of that test, Regan still had trouble accepting that a tiny life was taking shape in her womb. The queasiness and sore breasts that came a few days later were more tangible evidence, but still not irrefutable proof.

Or maybe she'd just been lingering in denial because the prospects of childbirth and parenthood—especially as a single mom—were so damn scary.

She hadn't had the first clue about being a mother. Numbers and balance sheets and cost flow statements were second nature, but babies were a completely foreign entity. Her sister had always wanted to get married and have a houseful of kids. Regan's lifelong dream had been to work at Blake Mining. She didn't *not* want kids, she just hadn't given the idea much thought. And, whenever she *had* thought about it, she'd always assumed it would happen after she'd fallen in love and married the father of her future children.

But there was a saying about life happening while you were making other plans, and the tiny life growing inside of her was proof of that.

So while being a single mom was never part of her

plan, she'd vowed to give it her best effort. And she would do it alone, because she had no other choice.

As a defense against the threat of tears, she'd grabbed a magazine from the table beside her. She opened the cover and began to flip through the pages, not paying any attention to the photos or articles, unable to focus on any of the words on the page where she paused.

"'Preparing Your Child for Kindergarten'," a familiar voice read from over her shoulder. "I know there's an old adage about planning ahead, but don't you think you should focus on getting ready for the birth before you worry about your baby's first day of school?"

She closed the cover of the magazine as Connor lowered himself into the vacant seat beside her. "What are you doing here?"

"I didn't want you to be alone for this."

"But how did you even know I'd be here?"

"You mentioned the appointment when our paths crossed at The Trading Post."

"And you remembered?" she asked incredulously.

"Well, you looked like you were ready to have a meltdown in the frozen food aisle, and I realized you were overwhelmed by the idea of doing this alone, so I noted the date in my calendar app."

That he'd done so and made the trip to Battle Mountain to be with her was a surprise—and her eyes filled with tears of relief and gratitude.

Because right now, at least in this moment, she wasn't alone.

"I should probably tell you to go, that I don't need someone to hold my hand," she said. "But...I'm so glad to see you."

He reached for her hand and linked their fingers together. "Everything's going to be okay."

It was a ridiculous thing to say—the words a promise she knew he shouldn't make and couldn't keep. And yet, she already felt so much better just because he was there. Connor Neal—former bad boy turned sheriff's deputy— so strong and steady, an unexpected rock to cling to in the storm of emotion that threatened to consume her.

"Regan Channing."

She rose to her feet, her heart knocking against her ribs.

Connor stood with her and gave her hand a reassuring squeeze.

"Are you going to come in?" she asked.

"Do you want *me to come in?"*

She nodded, surprised to realize that she did.

The technician had introduced herself as Lissa and led them to an exam room.

She'd explained that they were there to take a first look at the baby, reassuring Regan that Dr. Amaro didn't have any specific concerns, so the primary purpose of the scan was to take some measurements to get an accurate estimate of her due date.

When Regan had stretched out on the table and lifted her shirt, Lissa squirted gel onto her belly and spread it around with a wand-like device she'd called a transducer, explaining that the sound waves would be converted into black and white images on the screen and provide an image of the baby.

Regan had reached for Connor's hand again, and squeezed it a little tighter, as both anticipation and apprehension swelled inside her.

"Now I really have to pee," she said, as Lissa pressed the transducer against her belly and began to move it around.

"Sorry," the technician said. "The full bladder can be

uncomfortable for the expectant mom, but it does allow us to get a better picture of the uterus and baby."

She continued to move the device—and press on Regan's bladder—as she made notes of measurements.

"The baby's heartbeat is strong and steady," Lissa said.

Regan tried to focus on the screen, but it was hard to see through the tears that blurred her eyes. Again. *Since she'd taken that pregnancy test, she'd been quick to tears no matter what she was feeling. Happy. Scared. Angry. Sad.*

"Actually...both heartbeats are strong and steady," Lissa remarked.

Regan blinked. "I'm sorry... What?"

The technician smiled. "Yeah, that's the usual reaction I get when I tell an expectant mother she's going to have twins."

"Twins?" Regan echoed, uncomprehending.

Lissa moved the wand over her patient's abdomen with one hand and pointed at the monitor with the other. "There's one...and there's the other one."

"Ohmygod." Regan looked at Connor—as if he might somehow be able to make sense at what she was seeing, because her brain refused to do so. "There are two babies in there."

"I can see that," he acknowledged, sounding as stunned as she felt.

"I can't have two babies," she protested. "I don't know what to do with one."

"You'll figure it out," he assured her.

As Regan's eyes drifted shut now, she finally believed that she would figure it out—so long as Connor was by her side.

* * *

Lying next to his wife in bed, Connor found himself also recalling the fateful day that he'd made the trip to Battle Mountain for Regan's ultrasound appointment.

She'd asked him why he'd shown up at the clinic, and the answer might have been as simple as that he knew she was feeling a little scared and overwhelmed and he wanted to be there for her—as she'd been there for him when he'd been struggling in twelfth grade calculus. Or maybe he hadn't completely gotten over the crush he'd had on her when she tutored him in high school. Regardless of his reasons, seeing how freaked out she was at the sight of those two tiny little blobs on the screen—twins!—he'd been doubly (Ha! Ha!) glad that he'd cleared his schedule for the morning.

"You still look a little shell-shocked," he'd noted, as they walked out of the clinic.

"Only a little?"

He'd smiled at that. "Let's take a walk. There's an ice cream shop just down the street."

"I don't think a scoop of chocolate chip cookie dough is the answer."

"Considering the circumstances, I was going to suggest two scoops," he told her.

Her eyes had filled with tears then. "That's not funny."

"You're right. I'm sorry." He'd pulled a tissue out of his pocket and offered it to her. "But I have to admit—it was pretty cool to see those two little hearts beating on the screen."

"Sure," she'd agreed. "If cool is another word for terrifying."

"What are you afraid of?"

"Everything."

"C'mon." He slid his arm across her shoulders and steered her down the street.

She hadn't protested. She hadn't even asked where they were going—a sure sign to Connor that she was preoccupied with her own thoughts. At least until he'd stopped in front of Scoops Ice Cream Shoppe.

"You don't have to do this," she said, when he'd opened the door for her to enter. "I'm not one of those women who tries to drown my worries with copious amounts of chocolate."

"Well, I *am* one of those guys who believes that ice cream is essential for any celebration."

"What are we celebrating?"

"I would have thought that was obvious," he'd said. "But since you're feeling a little overwhelmed by the prospect of impending motherhood right now, we can focus on something else."

"Such as?"

He'd gestured to the sky outside. "The sun is shining."

"Do you celebrate every sunny day with ice cream?"

"I might, if we had a Scoops in Haven," he told her.

Regan had managed a smile as she moved closer to view the offerings in the glass freezer case.

She'd opted for a single scoop of chocolate chip cookie dough in a cup. He'd topped a scoop of rocky road with another of chocolate in a waffle cone. And they'd sat across from each other on red vinyl padded benches with a Formica table between them.

He'd enjoyed his ice cream in silence for several minutes, giving her some time to sort out whatever thoughts were creating the furrow between her brows.

"You're not eating your ice cream," he'd commented, as she continued to mush the frozen concoction with her spoon.

She lifted the utensil to her lips. "I was just starting to get my head around the fact that I was going to have a baby, only to find out that I'm going to have *two*," she'd finally shared.

"All the more reason to tell your family sooner rather than later," he'd pointed out. Because he knew that he was the only person she'd confided in about her pregnancy so far.

She'd nodded and swallowed another mouthful of ice cream. "I know you're right. I just can't imagine how they're going to react." Then she shook her head. "No, that's not true. I'm pretty sure my dad's going to flip."

Her comment had prompted him to ask, "Does your father have a temper?"

"Not that most people would know," she'd said. "Because it takes a lot to make him lose his cool, but I suspect my big news will do the trick."

He'd frowned at that. Even in a relatively quiet town like Haven, he'd responded to his share of domestic violence calls—and he knew, better than anyone, that some of the worst abusers presented a completely benevolent persona to the outside world.

"Would he… Has he ever…hit you?" he'd asked cautiously.

Regan's eyes had gone round with shock. "Ohmygod—no! He would never… I didn't mean… No," she'd said again.

Her automatic and emphatic denial rang true, which had been an enormous relief to Connor.

"When I said that he had a temper, I only meant that he'll probably yell a little," she'd confided. "Or a lot. But far worse than the yelling is that he'll be disappointed in me."

"And your mom?" he'd wondered aloud.

"She tends to be a little more practical—the 'no sense crying over spilled milk' type," Regan had told him. "She'll want to start interviewing nannies right away, so that I can get back to work as soon as possible, because nothing is as important to her as Blake Mining. And then we'll probably argue about that, because I may not know a lot about parenting, but I know I don't want a stranger raising my babies. I mean, I don't plan to be a stay-at-home mom forever, but I don't want my children to have to visit my office if they want to see me."

Which he'd guessed, from her tone, had been her experience. "Well, that's your decision to make, isn't it?"

"You'd think so," she'd said, a little dubiously.

He'd popped the last bite of cone into his mouth. "Are you ready to head back?"

She'd nodded and picked up her mostly empty ice cream container to drop it into the trash on their way out.

He'd walked her to her car, parked only a few spots away from his truck.

"I know you're not looking forward to the fallout, but you should tell your family," he'd encouraged her. "With two babies on the way, you're going to need not just their support but their help."

"You're right," she'd acknowledged. "I just wish…"

"What?"

She'd sighed and shaken her head. "Nothing."

"You shouldn't waste a wish on nothing," he'd chided gently.

And her lips had curved, just a little.

"What do you wish?" he'd asked again.

"You've already done so much for me," she'd said.

"Tell me what you need. I'll help you if I can."

Because he was apparently a sucker for a damsel in distress—or maybe it was just that he hated to see *this* damsel in distress, as he seemed unable to refuse her anything.

"Will you go with me...to tell my parents?"

Of course, he'd said "yes."

And ten days later, he'd said, "I do."

Chapter Five

He didn't feel any different. But as Connor drove back to Haven, the platinum band on the third finger of his left hand was visible evidence of his newly married status—and proof that everything was about to change.

"You've hardly spoken since we left the chapel," he remarked, with a glance at his wife, sitting silently beside him, her hands folded in her lap. "Having second thoughts already?"

"Are you having them, too?" Regan asked, sounding worried.

"Actually, I'm not. I mean, there were a few moments during the drive when I wondered if we were making a mistake—or at least being too hasty," he acknowledged.

But there were time constraints to their situation that had required quick action—not just because a twin pregnancy would likely show sooner than a single pregnancy but because of the deal he'd made with his now father-in-law.

He'd experienced a moment of hesitation after the legalities were done and the officiant invited Connor to kiss his bride. But it was just a simple kiss. Except that her soft lips had trembled as he brushed them with his own, and her breath had caught in her throat as her eyes lifted to meet his. In that moment, something had passed between them.

Or maybe Connor had just imagined it.

In any event, that moment was gone.

"But I have no doubt that we've done the right thing for your babies," he said to her then.

"What about us?" she'd wondered aloud.

"We'll make it work," he promised.

She twisted her rings around on her finger. "I never even asked if you had a girlfriend."

"Not anymore."

She gasped. "Ohmygod—"

"I'm kidding," he said.

"Oh." She blew out a breath. "For the record, not funny."

"Sorry."

"So…" she began, after another minute had passed in silence. "Why don't you have a girlfriend?"

"I'm not sure my wife would approve," he remarked dryly.

"Also not funny," she told him.

"I've had girlfriends," he'd assured her. "In fact, I dated Courtney Morgan on and off for several months earlier this year."

"What caused the off?"

He shrugged. "We had some good times together, but I think we both knew it was never going to be anything more than that."

"How do you think she'll react to the news of your marriage?" Regan wondered.

"Probably with disbelief, because I told her right from the beginning that I wasn't in any hurry to settle down." And that had been the honest truth at the time, but a lot of things had changed since his first date with Courtney Morgan.

"I think people will be less surprised by the news of our wedding when they realize I'm pregnant," she acknowledged, splaying a hand over her belly. "And with two babies in there, that probably won't be too long."

"There's going to be a lot of gossip," he acknowledged, reaching across the console to take her hand. "But we'll face it together."

But first they had to face her parents.

"I feel a little guilty," he'd admitted, when he pulled his truck into the stamped concrete drive of 1202 Miners' Pass.

"Why?"

"Because you're leaving all of this to come and live with me in a house that's only a fraction of its size."

"Your house is more than adequate," she said. "Although I wouldn't object if you wanted to update the kitchen. In fact, I encourage you to do so."

He opened the passenger-side door and offered his hand to her. "When you start cooking, I'll start thinking about renovating," he said teasingly.

"Just because I don't cook doesn't mean that I can't," she warned. "Celeste taught all of us to make a few basic dishes."

"Suddenly married life is looking a whole lot brighter."

She smiled, but the way she clutched his hand as they made their way to the door told him that she was uneasy anticipating her parents' reactions to the news of their impromptu nuptials.

He wished he could have reassured her that her father, at least, wouldn't object to their marriage. But before he'd exchanged vows with his bride, he'd made a promise to Ben Channing, and he knew that reneging on that promise could jeopardize everything.

As Connor listened to the quiet even breaths of his wife beside him, he knew that was as true now as it had been the day they'd married.

But now, he had so much more to lose.

* * *

Regan hadn't been asleep for long when soft plaintive cries penetrated the hazy fog of her slumber.

Immediately, she felt a tightness in her breasts that she'd started to recognize as the letdown reflex, readying her milk for the babies—because when one was awake and hungry, the other was soon to follow. She sat up, swinging her legs over the side of the mattress and reaching for the hungry infant.

Connor had plugged a night-light into the wall so that she wouldn't have to stumble around in the dark, and as she reached into the bassinet, her heart plummeted to discover there was only one swaddled baby inside.

She gasped and turned her head, searching for her husband in the dimly lit room.

"I'm right here," Connor said. His tone was quiet and reassuring, though the words emanated not from the bed but the rocking chair in the corner. "And Poppy's here, too."

She exhaled a shuddery sigh of relief as she reached into the hidden opening of her nursing gown to unhook the cup of her bra and set Piper to her breast. The baby, hungry and intent, immediately latched on to her nipple and began to suckle. Regan tried not to wince as she settled back on the mattress with the infant tucked in the crook of her arm.

"What are you doing up?" she asked. "Did Poppy wake you?"

"I wasn't really sleeping," he said. "So when she started fussing, I decided to change her diaper and sit with her for a little while in the hope that you'd be able to get a few more minutes' sleep."

"Did I?" she wondered.

"A very few," he told her.

But she was grateful for his effort. "What did I do to deserve a guy like you?" she teased in a whisper.

He rose from the chair and returned to the bed, sitting on top of the covers beside his wife, with Poppy still in his arms. "I'm the lucky one," he said. "I've got a beautiful wife and two gorgeous daughters."

She smiled to lighten the mood, because his tone—and words—had been more serious than she'd expected. "You mean a hormonal wife and two demanding babies?"

He tipped her chin up, forcing her to meet his gaze. "I say what I mean."

"No regrets?" she asked, then held her breath, waiting for his reply.

"Not for me," he immediately replied. "You?"

She shook her head. "Fears, worries and concerns—yes. Regrets—no."

Poppy started to squirm and fuss then, and he shifted her in his arms, offering his finger for her to suck on. That satisfied the infant for all of about ten seconds—until she realized no sustenance was coming out of the digit.

"I guess she's hungry, too," Regan remarked.

"She can wait a few minutes until her sister's finished. Or I could go downstairs and make up a bottle," Connor offered.

She shook her head again as she eased Piper's mouth from her breast and lifted the baby to her shoulder. "Switching back and forth between breast and bottle can cause nipple confusion."

"*Can* doesn't mean *will*," he pointed out.

Piper let out a surprisingly loud burp, then sighed and laid her head down on her mother's shoulder, her eyes already starting to drift shut.

Regan touched her lips to the infant's forehead, then exchanged babies with Connor.

He carried Piper to the dresser and laid her down on the change pad. There was an actual change table in the twins' bedroom, but while they were sleeping in here, it made sense to change them in here, too.

"Everybody talks about how natural breastfeeding is," she said, as she unfastened the other cup of her nursing bra for Poppy. "But that doesn't mean it's easy."

"It's also a personal choice," Connor said. "So you don't have to continue with it if you don't want to."

"I want to," she insisted. "I just worry that I'm not going to be any good at it."

"The lactation consultant at the hospital said you were doing just fine," he reminded her.

"But they seem to be eating all the time," she lamented. "They're eating all the time, and it's only day eight and..."

"And what?" he prompted.

A single tear slid down her cheek. "What if I can't do this?"

Regan's voice was barely a whisper in the quiet room, as if she was afraid to say the words aloud because that might make them true.

"Do what?" Connor asked gently.

Over the past few months, he'd learned that her fears and insecurities, though not unique, were real, and he tried to offer sincere support rather than empty platitudes.

"Feed my babies," she admitted. "What if my body doesn't make enough milk?"

She was his wife. He shouldn't feel uncomfortable having this kind of conversation with her. But theirs wasn't a traditional relationship in which they'd fallen in love after dating for a while. In fact, they'd never been on a date and had only married because she was pregnant and didn't want her babies to grow up without a father, so he didn't think any of the usual rules applied.

He plucked a tissue from the box beside the bed and gently blotted the moisture on her cheek. "The more they take, the more you'll make," he said, echoing the doctor's words. "But if you don't think they're getting enough, it's okay to supplement with formula."

"But Dr. Amaro said that breast is best."

He wished they were talking about something—*anything*—else.

Yes, breastfeeding was natural and normal, and maybe most guys could watch their wives nurse their babies and view it as a simple biological function, but Connor wasn't one of those guys.

He averted his gaze from the creamy swell of her breast and cleared his throat. "And nursing Piper at midnight while Poppy has a bottle is okay, because you'll nurse Poppy at three a.m. and give Piper a bottle then," he suggested reasonably.

"I'd feel like a failure," she admitted.

"You're not a failure," he assured her.

Another tear slid down her cheek. "My nipples hurt."

He really did *not* want to be thinking about her nipples. Or any other part of her anatomy that identified her as female, because his body, too long deprived of sex, couldn't help but respond to her nearness.

Maybe it was inappropriate, but it was undeniable.

He cleared his throat and tried to clear his mind. "Did you try the cream they gave you at the hospital?"

She shook her head.

"Why not?"

"Because—" she sniffled "—I forgot."

He laid the now-sleeping Piper down in her bassinet

and rummaged through the various pockets of the diaper bag until he found the sample size tube of pure lanolin that the doctor had assured them was safe for both mom and babies.

He set it on the bedside table, then picked up her empty water glass. "Do you want a refill?"

"If you don't mind," she said.

He took the glass, grateful for the excuse to escape the room so that he didn't have to attempt to avert his gaze while she rubbed cream on her breasts.

He stepped through the door—and muttered a curse under his breath as he nearly tripped over Baxter.

"What are you doing up here?" he demanded in a whisper.

The dog lifted his head and thumped his tail a few times.

Connor sighed and squatted down to rub the animal's head. "Yes, you're a good boy," he said. "But you're supposed to sleep on *your* bed in the living room, not outside *my* bedroom."

Baxter rose slowly to his feet and stretched.

"Living room," he said again, and pointed toward the stairs.

The dog looked at the stairs, then back to the bedroom again.

"The babies are fine," he promised.

Apparently Baxter was persuaded, because as Connor headed to the kitchen, the dog trotted down the stairs beside him.

"Can I help you find something?" Connor asked, when he returned from his morning walk with Baxter to see his sister-in-law digging through the cupboards in the kitchen.

"Coffee?" Brielle said hopefully.

He pointed to the half-full carafe on the warmer.

She shook her head. "No, I mean *real* coffee."

"Sorry," he said. "I switched to decaf when Regan did."

His sister-in-law frowned. "She doesn't like decaf."

"And therefore isn't tempted to sneak an extra cup," he pointed out.

"I couldn't finish a first cup," she said. "How do you survive on that?" She immediately realized the answer to her own question. "You get the real stuff at the sheriff's office, don't you?"

"Of course," he agreed. "You want to come in for a cup?"

"Desperately," she said, as she plugged in the kettle— and remembered to flip the switch this time. "But I'll settle for herbal tea and try to pretend my body isn't going through serious caffeine withdrawal."

"Have a cookie," he said, nudging the bakery box toward her.

She opened the lid and frowned. "There's only one left—I can't take the last one."

"I took two up to Regan earlier," he said.

"In that case—" she snatched up the cookie and bit into it. "It's not a cup of freshly brewed dark roast, but the sugar rush might give my system a boost."

"Did the babies wake you up in the night?" Connor asked, as he refilled his own mug.

Brie shook her head. "No, I'm a pretty heavy sleeper. But my body's still on Eastern Standard Time, so I've been up since three o'clock."

He'd been up at 3 a.m., too, but then he'd crashed again—at least for a little while. He'd never realized he could enjoy sharing a bed with someone solely for the purpose of sleep, but when he'd managed to tamp down on his inappropriate desire for his wife, he'd found himself comforted by her presence. If their circumstances had been different, he might have shifted closer and wrapped his arms around her. But their circumstances weren't different, so he'd stayed on his own side and only dreamed of breaching the distance between them.

"And by the time you get used to the time change, you'll be heading back to New York," he remarked to his sister-in-law now.

"Most likely," she agreed, as she poured the boiling water into her mug.

Regan wandered into the kitchen then, tightening the belt of her robe around her waist, and her sister pulled another mug out of the cupboard, dropped a tea bag inside, and filled it with water, too.

Brie pushed the mug across the counter. "Are the babies still sleeping?" she asked.

"Not still, just," Regan said, reaching for the tea. "They just went down for a nap. Hopefully, a long one." She lifted a hand to stifle a yawn. "You didn't hear them in the night?"

Brie shook her head. "How many times were they up?"

Regan looked at Connor.

He shrugged. "I lost count."

"Me, too," she admitted. "But I'm pretty sure one or the other was up...almost constantly."

"That sounds about right," he agreed. "And that's why you should go back to bed."

She looked him over, noting the uniform he wore. "I should go back to bed but you're going in to work?"

"I'd be going back to bed, too, if I had the option."

"Which is why you shouldn't have been up with me, every single time, in the night," she pointed out to him.

"I'm fine," he said. "And everyone else will be, too, so long as I don't have to pull out my weapon today."

"You're kidding—I hope."

He chuckled softly. "I'm kidding. And I'm going to pick up dinner on the way home, so you don't have to worry about anything but taking care of the babies and hanging out with your sister today."

"Didn't you say the freezer is full of casseroles from friends and neighbors?" Regan asked.

"It is," he confirmed. "But you mentioned that you've been craving Jo's Pizza."

"I did." She closed her eyes, as if picturing a pie with golden crust and melted cheese, and hummed approvingly. "And I am."

"Then Jo's Pizza it is." He bent down to give Baxter a scratch and started toward the door, then paused and turned back to kiss the top of Regan's head and wave to his sister-in-law before heading out.

"That's a good man you've got there," Brielle said to her sister when Connor had gone.

"He is," Regan agreed, lifting her mug to her lips.

"And yet…" Brie let the words trail off.

She sipped her tea, refusing to take the bait.

Her sister popped the last bite of cookie into her mouth and chewed.

Regan lasted another half a minute before she let out an exasperated sigh and finally asked, "And yet *what*?"

"That's what I'm trying to figure out," Brielle admitted.

"Well, let me know when you do."

"I know I've been gone a long time," Brie acknowledged. "But I know you, Regan. I know how you respond to men you like, and to men you *really* like. And I know there's more—or maybe less—going on here than you want everyone to believe."

"What are you talking about?" she asked.

"I'm talking about your relationship with your husband."

"Connor's amazing," Regan said. Because it was true—but it wasn't the whole truth, and she felt a little guilty that she wasn't being completely honest with her sister. "Since I told him that I was pregnant, he's been there for me. He rearranged his schedule to be at my first ultrasound appointment, and he even went with me to tell Mom and Dad that I was pregnant."

Brie's brows lifted. "*Before* he put a ring on your finger? He's even braver than I would have guessed. But I'm still missing something," she decided. "I'm adding two plus two and somehow only coming up with three."

"You were never particularly good at math," she teased her sister.

"That's why I'm the kindergarten teacher and you're the accountant," Brie agreed. "But as a teacher, I've become adept at knowing when one of my students is hiding something from me, and I know you're hiding something now."

"You're right," Regan acknowledged, almost relieved to say the words aloud, to confide in her sister. "There's something I haven't told you. Something nobody knows."

Brie laid a hand on her sister's arm, a silent gesture of support and encouragement.

"Connor married me because I was pregnant…but he didn't get me pregnant."

Chapter Six

Connor could empathize with his sister-in-law's craving for caffeine, and the always-fresh pot of coffee was his prime target when he arrived at the sheriff's office a short while later.

"I want to see pictures," Judy Talon, the sheriff's administrative assistant, demanded as soon as he walked through the door.

"I've got pictures," he promised. "But I want coffee first."

"Black?" Judy asked, rising from her chair.

When Connor had first been hired, the older woman had clearly and unequivocally stated that she was nobody's secretary or servant. While she had no objection to making coffee, she wasn't going to serve it to anyone else. And in four years, this was the first time she'd ever offered to pour him a cup.

He nodded gratefully. "That would be perfect. Thanks."

Along with the mug of steaming coffee, she brought him a glazed twist from the box of donuts that Deputy Holly Kowalski habitually brought in on Friday mornings.

"Thanks," Connor said again.

"You look like you've had a long day already and it's not yet nine a.m.," she noted.

"Long night," he clarified.

"One of the joys of being a new parent," Judy remarked.

"But these are the real joys," he said, unlocking the screen of his phone to show her the promised photos.

"Oh, they are precious," she agreed, leaning closer for a better look. "And so tiny."

He pointed to the baby with a striped pink cap on her head. "Piper was born at 3:08 a.m., weighing five pounds, eight ounces and measuring eighteen and a half inches." His finger shifted to indicate the baby wearing the dotted pink cap. "Poppy followed fourteen minutes later at five pounds, ten ounces and eighteen inches."

"Piper and Poppy are rather unusual names," Judy remarked.

"Unique," Connor agreed. "Although we did opt for more traditional middle names. Piper's is Faith and Poppy's is Margaret."

"Oh." Judy's lips curved as she glanced down at the phone again. "Your mom would be tickled pink to know that you shared her name with your firstborn."

The sheriff's admin had known his mom "way back when." They hadn't been friends, but Judy had been friendly to Faith, which was more than could be said about a lot of other women in town. They'd attended the same church—that is, his mom had attended when she wasn't required to work on a Sunday morning—and Connor knew there had been occasions when Judy had encouraged Faith to take her kids and leave her deadbeat husband. But Faith Parrish always replied that she'd promised to stick by Dwayne "for better or for worse," and she intended to honor those vows.

"She'd also be so proud of the man you've become," Judy told him now.

"Look at this one," he said, swiping the screen to show

the next photo—hopefully making it clear that he didn't want to talk about his mom.

Faith had been gone for almost five years now. The doctors had ruled her death an accidental overdose, suggesting that her mind had been muddled by the tumor growing on her brain, which resulted in her taking too many pills. Connor had a different theory. He'd overheard his mom talking to a neighbor about her grim prognosis and confiding that she didn't want her sons to watch her waste away. Six weeks later—ten days after Deacon's high school graduation—she was gone.

Connor still missed her every day. He missed her gentle smile and her wise counsel. No doubt she would have something to say about the predicament he'd gotten himself into, but he couldn't begin to imagine what that *something* might be.

Judy continued to *ooh* and *ahh* as she scrolled through the pictures. "Is that Regan—in the hospital?"

He glanced at the screen. "Yeah."

"She looks like someone who just went for a leisurely walk in the park, not someone who just gave birth to two babies."

"She was a trouper," Connor said, flexing the hand that had been clamped by her iron grip with each contraction. "But it was not a walk in the park."

"Says the man whose most strenuous task was probably cutting the cords," Judy said.

"I did cut the cords," he confirmed.

He'd been surprised when Regan asked him if he wanted to perform the task—and even more surprised to discover that he did. And still, he hadn't been prepared for the significance of the moment or how severing the tangible link between mother and child somehow seemed to forge a stronger bond connecting all of them.

"My husband did it when our son was born," Judy told him. "But he was in Afghanistan when our daughter was born. She's twenty-four now and regularly gripes that she's still waiting for him to cut the cord."

"Or maybe it's just hard for dads to let go of their little girls—even when they're not so little anymore," Connor said.

"That's probably true, too," she acknowledged. "And lucky for you that you have a badge and gun, because if those girls grow up to be as pretty as their mama, you're going to need both to keep the boys at bay."

"Don't I know it," he agreed.

"Hey, look who's back," Holly said, coming up from the evidence storage locker downstairs. "Congratulations, Deputy Daddy." She went to her desk to retrieve an oversize gift bag, then set it on top of his.

"What's this?" He eyed the package suspiciously.

She chuckled. "It's going to be fun watching you raise two little girls if just the sight of pink tissue makes you cower with fear."

"I'm not afraid," he denied. "I'm just…surprised."

"Surprised that I'd give a gift to my coworker's new babies?" she prompted, sounding hurt.

"Yes. I mean, no. I—"

"Why don't you shut up and open the gift?" Judy suggested.

Deciding that was good advice, Connor pulled out the tissue that was stuffed in the top of the bag and then two neatly folded blankets. He opened up the first, noted the patchwork of pale pinks and soft purples. The second blanket was a different pattern in the same colors. "Thanks, Kowalski. We can definitely use more blankets."

Judy shook her head despairingly. "Those aren't baby

blankets. They're handmade quilts. That one—" she nodded to the one that Connor was holding "—I recognize as a pinwheel pattern. But this one—" she traced a fingertip over a line of tiny stitches and glanced questioningly at Holly.

"That's a fractured star," she said.

"It's beautiful," the admin told her. "They both are. I especially love how you used the same fabrics in the different patterns so that the quilts coordinate."

Connor frowned and turned his attention back to the deputy. "You *made* these?"

"Kowalski's more than just a deadeye with her service pistol," Sheriff Reid Davidson remarked, as he entered the bullpen.

"Apparently," Connor agreed.

"Tessa won't go to sleep without the one you made for her," Reid told Holly.

She actually blushed in response to his praise. "I'm glad she likes it."

The sheriff shifted his gaze to encompass the other deputy and his admin. "And if you were going to have a baby shower in the office, you should have invited the boss."

"Your invitation must have gotten lost in the mail," Judy retorted.

"I'm sure it did," he remarked, his tone dry.

Connor folded the blankets—*quilts*—and put them back in the bag.

"You could have taken a few more days, Neal," Reid said.

"Regan's got her sister helping her out today, so I figured I'd come in and try to catch up on some paperwork."

The sheriff nodded as he filled his mug with coffee.

"Are you ready for your Stranger Danger presentation at the elementary school, Kowalski?"

"Is that today?" The female deputy feigned surprise. "Because I have a dentist appoint—"

"You don't have a dentist appointment," her boss interrupted. "Or if you do, you're going to cancel it, because this has been on your calendar since the beginning of the month."

She sighed. "Maybe you should send Neal," she suggested. "You don't want to depend on a sleep-deprived new dad to back you up if you have to take down a strung-out junkie."

The sheriff shook his head. "You're the only person I know who'd rather face a strung-out junkie than a room full of second-graders."

"Because no one would fault me for shooting the junkie," she pointed out.

"Stoney Ridge Elementary School. Eleven o'clock," Reid said. "And Kowalski?"

"Yes, sir?"

"Lock up your weapon before you go."

Connor coughed to cover up his laugh.

The sheriff lifted the lid of the donut box. "Dammit—who took my glazed twist?"

Kowalski didn't even try to disguise her snicker.

Regan held her breath in anticipation of Brie's response to her confession about the paternity of her twin babies.

"Wait a minute." Her sister held up a hand, apparently needing another moment to process the startling revelation. "Are you telling me that your husband isn't Piper and Poppy's father?"

"He's their father in every way that counts," Regan insisted. "They just don't share his DNA."

"Does he know?" Brie asked cautiously.

"Of course he knows," she said.

Her sister seemed relieved by her response, albeit still a little puzzled. "But if he's not the father and he *knows* he's not the father—biologically," she hastened to clarify, "why did he marry you?"

"Because I was a damsel in distress and he has a white knight complex?" Regan suggested.

Brie immediately shook her head. "I've never known a woman more capable of rescuing herself from any situation than you."

"I appreciate the vote of confidence, but you weren't here when I took the home pregnancy test," Regan reminded her. "Or when I finally told Mom and Dad."

But Connor had been—at least on the latter occasion—and she'd repaid his kindness by metaphorically throwing him to the wolves.

She'd taken his advice and told her parents the truth about the pregnancy. Except for one, tiny detail…

"What just happened in there?" he demanded when they left the house on Miners' Pass. "Why did you let your parents think I was the father of your babies?"

"Because if they hadn't assumed you were the father, they would have asked a hundred questions about him and our relationship."

"Questions you didn't want to answer," he realized.

"Questions I can't answer." She buried her face in her hands. "Not without admitting that I had an affair with a married man."

"You didn't know he was married," he said, repeating what she'd previously told him.

"But maybe I should have known. Maybe I didn't ask enough questions."

"All of that's academic now," he pointed out.

"I'll tell them the truth," she promised.

"When?" he demanded.

"Soon. I just need some time to figure out what to say."

"Here's a suggestion— 'Connor Neal isn't the father of my babies.'"

But then, before she'd had a chance to right the wrong, he'd apparently had a change of heart. Instead of distancing himself from the mess she'd made of her life, he'd offered to marry her—putting himself squarely in the middle of it.

"I was completely freaking out," Regan confided to her sister now. "I hated lying to Mom and Dad. I was having a really hard time processing the news that I was having twins! And although I wanted to believe that I could be a single mom, Connor's proposal gave me another option. A better option for my babies."

"Still, marriage is a pretty big step to take without any previous investment in the relationship," Brie noted.

Regan nodded. "But Connor grew up without a father—excluding the few years he lived with an abusive stepfather—and he didn't want Piper and Poppy to be subjected to whispers and speculation about their paternity."

"That's admirable," her sister said. "But it implies that he would have offered a ring to any unmarried woman who got knocked up."

"I wasn't any unmarried woman," she pointed out. "I was one who could bolster his standing in the community."

Brie frowned at that. "You're not seriously suggesting that he married you because our mother was a Blake?"

"It was a factor," Regan acknowledged. "Marrying into one of the town's founding families seemed like a surefire way for a man from the wrong side of the tracks to elevate his status in the community."

"He told you that?"

She nodded.

"That seems rather calculating," her sister noted. "On the other hand, it also makes a little more sense to me—a marriage of convenience for both of you."

"Except that it doesn't always feel convenient," Regan confided.

"Because you have feelings for him?" Brie guessed.

"Yes. No." She sighed. "I don't know."

"Well, as long as you're sure," her sister remarked dryly.

"I have all kinds of feelings," she said. "But I don't know if they're feelings *for* Connor or if the overwhelming love I feel for my babies is spilling over in his direction. Or maybe I'm just so grateful to him for everything he's done that I'm making something out of nothing."

"You could also be transferring your feelings for the biological father to the man who stepped up to take his place," her sister suggested as another alternative.

This time Regan shook her head. "I wasn't in love with Bo Larsen."

"So how did you end up in bed with him?" Brie wondered.

"He was handsome and charming, and it had been a really long time since a handsome and charming man showed any interest in me."

"Does he know…that you had his babies?"

"No," she admitted. "I mean, I told him that I was pregnant, because I thought that was the right thing to do."

"How did he respond?"

"He gave me money for an abortion."

Brie responded to that with a single word that questioned *his* paternity, and the fierceness of her response made Regan smile.

"I haven't seen or spoken to him since," she said.

"I assume that means he isn't from Haven?"

"No, he's not," she confirmed. "He was in town for a few months on a business contract, and when the contract ended he went back to Logan City—and his wife."

Brie's eyes went wide. "He was *married*?"

Regan felt her cheeks burn with a hot combination of guilt and remorse. "*Is* married," she corrected. "Though I had no idea, when we were together, that he had a wife." She swallowed. "And…two daughters."

"Wow."

She nodded, her face flaming with the memory of their confrontation—and her shame upon hearing his revelation.

"When did you find out?" her sister asked.

"When I told him that I was pregnant. Until then…I had no idea *I* was the other woman."

"Oh, honey." Brie wrapped warm, comforting arms around her. "I'm so sorry."

"I was such a fool," Regan noted.

"We all make mistakes when it comes to matters of the heart," her sister said. "And occasionally an overload of hormones."

She managed to smile through her tears. "You're the only one, besides Connor, who knows the whole truth."

"My lips are sealed," her sister promised. "But I have to admit, I'm curious about something."

"What's that?"

"Your platonic relationship with your husband."

The comment blipped on Regan's radar. She knew Brielle too well to assume this was an innocent question. "Why is that curious?" she asked, unwilling to admit that she was less-than-thrilled that Connor seemed determined not to stray beyond the friend zone. She should focus on what they had rather than wishing for more.

"Because it's obvious to me that there's some real chemistry between the two of you—and equally obvious that you're both pretending to be unaware of it."

"The only thing obvious to me is that your romantic heart is looking for a happy ending where one doesn't exist," Regan said.

But there was a part of her that wished her sister was right—and a happy ending wasn't outside the realm of possibility.

Chapter Seven

Connor hadn't thought to ask Brielle what she liked on her pizza, so he ordered two pies: one with bacon, pineapple and black olives—Regan's favorite, and one with only pepperoni. Of course, when he went into Jo's to pick up the order, he had to pull out his phone again and show pictures of the babies to everyone gathered around the counter.

Not that he minded—especially when Jo refused to take his money "just this once," suggesting that he should put it into a college fund for his daughters, because it was never too early to start saving. He knew that she was speaking the truth. He also knew that, even if he started saving right now, the spare pennies from a deputy's salary wouldn't add up to enough.

Thankfully, Piper and Poppy's maternal grandparents had expressed their intention to set up education funds for both of them, as they'd already done for their other granddaughter. He wanted to resent all the ways that the Channings threw their money around, but that would be rather hypocritical considering how he'd already benefited from their generosity.

When he finally got home, he found his wife and her sister snuggling with the babies in the living room. Baxter usually raced to the door whenever he heard Connor's truck pull into the driveway, but today the dog didn't move from his sentry position on the floor in front of the sofa.

"So much for man's best friend," he lamented, though he didn't really object to the dog's allegiance to the newest members of the family.

Baxter lifted his head to sniff the air—or, more likely, the pizza—then gave a soft *woof.*

He set the flat boxes on the coffee table and the dog rose to his feet, his nose twitching.

"Not for you."

Baxter looked at his master, pleading in his big brown eyes.

"He's had his dinner," Regan said. "So don't let him tell you any differently."

The animal swung his head to look at her, a wordless reproach.

"Well, you have," Regan said to him, as she rose to her feet to lay Poppy down in the playpen. "And you're not allowed people food, anyway."

Baxter let out a sound remarkably like a sigh and dropped to the floor again, his chin on top of his paws.

Connor went to the kitchen to get plates and napkins. When he returned, he saw that his sister-in-law hadn't moved from her position on the sofa.

"It will be easier to hold a plate without a baby in your arms," he remarked.

"Probably," Brielle agreed. "But I don't think I'm ready to let this little one go."

"Your nieces will still be here long after the pizza is gone," Regan pointed out, as she lifted a gooey slice covered with bacon, pineapple and olives onto her plate.

"A valid point," her sister acknowledged, and laid Piper down beside her twin.

"By the way, you can probably skip the w-a-l-k tonight," Regan said to Connor, as he loaded up his plate.

"Why's that?" he asked.

"We took him—and the babies—out this afternoon."

He frowned. "The wind was a little brisk this afternoon."

"It didn't seem to bother him," his wife remarked.

"I was thinking about Piper and Poppy," he clarified.

"They were wearing hats and mitts and tucked under a blanket in their stroller—even Mrs. Lopez approved," Regan assured him.

"I'll bet she was thrilled to get a peek at them."

"And Baxter was in doggy heaven because she kept slipping him treats while we were chatting."

"So you did the long route," he realized.

"And then some," Regan agreed. "Brie didn't believe me that the old Stagecoach Inn had reopened, so we went by there, too."

"It's been open a few months now, I think," Connor said.

"Since Valentine's Day, according to the brochure I picked up and which promises the ultimate romantic experience any day of the year," his sister-in-law noted.

"Well, Liam Gilmore's investment certainly seems to be paying off, because there are always cars in the parking lot."

Brie went still, then slowly turned and looked at her sister. "You didn't mention that Liam Gilmore owned the hotel."

"I didn't think it mattered," Regan said.

"It doesn't," Brie said, but the sudden flatness in her tone suggested otherwise.

Connor knew about the acrimonious history between the Blakes and the Gilmores, of course, but he sensed that his sister-in-law's reaction was based on something more recent.

"People rave about The Home Station restaurant, too," he said, in an effort to defuse the sudden tension.

"Have you eaten there?" Brie asked him.

He shook his head. "It's impossible to get a table without a reservation, and reservations aren't easy to get."

"That's hardly surprising. When I lived here, the only place you could go for a decent meal in this town was Diggers'. Or Jo's, if you wanted pizza," she added. "Which, by the way, was delicious."

"And now, instead of going to Battle Mountain for a special occasion, people from Battle Mountain are coming here to celebrate," Regan told her.

"And I thought nothing had changed in the seven years I was gone," Brie remarked lightly.

"For six of those years, nothing did," her sister agreed.

"But now I have a brother-in-law and two adorable nieces—and a pedicure appointment at Serenity Spa with my sister tomorrow afternoon."

"Really?" Regan was obviously surprised by this announcement.

"Two o'clock," Brie confirmed.

His wife sighed happily. "I haven't had a pedicure in…a very long time. Then again, for a very long time, I couldn't even see my feet, so pampering them seemed unnecessary."

"Pampering isn't ever necessary but it's always fun," her sister said. "And after our treatments, I'm going to take a closer look at the hotel, because it looks like the perfect place for a romantic getaway for new parents who never had a honeymoon."

It didn't require much reading between the lines to realize that Brie was thinking about her sister and brother-in-law.

Connor exchanged an uneasy glance with his wife before she looked away again, her cheeks flushed with color. Because she didn't want to imagine a romantic getaway with her husband? he wondered.

Or because she did?

They had their pedicures Saturday afternoon, then Brielle insisted on cooking dinner for her sister and brother-in-law Saturday night. The chicken simmered in a white wine sauce was tender and delicious—one of Celeste's recipes, Brie confided. After dinner the sisters stayed up late talking, trying to squeeze every possible minute out of a visit that was soon coming to an end.

On Sunday they went to Regan's parents' house for brunch, so that the whole family could celebrate the twins' birth together before Brie headed back to New York City.

Connor wouldn't have minded skipping the event. He always felt a little out of step around his in-laws—or maybe it was just that he didn't have a lot of experience with such family get-togethers. But he wanted Piper and Poppy to grow up with a strong sense of family and the security of belonging, so he tamped down on his own discomfort and carried the babies' car seats out to the truck.

It would be a tight squeeze for Brie in the backseat between the two babies, but it wasn't a long drive. Of course, nothing in Haven was too far from anything else, although the town was starting to expand and push out its long-established boundaries. The Channings' house—three towering stories of stone and brick—was an architectural masterpiece in the newest residential development. To a man who'd grown up in very modest circumstances, it was more than impressive—it was intimidating.

Connor pulled into the concrete drive behind a truck that he recognized as belonging to Regan's younger brother Spencer, a former bull rider turned horse trainer. The truck parked in front of Spencer's had the Adventure Village logo painted on the driver's side door, confirming that it belonged to Regan's older brother Jason, who owned the family-friendly recreational facilities. Jason was married to Alyssa—a West Coast native who, for reasons that no one could fathom, had willingly traded in the sun and surf of Southern California for the arid mountains of Northern Nevada.

"Looks like everyone's here," Brie remarked, sounding relieved as she lifted the twins' diaper bag onto her shoulder.

"I don't see Gramps's truck," Regan noted.

"Maybe he decided to stay at the ranch to watch over the cows."

Again, Connor suspected there was a deeper meaning to her words. Although Jesse Blake continued to supervise operations at Crooked Creek Ranch, the modest herd was more of a hobby than a livelihood now that the family's focus had shifted to mining.

Though Regan had lived in the fancy house on Miners' Pass prior to her marriage to Connor, she rang the bell and waited for the door to be opened rather than just walking in. And while he'd become accustomed to the formality—unheard of at his mother's house—it still gave him a start when the door was opened by a uniformed housekeeper.

Apparently it wasn't hard to find good help if you were able to pay for it, he mused, as Greta took their coats. And Ben and Margaret could definitely afford it.

If the Channings hadn't been filthy rich, they likely would have been viewed as neglectful parents. Because they owned and operated the mines that kept half the town employed, excuses were readily made for the parents who were simply too busy to attend teacher conferences, holiday plays, awards ceremonies and—in Spencer's case—even high school graduation.

If Ben and Margaret harbored any regrets about the milestone events they'd missed sharing with Jason, Regan, Spencer and Brielle, they never said as much. But it appeared to Connor that his in-laws were making a distinct effort to be involved in the lives of their grandchildren more than they'd ever done for their children.

They'd surprised Dani with the gift of a pony for her fourth birthday—and surprised Dani's father even more by actually attending the party rather than just sending the gift with their regrets. When Piper and Poppy were born, the maternal grandparents weren't the first visitors to the hospital—Alyssa and Jason took that honor—but they did show up on the first day. And now they'd cleared their schedules—because yes, even on a Sunday, their time was in demand—to host a family gathering where everyone could coo over and cuddle the newest additions to the family. (Though Connor noticed that his mother-in-law seemed more comfortable with cooing than cuddling.)

Of course, it was Celeste who'd done the real work. The Channings' longtime housekeeper and cook—solely responsible for planning and preparing meals since her employers had moved into a much bigger house—had prepared a veritable feast for the occasion, with breakfast items such as eggs benedict, bacon, sausage and pancakes. She'd also baked a ham, made cheesy scalloped potatoes, a green bean casserole and cornbread. An apparent new offering on the menu—fruit salad with mini-marshmallows—was a big hit with Dani, though Connor noted that his wife took a second scoop of the salad, too, after she'd polished off her first serving.

She'd frequently lamented the extra twelve pounds she still carried after giving birth—and that she was always hungry. The doctor had assured her that was normal for a nursing mom—and she was nursing two babies!

Connor didn't know how to reassure her that she looked great, because he didn't want to focus on how great she looked. He didn't want to acknowledge that he was wildly attracted to his wife or that he thought those new curves looked really good on her. Or maybe it was motherhood that added a softness to her features and a glow to her cheeks.

Conversation during the meal touched on numerous and various topics: Jason and Alyssa's recent trip to California over the spring break; the surprise visit of a famous actor to Crooked Creek with a request for Spencer to train his horses; excited recitations of Dani's riding lessons; a discussion of Brie's options for summer employment—because she couldn't imagine doing nothing for the ten weeks of her summer break.

Regan's maternal grandfather—known as Gramps—was in attendance, having driven over from Crooked Creek with Spencer's family, who now lived in the main house on the ranch. Connor noticed that the old man didn't contribute much to the various conversations that took place during the meal, but he kept a close eye on the little girl seated beside him, helping to fill Dani's plate with the foods she wanted, even cutting her pancakes and pouring the maple syrup. Though he hadn't been part of the family for very long, Connor had heard murmurs about a rift between Gramps and his granddaughter vis-

iting from New York City. The lack of any direct inter-
action between them gave credence to those murmurs.

"I can't believe you're going back to New York already," Jason said to Brielle, as he dug his fork into his
lemon pie. "It seems like you just got here."

"Because she did," Spencer agreed.

"I've been here four days," Brie reminded them.

"Four whole days?" her oldest brother echoed. "You've
definitely overstayed your welcome."

"And," she continued, ignoring his sarcasm, "I've got
fifteen six-year-olds who will be waiting for me at eight
thirty Monday morning."

"Because some people have real jobs," Alyssa teased
her husband.

"Just because I don't punch a clock doesn't mean I
don't work hard," he replied, a little defensively.

"I know, " she said soothingly.

"On the bright side, I think I've almost convinced Brie
to come back in June, for Piper and Poppy's baptism,"
Regan announced.

"Really?" Margaret looked at her youngest daughter,
her expression equal parts surprised and hopeful.

"So long as it's later in June, after school's finished,"
Brie said.

"We'll make it late June," Regan promised.

"And by then it will be time to look at flights for
Thanksgiving," Kenzie said. "Because they tend to book
up fast."

Brie shook her head. "I won't be coming back again
in November."

"But you have to," her friend and sister-in-law said.
"You set a precedent by coming home to meet Piper and
Poppy, so it's only fair that you do the same for your next
niece or nephew."

The silence that fell around the table was broken by Spencer's four-and-a-half-year-old daughter. "Can I say it now?" Dani asked. "Can I?"

Spencer put a finger to his lips, urging her to shush. "We're going to give Auntie Brie—and everyone else— another minute to figure it out."

The little girl crossed her arms over her chest, clearly unhappy with this decision. "But you said that *I* could tell everyone about our baby," she reminded him, obviously in protest of the change of plans.

"And you just did," Gramps remarked, evidently amused enough by the exchange to speak up.

At the same time Brie put the pieces together and said to Kenzie, "You're pregnant?"

Spencer's wife nodded, the wide smile that spread across her face further confirmation of the happy news. "Our family will be growing by one in early November."

"Or maybe we can have two babies, like Auntie Regan," Dani chimed in hopefully.

Connor and Regan shared a look, silently communicating amusement that anyone would wish for the double duty that came with twin babies—and a wordless acknowledgment that they'd been doubly blessed by the arrival of Piper and Poppy.

"We're *not* having two babies," her stepmother said firmly.

"Not this time, anyway," Spencer said, with a conspiratorial wink for his daughter.

Dani sighed. "Well, can we at least have a girl baby, then?"

"We won't know if we're having a girl or a boy until the baby's born," Kenzie cautioned.

"But the news of another baby—girl *or* boy—is cause for celebration," Ben said.

"And that means we're going to need a bottle of champagne," his wife decided.

"A great idea," Regan remarked dryly. "Let's celebrate Kenzie's pregnancy with alcohol that she can't drink."

"Well, we'll open a bottle of nonalcoholic champagne, too," Margaret said.

Celeste brought in the bottles of bubbly, along with enough champagne glasses for everyone. Corks were popped as best wishes and embraces were shared around the table.

Spencer, in charge of pouring the nonalcoholic bubbly, distributed glasses to his expectant wife, his young daughter and his sister—the nursing mom.

"I'll have a glass of that, please," Alyssa said, gesturing to the bottle in his hand.

"Why? Are you pregnant, too?" Spencer teased his brother's wife.

"Can't a woman decline alcohol without everyone assuming she's pregnant?" Alyssa countered.

"Of course," Regan spoke up in her sister-in-law's defense. "But it's interesting that you avoided answering his question by asking one of your own."

Alyssa, her cheeks flushed, turned to look helplessly at her husband.

"We were planning to wait awhile longer before sharing our news," Jason said. "But yes, we're going to have a baby before the end of this year, too."

"When?" Kenzie immediately wanted to know.

"Late November," Alyssa confided.

Of course, this news was followed by more hugs and congratulations as the rest of the glasses were passed around the table.

"Champagne?" Margaret asked, offering her youngest daughter a glass.

"I definitely want alcohol," Brie replied. "Because I'm beginning to suspect that there's something in the water in this town, and I'm not taking any chances."

Chapter Eight

It was harder than Regan expected to say goodbye to her sister. For the past seven years, she'd had regular if not frequent contact with Brielle via text, email and FaceTime, but visits had been few and far between.

She'd gone to New York a couple of times, but it was different there. Brielle had been pleased to have Regan stay with her and her roommates hadn't voiced any objections—they were happy to include her in all their plans. But that was the problem: they always seemed to have plans, which meant that Regan had little one-on-one time with her sister.

Regan didn't begrudge her sister these friendships. In fact, she genuinely liked Lily and Grace, and she had other friends of her own, too. But none that she was particularly close with or would confide her deepest secrets to.

Had she ever shared that kind of kinship with anyone other than Brielle? Maybe, when she was younger. But once she'd set upon her career path, she'd focused on that to the exclusion of all else. And anyway, there were some secrets that she didn't feel she could entrust to anyone outside the family—such as the truth about Piper and Poppy's paternity.

When Ben and Margaret left to take Brielle to the airport, the rest of the siblings said their goodbyes to one another and went their separate ways. Celeste had packed up various leftovers for each family, instinctively knowing who would want what. Which was why Dani happily skipped out the door with a Tupperware container of marshmallow fruit salad in her hands.

Regan and Connor were the last to leave, taking longer than everyone else who wasn't carting around twin babies. For the new parents, the cook had prepared plates of baked ham, scalloped potatoes and beans that could be easily reheated in the microwave for their dinner.

"Are you sure you don't want to come home with us?" Connor asked as he accepted the plates.

"Don't think I'm not tempted," she told him, her wistful gaze shifting to the twins securely buckled into their matching car seats. "But I promise, anytime you want to bring those babies for a visit, you won't leave here hungry."

Celeste gave an extra hug to the new mom before she left. "You used to spend so much time working, I was afraid you'd never meet and fall in love with a wonderful man," she said quietly, her words for Regan alone. "I'm so glad to see that I was wrong. And so happy to know that he loves you, too."

Regan hugged her back, saying only, "Thank you for everything today."

Because while there was no denying that Connor was a wonderful man, their marriage wasn't the love match that Celeste obviously believed it to be—and that Regan found herself starting to wish it *could* be.

Baxter was waiting at the door, fairly dancing with excitement as he greeted them upon their return. He didn't wait for Connor to put the car seats down, but walked all the way around them, sniffing, his tail wagging happily because his favorite little humans were finally home. When the sleeping babies were transferred from their car seats to the bassinet in the master bedroom, Baxter immediately settled down beside it.

The parents retreated to the living room, where Regan dropped onto the sofa and stretched her legs out in front of her.

"What are your plans for the rest of the day?" Connor asked her.

"To do as little as possible," she admitted.

"Do you mind if I join you?"

She patted the empty space beside her.

"Are you up for a movie?" he asked, reaching for the television remote.

"Put on whatever you want," she said. "Because there's no guarantee I'll stay awake to watch anything."

He grinned. "That means I don't have to worry about picking something you'll like."

She smiled back, grateful and relieved for the easy camaraderie they shared. Maybe this wasn't quite how she'd imagined marriage would be, but she had no cause for complaint.

It had taken some time for them to become comfortable with one another and their new living arrangement, and adjustments had been made on both sides. They shared some common interests, including a love of dogs, action movies, baseball games and Jo's pizza. And they respected their differences with regard to musical preferences, literary genres and art appreciation. Most important, they talked and laughed together, and she knew that he loved Piper and Poppy as much as she did.

And—except for that one time, during the Christmas holiday three months earlier—he seemed completely oblivious to the fact that she was female. Which maybe wasn't something she should complain about, she acknowledged, recalling a conversation she'd overheard between two of her coworkers.

The women had been complaining about the unrealistic expectations of their respective husbands. As if, after working at an office all day and then running around after the kids at home, the wives wanted nothing more than to indulge the sexual fantasies of their partners.

"I might feel a little more energetic in the bedroom if he put a load of laundry in the washing machine while I was making dinner," Becky had said.

Sandra nodded. "Or pulled out the vacuum every once in a while instead of waiting for me to do it."

Regan had listened to their chatter with sympathy but she had nothing to add. Because the truth was, Connor probably did twice as much laundry as she did. He even hung up her delicates, as recommended by the labels, instead of tossing them into the dryer. And if he spilled crumbs on the floor, it was likely that Baxter would clean them up before the vacuum could be plugged in. But when it came to other household chores, he was more than willing to do his share, if not more.

No, she had no cause for complaint, she reminded herself.

Except...wasn't it unusual for a man not to express an interest in sex? Even if there was a lot about their marriage that wasn't usual.

They hadn't specifically discussed sleeping arrangements before their impromptu wedding ceremony, but he'd vacated his bed for her, confirming that physical intimacy wasn't part of their bargain—and maybe not even desired. But if "separate rooms" was a marriage of convenience "rule," she was starting to think they should throw out the rule book.

Of course, she'd already been pregnant when they got

married, and maybe Connor was turned off by the idea of making love with a woman who was carrying another man's baby. Or maybe he just wasn't attracted to her at all—although the passionate kiss they'd shared in December certainly suggested otherwise.

She tipped her head back and closed her eyes as the memory of that kiss played out in her mind and stirred her body.

"You might be more comfortable upstairs, if you want to take a nap," he suggested.

And the tantalizing memory slipped away, leaving only the remnants of an unsatisfied hunger.

Regan held back a regretful sigh as she shook her head. "If I go upstairs, the babies might wake up. It's almost as if they can sense when their food supply is in close proximity."

"You nursed them before we left your parents' place, though, so they should be okay for a while, I'd think."

She held up her hand, showing her fingers were crossed.

And though she tried to hold back a wistful sigh, she must have made some sound because Connor asked, "Are you okay?"

"Yeah," she said, albeit not very convincingly.

"I know you're going to miss your sister, but she's going to come back in a couple of months for the baptism, and probably again in November, after Spencer and Kenzie's baby is born. Or maybe at Christmas, to meet Alyssa and Jason's baby at the same time."

Regan nodded. "I'm sure you're right. And I am going to miss Brie, but…it's more than that," she admitted.

He shifted on the sofa, so that he was facing her, and took her hands in his. "What's more than that?"

Her eyes filled with tears. "Everyone was so happy

to hear the news about Spencer and Kenzie's baby—and then Jason and Alyssa's baby."

"You mean, unlike your parents' reactions when you told them about your pregnancy," he guessed.

She nodded again. "Obviously my situation was different," she acknowledged. "And although I wouldn't change anything that happened, because we've got Piper and Poppy now, I sometimes wish I'd been able to savor the joy of discovering that I was going to be a mother. Instead, I was too busy being worried that I was going to have to do everything on my own."

Connor squeezed her hands gently. "You're not on your own now."

Regan smiled. "I know. And thanks to you, I was able to relax and prepare for the babies during the last five months of my pregnancy."

His brows lifted. "When were you relaxed? Was I out of town that day?"

She elbowed him in the ribs.

He chuckled.

"Seriously, though, I hope you know how grateful I am to you. For everything."

"We entered into a mutually beneficial arrangement," he reminded her.

"It sounds so romantic when you phrase it like that," she said dryly.

He shrugged. "Romance isn't really my thing."

"It was never mine, either." She lifted her head to meet his gaze. "But lately I've found myself wondering if that could change."

Then, before she could think about all the reasons it might be a mistake, she leaned forward and pressed her lips to his.

It wasn't the first, or even the second, time they'd

kissed, but somehow Connor had managed to forget how potent her flavor was. Now her sweet taste raced through his veins like a drug, making his heart hammer and his blood pound. And like an addict coming down from that first euphoric rush, he wanted more.

She sensed his desire, and willingly gave more. She didn't hold anything back. When he touched his tongue to her lip—testing, teasing, she sighed softly and opened for him—readily, eagerly. Her hands slid over his shoulders to link behind his head, her fingers tangling in the hair that brushed the collar of his shirt. The gentle scrape of her nails against his scalp had all the blood draining out of his head and into his lap.

His arms banded around her, pulling her closer. Her breasts, full and plump, were crushed against his chest. Their tongues touched, retreated. Once. Twice. More. The rhythmic dance mimicked the sensual act of lovemaking and somehow made him impossibly harder.

He wanted her—more than he could ever remember wanting another woman. But she wasn't another woman; she was his wife. And not even two weeks had passed since she'd given birth to their twin baby girls. Maybe he didn't share any of their DNA, but his name was in the "father" box on their birth registration. That status not only gave him certain rights and responsibilities, it was a gift that he was trying to prove himself worthy of.

With a muttered curse and sincere regret, he eased his mouth from hers.

Regan exhaled, slowly and a little unsteadily, before lifting her gaze to his. "What's wrong?"

"We got married so that your babies would have a father," he reminded her. "I didn't—*don't*—expect anything more."

He saw a flicker of something—disappointment?

hurt?—in her eyes before she looked away. "Are you seeing someone else?"

"What?" He was shocked that she would even consider such a possibility. "No! Of course not."

"So you're being faithful to a wife you're not even sleeping with?"

"We exchanged vows," he reminded her. "And I don't make promises lightly."

She considered his words for a moment. "I can appreciate that," she said. "But what I really want to know is—are you at all attracted to me?"

Connor was baffled by the question.

How was it possible that she couldn't know how much he wanted her?

But apparently she didn't, and he decided that admitting the truth and intensity of his desire for her might do more harm than good at this point.

"Regardless of my feelings, there are times when it's smarter to ignore an attraction than give in to it," he said.

"Maybe—if you're attracted to your best friend's sister or another man's girlfriend," she allowed. "But I don't think there's any danger in acting on feelings for your own wife."

"Honey, you are the most dangerous woman I've ever known," he assured her. "Not to mention that anything we start here is doomed to remain unfinished."

"There are various ways to finish," she pointed out. Then, in case he needed more convincing, she leaned forward to nibble playfully on his lower lip.

"There are," he agreed hoarsely, and his body was more than ready to accept any variation that she wanted to offer.

This time he reached for her. His hand slid beneath the curtain of her hair to cradle the back of her head, holding her in place while his mouth moved over hers. His kiss was hot and hungry. Desperate and demanding.

Somehow she found herself in his lap, where she could feel the solid evidence of his arousal pressed hard against her, stoking the embers of her own desire. His hands were on her breasts now, gently kneading, his thumbs brushing over her peaked nipples. Even through the lightly padded cups of her nursing bra, she was hyperaware of his touch, as arrows of sensation shot from the tips of her breasts to her core, stirring an unexpectedly urgent hunger.

She arched into him, wanting, *needing*, more. More of his touch. More of his taste. More everything.

She reached between their bodies to unfasten his belt, then released the button of his jeans. The zipper required more effort and attention as the fabric was stretched taut over his straining erection, but she finally succeeded and rewarded herself by sliding her hand beneath the band of his briefs to take hold of her prize.

As her fingers wrapped around him, his groan of approval reverberated through her, encouraging and emboldening her. In the far recesses of her mind, she thought she heard something—maybe a sound coming from the baby monitor? But it was a vague inkling that failed to draw her attention away from her task.

Then Baxter woofed—a sound not so vague or distant.

Regan tried to ignore the dog and concentrate on the task in hand, but Baxter, apparently displeased that she wasn't already racing up the stairs in response to the sounds of a baby stirring, put his paws up on the edge of the sofa and nudged her arm with his nose.

She couldn't help it—she giggled. Her husband cursed. The dog nudged her again, more insistently this time. Connor put his hand over hers, halting her motions.

"You better go check on the babies," he said. "Because Baxter isn't going to give us any peace until you do."

She knew he was right, and she appreciated the animal's diligence —although not as much as she resented the interruption right now. "I'll be quick," she promised.

But the twins conspired to thwart her efforts.

When she reached the bedroom, Poppy was wide awake and demanding attention. Regan changed the baby's diaper, then settled into the rocking chair with the hungry infant at her breast.

Of course, by the time Poppy was sated, Piper was awake, so Regan had to go through the whole routine again. She was fastening a fresh diaper around the infant's middle when Connor popped his head into the room.

"Everything okay?" he asked.

"Yeah, but the girls both decided it was dinner time—again, and I'm just getting started with Piper."

"In that case, I might as well take Baxter out," he said. "He's pacing by the door, eager for his w-a-l-k."

She nodded and returned to the rocking chair to feed her firstborn daughter. When Piper was finished nursing, Regan laid the now-sleepy baby down in the bassinet beside her twin.

Then she stretched out on the bed to eagerly wait for her husband's return...and was fast asleep only minutes later.

Chapter Nine

Connor wasn't surprised to find his wife completely out when he returned home. To be honest, he might even have been relieved to discover that Regan had succumbed to her obvious exhaustion. After all, wasn't that one of the reasons he'd decided to treat Baxter to an extra-long walk?

Well, that, and to give himself the necessary time and distance to cool the heat that pulsed in his veins. Because while she'd given every indication that she craved physical intimacy as much as he did, he worried that he'd taken advantage of her vulnerable state.

She'd been through a lot over the past couple of weeks, and giving birth to Piper and Poppy was only the beginning of it. In addition to the physical toll of the experience, her emotions had ebbed and flowed like the tide. Except that suggested a predictable and almost gentle rhythm, whereas her moods had been anything but. Perhaps a more appropriate analogy would be the heart-pounding climbs and breath-stealing plunges of a roller coaster—like Space Mountain, completely in the dark.

Not that any of that dampened his desire for her. He only had to look at her to want her again. In fact, his body was already stirring, urging him to stretch out beside her and pick up where they'd left off.

Instead, he picked up the blanket that was neatly folded at the foot of the bed and gently draped it over her sleeping form, accepting his own unfulfilled desire as the price he had to pay for the bargain he'd struck. Because he knew that getting tangled up in a physical relationship with his wife would only make it that much harder for both of them when she eventually decided that she wanted to extricate herself from their marriage.

Because he'd been convinced, when they exchanged their vows, that the arrangement was only a temporary one. Not that she'd suggested any particular time frame, but he felt certain the day would come when she no longer wanted to be tied down to a man who was so wholly unsuitable. When she was more comfortable with and confident in her role as a mother and accepted that the difficulties of raising twin daughters on her own was less of a trial than staying with a man she didn't love.

Maybe, lately, he'd started to let himself imagine that they could make their marriage work—and admit to himself that he wanted to. Since sharing his home with Regan—and now their babies—he'd realized how empty his life had been before, without her in it. But Regan had given him no indication that the vows they'd exchanged meant anything more to her than a means to an end.

As Connor made his way back down the stairs, leaving his exhausted wife sleeping, he silently cursed Ben Channing for forcing him into this impossible situation.

Except that no one had forced him to do anything, his conscience reminded him. He'd taken the easy way. He'd sold out.

His conscience was right.

He should have spoken up and corrected the assumption that he was the father of Regan's babies when she first told her parents about the pregnancy. He should have made the truth known, loudly and clearly, because even when he'd acceded to her wordless request, he'd suspected his silence in that moment was going to come back to bite him.

As he passed the laundry room, he noticed an empty basket beside the dryer—a telltale sign that there was a load in need of folding. Diaper shirts and sleepers, he guessed. Because there always seemed to be a load of diaper shirts and sleepers in the laundry.

He transferred the contents of the dryer to the basket and carried it into the living room. He found a baseball game on TV and listened to the play-by-play as he folded the tiny garments—and a couple of even tinier pairs of bikini panties that obviously belonged to his wife.

He didn't know how to fold women's underwear—or even if they should be folded—so he simply made a neat pile of the panties and tried not to notice the silkiness of the fabric and peekaboo lace details. Because being in a marriage of convenience with a woman he wanted more than any other was painful enough without thinking about the sexy garments that hugged her feminine curves.

The fact that she wanted him, too—as she'd made abundantly clear before Baxter's interruption—only made their situation more difficult. While the sharing of physical intimacy would satisfy certain needs, Connor knew that the secret he continued to keep prevented them from developing a real and honest relationship.

A secret that dated back to the day after Regan's ultrasound, when Connor looked up from the report he was writing to see her father striding toward his desk. He'd been pretty sure he could guess why the man was there—but at least he wasn't carrying a shotgun.

The sheriff had offered his office for a more private conversation, and Connor had braced himself as he closed the door.

Regan's father had surprised him then by asking how

his brother was doing at Columbia and commiserating with the deputy about the outrageous costs of a college education—especially a top-notch law school like Columbia. And just when he'd started to think that he might have been mistaken about the reason for this visit, the other man asked if Deacon knew that Connor had put a second mortgage on his house to pay his brother's tuition.

Connor had admitted that he didn't and that he'd prefer to keep it that way. He hadn't bothered to ask how Regan's father knew about his financial situation. Ben Channing was a major shareholder in the local bank and his signature was required for most mortgages and loans.

The other man had acknowledged his request with a nod before unnecessarily pointing out that there wasn't enough equity in the property to finance a second year at Columbia.

And then he'd spoken the words that changed everything.

"Blake Mining is always looking for ways to give back to the community," Ben said. "And I'm confident that a scholarship fund to help with your brother's education would be a good use of our resources."

Connor had been intrigued by the idea—and more than a little wary. "Do you really think your company would be willing to give Deacon a scholarship?"

"If you help me, I'll help him."

Said the spider to the fly, Connor mused.

But still, he had to know: "What is it you think I can do for you?"

"Marry my daughter," Ben said.

Connor had, of course, anticipated this demand. And if the man had shown up with a shotgun in hand, he would have refused, for a lot of valid reasons. Instead,

Regan's father had come armed with something much more dangerous.

"How do you think your daughter would feel if she knew you were here trying to buy her a husband?" Connor had asked him.

"I don't imagine she'd be too happy," Ben admitted. "Which is why I'd appreciate your discretion."

"The situation isn't as black-and-white as you seem to think," he cautioned.

"I'm aware of the many shades of gray," the other man assured him. "And I'm not nearly as oblivious to what goes on in my daughter's life as she thinks. Thankfully, no one else knows about the short-term romantic relationship she ended a few months back.

"So when news of her pregnancy spreads, there's going to be talk and speculation about the father. If you put a ring on her finger, people will assume that the two of you did a remarkable job of keeping your relationship discreet."

"Why me?" Connor asked.

"Aside from what I said earlier about each of us being able to help the other, it occurred to me that you must care about Regan if you were willing to let her drag you into our home to announce her pregnancy, and then not correct our mistaken assumption that you were responsible."

"I didn't want to be there," Connor admitted. "But your daughter can be rather persuasive."

"Now it's your turn to persuade her that marrying you would be the best thing for her unborn children."

"How am I supposed to do that?"

"I don't think it will be too difficult," Ben said. "For all her courage and conviction, Regan's very much a traditional girl at heart. Given the choice, she'll want her babies to have both a mother and a father. A family."

Then he reached into his pocket and pulled out a check in an amount that made Connor's brows lift.

"I'm on my way to the bank now, to give the manager this. It only represents about half the costs of your brother's first year of law school," Ben acknowledged. "Consider it a sign of good faith. As soon as Regan's wearing your ring on her finger, your brother will get the other half. Just remember—she can't know that we had this conversation."

"You want me to lie to my prospective bride—your daughter—about my reasons for proposing to her? *If* I decide to go along with this plan," he hastened to clarify.

"I want you to make a case in favor of a legal union that will give her and her babies the security of a family and that will give you legitimacy in the eyes of the community."

And there it was—the acknowledgment that no matter how hard Connor had worked to turn his life around, to most of the residents of Haven, he was still just Faithless Faith's bastard son.

"I'm surprised you'd want your daughter to marry a man of questionable reputation," he'd remarked.

"I put more stock in character than reputation," Ben told him.

"A man of strong character wouldn't let himself be bought," Connor noted.

And before Ben Channing had pulled out that check, he would have said that he wasn't for sale. He was ashamed to acknowledge now that his assertion would have been wrong.

"Every man can be bought for the right currency."

For Connor, that currency had been his brother's education. Because Ben Channing was right—he'd had no idea how he would manage to pay for Deacon's second year of law school when he'd barely been scraping by after helping to finance his first semester.

And maybe, selfishly, he did crave the legitimacy that he knew marriage to Regan would bring.

So he'd taken the last of his meager savings and bought a ring.

He'd sold out.

He'd convinced himself that he was doing Regan a favor. That he was being noble and self-sacrificing. But the truth was, his actions had been selfish and self-serving. And yet, he'd been rewarded with a beautiful wife and two adorable babies.

He'd been fascinated by the twins since that very first ultrasound, and he'd become more and more enchanted as their growth and development was reflected in the changes to Regan's body. And when Piper and Poppy were finally born, the rush of emotion filled his heart to overflowing. He truly did love those baby girls as if they were his own. And watching his wife with their babies, he realized that he was developing some pretty deep feelings for Regan, too.

And that was before she'd kissed him tonight, tempting him with possibilities that he hadn't let himself even dream about.

There were days when he wondered how he'd let himself get caught up in the drama of her life and what his life would be like if he'd never made the trip to Battle Mountain for her ultrasound. But he couldn't imagine not having been there every day over the past several months.

And maybe that had been his punishment: being married to a warm, sexy woman that he couldn't touch.

Until today, when she'd suddenly changed all the rules.

When she'd turned his whole world upside down with a kiss.

Just thinking about those soft, sweet lips against his was enough to have the blood in his head migrating south. He didn't dare remember the press of her body against his, the glorious weight of those plump breasts filling his palms, the tantalizing rhythm of her pelvis rocking against his. The not remembering required so much effort that perspiration beaded on his brow.

As she'd pointed out to him earlier, there were different ways to finish, and he was going to have to utilize the old standby of teenage boys if he hoped to get any sleep tonight. But there would be no pretending that his callused hand could replicate her soft, tempting touch.

And that was probably for the best.

By her own admission, Regan had been feeling a little out of sorts after the family gathering at her parents' house. Maybe she wanted to pretend—at least for a while—that she had a real marriage like each of her brothers with their respective wives. The important thing for Connor to remember was that whatever she was feeling, it wasn't about him.

It had never been about him.

Theirs was just a marriage of convenience that was becoming more and more inconvenient with every day that passed.

Chapter Ten

Connor was up early after a restless night. As he moved down the hall past the master bedroom, he heard no sound from inside, suggesting that Regan and the twins were still asleep. He'd heard the babies in the wee hours and had felt a little guilty for leaving Regan to respond to their demands on her own. But apparently his self-preservation instincts were stronger than his sense of responsibility, because he hadn't gotten up to help. Because he didn't trust himself to walk away from her again if she invited him to share her bed.

He poured water into the coffeemaker, measured the grounds into the filter, then retrieved Baxter's leash from the hook by the door. The dog trotted happily along with his tongue hanging out of his mouth and his tail wagging.

As they made their way down Elderberry Lane, Connor noted an unfamiliar red Toyota pull into Bruce Ackerman's driveway. A slender woman with long blond hair got out of the driver's side and moved around to the back of the vehicle.

As she lifted a bucket of cleaning supplies out of the trunk, Connor thought there was something familiar about her. A gust of wind swept through the air, and she lifted a hand to tuck an errant strand of hair behind her ear.

The movement afforded him a clearer view of her profile and revealed why she seemed familiar. Mallory

Stillwell had lived across the street and two doors down from Connor while they were growing up. Though she was two years younger than he, they'd frequently hung out together and even dated for a brief while.

He'd lost touch with her after high school. The last he'd heard, she'd taken off for Vegas in the hopes of making a fortune—or at least a better life for herself. He didn't know if she'd found what she was looking for, but she was obviously back in Haven now.

"Mallory." He called out her name as he made his way down the street.

She didn't hear him.

Or maybe she was ignoring him, because she slammed the lid of the trunk and hurried toward the front of the house with the bucket in hand.

"Mallory," he called again, jogging to catch up with her.

Baxter barked happily, always eager to run.

She'd ignored Connor—twice, but the bark seemed to give her pause, reminding him that she'd always had a soft spot for animals.

In fact, she'd volunteered at the local animal shelter twice a week throughout high school. Of course, she'd said that anything was better than hanging around at home, deliberately downplaying the value of her efforts. He'd stopped by the shelter a couple of times to see her and noticed that she had tremendous empathy for all the animals, especially those that exhibited obvious signs of abuse.

She wasn't looking at him now, but at his canine companion. "Rusty?" she said, her voice hesitant.

Baxter barked and wagged his tail.

"Ohmygod…it *is* you." She dropped to her knees on

the driveway to embrace him, tears sliding down her cheeks.

"How do you know my dog?" Connor asked cautiously.

She wiped the backs of her hands over her tear-streaked cheeks before finally looking up at him. "He used to be my dog," she admitted. "Where did you find him? *When* did you find him?"

"Last April," he said. "Out at the train yard."

"Oh, Rusty," she said, her eyes filling with fresh tears.

"His name's Baxter now," Connor told her.

"Baxter," she echoed, and nodded. "It's a good name. He's a good dog."

"The best," Connor said. "So…how did he end up at the train yard?"

Her gaze skittered away. "I don't know."

"But you have a theory," he guessed.

"Evan said he ran away." She shrugged her narrow shoulders. "I suspected he left the door open on purpose, so that Rusty could do just that."

"Evan?" he prompted.

"My husband."

He glanced at her left hand, noted there was a thin gold band encircling her third finger.

"He was tied to a fence post," Connor told her. "Shivering. Starving."

She flinched, as if each word was a physical blow. "Evan never wanted a dog," she admitted, stroking her hands over Baxter's glossy coat as she spoke. "I picked Rusty—*Baxter*," she immediately corrected herself, "out of a litter of puppies that I helped take care of at the SPCA in Vegas, where we were living at the time. Evan was driving a rig and sometimes gone for weeks at a time, and I thought a dog would be good company for me and my daughter."

"I didn't know you had a child," he admitted.

Mallory nodded, her expression brightening slightly. "Chloe's almost six and the light of my life. When Rus—*Baxter* went missing, we were out all night looking for him. And again the next day, and the day after that."

She tipped her head forward, so that her face was curtained by her hair. "I thought Evan—" her voice broke and she shook her head, as if unable to complete the thought. "I'm so glad he's got a good home now." She looked up at him then and managed a tentative smile. "Good people."

"He does," Connor agreed. Then, "So what brought you back to Haven?"

"My mom died and left the house to me and my sisters, but they have better places to live. Madison's in Houston and Miranda's in Battle Mountain, so now I'm paying them rent to live in a house I didn't ever want to come back to." This time her shrug was one of resignation. "But Evan didn't grow up in Haven, and he figured that if we missed one or two rent payments here, my sisters wouldn't evict us."

"Is he still driving a rig?"

She shook her head. "His CDL was yanked for DUI. He's applied for a few jobs around town, but there aren't many."

They both knew the town's biggest employer was Blake Mining and that his wife was a Blake, so Connor had to give her credit for not attempting to leverage their shared history into a job for her husband.

"You've done good for yourself, though," Mallory noted, in an obvious effort to shift the conversation. "Working in the sheriff's office now, living in a house on the right side of town, married with children. Of course, no one was more surprised than me to hear that the Channing ice princess went slumming and got herself knocked up by my first boyfriend."

"Regan's a good person," he told her. "And a wonderful mother."

"Maybe, but those names—" she rolled her eyes "—Piper and Poppy? What were you thinking?"

"Piper's full name is Piper Faith Neal."

"Oh." Her sneer immediately faded. "For your mom. That's nice."

"It was Regan's idea."

"So maybe she's not all bad," Mallory allowed.

"She's amazing," Connor said.

She tilted her head to look at him. "Huh."

"What's that supposed to mean?"

"I guess I just assumed that you'd married her because she was pregnant. I never considered that you might actually have feelings for her."

Before he could respond to that, the front door opened and Mr. Ackerman poked his head out. "Everything okay, Mallory?"

"Just catching up with an old friend," she told him.

"I'm not paying you to chitchat, you know."

"I also know that you pay me by the job not the hour," she retorted. "So it doesn't really matter when I get started as long as the job gets done."

"Cheeky girl," the old man grumbled, with a twinkle in his eye.

"But I probably should get started," Mallory said, when Mr. Ackerman had disappeared back inside. "This is only the first of three houses I have to do today."

Connor nodded. "It was good to see you, Mallory."

"You, too." She looked at the dog at his feet and gave his head a quick rub. "And especially you, Baxter."

As Connor headed toward home, Mallory's comment about his feelings for Regan continued to echo in the back of his mind.

Of course he had feelings for Regan—but he wasn't inclined to put a label on those feelings.

He cared about her and enjoyed spending time with her. And why wouldn't he? She was beautiful and smart, with a generally sunny disposition and good sense of humor. She was also sexy as hell, and his attraction to her often felt like more of a curse than a blessing.

But for the better part of seven months, he'd managed to ignore the attraction. He'd ruthlessly shoved it aside, reminding himself that she'd married him not because she wanted a husband but because she wanted a father for her babies.

Their hasty vows had offered her a degree of protection when she could no longer hide her pregnancy. Sure, there was plenty of gossip as residents pretended to be shocked when they counted the months between the wedding and the birth of her babies and came up with a number less than nine. But the revelation that Regan Channing *had to* marry Connor Neal was scandalous enough that they didn't suspect there was more to the story.

Connor knew the whole truth, and that was a burden he carried alone. Regan had shared her deepest secrets with him, trusting that he would keep them safe. But he couldn't do the same, because his secrets—if revealed—could tear apart the fragile foundation of their family.

Maybe that foundation would be stronger if he'd been honest with her from the beginning. Instead, they'd built their marriage on secrets and lies. It was ironic, because he'd urged her to tell the truth to her parents, and when she'd stopped by to tell him that she was going to do just that, he was the one who backtracked from his own advice.

Twenty-four hours after Ben Channing's visit to the sheriff's office, Connor had been mulling over the man's proposition when Regan showed up at his door.

She'd offered him two containers of ice cream and a tempting smile. "Rocky road and chocolate."

"What's the occasion?" he'd asked.

"I've decided to tell my parents the truth tonight," she told him.

Baxter had been out in the backyard taking care of business, but he came through the doggy door then, and sensing—or maybe scenting—they had a visitor, raced to the front entrance as Regan stepped inside.

Before Connor could caution her or restrain the dog, Regan had dropped to her knees to fuss over the excited canine.

"Oh, aren't you just the cutest thing?" she'd said, clearly talking to the dog and not him. "And friendly," she noted with a chuckle, as she rubbed the back of her hand over her cheek to wipe away his slobbery doggy kisses.

"Baxter, sit."

The dog plopped his butt on the floor, but his tail continued to wag.

"He's very well trained," she'd remarked, rising to her feet.

"If he was well trained, you wouldn't have dog hair all over you," he'd noted.

Regan had glanced down and, with a dismissive shrug, brushed her hands over the thighs of her pants.

It might have been that moment, Connor realized now, when he really started to fall for her. Because who wouldn't fall for a beautiful, sexy woman who showed up at his door with ice cream and didn't mind his canine companion shedding all over her clothes?

His own hands had started to go numb from the cold, reminding him of the ice cream he was holding.

"What kind do you want?" he'd asked, leading the way to the kitchen.

"Can I have a scoop of each?"

He took two bowls out of the cupboard. "I thought you weren't one of those women who drowns her worries with copious amounts of chocolate."

"If I wanted to do that, I would have stayed home with both containers and a spoon," she'd said.

He'd chuckled at her remark as he pried the lid off the first container and dipped the scoop inside.

"So why today?" he'd asked, when he handed her the bowl full of ice cream and a spoon.

"I figured, after three days, my father's blood pressure should have come down to something approximating normal. And I know you're anxious for me to rectify their misunderstanding."

Of course, he'd urged her to do exactly that—but that was before Ben Channing had shown up at the sheriff's office with his intriguing proposition.

"So tell me," she said, apparently wanting to discuss something other than the impending visit with her parents. "Was this circa 1980 kitchen a deliberate design choice?"

"Actually, I think it's circa 1972, because that's when the house was built."

She glanced around. "You're not interested in updating the look?"

"It's functional," he said, well aware that the space was in desperate need of a major overhaul. But right now,

Connor could hardly afford a can of paint, never mind a more substantial renovation.

Except that Deacon had called him that afternoon, practically bursting with excitement over the news that he'd been awarded another scholarship—confirming that Ben Channing had honored at least the first part of his promise. Deacon wanted to send the money back to his brother, to repay him for his first-term tuition. But Connor had suggested that he hold on to the funds for second term, because he knew it might be the last "Aim Higher" check he ever saw.

Of course, that scholarship depended on Connor more than Deacon. All he had to do was convince Regan to marry him, and her father would ensure that Blake Mining continued to fund the scholarship.

Sure, he had qualms about proposing for mercenary reasons. Truthfully, he had qualms about marriage in general. And a lot of reservations about his ability to fulfill the responsibilities of parenthood. Because what did he know about being a father? His biological father had never been part of his life and his stepfather had been an abusive drunk, ensuring he had no role models he'd want to emulate.

But something had happened when he'd seen Regan's babies on the ultrasound monitor. He'd felt an unexpected swell of emotion, a desire to help and protect both the mom and her babies. Maybe he didn't know anything about being a dad, but he knew that if he was ever entrusted with the care of a child—or children, he would do everything in his power to be the best dad that he could be.

"Did you stop by to critique my decor?" he'd asked Regan, picking up the thread of their conversation.

"No." She'd sighed. "My visit was solely for the purposes of procrastination—and ice cream."

"You're not eager to tell your parents the truth," he'd guessed.

"Definitely not," she agreed. "When my dad hears that you're not the father of my baby, he's going to demand to know who is, so that he can force me to marry him."

"You don't want to marry the father?"

"Not an option," she said bluntly.

"Why not?" he wondered.

"Because bigamy's illegal in Nevada."

And he'd thought nothing could have surprised him more than her pregnancy. "He's married?"

She'd nodded slowly. "I didn't know he was married when we were together," she explained. "But maybe I should have suspected something was up.

"He was an environmental consultant in town on a contractual assignment, and because he was only going to be in town for a short while, he wanted to be discreet. To protect my reputation, he said, because he understood how gossip worked in small towns and he didn't want people talking about me.

"In retrospect, it was obvious that he didn't want people talking about *us*, because some people did know that he was married."

"When did you find out?" Connor asked her.

"When I told him that I was pregnant," she admitted. "Our relationship was already over, but when I realized I was going to have his baby, I went to see him."

She shoveled another spoonful of ice cream into her mouth. "I didn't want or expect anything from him—not that I was willing to admit, anyway—but I felt I had an obligation to tell him that he was going to be a father." She swirled her spoon inside the bowl. "Turned out he didn't just have a wife but two kids—and he didn't want any more. And he definitely didn't want me causing any trouble for his perfect little family.

"He used me," she said quietly. "And I was foolish enough to let him."

He'd never seen her like this—so vulnerable and insecure. Even when she'd been throwing up outside of Diggers', she'd given the impression of a woman in control of her life—if not her morning sickness. Even at the clinic for her ultrasound, she'd seemed appreciative of his support but not in need of it. And her sudden openness and uncertainty now brought out every protective instinct he had, urging him to help her in any way that he could.

She dropped her gaze to the remnants of the ice cream, then pushed the bowl away, her craving sated—or maybe her appetite lost.

"I just wish there was a way to be sure he couldn't ever make a claim to my babies."

"Do you have any reason to suspect that he would?"

"No," she admitted. "He was pretty adamant that he wanted nothing to do with another child. I just hate to imagine what might happen if he ever changed his mind."

And Connor hated that she'd just given him leverage to push his own agenda, but that didn't prevent him from using it. "I'm not a lawyer, but I know there's something called a presumption of paternity," he'd told her. "If a man is married to a woman when she gives birth, he is presumed, in the eyes of the law, to be the father. If you want to be sure this guy can't make a claim to your babies, you could marry someone else before they're born and put your husband's name on their birth certificates."

Regan had seemed intrigued by the idea at first, but after another moment of consideration, she'd shaken her head. "I don't think I could trick some hapless guy into marrying me."

"You don't have to trick anyone," Connor had assured her then. "You could marry *me*."

Chapter Eleven

"I was starting to worry that you might have gotten lost," Regan said to Connor, when he returned from his walk the next morning.

Baxter raced over to her chair for the pat on the head that he figured was his due. Then he raced into the living room, no doubt looking for the twins, and upstairs to the master bedroom, where he dropped to the floor to stand guard in his usual position outside the door after finding them.

Connor washed his hands at the sink, then retrieved a mug from the cupboard and filled it with coffee. "I ran into an old friend from high school."

She didn't ask if it was anyone she knew, because there had been little—if any—overlap between their social circles when they were teenagers.

"Do you want me to make you some breakfast?" she asked.

"Mmm…" He sounded intrigued by the offer. "Belgian waffles with fresh berries and powdered sugar would be good."

"You had Belgian waffles at brunch yesterday," she reminded him. "How about scrambled eggs and toast?"

"Eggs and toast sound good, too," he agreed. "But I'll make them."

"I know how to break eggs," she remarked dryly.

"You're also going to be up and down with the twins

all day, so why don't you sit for ten minutes and let me take care of breakfast?"

It sounded perfectly reasonable—considerate, even. And yet, she couldn't help but wonder if this was another example of her husband attempting to ensure that they didn't fall into any kind of usual married couple routines.

"I'm not fragile, Connor."

"I know."

"And I don't need you to take care of me."

"Maybe I want to," he said. "It seems only fair, since you spend so much time taking care of Piper and Poppy."

She shrugged. "In that case, I like my eggs with Tabasco mixed in and cheese melted on top."

He set a frying pan on the stove to heat, then retrieved the necessary ingredients from the fridge.

"I'm sorry about last night," she said, as he whisked the eggs. "Not about what happened—or almost happened—but about the interruption."

"There's no need to apologize." He shook a few drops of Tabasco into the egg mixture and continued whisking. "And anyway, it was probably best that we didn't take things too far."

She frowned at that. "How's that best?"

"Getting intimate would only complicate our situation," he explained, as he dropped bread into the slots of the toaster.

"We're married. Isn't physical intimacy usually a key component of that situation?"

"Except that ours isn't a usual marriage," he reminded her.

"I'll concede that sex usually comes before marriage and children," she said.

He poured the egg mixture into the hot pan. "And you only gave birth two weeks ago," he reminded her.

"What does that have to do with anything?"

"Pregnancy and childbirth take a toll on your body, not just physically but emotionally, and it's going to take some time for your hormone levels to recalibrate and—"

"You're not seriously trying to explain postpartum physiology to me, are you?" she asked, cutting him off.

"Of course not," he denied, as he pushed the eggs around in the pan with the spatula. "I just want you to know that I understand what happened last night wasn't really about us as much as it was a reaction to the emotional stresses of the day."

"Have you been reading my pregnancy and childcare books again?"

"I thought you wanted me to read them."

"To learn about the growth and development of the babies—not about what exercises help strengthen pelvic floor muscles or how long it takes for a uterus to shrink back to its normal size," she told him.

"Kegels, and about a month," he said, as he grated cheese over the eggs.

She huffed out a breath. "Okay, you get a gold star for that. But the implication that what happened last night was about nothing more than hormones is insulting to both of us.

"Maybe I was an idiot for wanting to feel close to my husband," she continued. "But you don't need to worry—it's not likely a mistake I'll make again."

She pushed back her chair as the toast popped up.

Connor transferred the eggs to a plate. "Your breakfast is ready," he said.

"I'm not hungry," she snapped, as she moved past him toward the stairs.

Which, of course, only proved that he was right.

* * *

Regan was just sliding Estela Lopez's chicken pot pie into the oven when her husband got home from work. She'd moved the babies' bassinet into the kitchen so that she could keep an eye on them while she peeled potatoes—which meant that Baxter was close by, too.

Connor offered her a smile when he entered the kitchen, then set a cylindrical tube on the table as he bent to give Baxter a scratch.

He'd made the first overture, and she knew that the next step needed to be hers.

"I'm sorry," she said.

He rose to his full height again and turned to face her, tucking his hands into his front pockets. "Isn't this how our conversation started this morning?" he asked warily.

She poked at the potatoes with a fork, checking them for doneness. "That's why I'm apologizing."

"Should I tell you again that it's not necessary?"

"But it is," she insisted, setting the fork down again and moving away from the heat of the stove. "Once I had some time to calm down and think about what you were saying, I realized that you were trying to be considerate of my feelings—physically and emotionally."

He nodded slowly.

"So I apologize for overreacting and storming out of the room," she said. And though she knew she should leave it at that, she couldn't resist adding, "But I'm still annoyed that you didn't give me credit for knowing my own feelings."

"Then I will apologize for that," he told her. "And, since we're clearing the air…"

She looked up, waiting for him to continue.

But instead of saying anything else, he pulled her close and kissed her.

It happened so fast—or maybe the move was just so completely unexpected—that she wasn't sure how to respond.

The touch of his mouth, warm and firm, wiped all thought from her mind. Desire tightened in her belly, then slowly unfurled like a ribbon, spreading from her center to the tips of her fingers and toes and every part in between. Just as she started to melt against him, he lifted his mouth from hers and took a deliberate step back.

She caught her bottom lip, still tingling from his kiss, in her teeth and lifted her gaze to his.

"What—" She cleared her throat. "What was that about?"

"I didn't want there to be any doubt about my attraction to you."

"Point taken," she told him.

He nodded. "Good. Also—" he picked up the tube again "—I have a peace offering."

"It doesn't look like flowers or jewelry," she noted, trying to match his casual tone though her insides were all tangled up from his kiss.

"I think it's something you'll like much better."

"Now my curiosity is definitely piqued."

He lifted the cap off the tube and pulled out—

"The blueprints for the kitchen?" she guessed.

He nodded.

He'd shown her the plans a few months earlier, when she'd lamented the sorry state of the kitchen cabinets after one of the doors almost came off its hinges in her hand. Apparently he did aspire to a cooking and eating space that was more than functional, but the price tag of a major renovation had forced him to delay implementing his plans.

"But...you said you couldn't afford to make any big

changes right now," she said, hating to remind him of the fact.

"Because I couldn't, but Deacon paid me back for his tuition when his scholarship came through, and now I can."

"I'd say that scholarship was a stroke of luck, but I have no doubt Deacon earned it through hard work rather than good fortune."

Connor busied himself unrolling the papers. "He's always been a good student—diligent and conscientious."

"And it paid off," she said.

"So it would seem," he agreed.

"I know I've said it before, but I'd be happy to—"

"No," he interrupted.

"But I could easily—"

"No," he cut her off again.

Regan huffed out a breath. "Why are you being so bullheaded about this?"

"Because I don't want you to think that I married you for your money."

"The prenup you insisted on made that perfectly clear."

"Good." He nodded again, indicating that the subject was closed. "But there is one other thing we need to discuss."

"What's that?" She dumped the potatoes into a colander to drain the water, then returned them to the pot and added butter and milk.

"If we're going to move ahead with the renovations, you can't stay here," he told her.

She frowned as he retrieved the masher from the utensil holder and took the pot from her to finish the potatoes.

"Why not?"

"Because it's not healthy for you and the babies to be living in a construction zone."

"Where are we supposed to go?" she asked.

"The easiest solution would probably be Miners' Pass." He added salt and pepper to the pot.

"You want me to take Piper and Poppy and move back to my parents' place?"

"Only temporarily," he said.

"Now I have to wonder if your impulsive decision to renovate is about updating the kitchen or putting some distance between us."

"Maybe both," he acknowledged.

"Well, at least you're honest."

Maybe he was right. Maybe the forced proximity during Brielle's visit had stirred up something that would have been better left alone. And maybe a couple of weeks apart would be good for them—with the added benefit that she would come home to a new kitchen.

"So which plan are you going with?" she asked. "The one with the walk-in pantry or the one with the island?"

"Which one do you want?"

"You're letting me choose?"

"It's your kitchen, too," he reminded her.

"I want the island," she immediately responded. Then reconsidered. "But the walk-in pantry is a really nice feature, too."

"I thought you'd say that." He gestured to the blueprints, encouraging her to look at them again.

It was then that she noticed there were now *three* sets of plans.

"I asked Kevin to come up with a new design that incorporated all of the elements you seemed to like best from the first two plans."

She moved for a closer look. "Oh, Connor...this is perfect!"

"And now you know my decision to renovate wasn't

as impulsive as you think. In fact, the cabinets should be ready next week, which means these ones need to be ripped out this weekend so the tile people can come on Monday."

She threw her arms around him. "Okay. I'll take the babies to my parents' house," she agreed, because she definitely didn't want their newborn lungs breathing in construction dust and paint fumes. "But I want to help. What can I do?"

"You can pick out the paint."

She was tempted to roll her eyes but managed to restrain herself, because she did like the idea of choosing the color for the walls. And they'd need a new covering for the window—maybe a California-style shutter to replace the roll-up bamboo shade that she suspected had been put in place by the original owners.

The plans called for slate-colored floor tiles, glossy white cabinets with stainless-steel handles and countertops of dark gray granite with blue flecks. She could already picture the finished room with cobalt blue and sunny yellow accents.

"And maybe I can get new dishes for the new kitchen," she said.

"What's wrong with my dishes?"

"Aside from the fact that they're *your* dishes, I don't think there are any two plates or bowls that match."

"Who cares if they match?" He immediately read her response to that question in her expression. "Okay, if you want new dishes for your new kitchen, you can buy new dishes."

"And glasses and cutlery?"

"And glasses and cutlery," he confirmed.

She narrowed her gaze. "Why are you suddenly letting me do this?"

"Because you're right—everything in this kitchen, in this house, was here before you moved in, when it was *my* house. Now it's *our* house, and I want you to do whatever you need to do to feel as if it's your home, too."

"That makes me feel a little bit better about the fact that you're kicking me out of *our* house for the next couple of weeks," she said.

"You wanted the new kitchen," he reminded her.

"Then I guess the lesson to be learned from this is that I shouldn't give up hope of getting what I want." She leaned across the counter and brushed her lips over his. "A lesson I will definitely keep in mind."

With a light step and smug smile, she moved away to take the casserole out of the oven, making Connor suspect that she wasn't only thinking about the kitchen renovation.

It felt strange to be back in her parents' house again.

Though she'd lived there for three years prior to marrying Connor and moving in with him, the mansion had never felt like home. It was an impressive structure built with meticulous attention by reputable craftsmen, the interior professionally finished and elaborately decorated with no expense spared. The result was a stunning presentation suitable to a spread in *Architectural Digest* but lacking any sense of history or feeling of warmth.

She'd set up the portable playpen in the great room, close enough to the fire to ensure the babies wouldn't catch a chill, while she brought in the rest of their things. The housekeeper had helped unload the cases from her trunk and promised to move them upstairs as soon as she had Regan's bed made up. Ordinarily Regan would have insisted on carrying them herself, but as the babies were starting to fuss for their dinner, she was grateful for Greta's help.

She'd finished nursing and had settled them down again when she heard the door from the garage open and the voices of her parents as they came in. From the sound of it, she was the topic of their conversation.

"—she was coming?" Ben asked.

"No," his wife replied. "If I'd known she was coming, I would have told you."

"Maybe it's not her car."

Margaret huffed out a breath. "Of course it's her car."

"Hi, Mom. Hi, Dad," she called out.

Her mother's heels clicked on the marble tile as she drew nearer.

Margaret stopped abruptly and pivoted to look at her husband. "I told you this would happen."

"Let's not jump to conclusions," Ben cautioned.

"What do you think happened?" Regan asked curiously.

Her mother waved a hand at the pile of bags and baby paraphernalia beside the door—the size of which had already been reduced by half by the diligent efforts of the housekeeper.

"Obviously you've left your husband. Not that I'm surprised, really, except maybe by the fact that the marriage lasted a whole six months."

"Please, Mom. Don't hold back—tell me what you really think."

"I'm sorry," Margaret said, not sounding sorry at all. "But if you'd bothered to talk to me before running off and getting married, I would have told you that you were making a mistake and you wouldn't be in this mess right now."

"I didn't leave my husband, and I'm not in a mess,"

Regan told her, speaking slowly and carefully so as not to reveal the hurt and disappointment elicited by her mother's assumptions. "The only mess is going to be in our kitchen, while Connor oversees the renovations. He suggested that I bring Piper and Poppy here for a couple of weeks so that we're not living in a construction zone."

There was a moment of stilted silence as her parents digested the information.

"Well, what was I supposed to think?" Margaret demanded without apology.

"I don't know," Regan admitted. "But I didn't expect you would immediately jump to the conclusion that my marriage had fallen apart."

"You might have called first to let someone know your plans," Ben suggested, his effort to smooth over the tension clearly placing the blame at Regan's feet.

"I did," she said. "I talked to Celeste."

"Has Greta made up your room?" Margaret asked.

"She said that she would," Regan replied. "But I can probably stay at Crooked Creek with Spencer and Kenzie, if you'd prefer."

"Don't be silly," her mother chided. "You don't want to be out in the middle of nowhere. Not to mention that we've got a lot more room for you and the twins here."

Regan nodded, because the latter statement at least was true. As for being out in the middle of nowhere—right now she wanted to be anywhere but here, but she wasn't foolish enough to bundle up her babies and pack up all their stuff again just because her feelings were hurt.

"I'll let Celeste know she can put dinner on the table," Margaret said now.

"She didn't mean anything by it," Ben said, when his wife had gone.

Regan just shook her head. "I don't understand. I thought you were happy that I married Connor."

"Under the circumstances, it seemed the best course of action," he said.

The circumstances being that she was pregnant, and they'd assumed—because she'd let them—that Connor was the father of her babies.

"He's a good man," Regan said now. "And I wouldn't have married him if I didn't believe we could make our marriage work."

He nodded. "I'm glad to hear it."

"And he's a wonderful father."

"Anyone who's ever seen him with your babies would agree with that," Ben assured her.

It was only later, when she was alone upstairs in her bed, that she wondered about his reference to Piper and Poppy as "her" babies.

Was it possible that her father knew more about her relationship with Connor than she'd told him?

"Damn, the house is quiet."

Connor didn't realize he'd spoken aloud until Baxter lifted his head off his paws and whined in agreement. He didn't believe the dog actually understood what he was saying, but he suspected his canine companion was responding to the regret in his tone.

"Maybe I didn't think this through enough," he acknowledged with a sigh. "I wanted to get the kitchen done because it seemed to mean a lot to Regan, but I also figured it would be easier to keep my hands off her if she was out of the house." He shook his head. "I just didn't expect it to feel so empty without her."

Baxter belly-shuffled closer, so that he was at his master's feet. Connor reached down and patted the dog's head.

Baxter immediately rolled over, exposing his belly for a rub.

Connor laughed and obliged. "Just like old times, huh? Just you and me?"

The dog whined again.

"It wasn't so bad back then, was it? At least we got to sleep through the night without being awakened by babies wanting to be fed or changed."

The dog looked at him with soulful eyes, clearly unconvinced.

"Okay, yeah. Maybe it didn't seem so bad back then because we didn't know anything different."

Baxter lowered his chin onto the top of Connor's foot.

"I'll get to work on the kitchen first thing in the morning," he promised. "Because the sooner I get started, the sooner I can finish, and Regan and Piper and Poppy can come home."

Chapter Twelve

Connor had just poured his first cup of coffee—not decaf but the real stuff, which he'd snuck into the house after a string of sleep-deprived nights made it almost impossible to keep his eyes open during the day—when there was a knock at the door.

"We've got an early-morning visitor," he said to Baxter, who was already jumping up at the front door.

"None of that," he said, giving the hand signal for sit.

The dog sat, though his body fairly vibrated with suppressed energy.

Connor unlocked and pulled open the door, surprised to see his boss on the other side of the threshold. "Good morning, Sheriff."

"Reid," he said, confirming that he wasn't at the door for any kind of official business. "I heard you talking to Kowalski about a demolition project you're tackling this weekend and thought maybe you could use a hand."

"Your wife doesn't have a list of chores for you at home?" Connor asked, opening the door wider to let him in.

"There's always a list," Reid said, and grinned at the dog sitting but not at all patiently inside the foyer.

He offered his hand for the dog to sniff, which Baxter did and gave his approval with a lick. The sheriff chuckled and scratched him under the chin.

"But Katelyn took Tessa out to the Circle G for a visit,"

Reid explained. "So she's not home today to remind me about all the things on the list."

Connor led the way to the kitchen. "So you came here to help with my list instead?"

"Tearing things apart is always more fun than putting them back together," Reid noted. "Although I have to say, it seems like an odd time to be tackling kitchen renovations—barely three weeks after the birth of twin daughters."

"Yeah," Connor agreed. He found another coffee mug in one of the boxes that he'd used to empty the cabinets and held it up, a silent question.

Reid nodded.

"But Regan would argue that updating the space is twenty years overdue," Connor continued, as he filled the second mug. "Notwithstanding the fact that I've only owned the house for three."

"Katelyn wouldn't move into our new place until all the work we wanted to do had been done. Thankfully, most of it was cosmetic."

"This is going to be a complete overhaul," Connor told him.

"You want to salvage the cabinets?" Reid asked.

He shook his head. "Not worth salvaging. Everything's going in the Dumpster."

"That will speed things up considerably," Reid said.

What also sped things up considerably was having an extra body pitching in. By the time they broke for lunch—Connor popped out to pick up Jo's Pizza—all of the top cabinets and half of the bottom had been removed and hauled out to the Dumpster.

As Connor closed the lid on the empty pizza box, the sheriff's phone chimed to indicate a message.

"Kate texted me a picture of Tessa with Ava, Max

and Sam," Reid said, turning his phone around so Connor could see the screen. "Tessa absolutely adores the triplets and is constantly asking to go see the babies. In fact, I think her favorite word now is *babies*. Although her first word was *Da-da*," he added, with a grin.

"Does it make you think about giving her a brother or sister?" Connor wondered.

"Sure," Reid agreed, as he tucked his phone away again. "But Katelyn's not yet on board with that plan. In all fairness, that might be because she tackles most of the childcare responsibilities. I've been encouraging her to check out the new daycare, but she insists that Tessa's too young to be left with strangers."

"A valid consideration," Connor noted, tugging his work gloves on again. "Though not a choice all parents can make."

Reid nodded. "But getting back to your question, yeah, I think Tessa would benefit from having a sibling."

"It is a unique bond," Connor noted. "Though I'll be the first to admit, I was a little panicked about the prospect of twins—"

"Especially twin girls, I'd bet," the sheriff interjected.

"You'd be right," Connor agreed. "But now I can appreciate how lucky Piper and Poppy are to have one another."

"They are lucky," Reid remarked. "I was an only child, so I didn't grow up with the benefit of knowing there was someone else who would always have my back. Of course, Katelyn had a sister and two brothers, so she wished sometimes that she was an only child."

Connor chuckled at that. "Well, there were eight years between me and Deacon, so that likely helped minimize any sibling rivalry."

"Speaking of—is your brother coming home for the summer?"

He nodded. "He was hoping to land a job in New York, something in the legal field for experience to add to his résumé, but nothing panned out."

"Katelyn's practice is growing like crazy, and she's been talking about wanting to hire a junior lawyer to help with research and case prep," Reid said. His wife was widely regarded as one of the top attorneys in the area and, as a result, her services were in great demand. "You should tell him to send his résumé to her."

"Deacon's hardly a junior lawyer," Connor pointed out. "He's only just finishing his first year of law school."

"First year at Columbia," his boss clarified. "That seems to me a pretty good recommendation right there."

"Well, he's obviously smarter than me, or I would have waited to tackle this renovation until he was home to help."

"On the other hand, there are certain therapeutic benefits of physical labor, which I'm sure you can appreciate right now."

Connor paused with the sledgehammer on his shoulder. "You're not really asking about my sex life, are you?"

"I don't need to ask," Reid told him. "I've been there. And I swear, those six weeks postpartum while we waited for the doctor to give us the green light were the longest six weeks of my life."

Six weeks?

Connor and Regan had been married for more than *six months* and hadn't even consummated their marriage— not that he had any intention of admitting that to his boss.

Instead, he responded by lifting the sledgehammer off his shoulder and heaving it at the wall marked to come down.

The plaster cracked and the sheriff laughed.

* * *

By her third day at Miners' Pass, most of the sting of her mother's words had faded, allowing Regan to acknowledge that it wasn't a horrible place to wait out the renovations. She didn't see much of her parents, who always went to the office early and came home late, but Celeste and Greta were more than happy to help with anything she needed or even just spend some time cuddling with the babies when they had nothing else to do.

But Monday was Celeste's grocery shopping day, so Regan had decided to go into town, too. She'd only been back a little while when Greta escorted a visitor to the great room, where Regan spent most of her time hanging out during the day.

"What are you doing here?" she asked, as pleased as she was surprised to see her husband.

"I came by to see if you've picked a paint color yet."

"As a matter of fact, I have." She reached into the side pocket of the diaper bag that was always close at hand and pulled out an assortment of paint chips. "I finally tried out that twin baby carrier we got from Alyssa and Jason, and Piper and Poppy had a great time being carted around the hardware store." She fanned out the samples, looking for the one she'd marked, then plucked it out of the pile and offered it to him. "Are you prepping to paint already?"

"Not even close," he admitted.

She lifted a brow. "So why are you really here?"

He shoved the paint chip in his back pocket without even looking at it. "Because I missed you."

"Oh." She felt an unexpected little flutter in her belly.

"Even with all the hammering and banging going on, I find myself listening for the familiar sounds of Piper and Poppy waking up or growing restless," he told her.

"You miss the babies," she realized, as the flutter faded away.

"I miss all of you," he clarified. "I miss the scent of your shampoo in the bathroom in the morning, the sound of your humming in the kitchen and the way your smile shines in your eyes."

And the flutter was back.

But still, she felt compelled to point out: "I don't hum."

He smiled. "Yeah, you do."

"And if you miss me, it's your own fault," she said. "Because you sent me away."

"I didn't know how empty the house was going to feel without you."

"You still have Baxter."

"He misses you as much as I do," he told her. "And a moping dog isn't very good company."

"You could bring him with you for a visit sometime," she said.

He looked pointedly at the cream-colored suede furniture on the ivory carpet and shook his head. "I don't think so."

"Then maybe I'll bring Piper and Poppy to your place—"

"*Our* place," he reminded her.

"—and take him out for a walk one day."

"He'd love that," Connor said. "But are you sure you can manage two babies and a dog?"

"With the twin carrier, I can," she assured him. "And speaking of the twins, I'm guessing you'd like to see them."

He grinned. "Well, I have no intention of leaving until I do."

She took his hand and led him upstairs. "Not because I want you to leave," she assured him. Piper and Poppy were sharing her former bedroom, where she'd taken up temporary residence again, and were snuggled together in the bassinet near the head of her bed. On the other side of the room was a rocking chair that Greta had brought up for the new mom.

Connor stood for a long moment, just looking at the sleeping babies. "I swear they've grown in the past three days." Though he whispered the remark, Piper stirred as if she'd heard and recognized her daddy's voice.

"Considering how often they're eating, I wouldn't be surprised," Regan told him. "But they're sleeping a little bit longer now. Last night it was almost five hours."

"Have they been asleep for long now?" he asked.

"I think what you really want to know is, are they going to be waking up soon?"

"Are they?"

She lifted a shoulder. "New moms who have their three-week-old babies on any kind of schedule are obviously better moms than me."

He shook his head. "There is no better mom than you."

"And that's why I'm going to risk breaking the rule about not disturbing a sleeping baby," she said, reaching down and gently lifting Piper out of the bassinet.

"But the books—"

"I'm going to hide those books from you," she said, gesturing toward the rocking chair.

He sat down and she transferred Piper to him, then went back to the bassinet for Poppy.

"They've had their baths already today," he noted.

"Maybe it's the scent of *their* shampoo that you remember," she teased.

"I can remember more than one scent," he told her. "Your shampoo smells like apples."

Poppy exhaled a quiet sigh and snuggled closer to her daddy's chest. Piper yawned.

"I think they missed you, too," Regan said quietly.

"I could sit here like this for hours," he said. "But that isn't going to get the new drywall taped and mudded."

"You're doing that yourself?"

He nodded. "It's not hard work, just messy, and it cuts down on the cost of labor."

"And you're going to tackle that tonight?"

"I'm going to get started anyway, as soon as I figure out what I'm doing for food."

"You could stay and have dinner with me," she suggested. "You know Celeste always makes enough for unexpected guests."

"I didn't come here to beg a meal," he assured her. "But it would be nice to eat something that wasn't Wheaties."

"Your dinner plan was Wheaties?"

"No, but I probably would have ended up eating Wheaties because I didn't have a dinner plan. And because I don't have a stove," he said, reminding her that the appliances had been taken out of the kitchen along with everything else.

"Then this is your lucky day," Regan said. "Because Celeste has a box of Frosted Flakes in the cupboard."

"Frosted Flakes are more a dessert than a main course."

"Beggars can't be choosers," she said.

Connor knew she was only teasing in quoting the old proverb, but there was something about being in this house that made him feel like a beggar—though he suspected a vagrant would never get past the housekeeper at the front door.

His mother, a big admirer of Eleanor Roosevelt, would

have pointed out that no one could make him feel unworthy without his consent. He knew it was true, that his insecurities said more about him than anyone else. And Regan had never said or done anything to indicate that she thought any less of him because he was "that no-good Neal boy" from "the wrong side of the tracks."

So he shook off the unease and carefully settled Piper and Poppy back in their bassinet, then followed his wife downstairs again and into the kitchen.

"Connor's going to stay for dinner," Regan said to the cook, who was drizzling caramel sauce over the top of a pie.

"And dessert," he added.

"You like pecan pie?" Celeste guessed.

"I like everything you make," he assured her.

She set the pie aside and reached into the cupboard for two plates. "It'll just take me a minute to set the table."

"The kitchen table is fine," Regan said, pulling open a drawer to retrieve cutlery.

"You know how your parents feel about eating in the kitchen," Celeste chided.

"I do, and since they're not going to be home for dinner, we'd like to eat in the kitchen—with you."

"You can eat wherever you like," the cook agreed. "But I'm having dinner in my room with *Top Chef.*"

"This is the first you've mentioned wanting to watch a cooking show tonight," Regan remarked.

"Because I didn't want you to have to eat your dinner alone. Since you now have the company of your handsome husband, you won't miss mine."

"Did you hear that?" Connor said to his wife. "She thinks I'm handsome."

"Just about handsome enough for my beautiful girl," Celeste confirmed.

"That's me," Regan told him.

The cook chuckled. "Now you two sit down and enjoy your dinner," she said, as she filled their plates with crispy honey garlic chicken, roasted potatoes and steamed broccoli.

Connor and Regan lingered over the meal, discussing all manner of topics.

"I'm doing all the talking," Connor realized, when his plate was half empty.

"Because your life is so much more interesting than mine right now," she told him. "You have an exciting job, a construction project underway and a faithful canine companion at home. My days are taken up by two admittedly adorable infants who eat, sleep, pee and poop—not necessarily in that order."

He chuckled, but then his expression turned serious. "Do you miss work?"

"Not yet," she said. "Right now I'm so tired out from keeping up with Piper and Poppy that the idea of going into the office and trying to make sense of numbers makes my head hurt."

She frowned as she lifted her glass of water to her lips. "But now that I think about it, there was a weird message on my voice mail the other day from one of the junior accountants at work. I haven't had a chance to call him back yet, but Travis's message said something about a scholarship fund."

The delicious chicken dinner suddenly felt like a lead weight in Connor's stomach. "He shouldn't be bothering you with trivial inquiries when you're on mat leave," he said. "Isn't there someone else who can answer his questions?"

"My father, probably," she said.

"Then you should let your father deal with it."

She nodded. "Yeah. When I get a chance to call Travis back, I'll tell him to talk to my dad."

"Or tell your dad about the call," he suggested. "And let him handle it."

"That's another option," she agreed.

He pushed his chair away from the table and stood up to clear away their plates.

"I suppose you want that pie now?" Regan asked.

"Actually, I didn't realize how late it was getting to be," he said. "If I want to make any progress with that drywall tonight, I should probably be heading out."

"You could take a slice with you," she offered. "We won't call it a doggy bag, so you won't feel obligated to share it with Baxter."

"I'd love to," he said. "It'll be my reward for getting the first layer of mud done."

She found a knife and cut a thick wedge of pie, which she slid into a plastic container. Just as she snapped the lid on, a soft, plaintive cry came through the baby monitor on the table.

"Well, we actually got through a meal without interruption," she said.

"It was a great meal," he said. "Thanks for asking me to stay."

"Thanks for stopping by." She started to walk with him to the door, but even he could tell that the cries were growing louder and more insistent. She folded an arm across her chest, her cheeks suddenly turning pink. "Letdown."

And because he'd read the books, he knew what that meant. "You better go see to the babies."

She nodded and turned to hurry up the stairs.

Connor was admittedly sorry that he hadn't had the chance to steal a goodbye kiss, but at the moment he had more pressing concerns. And a call to his father-in-law was at the top of the list.

When the two men had struck their deal, Connor hadn't given any thought to the possibility that Regan—Blake Mining's CFO—might question why a check written by her father from a company account had been deposited into an account with her husband's brother's name on it. So he hoped like hell Ben Channing had given the matter some thought—and had a credible explanation ready for his daughter if one was required.

Chapter Thirteen

Detouring to Miners' Pass became part of Connor's routine over the next couple of weeks. He never stayed long, as he was anxious to get back to work on the kitchen so that Regan and the twins could come home. But it was always worth the trip, just to spend a few minutes with them—with the added benefit of a fabulous meal that beat any kind of takeout.

He was usually gone before Regan's parents got home from the office. It seemed a shame to him that they'd spent so much money to build a beautiful home that was empty most of the time, but he got the impression that the display of wealth was almost more important to Margaret than the enjoyment of it.

In any event, he didn't mind not crossing paths with Ben and Margaret—no doubt at least in part because of his own guilt with respect to the secret he was keeping from his wife. No matter how many times Connor tried to reassure himself that the money Ben Channing had put up for Deacon's scholarship had nothing to do with his relationship with Regan, he knew it wasn't really true.

There would have been no scholarship if he hadn't convinced Regan to marry him, and lately, he'd found himself wishing that he'd never entered into any sort of agreement with his now father-in-law. He didn't regret his marriage to Regan. He just wished the exchange of vows had happened for different reasons.

"You're rather introspective tonight," she noted.

"Sorry," he said. "I was just making a mental list of a few last things that I need to pick up at the hardware store on the way home."

"Does *a few last things* mean that the renovation is almost complete?"

He nodded. "Fingers crossed, you'll be able to see the completed project on Saturday."

"You've made a lot of progress in two weeks, then," she said.

"I had a powerful incentive."

Regan smiled. "I can't wait to see it."

"You really haven't checked on the progress at all?"

He found it hard to believe that she hadn't even peeked when she'd come by the house, as she'd done a few times, to take Baxter for walks in the middle of the day. He had all entrances to the kitchen area blocked off with plastic to keep the dust and debris contained, but it would be easy enough to pull back the plastic and take a look. He'd taken pictures to document the progress, but she'd insisted that she didn't want to see those, either, until after.

She shook her head now in response to his question. "I was tempted," she admitted. "But I decided I'd rather wait."

"Well, I think you're going to be pleased. And Baxter is going to be so excited when you come home—the house has been so empty without you."

"Remember you said that," Regan teased. "Because we'll all likely be tripping over one another when your brother comes home."

"It won't be so bad," Connor said. "Especially as he has a full-time job for the summer."

"Where's he going to be working?"

"At Katelyn Davidson's law office."

"That's great," she said.

Her enthusiasm seemed genuine, prompting him to ask, "You don't mind that he's going to be spending his days with your archenemy."

"Archenemy?" she echoed, amused. "Am I a comic book character now?"

"Hmm…now that you mention it, I wouldn't mind seeing you in a spandex jumpsuit."

"Not going to happen," she assured him.

"Disappointing," he said. "But I was only referring to the history between the Blakes and the Gilmores."

"There's some bad blood there, as a result of which I can't imagine ever being best friends with a Gilmore," Regan acknowledged. "But it has nothing to do with me or Katelyn, even if she was a Gilmore before she married the sheriff."

"What about your sister and Liam?" he asked.

She seemed taken aback by the question. "Why would you ask that?"

"The way she reacted to the mention of his name when you were talking about the inn, I got the impression there might be some history there."

"No." She shook her head. "There's no history between Brie and Liam."

"Brie and Caleb, then," he guessed.

"So when is Deacon coming home?" she asked.

It was hardly a subtle effort to shift the topic of conversation, but Connor obliged. "His last exam is May ninth, and he flies back on the tenth."

"I'm sure he's eager to get home."

"And excited to meet his nieces," Connor told her.

"I'm glad you think so," Regan said. "Because I was hoping we could ask him to be Piper and Poppy's godfather."

"Really?"

She nodded. "Brie was the obvious choice for god-mother, because she's my only sister, and since Deacon is your only brother, well, it just made sense to me. What do you think?"

"I think it's a great idea," he agreed.

"Then the next order of business is to actually sched-ule a date for the baptism."

"You can work that out with your sister," he said. "Just tell me when and where."

She nodded. "And you should be forewarned—my parents have already said they'd like to have a party here after the event."

"You say that as if you expect me to object," he noted.

"I just thought we should do something for our daugh-ters at our house."

"Which I wouldn't object to, either," he assured her. "But your parents have a lot more space—especially if the party had to be moved indoors."

"They also have Celeste," she realized.

"Well, yeah."

"I think she's the real reason you want to have the party here, because you know she'll be in charge of the food."

"That might have been a consideration," he allowed.

She grinned. "In which case I will say, you're a very smart man, Connor Neal."

"What's going on here?" Regan asked, sidling between a vacant stool at the bar and the one upon which her hus-band was seated.

It was Friday—the day before the big unveiling he'd promised—so she'd been understandably surprised to get the call from the owner of Diggers' Bar & Grill revealing that Connor was at the bar. Duke had asked if she could pick up her husband because he was in no condition to drive home and he didn't trust the deputy would be able to find his way if he walked.

"We're shelebrating."

She looked pointedly from the empty stool on her side to the trio of vacant seats on his other side. "We?"

"Well, everyone elsh is gone now."

Duke carried a steaming carafe of coffee over to top up the cup on the bar in front of Connor.

"He didn't have a lot to drink," the bartender said, shaking his head. "I've never known a grown man who was such a lightweight."

"How much isn't a lot?" she asked.

"Two beers, and then a couple of shots. It was the shots that seemed to do him in."

"Well, you said it," agreed Regan. "He's not much of a drinker."

And knowing that he grew up with a stepfather who got angry and belligerent when he was drunk, she understood why.

She turned her attention back to her husband. "What were you celebrating?"

"Kowalshki's gettin' married."

"That's happy news—and a good reason to celebrate," Regan acknowledged.

"Everyone was goin' for drinks," he explained. "I couldn't say no."

"Of course not," she agreed. "Though next time you might want to say no to the shots."

"Damn Shack Daniels."

She bit back a smile and looked at the bartender again. "Has he paid his tab?"

"Sheriff took care of it," Duke said.

She nodded and nudged her hip against Connor's thigh. "Let's get you home."

He put his feet on the ground, then reached out to grasp the edge of the bar to steady himself.

"You are a lightweight, aren't you?" she mused.

"Tired," he said. "Didn't sleep mush last night. Wanted to get the kitshen done."

She took his arm to guide him to the door. "Is it done?"

He nodded. "Celeste gave me a reshipee so I could make dinner for you tomorrow."

"A nice idea," she said, touched that he would want to cook the first meal for her in the new kitchen. "But maybe we should wait and see how hungover you are in the morning before we make any plans."

"You can come home now," he said.

"I'm taking you home right now," she promised, opening the passenger-side door of her SUV for him.

He folded himself into the seat, then turned to look behind him. "Where's the girls?"

"At my parents' place."

"Your parents are lookin' after them?"

She snorted. "I'd have to be drunker than you are to let that happen."

He frowned, clearly not understanding.

"Celeste is looking after them."

"Ahh." He nodded. "Celeste took care of you when you were a baby."

"Celeste still takes care of me—of all of us," Regan said.

"I wish we had a Celeste."

"My parents offered to pay her salary and have her help us out for a year," she reminded him.

"Your father thinks he can buy anything...or anyone."

She frowned at the bitter edge underlying the muttered words. "What are you talking about?"

"Nothin'."

"It sounded like something to me."

But he'd closed his eyes, and he didn't say anything else until they were almost home. "I have a 'feshun to make."

She turned into the driveway. "Is it something you're going to regret telling me when you're sober?" she wondered.

"I didn't jus' marry you to give your babies a father," he confided.

She turned off the ignition. "So why did you marry me?"

"I've hadda crush on you sinch high shcool."

"High school?" she echoed, surprised. "We barely knew each other in high school."

"You don't remember." He slapped a hand against his chest. "I'm wounded."

"I have no doubt your head is going to feel wounded in the morning," she told him. "But what is it you think I don't remember?"

"Twelfth grade calculus."

She got out of the car and went around to the passenger side to help him do the same. "I remember," she assured him. "I tutored you during lunch period on Tuesdays and Thursdays, and sometimes after school on Wednesdays."

"I got an A. Well, an A-minus, acshally, but I figured it counted."

"I know. You offered to take me out for ice cream to celebrate."

He nodded, paying careful attention to the steps as he climbed them. "But you had plans with Brett Tanner. Goin' to see 'Bill & Ted's Exshellent Avenshure.'"

She paused with her key in the lock. "How could you possibly remember such a trivial detail after so many years?"

"I hated Brett Tanner," he said. "Or maybe I jus' hated that you liked him."

She opened the door and hit the light switch inside.

Baxter, waiting—as always—on the other side of the door, gave a happy bark and danced around them in circles.

Regan fussed over the dog for a minute while Connor struggled to take off his boots. When he'd finally accomplished that task, she followed him up the stairs.

Apparently he'd resumed sleeping in the master bedroom after she'd gone, because he headed in that direction and collapsed on top of the mattress.

"Don't fall asleep just yet," she warned.

"'kay."

She went across the hall to the bathroom, returning with a cup of water and a couple of Tylenol. "Sit up and take these."

He eased himself into sitting position against the headboard. She dropped the tablets in his hand, then gave him the cup. He tossed back the pills and drank down the water.

She took the empty cup back to the bathroom and refilled it, then set it on the table beside the bed.

"Are you going to get under those covers or sleep on top of them?" she asked.

"You sleep with me?"

"Not tonight," she said. "I need to get back to our babies."

"Pretty babies," he said. "Jus' like their mama."

"You're talkative when you're drunk," she mused. "I'll have to remember that."

"I don't get drunk," he denied. "No more'n two beers—" he held up two fingers and squinted at them as if he wasn't quite sure it was the right number "—ever."

"You should have told that to your pal Shack Daniels."

He shook his head. "Not my pal."

She really did need to get back to Piper and Poppy, but she was curious about something he'd said earlier. She perched on the edge of the mattress and said, "What does your high school crush have to do with your proposal?"

"I finally got the mos' pop'lar girl in shcool to go out with me."

"I wasn't the most popular girl," she denied. "In fact, I hardly dated in high school." Because even as a teenager, she'd been focused on getting into a good college and earning a degree so that she could go to work with her parents at Blake Mining.

"You were tight with Brett Tanner."

"Not as tight as he wanted people to think," she confided.

"It doesn' matter. You lived in one of the biggest houses in town…an' I was a loser from the wrong shide of the tracks."

"You were never a loser," she said, shocked that he could ever have thought so little of himself. "And that expression—the wrong side of the tracks—never made any sense to me. Especially considering that the trains stopped running through Haven more than fifty years ago."

"But people still 'member where they ran."

"For what it's worth, I thought you were kind of cute back in high school," she confided.

"Cute?" he echoed.

"All my friends did, too," she told him.

"Cute?" he said again, as if the word was somehow distasteful.

"But in an edgy kind of way," she said. "Of course, bad boys have always been the downfall of good girls."

"An' you were the goodest of the good girls, weren't you?"

"I was a rule follower," she acknowledged. "Most of the time, anyway."

"When have you not followed the rules?" he wondered.

"My first date with you."

His brow furrowed, as if he was struggling to remember. "The wedding chapel in Reno?"

She nodded. "Getting married was the craziest thing I'd ever done on a first date."

"Prob'ly mine, too."

"Only probably?"

"I'm a bad boy, 'member?"

She took the throw from the rocking chair and draped it over him. "You keep telling yourself that."

"But it was defin'ly—" his eyes drifted shut "—my best first date ever."

She waited until she was sure he was asleep, then she leaned over and touched her lips to his forehead. "Mine, too."

"You don't look any the worse for wear," Regan remarked when Connor came outside to greet her the next day.

"I figured it was too much to hope that you'd let me forget about last night."

"Actually, I'm curious to know how much you remember."

"All of it." He opened the back door of her SUV and reached inside to unclip Piper's car seat, then he went around to the other side and did the same to Poppy's. "I think. After a handful of Tylenol and a gallon of water this morning, my head stopped pounding enough for the memories to become clearer."

She hefted the diaper bag onto her shoulder and followed him into the house.

Baxter could barely contain his excitement when Connor took the babies into the house. Although Regan had brought the twins with her when she came to take him for his walks, he seemed to sense that this time was different—that they were finally home—and he was in doggy heaven.

"But thank you," Connor said to her now. "Although I'm fairly confident I could have found my own way home last night, I appreciate you coming to get me."

"It was my pleasure," she said.

His gaze narrowed. "And now I'm wondering if there are some gaps in my memory."

"Maybe I'm just happy to be home," she told him. "And eager to see the new kitchen."

"Then I won't make you wait any longer," he said, leading the way.

She'd seen the plans, of course, so she had a general idea of what to expect. She'd approved of the floor tile and cabinet style and granite he'd chosen, but the mental image she'd pieced together in her mind didn't do justice to the final result.

"This is incredible," she said, gliding her fingertips along the beveled edge of the countertop. She opened a cupboard, appreciating the smooth movement of the hinge, and smiled when she saw that the new dishes she'd ordered were stacked neatly inside.

But not all of them.

Two place settings had been set out on the island,

with the shiny new cutlery set on top of sunny-yellow napkins. A bouquet of daffodils was stuffed into a clear vase in the corner.

"You do good work, Deputy."

He looked pleased with the compliment.

"And—do I smell something cooking?"

He nodded. "Chicken with roasted potatoes. Celeste promised it was a foolproof recipe, so if it doesn't taste as good as hers, I'm blaming the new oven."

"Don't you mean she promised it was a foolproof re-shipee?" she teased.

He shook his head. "Are you ever going to let me forget about last night?"

"I won't say another word."

But truthfully, she didn't want to forget about last night—or at least not about the revelation he'd made. Because if it was true that he'd had a crush on her in high school, maybe it wasn't outside the realm of possibility that he might develop real feelings for her now. As she'd developed real feelings for him.

And then maybe, someday, their marriage of convenience would become something more.

Chapter Fourteen

Every detail of The Stagecoach Inn reflected elegance and indulgence, and excited butterflies winged around inside Regan's belly as she checked in at the double pedestal desk. After the formalities were taken care of, she'd been invited to a wine and cheese reception for guests in the library, but she'd opted to explore the main lobby on her own while she waited for her husband to arrive.

She glanced at her watch. 5:58.

Connor was supposed to meet her at six o'clock, but because she'd gotten there early, she'd spent the last twelve minutes pretending she wasn't watching the time. She thought about taking a leisurely stroll down the street, to distract herself for a few minutes, but she didn't trust Connor to wait if he showed up at six o'clock and she wasn't there.

Instead she perched on the edge of a butter leather sofa facing the stone fireplace and pulled her phone out of her pocket to send a brief text message to her sister.

Maybe this was a bad idea.

Brie immediately replied:

Don't u dare chicken out!

I'm not chi

That was as far as she got in typing her reply before Connor stepped through the front door.

She tucked the phone back into her pocket and stood up.

"Hey." He smiled when he saw her, and the curve of his lips somehow managed to reassure her while also releasing a kaleidoscope of butterflies in her belly.

"What's going on?" he asked. "Where are Piper and Poppy?"

"They're at home with the babysitters."

His brows lifted. "We have babysitters?"

She nodded. "Alyssa and Jason thought looking after the twins would give them a crash course in parenting, to help prepare them for the arrival of their own baby."

"Okay, but why are we here?"

"Because it's our anniversary."

He frowned at that. "We got married in September."

"The twenty-sixth," she confirmed. "Which makes today our seven-month anniversary."

"I didn't know that was a thing," he said, sounding worried. "Was I supposed to get you a card? Send flowers?"

She shook her head. "I didn't get you anything, either. This—" she held up an antique key "—is a belated-wedding-slash-early-anniversary gift from my sister."

He swallowed. "She got us a hotel room?"

"The luxury suite," Regan clarified, taking his hand and leading him up the stairs toward their accommodations on the top floor.

"It's a nice idea," he acknowledged, his steps slowing as they approached the second-floor landing. "But..."

She nodded, understanding everything that was implied by that single word. But theirs wasn't a traditional marriage. It wasn't even a *real* marriage. Although she knew that Brie had booked the suite for them in an effort to change that.

"Just come and see the room," she urged.

She'd already checked in and been escorted to the suite by Liam Gilmore, the hotel's owner doing double-duty as bellhop. He'd given her a brief history of the hotel as they climbed to the upper level, a scripted speech that filled what would likely have been an awkward silence otherwise.

She might have made some appropriate comment when he was done, but then he opened the door of the suite and she'd been rendered speechless. The plaque on the wall beside the door identified Wild Bill's Getaway Suite, but everything inside the space screamed luxury and elegance.

The floor of the foyer was covered in an intricate pattern of mosaic tile; the walls were painted a pale shade of gold and set off by wide white trim. Beyond the foyer was a carpeted open-concept sitting area that Liam had called a parlor, with an antique-looking sofa and chaise lounge facing the white marble fireplace over which was mounted an enormous flat-screen TV. Beyond the parlor was the bath, with more white marble, lots of glass and shiny chrome and even a crystal chandelier. On the other side of the bath was the bedroom, which boasted a second fireplace—this one with a dark marble surround, a king-size pediment poster bed flanked by matching end tables, a wide wardrobe and a makeup vanity set with padded stool.

"This is…impressive," Connor said. Then, his tone almost apologetic, he added, "But we can't stay."

"Do you want to explain why to my sister, who prepaid for two nights?" she asked.

"She knows you're nursing Piper and Poppy. It should

be simple enough to explain that you can't be away from them for two days."

"She also knows I've got a pump. And there's enough breast milk in the freezer at home for a week." She'd finally overcome her opposition to occasional bottle feeding after a visit from Macy Clayton—a single mom of triplets—who wanted to reassure Regan that there were other "moms of multiples" out there who could be a great resource when she had questions or concerns about raising her twins. (Coincidentally, Macy was also the manager of the Stagecoach Inn—and dating Liam Gilmore.) Macy had urged Regan not to demand too much of herself and suggested that if her husband was willing to give a baby a bottle, she should let him—and not feel guilty but grateful.

"What about Baxter?"

"Jason promised to walk him twice a day. I even mapped out Baxter's usual route for him."

"But all I've got are the clothes on my back."

"I packed a bag for you," she said. "It's in the bedroom."

"I guess that shoots down all my arguments," Connor acknowledged, sounding more resigned than pleased at the prospect of being alone with his wife.

And Regan was suddenly assailed by doubts, too.

Being married was both easier and harder than she'd anticipated when she'd accepted the deputy's impulsive proposal.

It was easier because Connor had truly become her partner in parenting Piper and Poppy. He obviously adored the two little girls—and the feeling was mutual. Their faces lit up whenever he walked into a room and they happily snuggled against his broad chest to fall asleep, assuring Regan that she couldn't have chosen a better father for her children.

And it was harder because of the deep affection and growing attraction she felt for her husband. She'd agreed to marry Connor because she'd been alone and scared. She hadn't worried that she might fall in love with her husband. In fact, she would have scoffed at the very idea that she could.

But over the past seven months, her awareness had grown and her feelings had changed, and she was hoping that his had, too. However, if she'd harbored any illusions that Connor would be overcome by desire when he found himself in a romantic hotel suite with his wife, his lukewarm response quickly dispelled them.

"Maybe we should go out to grab a bite to eat," he suggested to her now.

"We could go down to The Home Station," she said. "Unless you'd rather have something sent up here?"

"I heard it's next to impossible to get a table in the restaurant."

"Mostly because priority is given to hotel guests," she explained. "When I checked in, they told me to call down to the desk if we wanted to make a reservation."

"Then we should take advantage of that," he decided.

"Or we could take advantage of this luxurious suite," she suggested. "Because the restaurant menu is also available through room service."

He didn't take the hint. "But the restaurant is closer to the kitchen, so the food will be hotter and fresher when it gets to a table down there."

It sounded like a reasonable argument. And it was possible that he wasn't deliberately being obtuse but was simply hungry. Wasn't it?

"In that case, why don't you call down to the desk for a reservation while I go freshen up?" she said.

"Okay," he agreed, sounding relieved.

While he reached for the phone, Regan retreated to the bedroom.

She opened up her suitcase, trying to remember if she'd packed something suitable for a fancy dinner. Truthfully, she hadn't worried too much about what she'd thrown into the case, optimistic that she wasn't going to need a lot of clothes over the next couple of days. She'd been more concerned about ensuring that she had all necessary personal items—including the box of condoms that she'd bought in hopeful anticipation of finally consummating their marriage.

Was she being too subtle? Or was Connor simply not interested? Over the past few weeks, he'd sent so many mixed signals she could hardly figure which way was up. One day he was kissing her senseless, the next he was moving her out of his house. While she was gone, he could hardly stay away from her, but since her return, he'd gone back to sleeping in his brother's room.

Of course, that escape wouldn't be available to him for much longer. Deacon was studying for his final exams now and would be on his way home soon. But that was little consolation to Regan, who didn't want Connor to share her bed out of necessity but choice, and she hated that he seemed to want an escape.

The television came on in the other room.

With a resigned sigh, Regan picked up her phone again and sent another text to her sister.

I'm about to chicken out.

She waited for Brie to reply—and nearly dropped the phone when it rang in her hand.

"Don't you dare," her sister said without preamble when Regan connected the call.

"It's just…maybe it's too soon."

"You've been married seven months," Brie reminded her. "Or do you mean too soon after the babies? Because I thought you said the doctor gave you the thumbs-up."

"She did," Regan confirmed.

"So what's your hesitation?"

"I'm not sure," she admitted. "It just seems like a big step."

"It *is* a big step," her sister agreed.

"And if we have sex…it's going to change everything."

"Don't you want things to change?"

"Some things," she acknowledged.

"Such as the fact that you're not having sex with your husband?"

She sighed. "Okay, yes. But we've actually got a pretty good relationship otherwise."

"Just think about how much better it will be when you add naked fun to the mix," her sister urged.

"Maybe that's the part that's holding me back," she said.

"You're opposed to having fun?" Brie teased.

"I meant the naked part," Regan clarified.

"Well, it's been a long time since I've had sex," her sister offered. "But as I recall, it's easier without clothes on."

"You seem to be forgetting that I had two babies four and a half weeks ago."

"I'm not forgetting anything. The whole point of getting you out of the house was to ensure that my adorable nieces wouldn't put a damper on your love life—at least not this weekend."

"The babies have hardly put a damper on our love life," Regan assured her.

"Only because you don't have one…yet."

"I guess that's what I get for telling you the truth," she muttered.

"Or at least part of the truth."

"What do you think I left out?"

"How much you care about your husband," Brie suggested.

"Of course I care about him," Regan said.

"And that you're seriously attracted to him," her sister added.

"He's a good man with a lot of attractive qualities," she admitted.

"And a smokin'-hot body," Brie noted.

That gave her pause. "You checked out my husband?"

"I needed to be sure he was worthy of my sister."

Regan sighed. "What am I going to do?"

"Your smokin'-hot husband?" her sister suggested.

She choked on a laugh. "If only it were that simple."

"It's only complicated because you're making it complicated," Brie insisted.

"We're in a seriously fancy hotel room and I'm on the phone with my sister while he's watching TV in another room."

"I'm sure, if you put your mind to it, you could make him forget about whatever was on the screen—even if he was a diehard football fan and it was Super Bowl Sunday," Brie said. "But if you need a little confidence boost, look inside the drawer of the bedside table."

Curious, she tugged open the drawer and found a lingerie-size box wrapped in pink-striped paper. The tag attached read:

For Regan (& Connor)—Enjoy! Love, Brie XO

"Is it sexy or slutty?" she asked.

Brie laughed. "A little of both. Now go put it on—

and I don't want to hear from you again until the week-end's over."

With that, her sister disconnected.

Regan stared at the package for a long minute, debating.

Brie had gone to a lot of effort to make this weekend special for her sister and brother-in-law, so Regan decided that she could at least do her part.

Connor had thought the first seven months of his marriage to Regan—living in close proximity but not being able to touch her—had been torturous enough. He suspected the next forty-eight hours were going to make those seven months seem like a walk in the park.

While she was in the bedroom, he'd checked to see if the sofa in the sitting area folded out to a bed. It did. But even if it didn't, he figured that squeezing his six-foot-four-inch frame into a five-foot sofa would likely be easier than trying to keep his hands off Regan if they were sharing a bed.

But maybe she didn't expect him to keep his hands to himself. Maybe she wanted to celebrate their anniversary the way most other couples celebrated anniversaries—naked together. Certainly she hadn't seemed the least bit reluctant to show him around the suite—including the luxurious bedroom dominated by the fancy bed. She might have been a little apprehensive if she'd known it had taken more willpower than he'd thought he possessed not to throw her down on top of that enormous mattress and have his way with her. Because he'd imagined a lot of various and interesting ways over the past seven months.

But Piper and Poppy were barely four weeks old, which meant that it would be another two before her body would be recovered enough from the experience of childbirth to engage in intercourse.

The longest six weeks of my life, Reid had remarked, in apparent sympathy with his deputy.

Of course, there were a lot of ways to share physical intimacy and sexual pleasure aside from sex. But Connor also knew that six weeks was only a guideline, that some women required a lot more time than that before they experienced any sexual desire.

He'd turned on the TV in a desperate effort to distract himself from the tantalizing thought that they were alone in a hotel room—at least until they could escape to the restaurant for their eight o'clock dinner reservation.

"Connor?"

"Hmm?" he said, his gaze fixed on the TV as he feigned interest in the action on the screen, though he couldn't have said if it was a movie or a commercial or a public service announcement.

Regan stepped forward then, so that she was standing directly in front of him, and his jaw nearly hit the floor.

The remote did slip from his hand and fall to the soft carpet.

He didn't notice.

He didn't see anything but Regan.

She was wearing something that could only be described as a fantasy of white satin and sheer lace. The lace cups barely covered the swell of her luscious breasts; the short skirt skimmed the tops of her creamy thighs.

He lifted his gaze to her face and swallowed. "I thought you were getting ready to go out for dinner."

"I decided that I don't want to go out for dinner."

"That's good," he said. "Because you'd start a riot if you walked into the restaurant wearing that."

She tilted her head to study him. "I can't tell if that means you approve or disapprove."

"Do you want my approval?"

"I want to know if you want *me*."

"Only more than I want to breathe," he admitted hoarsely.

Her glossy pink lips curved as she moved closer. "That's just the right amount," she said, as she straddled his hips with her knees and lowered herself into his lap.

The position put her breasts, practically spilling out of her top and rising and falling with every breath she took, right there at eye level. But he wanted to do more than just look.

He wanted to touch, taste, take.

Instead, he curled his fingers around the edge of the sofa cushion, desperately trying to hold on to the last vestiges of his self-control, but it was rapidly falling away like a slippery thread.

She leaned closer, so that her mouth was only a whisper from his, and he was about half a second from losing his mind.

But instead of touching her lips to his, she touched them to his cheek, then his jaw and his throat. Light brushes that teased and tempted.

His hands gripped the leather cushion tighter.

"Six weeks," he said hoarsely.

She lifted her head, her eyes dark with desire and sparkling with playfulness. "What?"

"It hasn't been six weeks."

She laughed softly and nipped at the lobe of his ear. "Six weeks is only a guideline, not a rule," she told him.

"You're sure?" he asked.

Please be sure.

She nodded. "I saw Dr. Amaro on Tuesday."

He exhaled an audible sigh of relief. "Thank you, Dr. Amaro."

"Your sentiment is noted," she said. "But I'd prefer you to focus on me right now."

"I can do that," he promised.

And in one abrupt and agile motion, Connor rose to his feet, taking her with him.

Chapter Fifteen

Regan yelped in surprise; Connor responded with a chuckle. One of his arms was banded around her waist while the opposite hand cupped her bottom, and though she didn't think she was in any danger of falling, she wrapped her arms and legs around him like a pretzel and held on.

He carried her to the bedroom and tumbled with her onto the mattress, pinning her beneath his lean, hard body. Her heart hammered against her ribs, not with fear but desire. Desperate, achy desire.

He eased back to hook his fingers in the satin straps of her baby doll, pulling them down her arms so that her breasts spilled free of their constraint. But then he captured them in his hands, exploring their shape and texture with his callused palms and clever fingers. His thumbs traced lazy circles around her already taut nipples, making everything inside her clench in eager anticipation.

"It's been torture, sleeping next to you night after night, not being able to touch you like this," he said.

"No one said you couldn't touch me like this," she pointed out.

"Well, it seemed to be implied that there were... boundaries...to our relationship."

"Tonight, let's forget about the boundaries," she suggested.

"That sounds good to me," he said.

And then he was too busy kissing her to say anything more.

He was a really good kisser: his mouth was firm but not hard; his tongue bold but not aggressive. At another time, she thought she could happily spend hours kissing and being kissed by him. But after so many months of wanting and waiting, it wasn't enough. She wanted more.

As if sensing her impatience, he eased his mouth from hers, skimming it over her jaw, down her throat. He traced the line of her collarbone with his tongue, then nuzzled the hollow between her breasts. His shadowed jaw rasped against her tender flesh, like the strike of a match. Then his mouth found her nipple, and the shocking contrast of his hot mouth on her cool skin turned the spark to flame. He licked and suckled, making her gasp and yearn.

Oh, how she yearned.

As his mouth continued to taste and tease, his hands slid under the hem of her nightie to tug her panties over her hips and down her legs. He tossed the scrap of lace aside and nudged her thighs apart. His thumbs glided over the slick flesh at her core, parting the folds, zeroing in on the center of her feminine pleasure.

Was it post-childbirth hormones running rampant through her system that were responsible for the escalation in her desire, the intensity of her response? Or was it finally being with Connor as she'd so often dreamed of being with him?

Had he dreamed of her, too? Had he imagined touching her the way he was touching her now? Or did he just instinctively know where and how to use his hands so that she couldn't help but sigh with exquisite pleasure?

She should have guessed that he'd approach lovemaking the same way he did everything else—thoroughly and with great attention to detail. But she wanted to touch him, too, so she yanked his shirt out of his pants and made quick work of the buttons.

She finally managed to shove the garment aside and put her hands on him. The taut muscles of his belly quivered as she trailed her fingers over his torso; a low groan emanated from his throat as she scraped her nails lightly down his back. When she reached for his belt, he pulled away to assist with the task—quickly discarding his pants, briefs and socks in a pile on the floor.

"Condom," she said, when he rejoined her on the bed.

It was widely accepted that nursing moms couldn't get pregnant, but with four-and-a-half-week-old twins at home, she didn't want to take any chances.

He reached for the square packet she'd set on top of the bedside table in anticipation of this moment, and quickly sheathed himself.

His eyes were dark and intently focused as he rose over her again.

"I feel as if I've been waiting for this moment forever," he confided. "I don't want to rush it now."

"And I don't want to wait a second longer."

His lips curved as they brushed against hers. "Demanding, much?"

But he gave her what she wanted—what they both wanted. In one smooth stroke, he buried himself deep inside her.

She cried out at the shock and pleasure of the invasion as he filled her, as new waves of sensation began to ripple through her. He held her hands above her head, their fingers entwined, then lowered his head and captured her mouth. She wrapped her legs around him, so that they were linked from top to toe and everywhere in between. Two bodies joined together in pursuit of their mutual pleasure…and finding it.

Regan awoke in the night, her breasts full and aching.

A quick glance at the clock beside the bed confirmed that it was 4 a.m. Poppy habitually woke up around 3:30 and Piper about half an hour later. The staggered times meant that each twin got individual attention, but it also meant that their mom spent twice as much time nursing. Regan knew that it was possible to nurse two babies at the same time, but she couldn't imagine ever being that coordinated—or able to sync their schedules.

She slipped out of bed, leaving Connor sleeping, and retreated to the bathroom with her breast pump. Her initial concerns about not being able to produce enough milk to satisfy the twins had proved to be for naught, and she'd left a more than adequate supply for the weekend in the freezer and detailed instructions for Alyssa about how to prepare it.

Regan was genuinely happy that Jason and Alyssa were starting a family. And that Spencer and Kenzie were expanding theirs. It was apparent that both of her brothers had fallen in love with their perfect mates. Not that either of them had followed a short or easy path to happily-ever-after, but they got there eventually.

Love hadn't been anywhere on Regan's radar when she'd exchanged vows with Connor at the little chapel in Reno. She'd been alone and scared—terrified of being a single mom to two babies, drowning in doubts and insecurities when he tossed her a lifeline in the form of his proposal. She'd snatched it up desperately, gratefully, never hoping or even imagining that their marriage of convenience would ever become anything more.

But over the past seven and a half months, her feelings for her husband had changed and deepened so much so that she knew she was on the verge of falling in love with him.

Or maybe she'd already fallen.

There wasn't any one moment or factor she could pin-point as the time or reason why, although she knew a big part of it was that she loved him for loving their babies. It took a special kind of man to step up and be a dad in the absence of any biological connection to the child, but Connor had never hesitated or wavered.

Regan knew he loved Piper and Poppy—the only question that remained was: could he ever love her?

The next time she awakened, sunlight was trying to peek around the edges of the curtain. Beneath her cheek, she could feel Connor's heart beating—a slow and steady rhythm. She idly wondered how long it would take her to get his heart racing again, like it had raced the night before.

Not long, was the answer, as he proved when he woke up only a few minutes later.

Regan had never been a big fan of morning sex, but as she'd begun to realize, everything was different with Connor.

Afterward, when she was snuggled close to him, she stroked a hand down the arm that was wrapped around her, following the contours of taut muscles. It amazed her that a man so physically strong could be so tender and gentle, as he'd proved last night and again only a short while ago.

"What happened here?" she asked, her fingers skimming over the vertical line of puckered skin that ran down his forearm.

He glanced at the jagged scar, almost as if he'd forgotten it was there. "Broken glass."

"What'd you do? Put your arm through a window?"

"No."

"Did it happen on the job?" she prompted, when he offered no further explanation.

"No," he said again, adding a shake of his head this time. "It was a long time ago."

"How long?" she asked curiously.

"Ten…maybe twelve…years ago."

She was surprised and dismayed by the result of the quick mental calculation. "When you were a teenager?"

"Yeah."

Another single syllable response, but she refused to be dissuaded. "I know we're both adjusting to the new parameters of our marriage, but I believe communication is key to the success of any relationship."

"Words aren't the only means of communication," he said, with a suggestive wiggle of his brows.

"Yes, and you've proven that you're quite adept at other forms of communication," she assured him. "So if you don't want to talk about it, just say so."

"And you'll let it go?" he asked dubiously.

"Probably not," she admitted. "I can be like Baxter with a juicy T-bone when I want to know something."

He chuckled. "Yeah, that's what I figured." His expression grew serious as he looked at the scar on his arm again. "Do you know Mallory Stillwell?"

"The name sounds vaguely familiar," she admitted, already second-guessing her decision to push for an explanation. She'd thought she wanted to know everything about him, but she hadn't anticipated that his answer might involve another woman.

"She grew up in my neighborhood," he explained. "Across the street and two doors down."

"You took her to prom," Regan suddenly remembered.

"Only because Dale Shillington ditched her two days before the event and she was devastated about not being able to go—especially after she'd worked three weekends of overtime shifts at Jo's to buy a new dress."

"Dale Shillington always was a dick."

"I won't argue with that," Connor said.

"So you stepped in to help out a…friend?" she asked, blatantly fishing for more information about the nature of her husband's relationship with the girl-almost-next-door.

"We were friends," he confirmed. "And, for a while, we were more."

"You can spare me those details," she said quickly.

"I wasn't planning on sharing them."

Which she should have realized. Connor had never been the type to kiss and tell—which only made her that much more curious.

"And you went to prom with Brett Tanner that year," he noted.

"Because he asked."

"You wore a black dress," he said. "All the other girls were in shades of pink or purple or blue, heavy on the makeup and tottering around on too-high heels as if playing at being grown-up. Then you walked in—in your black dress with skinny straps and long skirt, and you were so straight-up sexy, you took my breath away."

"That's quite the memory," she remarked, embarrassed to admit that she couldn't summon an image of him at prom. She knew he'd been there, because she'd heard the stories that circulated, not just that night but for several weeks afterward, but it was possible she hadn't actually seen him.

"You made quite the impression," he assured her.

"And you got kicked out," she said, as her hazy memories slowly came into focus.

"What else would anyone expect from that no-good Neal boy?"

"Did you ever really do anything to earn that reputation?"

"I got kicked out of prom," he reminded her.

"What does any of this have to do with your scar?" she asked, in an effort to steer the conversation back on topic.

"Like my stepfather, Mallory's mom was a heavy drinker—and a mean drunk. And when she'd been drinking, she liked to knock her kids around. Mallory, being the oldest, usually took the brunt of the abuse."

Regan's fingers skimmed down his arm again, over the jagged scar, to link with his.

"One day she went at Mallory with a broken bottle and I stepped between them—and got thirty-four stitches for my efforts."

She winced, not wanting to imagine the bloody scene. "Was she arrested?"

He shook his head. "Mallory begged me to say that it was an accident."

"Why?"

"Because if her mother had gone to jail, family services would have come in and taken her sisters away."

"Considering their mother's violent abuse, that might have been better for them," she remarked.

"Says the girl born with a silver spoon in her mouth."

She nudged him away. "You're going to hold that against me?"

He shook his head. "No, I'm just pointing out why you can't understand the realities of life for those of us who grew up without the same privileges."

"You don't think Mallory and her sisters would have been better off in a different environment?"

"Maybe," he allowed. "Except that no one worried too much about separating siblings back then, and that might have been even more traumatic for all of them."

"I never thought about that," she admitted.

"And I don't want you thinking—and worrying—about it now," he said. "I just wanted to give you a complete picture."

"Got it."

"Good. Now can we stop talking about ex-girlfriends and high school and focus on the here and now?" he suggested, rolling over so that he was facing her.

"What, exactly, in the here and now do you want to focus on?"

"I'd like to start here," he said, and nibbled on her throat.

Her head dropped back and a sigh slipped between her lips. "That's a good place to start," she agreed.

"And here," he said, skimming his lips along the underside of her jaw.

"Another good place."

As his mouth continued to taste and tease, his hands moved lower. A quick tug unknotted the belt at her waist, and the silky robe fell open. She immediately tried to draw the sides together again, but he caught her wrists and held them in place.

"Why are you suddenly acting shy?"

"Because you opened the curtains and it's broad daylight."

"We're on the third floor. No one can see in," he told her.

"But you can see me," she protested.

"That was the point," he said. "I want to see and touch and taste every part of you."

"Some of those parts aren't as firm or smooth as they used to be."

"All of your parts are perfect." He brushed his lips over hers. "You're perfect."

She wasn't, of course. But it was nice of him to say so, and to sound as if he really believed it.

She'd had several boyfriends and a few lovers, but she'd always been careful to keep them at an emotional distance. She enjoyed sex but was wary of messy emotional entanglements. She hadn't been able to keep Connor at a distance. Or maybe she hadn't wanted to.

"What are you thinking about?"

"I was just wondering…do you think we can make our marriage work?"

"I think we've been doing a pretty good job of it so far," he pointed out. "And that was without the added benefits of sex."

"I guess I just worry sometimes—"

"You worry all the time," he interjected.

She managed a small smile. "Well, sometimes I worry that you might wake up one day and regret marrying me."

He shook his head. "Never."

"How can you be so sure?"

"Because I love the life we have together," he said.

It wasn't a declaration of feelings for her, but she decided it was close enough—at least for now.

"I'm really glad you were there when I was puking in the bushes outside of Diggers'," she said softly.

He chuckled and brushed his lips over her temple. "Me, too."

Chapter Sixteen

Two weeks after their weekend at The Stagecoach Inn—two weeks during which he'd continued to enjoy the many benefits of sharing a bed with his wife at home—Connor drove to the airport in Elko to pick up his brother. For a lot of years, it had been just him and Deacon, and it had been a big adjustment for both of them when his brother went away to school.

It wasn't just that Deacon was gone, but that he was so far away, and the cost of travel meant that he'd only been home once in the past eight months. And when he'd made that trip at Christmas, Connor hadn't been able to relax and enjoy his brother's company because Deacon's presence meant he had to move back into his own room, occupied by an incredibly sexy and far-too-tempting woman who just happened to be his wife.

This time there was no similar apprehension about Deacon's homecoming, just anticipation for the chance to reconnect with his only sibling.

The first night, after Deacon had finally been introduced to his nieces and made a suitable fuss over "the cutest babies ever"—and then an equal fuss over Baxter, reassuring the dog that he was also loved and adored—they stayed up late talking. Regan lasted until ten o'clock, explaining to her brother-in-law that Piper and Poppy didn't just get up early but continued to wake a couple of times through the night.

"I didn't say it at Christmas, because I was still trying to wrap my head around the fact that you were married," Deacon said, after his brother's wife had gone upstairs. "But I'm really happy for you and Regan."

"Thanks," Connor said.

"And I think it's pretty cool that I'm an uncle—times two."

"With twins, everything is times two," Connor told him. "Twice as many feedings and dirty diapers and loads of laundry."

"Twice as much cuteness," his brother added. "Of course, that's only because they look so much like their mom."

"Lucky for them," Connor agreed.

And lucky for him, because if Piper and Poppy didn't look so much like Regan, people might start to wonder why they didn't look anything at all like their dad.

"Seriously, though, those kids are lucky they've got you for a dad," Deacon remarked.

"I'm the fortunate one," he said. "When I married Regan, I got everything I never knew I wanted."

"She seems pretty great," his brother acknowledged. "I have to admit, when I first got the letter about my scholarship, I didn't realize that it was my sister-in-law's family that was responsible for the fund."

"Blake Mining throws a ton of money around," Connor told him, attempting to downplay the familial connection. "Probably in the hope of some positive PR to combat the negative environmental impact of the business."

"So Regan didn't pull any strings to get me the scholarship?" Deacon asked, wanting to be sure.

"I promise that she didn't," Connor said.

Because Deacon returned to Haven in the middle of the week, he had a few days off before he was scheduled to start working at Katelyn Davidson's law office the following Monday. Unfortunately, Connor didn't have any of those days off. Not even the weekend, because it was his turn in the rotation.

"I know it sucks that it's your first week back and your brother's hardly been home," Regan said to him, after a leisurely breakfast Saturday morning.

"We'll have plenty of time to catch up over the summer," Deacon said. "And I've kind of enjoyed hanging out with you and Piper and Poppy. And Baxter," he added, with a glance at the dog sprawled by his feet.

"I was worried that you might feel uncomfortable, coming home to a place where so much has changed."

"You mean because I came back at Christmas and met my brother's wife? Then, four months later, when I finished the school term, there were two babies in the house?"

"Something like that," she agreed.

"There have been a lot of changes," he acknowledged. "But all for the better."

"I'm glad you think so."

"It's good to see Connor happy," Deacon said. "Not that he ever seemed unhappy, but he smiles a lot more now. Laughs more.

"I have to be honest, I wasn't sure he'd ever want to take on the roles of husband and father. It was pretty rough for him," he explained. "Growing up without a father."

"I doubt it was any rougher than you growing up with yours," Regan said gently.

He seemed startled by her remark. "He told you about Dwayne?"

She nodded.

"I don't really remember much about him. Or maybe

I don't want to remember much, because what I do remember—" He cut himself off with a shake of his head.

"Anyway, it was Connor who mostly raised me," he continued. "Despite the fact that there's only eight years between us, he was the closest thing I had to a father. My own was useless on a good day, and our mom was always working.

"It was Connor who made sure I had clean clothes and a lunch packed for school. He filled out the trip forms and gave me milk money from his own savings."

"He never told me any of that," Regan admitted.

"He's always been the first one to step up to help someone else and the last one to want any credit for his actions," Deacon said.

She nodded, agreeing with his assessment.

"Do you know why I applied to Columbia?" Deacon asked.

"Because it's one of the top law schools in the country?" she suggested.

"Well, yeah," he acknowledged. "But I never actually planned to go there. Truthfully, I didn't even think I'd get in. But if I did, what an interesting story I'd have to tell the other lawyers in the barristers' lounge. Over single-malt scotch and imported cigars and conversations about our alma maters, I could casually mention that yes, I'd graduated from UNLV, but I could have gone to Columbia."

"You don't drink or smoke," she said, pointing out the obvious flaws in his story.

He chuckled. "In this futuristic scene of my imagination, I did. But Connor changed that futuristic scene for me. He changed that 'could have gone' to an 'am going.'"

"I know he's incredibly proud of you," she told him.

"And I'm incredibly grateful to him," Deacon said.

"How grateful?" Regan wondered.

"Uh-oh. That sounds like the prelude to a request for a big favor," he remarked.

"It is," she admitted. "Piper and Poppy's baptism is scheduled for June thirtieth and we'd like you to be a godparent."

A smile—quick and wide—spread across his face. "Me? No kidding?"

"No kidding," she assured him. "What do you say?"

"I'd be honored," he said. "But now I have a question for you."

"What is it?"

"What exactly is a godfather supposed to do —and does it include having to change stinky diapers?"

The middle of the following week, Piper and Poppy had their two-month checkup with their pediatrician in Battle Mountain.

"I appreciate the company on the drive," Regan said to Connor, when they headed back to the car with their healthy and happy baby girls after the appointment. "But you really don't have to come to every checkup with me."

"I know," he said. "But it's a long way for you to come on your own, especially if they start fussing. Plus, booking half a day off work gives me an excuse to take my wife out to lunch."

"Now that you mention it…I am kind of hungry."

"What are you in the mood for?"

"Pizza from Jo's," she decided.

"I thought you'd want to take advantage of the fact that we're in a town that offers a few more dining options than the Sunnyside Diner, Diggers' Bar and Grill, and Jo's Pizza."

"But if we pick up a pizza on the way home, I can

take advantage of my husband before he has to go into work later."

He grinned. "I like the way you think."

By the time they got around to eating the pizza, it was cold, but neither of them complained. After lunch, Regan wrapped the leftover slices while Connor went upstairs to get dressed.

She was startled when the doorbell rang, because Baxter was out in the backyard and hadn't given her any warning that someone was approaching the house. Although it was unusual to get visitors in the middle of the day, she was more curious than concerned when she responded to the summons.

Until she opened the door and discovered Bo Larsen on the other side.

"Hello, Regan."

There were at least a dozen random questions spinning through her mind, and she blurted out the first one she latched on to: "What are you doing here?"

"I was in town and thought I'd stop by to congratulate the new mother," he said.

Though the words sounded pleasant enough, she remained wary. "Thank you."

"You don't want to know who told me?"

"It's a small town and hardly a big secret," she pointed out.

"True," he acknowledged. "And it wasn't really a surprise to me, either. At least, not after I received a tax receipt for my generous donation to The Battle Mountain Women's Health Center.

"You can imagine how awkward it was," he continued in a conversational tone, "trying to explain that to my wife."

"I can," she agreed. "But I have to say, I approve of your philanthropy."

"Don't you mean *your* philanthropy?" he asked. "You took the money I gave you and turned it over to the clinic."

She didn't deny it. "You wanted to pay for an abortion, and I wasn't interested in having one."

"You might have told me that."

"Why? You made it perfectly clear that you had no interest in my baby."

"Don't you mean babies?"

She swallowed. "What do you want, Bo?"

"I just wanted to make sure—" His words cut off as his gaze shifted to focus on something—or someone, she guessed—over her shoulder.

"Everything okay?" Connor asked, as he came down the stairs to take up position behind her.

"Everything's fine," Regan said, breathing a silent sigh of relief that her husband wasn't carrying one or both of their daughters. "And Bo was just leaving."

"I don't want to rush off without being properly introduced to…" He paused, obviously waiting for her to fill in the blank.

"My husband," Regan told him. "Connor is my husband."

"Husband," Bo echoed, sounding surprised. "When we…worked together, I didn't get the impression that you were looking for a long-term commitment. But I guess parenthood changes a lot of things."

"Meeting the right person changes everything," Regan said pointedly.

Bo nodded. "Apparently so."

Regan turned to her husband then. "This is Bo Larsen, a former colleague."

"Oh, we were more than colleagues," he chided.

Regan narrowed her gaze.

Of course, Connor knew exactly what she and Bo had been. When she'd told him about her pregnancy, she'd told him everything. What he didn't know, because she'd only recently realized it herself, was that her relationship with Bo had been a mistake from the beginning.

And yet, even if she could go back in time, she wouldn't change a thing, because Bo was the reason she had Piper and Poppy—and they were the reason Connor had married her.

"We were also friends," her ex continued.

"And now we're not," she said pointedly.

Bo nodded. "I'm glad I got to meet your husband." He looked at Connor then. "Congratulations on your wedding. And your new family."

"Thank you," Connor said.

As soon as Bo turned away, Regan closed the door and turned the lock.

Connor stood behind her, watching Regan as she watched, through the glass, her former lover drive away. He could see the tension in the rigid line of her shoulders and practically feel it emanating from her body.

Did she want to be sure that he was gone?

Or was she wishing that he'd stayed?

"Are you okay?"

She turned around quickly and nodded. "I'm fine." She added a smile. "And reassured."

"Reassured?" he echoed dubiously.

She nodded again. "I always suspected he'd show up someday. Now that day has passed, and I don't have to worry that he'll come back again."

"How can you be sure?" he wondered.

"Because I saw how relieved he was to learn that we were married."

Connor hoped she was right and they'd seen the last of the other man. But even if it was true, that didn't eliminate the last of his concerns.

He hated to ask the question, but he needed to know: "Do you still have feelings for him?"

Regan shook her head. "Of course not. After the way he lied to me and used me? How could you even imagine that I would?"

"You said you knew he'd show up someday... I guess I just wondered if maybe that's why you made the donation to the women's health center in his name—to ensure that he would? To give him a reason to find you and force this confrontation?"

"No," she said again. "At the time, I was only thinking of getting rid of the money. Maybe I should have just torn up the check, but I was hurt and angry and obviously not thinking very clearly."

He wanted to believe it was as simple as that, but the other man's appearance at the door had shaken Connor more than he wanted to admit. He'd known about the relationship. She'd been honest with him about her former lover, but now that abstract persona had taken a specific form in a suit and tie, with a preppy haircut and neatly buffed nails.

Bo Larsen was exactly the type of guy he would have imagined Regan falling for—and a living reminder that, had her circumstances been different, she would never have chosen to get involved with a guy from the wrong side of the tracks.

Yet it was Connor she turned to in the night, not just willingly but eagerly. And when they came together, their passion was honest and real.

If that was all they ever had, he vowed it would be enough.

* * *

The next morning, as Connor made his way to the kitchen to start the coffee brewing, he found his brother in front of the mirror in the hall.

"You're up early today," he noted. "And all dressed up like a grown-up."

Deacon grinned into the mirror as he finished adjusting his tie. "What do you think?"

Connor, looking over his brother's shoulder, nodded. "I think you look like a lawyer."

"I'm a long way away from that, but I thought I should dress the part for my first day in court."

"I guess this is a pretty big opportunity, huh?"

"Huge," Deacon agreed. "And something else I owe to you."

"I didn't do anything except pass your résumé on to the sheriff, who gave it to his wife," Connor pointed out.

"That's the least of what you did," his brother said. "You always encouraged me to follow my dreams."

"I'm glad to see that you are."

"Actually, this is beyond my dreams." Deacon turned to face Connor now. "But you said that I could use the past to guide my future, but I should never let the past limit it."

"That sounds like pretty good advice," he said, lifting Baxter's leash off the hook by the door. "Here's some more—don't be late for your first day in court."

Deacon grinned in response to the not-so-subtle prompt. "I'm on my way."

When Connor and Baxter headed down Elderberry Lane, he saw a now-familiar red Toyota pulling into Bruce Ackerman's driveway.

"I haven't seen you around here in a while," he said,

when he caught up to Mallory as she was lifting her bucket of cleaning supplies out of the trunk.

She didn't look at him when she responded. "I picked up a couple more jobs, so my schedule isn't as regular as it used it be."

Baxter barked, as if to ask why she was ignoring him.

She turned to scratch his head, but dropped her chin so that her hair fell forward to curtain her face.

The deliberate motion set off Connor's radar. He took a step closer and tipped her chin up, the muscle in his jaw tightening as he noted the faded bluish-green bruise on her cheekbone. "What happened?"

She shrugged. "I ran into a fist."

At least her flippant response was honest. Of course, she had to know that he'd never believe that she ran into a door. They'd both heard that lie too many times, and he was furious and frustrated and sorry and sad for the sweet girl he'd known.

"Your husband's?" he guessed.

"Yeah, but it's really not a big deal," she said. "I mean, it doesn't happen very often. Usually, he treats me pretty good."

Connor shook his head. "Are you hearing yourself, Mallory? Do you realize how much you sound like your mother? Do you remember how much you hated the way she always made excuses for the men who knocked her around? The same excuses she made when she knocked you around?"

"Well, I guess it's true what they say about the apple not falling far from the tree," she said, though the color in her cheeks suggested that she was more ashamed of succumbing to the cycle of abuse than she wanted to admit. "But anyway, I'm fine."

"You mentioned a daughter."

"What about her?"

"Is she fine?" he wondered. "How do you think she feels when she sees her mother get knocked around?"

"He's never hit me in front of Chloe."

"Yet."

"Save the lecture for someone who needs it, Deputy," she advised.

"I'm not lecturing, I just—" he cut himself off, realizing that he was about to do exactly that. Because she'd heard it all before, and there was nothing to be gained by putting her on the defensive now. "Just promise that you'll call me if you ever need anything."

He handed her a card with his cell phone number on it; she tucked it into her pocket without even looking at it.

"Sure," she agreed.

But they both knew she was lying.

Chapter Seventeen

The day of the baptism dawned clear and bright.

The ceremony happened after the morning church service, by which time both Piper and Poppy were feeling a little restless and out of sorts. Everyone agreed the twins looked like perfect little angels in their matching christening gowns, but when it came time for the sprinkling with water, they screamed like little devils.

After the ritual had been completed, everyone gathered at the twins' grandparents' house on Miners' Pass. It was mostly a family event, although some of Regan's co-workers from Blake Mining and some of Connor's from the sheriff's office had been invited to attend. Holly Kowalski was there with her fiancé, and Regan was pleased to have the opportunity to thank her personally for the beautiful quilts she'd gifted to Piper and Poppy—and to offer her congratulations on the deputy's recent engagement.

"Why do I feel as if I've lost something?" Regan asked her husband, when Connor returned with the glass of punch she'd requested.

"Probably because you don't currently have a baby attached to your body," he noted.

"That might be it," she acknowledged, scanning the crowd for their daughters.

They'd been passed around from one person to the next all day and had held up pretty well—after they'd gotten back to the house and had their empty bellies filled. She located them quickly enough. Piper was in Auntie Brie's arms and Poppy was being cuddled by her cousin Dani, under the watchful eye of Auntie Kenzie. No doubt the little girl was going to be a great big sister when Spencer and Kenzie's baby was born.

"You were thirsty," Connor noted, when she quickly drained the contents of her glass. "Want a refill?"

She shook her head. "No, but I'm going to head inside to the powder room." She pitched her voice to a whisper, so that no one could overhear. "I have to adjust my nursing bra."

"Do you want me to come with you?" he whispered back. "I've got some experience with your undergarments."

"Taking them off," she acknowledged. "And that will have to wait until later."

"Promises, promises."

She was smiling as she walked into the house. And why not? She had a wonderful life and she was grateful for every bit of it. Okay, maybe not the bulky bra, she mused, as she adjusted the garment. But everything else was pretty darn good.

She exited the powder room and caught a snippet of conversation from the great room.

"—personally thank you for funding the Aim Higher Education Scholarship."

Regan stopped in her tracks.

She immediately recognized Deacon's voice—but who was he talking to?

"Blake Mining believes in giving back to the community."

Her father?

"Well, I'm grateful for that," her brother-in-law said now. "The funds have been of tremendous assistance."

Regan took a step back, her mind spinning.

She knew about Deacon's scholarship, of course, but she'd had no idea that the money had been put up by Blake Mining.

Was it a coincidence?

She didn't think so.

Especially when she recalled part of a conversation that she'd had with her husband several weeks earlier.

"...there was a weird message on my voice mail the other day from one of the junior accountants at work," she'd told him. *"...something about a scholarship fund."*

"He shouldn't be bothering you with trivial inquiries when you're on mat leave...let your father deal with it."

Had Connor known?

And if so, why hadn't he told her?

Determined to get answers to those questions from her husband right now, she pivoted quickly and nearly bumped into him.

"Hey." He caught her arms to steady her. "Are you all right?"

She nodded, then shook her head. But she didn't want to have a private conversation in the middle of the foyer, so she took his hand and pulled him into the library, closing the door behind them.

"If you wanted to be alone with me, you only had to say so," he teased, smiling as he moved in to kiss her.

She put a hand on his chest, halting his progress. "I heard your brother talking to my father."

His smile faded, his gaze shuttered. "Is that a problem?"

"That's what I'm trying to figure out," she admitted, as the hollow feeling in her stomach grew. "Did you know that Blake Mining paid for Deacon's scholarship?"

To his credit, Connor hesitated only briefly before nodding. "Yes, I knew."

Maybe he deserved some credit for being honest, but his truthfulness didn't lessen her feelings of betrayal. "And yet, I didn't."

"You've had more important things to think about over the past several months," he said reasonably.

She couldn't deny that was true, but she still had questions that she wanted answered. The most important one being: "When did you know about it?"

"Your dad mentioned the possibility of a scholarship to me shortly after Deacon headed to New York for his first term," he admitted.

"In the fall, then?"

He nodded again.

"Before or after you asked me to marry you?" she wanted to know. *Needed* to know.

Except that, in her heart, she suspected that she already knew. But she fervently hoped his response would prove her instincts wrong.

"Does it matter?" he asked.

"Of course it matters," she said. "And I'm guessing, from your deliberate effort to sidestep the question, the answer is before."

She read the truth—and maybe regret—in his gaze before he responded.

"Yes," he acknowledged quietly. "It was before."

Now she nodded, even as her heart sank impossibly deeper inside her chest. "How much?"

"How much what?" he asked warily.

Her eyes stung; her throat ached. "How much did it cost my father to buy me a husband?"

"It wasn't like that, Regan," he denied, reaching for her.

She stepped back, away from him. "Or maybe he was

more worried about the legitimacy of his grandchildren than his daughter's happiness?" she suggested as an alternative. Then she shook her head. "I can't believe I was such an idiot. That I actually believed you wanted to marry me and be a father to my babies, so they wouldn't grow up with unanswered questions about their paternity, like you did."

"I *did* want to marry you and I *am* their father," he said, sounding so earnest she wanted to believe him. "And even if you're upset that you didn't know about the scholarship, you have to know how much I love Piper and Poppy."

She nodded, because she did know. There was no denying that Connor loved their daughters. He'd also told her that he loved their life together, being a family.

But he didn't love *her*.

She hadn't expected happily-ever-after when they'd exchanged their vows. It wasn't part of their deal. Then again, she hadn't known he'd made a completely different deal with her father. And while they'd lived and worked together over the past eight and a half months—first preparing for the birth and then taking care of the twins—she'd been falling in love with him, and he'd been in it for the financial reward.

"You're right about the latter part," she acknowledged. "You are a wonderful father to Piper and Poppy. I just wish I'd known the real reasons you'd agreed to take on that role."

"I never lied to you, Regan." His tone was imploring, as if it really mattered to him that she believed him.

As if she could.

"Really? Is that how you justified the deception in your own mind? That you never actually lied?" she challenged. "Because you weren't completely honest with me, either."

"We each had our own reasons for wanting to get married," he reminded her. "And neither of us was under any illusions that it was for love."

"You're right again," she said.

"And everything I told you, all the reasons I gave for wanting to marry you, were true."

"But not the whole truth."

"You would never have agreed to marry me if you'd known the whole truth," he said.

"I guess we'll never know, will we?" she countered. "But one thing I do know is that I never would have assumed you were noble and honorable and—" She shook her head. "I was such an idiot. When I offered to pay for the kitchen renovation, you assured me you didn't marry me for my money. Because you married me for my father's money."

He flinched at the harshness of her words, but she refused to feel guilty for speaking the truth.

She swiped impatiently at the tears that spilled onto her cheeks. "If I'd known, I might still have married you," she decided. "I was so scared and desperate and alone, I might not have cared about your reasons. But at least then I would have gone into the marriage with my eyes wide open.

"And I wouldn't have been foolish enough to fall in love with you."

Before Connor could wrap his head around what she'd said, she was gone.

He was staring at the door through which she'd disappeared when her sister entered. "I came in to ask Regan where she put the diaper bag, and she walked right past without even seeing me," Brie remarked.

"Over there," he said, pointing to a chair in the corner.

His sister-in-law opened the top of the bag, took out a diaper and the package of wipes. "Why did she storm out of here?"

"Maybe you should ask your sister," Connor suggested.

"I'm asking you," she said.

He sighed wearily but knew there was no point in denying the truth. "I screwed up."

"Yeah, that was a given," she noted. "How badly?"

He just shook his head.

He should have ignored her father's directive and told her the truth in the beginning. But he'd been afraid that she'd say no and he really wanted her to say yes. Not just because he'd needed the money for Deacon's education, but because he'd wanted a chance to be with Regan. Of course, he never would have admitted that was a factor at the time, because he hadn't been willing to acknowledge his feelings for her.

"Regan can forgive a lot of faults," Brie said to him now. "But she can't tolerate dishonesty. She was involved with a guy once who had a pretty big secret, and when it was finally uncovered, she was devastated—by the deception even more than the truth."

He guessed that she was referring to Bo—the ex-colleague, ex-lover, with the secret family. And he realized that it didn't matter how he'd managed to justify, in his own mind, keeping the truth about the scholarship from Regan. She'd trusted him with her deepest secrets, and he hadn't done the same.

"I screwed up really, really badly," he confessed.

"Then you better come up with a really, really good

plan to fix it," she said. "Assuming you want to fix it because you're head over heels in love and can't imagine your life without her?"

"I am," he confirmed. He wasn't sure how or when it had happened, but he knew it was true.

"Then you might want to lead with that," Brie suggested.

When Connor got home, he found his brother in the living room with books spread out on the coffee table, a dog at his feet and a baseball game on TV. Deacon had left the party early to work on a pretrial memo that his boss had asked him to prepare, so he had no idea that his brief conversation with Regan's father had resulted in lasting fallout for his brother.

"Where's everyone else?" Deacon asked, noting that Connor was alone.

"They're staying at Miners' Pass tonight."

His brother hit the mute button on the TV to give Connor his full attention. "Why?"

"Because Regan's mad at me," he admitted.

"About?"

He shook his head. "It doesn't matter."

"Regan doesn't strike me as the type to go off in a tiff, so I'm guessing it was something that matters to her."

"Yeah." Connor scrubbed his hands over his face. "Maybe my mistake was in ever thinking we could make our marriage work."

Deacon frowned. "Why would you say something like that?"

"Because we're way too different."

"So?"

"So Regan's a Blake," he reminded his brother. "And that puts her way out of my league."

"Obviously Regan doesn't think so, or she would never have married you."

"She was pregnant and overwhelmed by the prospect of raising her babies alone."

"I don't have enough worldly experience to translate into words of wisdom," Deacon said. "So I'll suggest that you take your own advice."

"What advice is that?" he asked, a little warily.

"Let the past guide your future but don't let it put limits on it."

"I'm not sure that's really applicable to this situation."

"Well, it's all I've got," Deacon said. "Except to say that you owe it to yourself as much as Regan to fight for the family you've made together."

Regan was miserable.

She'd told Connor that she needed space and time to think about things, and he'd given it to her.

Idiot.

Why couldn't he know that what she really wanted was for him to fight for their marriage? To prove to her that she was worth fighting for. Or, if not her, at least Piper and Poppy.

Two days had passed since the party with no communication from him. On day three—Greta's day off—she responded to a knock on the door.

"Deacon, what are you doing here?"

"If the mountain won't come to Muhammad," he began.

She smiled at that. "Come in, Muhammad."

He stepped through the door and gave her a warm hug.

Inexplicably, her eyes filled with tears. Although she was mad at Connor and still feeling hurt and betrayed, she missed Deacon (and Baxter) and the rhythms and routines they'd established as a result of living together, and she really wanted to go home.

She'd only lived with her husband in the house on Larrea Drive for nine months, but it truly felt like home. And not only because Connor had renovated the kitchen in accordance with her preferences, but because being there with him—being his wife and a mother to their babies—she truly felt as if she was where she belonged. It didn't seem to matter why or how they'd connected, all that mattered was that they were a family together.

Without him, she felt alone and incomplete.

But she pushed that thought aside for now to focus on her visitor. "Can I get you something to drink?" she offered. "Soda? Coffee? Beer?"

"I'm not thirsty," Deacon said. "I just wanted to come by to make sure you were okay."

The unexpected overture and genuine concern in his expression caused her throat to tighten. "I'm fine," she said, though her tone was less certain than her words.

"And to ask how long you intend to punish my brother," he added.

"Is that what you think I'm doing?" she asked, startled by the question—and perhaps his insight.

"Isn't it?" he prompted gently.

Regan sighed. "I don't know. I mean, it wasn't a conscious decision, but maybe I did want him to feel some of the hurt I was feeling."

"He knows he screwed up," her brother-in-law said.

"I screwed up, too," she admitted.

Growing up a Blake in Haven—because despite her last name being Channing, everyone knew Regan was a Blake—everything had come easily to her. So much so that she'd taken a lot of things for granted. She hadn't delved too deeply into Connor's reasons for marrying her because she'd wanted a husband for herself and father for her babies, and she usually got what she wanted.

She was spoiled and entitled, and she'd proven it by running away when Connor didn't respond to the shouted declaration of her feelings with an equally emotional outburst. She'd wanted him to fight for their marriage, but why would he when she hadn't fought to stay with him?

"Well, for what it's worth, he's miserable," Deacon told her now.

"That makes two of us," she confided.

"So come home," he urged. "It will be more fun to watch him grovel up close."

She managed a laugh. "I'll think about it. Now, that's enough about your brother—tell me about your job."

"Katelyn's got a ton of cases on the go, so I'm working my butt off—and loving every minute of it."

"That's great," she said sincerely.

"We're doing jury selection in court tomorrow."

"That sounds like fun—unless you're in the jury pool."

He chuckled. "Yeah, most people grumble about getting the summons. But it really is a fascinating way to see the legal system at work."

They chatted a little bit more about his work, until Regan lifted a hand to stifle a yawn.

Deacon immediately rose to his feet. "That's my cue."

"It wasn't a cue," she protested. "I'm a new mom of twins—I'm always tired."

"Another reason to come home," her brother-in-law said, with a conspiratorial wink. "Make the dad do his fair share."

Chapter Eighteen

Connor was scowling at the coffeepot when Holly took the pot off the burner and filled a mug that she then pressed into his hands.

"You have to actually drink it for the caffeine to take effect," she told him.

He lifted the mug to his lips. "I didn't get much sleep last night."

"The twins keep you up?" she asked sympathetically.

He swallowed a mouthful of coffee. Missing the twins and their mother was what kept him up, though he didn't say as much. He didn't want anyone to know that his wife had left him because he was hoping it was a temporary situation soon to be rectified.

Regan had asked for time—but how much time was he supposed to give her? How much was enough and—

"Neal, Kowalski—you're with me," the sheriff said, striding briskly through the bullpen.

Connor put the mug down and automatically checked for his weapon and badge.

Holly did the same as she asked, "What's up?"

"Domestic," Reid said grimly.

"Damn," Connor muttered, falling into line behind his boss, who was already halfway out the door. "Who called it in?"

"Six-year-old kid hiding in the closet of her bedroom."

Connor swore again.

"It gets worse," Reid warned. "She claims her dad has a gun."

"Shotgun," Holly said.

Connor frowned as he reached for the passenger-door handle of the sheriff's SUV. "How do you know?"

"I don't." She nudged him aside with her hip. "I was claiming the front seat."

With a philosophical shrug, Connor moved to the rear door.

"Where are we going?" he asked, when the sheriff slid behind the wheel.

"Southside."

Connor's old neighborhood.

"Second Street."

He suddenly had a knot in his stomach the size of a fist. "Number?"

"Sixty-eight."

Mallory's house.

As the sheriff turned onto Second Street, Connor considered the possibility that the caller—the daughter Mallory had described as the light of her life—might be wrong about the gun. Sometimes kids had trouble separating fantasy from reality. And sometimes, he knew from personal experience, kids saw things that everyone else chose to ignore.

Either way, they were going to go in assuming the dad was armed—and hope like hell he didn't have more than one weapon.

Reid pulled the SUV over in front of number sixty-two so as not to tip off anyone inside number sixty-eight. He opened the back and handed out vests.

"The 911 operator said the kid was calling from her bedroom at the back of the house. Apparently there's a window accessible from the ground. Kowalski, go in and get the girl and let us know when she's safe.

"And no, I'm not keeping you out of harm's way," he said, before she could protest her assignment. "I'm sending you because the kid's terrified that her dad has a gun, so I don't want to send in another man with a gun."

Holly nodded. "Yes, sir."

"Neal, as soon as we get word that the kid's out of the house, you're going in the side door, I'm going in the front."

Though Haven was hardly a hotbed of criminal activity, bad things did occasionally happen in the town, and Connor had learned early on to trust his instincts when reading a situation. He was struggling to read this one. Although human nature was predictable, individuals often bucked the trends—especially when emotions were running high.

Evan Turcotte's emotions were running high, as evidenced by the pained expression on his face and the real tears in his eyes as he held his gun pointed at his wife. "You called the cops?" The gun shook in his hand. "How could you do that to me?"

"I didn't." Mallory's voice pleaded with him to believe her. "You know I didn't, Evan. I've been here with you the whole time."

Unable to argue with her logic, he shifted blame to the neighbors, using several choice adjectives to describe their interference in things that were none of their goddamned business.

"Do you have a daughter, Mr. Turcotte?" The sheriff spoke up now, attempting to engage the man and defuse the situation.

"Yeah," Turcotte admitted. "So what?"

"So maybe yelling at her mom and waving a gun around might have scared your little girl," Reid suggested.

Turcotte swore again and blinked hard, attempting to clear the moisture from his eyes. "Aww, man. Chloe called you?"

"She did," Reid confirmed. "Because she wants everyone to be safe."

"I've never laid a finger on Chloe," Turcotte said. "I wouldn't ever hurt my little girl."

"I'm sure it would be a lot easier for Chloe to believe that if you put the gun down," the sheriff continued in the same patient tone.

"Where is she?" Turcotte demanded. "Where's my daughter?"

"She's outside with Deputy Kowalski," Reid said.

"I want to see her."

"You put the gun down, and we'll make that happen," the sheriff promised.

"If I put this gun down, you're gonna put cuffs on me and haul me off to jail," Turcotte said. "I know how this works—I'm not an idiot."

"You're obviously upset about something, Mr. Turcotte. Why don't we talk about what that is?"

"I only want to talk to Mallory," he said, his voice filled with despair. "I want you guys to go so I can talk to my wife."

"If you know how this works, you know we can't do that," Reid said. "This is what's considered an active threat situation."

"It's okay, Sheriff," Mallory said, but the trembling of her voice suggested otherwise. "You should go so me and Evan can talk."

Connor stepped out of the shelter of the doorway, hoping the sight of a familiar face would reassure her. "We're not going anywhere."

She shook her head. "Please, Connor. This isn't—"

"Connor?" Turcotte's interjection sounded pained. "Oh, this is just perfect. My cheating wife—" his voice broke a little as he swung the gun from Mallory to the deputy "—and her lover."

"I'm afraid you've been given some misinformation," Connor said calmly.

Unfortunately, Mallory didn't exhibit the same coolness. She threw her arms up in the air. "Ohmygod— where do you come up with this stuff?"

"I found his card on your dresser and I know you're sleeping with somebody," Turcotte snapped at her.

It was obvious to Connor that the man was at the end of his rope—desperate to hang on to his family and unable to see that his actions were pushing them away. So he took another step forward, attempting to draw the man's attention back to him.

"If you want to be mad at someone, Evan, be mad at me." He deliberately used the man's first name and a friendly tone, attempting to establish a rapport. To encourage him to look for a peaceful resolution to whatever conflict had driven him to this point.

But Mallory's husband wasn't interested in rapport. "I've got enough mad—and enough bullets—to go around," he promised grimly.

"Come on now," Connor said, in the same placating tone. "Put the gun down so that we can talk."

"I don't wanna talk to you."

"Well, you don't want to be making threats—especially against an officer of the law."

"I'm done making threats," Turcotte said, and pulled the trigger.

* * *

Ben and Margaret hadn't said anything when Regan told them that she was going to be staying at Miners' Pass with her babies again. Or maybe her parents had said plenty—just none of it to her. And for the first couple of days, she was happy to avoid any kind of confrontation with them. She just needed some time to sort through her own emotions—the most prominent of which were hurt and anger.

Although she was furious with Connor, she suspected that the marriage idea hadn't originated with him. Not that she intended to let him off the hook on that technicality when he'd proven only too willing to go along with the plan, but right now, her attention was focused in another direction.

"This is a surprise," Ben said, glancing to his wife for confirmation when Regan walked into his office four days after the baptism.

"We didn't have a meeting scheduled," Margaret assured him.

"No," Regan agreed. "But I needed to talk to you and I didn't want to wait until dinner."

"Talk to *me*?" her father asked, his tone wary.

She nodded. "But it's good that you're both here."

"What can we do for you?" her mother asked.

"I'm trying to understand—" she broke off, mortified to discover that her eyes were filling with tears. *Again.*

"Regan?" Margaret prompted gently.

She tried to focus on her father through her tears. "I need to know—was it your idea or his?"

"I've only ever wanted what's best for you," Ben said.

"Yours then," she realized.

Margaret frowned and turned to her husband. "What was your idea?"

Regan's brows lifted. "Mom doesn't know?"

Her father sighed. "No one was supposed to know."

"Know what?" Margaret demanded.

Ben seemed to be struggling to find the words to tell his wife what he'd done, so Regan explained, "Dad paid Connor to marry me."

Margaret gasped. "Is it true?"

"No," he immediately denied. "I never gave Connor any money."

"Not directly," Regan acknowledged. "But you wrote a hefty check to his brother."

"The Aim Higher Scholarship," Margaret murmured, putting the pieces together.

Regan nodded.

"You can't seriously be upset that your father wanted to help your brother-in-law with his law school expenses," her mother chided.

"Except that Deacon wasn't my brother-in-law at the time and Dad didn't offer the money out of the goodness of his heart—he did it so Connor would marry me." She shifted her attention back to her father then. "But how did you know he'd go along with your plan?"

"I knew he'd put a mortgage on his house to pay Deacon's tuition," Ben confessed. "And I saw the way he looked at you, the day you told us you were pregnant, and I knew he'd do almost anything for you—even give his name to your babies."

There it was again, the reference to "your babies," as if her father knew—or at least suspected—that Connor wasn't their biological father.

"I don't understand," Regan said now. "For most of my life, you barely showed any interest in where I was or what I was doing, and now suddenly you're not only interested but interfering."

"We've always wanted what's best for you," Ben said again.

"Maybe you should have conferred with Mom first, because I don't think she believes Connor fits the bill."

"I'll admit I had some reservations when you first brought him home," Margaret said. "But only because he's not your usual type."

"What's my usual type?" Regan wondered.

"Well…" Her mother faltered a little. "You never really brought anyone home before."

"Or maybe you were just never there to meet the friends I did bring home."

"And if I had some reservations," Margaret continued, pointedly ignoring the truth of her daughter's remark, "well, the fact that you moved back home after only a few months proves they weren't unfounded."

"I didn't move," she denied. "I only needed some time to think about the fact that my husband had reasons for marrying me that I knew nothing about."

"How much time do you think you need?" her father asked. "Because you can't expect him to sit around waiting for you to stop being mad at him."

"I'm also mad at you," she pointed out.

"Do you want me to apologize?"

"Are you sorry?" she challenged.

"No," he admitted. "Because he's a good man—and a good husband to you and father to your babies."

She felt the sting of fresh tears. "He is a good husband and father."

"Do you love him?" her father asked gently.

She swiped at the tear that spilled onto her cheek. "Yes, but that doesn't make what you did okay."

"He loves you, too," he said. "Even if he hasn't told you so."

Another tear; another swipe. "How do you know?"

"Because your husband and I have more in common than you know."

"What do you have in common with Connor Neal?" Margaret asked.

Ben smiled at his wife. "For starters, we both fell in love with women who were way out of our league."

She smiled back. "It's true," she told their daughter now. "We've been together so long, I sometimes forget how socially awkward and financially challenged Benjamin was when we first met."

"That's your mother's way of saying I was a geek—and broke."

"But you were a cute broke geek," Margaret noted affectionately.

"And you were popular and beautiful and a Blake, and I fell head over heels the first time I saw you."

"And six months later, I finally agreed to go out with you—just so you'd stop asking," Margaret recalled fondly. "Then you kissed me good-night, and I was so glad I'd finally said yes."

Maybe it did warm Regan's heart to see the obvious and enduring affection between her parents, but she'd come into the office today to try to figure out what she was going to do about her own marriage.

"I need to go home," she suddenly realized.

"We'll see you at dinner then," Margaret responded, without looking away from her husband.

Regan shook her head. "No. I need to go home to Connor—to tell him that I want to make our marriage work."

"I think that's the right decision," Ben told her.

Before she could say anything else, her cell phone buzzed.

A quick glance at the screen revealed Connor's name on the display, and her heart skipped a beat.

"Are you going to answer it?" Margaret asked.

She nodded and swiped her finger across the screen. But when the call connected, it wasn't her husband on the other end of the line.

It was the sheriff.

"What's wrong?" Ben asked, when Regan disconnected.

She opened her mouth, then closed it again, unable to say the words.

"Regan?" her mother prompted, concern evident in her tone.

"He… Connor… He was shot."

"Shot?" Ben and Margaret echoed together.

Regan nodded. "He's okay," she told her parents, desperately clinging to that belief. "The sheriff said he was wearing a vest, but they took him to the hospital in Battle Mountain to be checked out, just as a precaution. I need to go there. To Battle Mountain."

"We'll all go," Margaret said.

Regan nodded again, but her feet remained glued to the floor while the upper part of her body seemed to be swaying.

"Sit down." Her mom nudged her into a chair. "I'm going to get you a glass of water."

Regan sat. She felt simultaneously hot and cold— empty inside and somehow full of churning emotions. But she didn't realize she was crying until her dad handed her a tissue as her mom returned with a glass of water.

"I wasn't done being mad at him," she said, dabbing at the wetness on her cheeks.

"So those are angry tears?" Margaret asked.

"I don't know why I'm crying," she admitted.

"Maybe they're tears of relief," Ben suggested. "Because you know he's okay."

"Maybe," she allowed.

"And maybe, somewhere deep beneath the hurt and anger, you're realizing that the phone call could have given you very different news," her dad said gently.

Fresh tears began to fall. "Ohmygod—he could have died."

"But he didn't," Margaret pointed out in a matter-of-fact tone. "And the sheriff said he's going to be fine."

But Regan knew she wouldn't believe it until she saw him for herself.

"I do love him," she sniffled.

"Then tell him that," Ben advised.

"I will," she vowed. "The first chance I get."

Connor didn't see why he needed to go to the hospital, but the sheriff had stood firm.

"You're going to get checked out," Reid insisted. "Then you're going to go home where your wife can fuss over your bruises."

Which didn't really sound so bad, except that Connor knew better than to count on Regan fussing over him. He was still trying to figure out how to convince her to come home.

"Knock knock."

He glanced over as the curtain was pulled back.

Mallory, a little girl he guessed was her six-year-old daughter, and another woman he vaguely recognized stepped into the exam area.

Though the effort made his chest hurt, he sat up on the table. "Hey," he said, not sure what else to say in the presence of the child.

"Hey," Mallory said back, and offered a wan smile. "You remember my sister Miranda?"

He nodded. "It's good to see you again."

"Same goes, Deputy," Miranda said.

"And this is my daughter, Chloe," Mallory said, brushing a hand over the little girl's hair.

"It's nice to meet you, Chloe."

The child watched him with wary eyes.

"The sheriff said you were okay," Mallory noted. "But we needed to see for ourselves."

"I'm okay," he confirmed.

Chloe didn't look convinced. "Daddy had a gun," she said quietly.

He nodded. "And you were very brave to call the police and tell them that."

"We learned about 911 at school," she said.

"Now you know why it's important to pay attention in class."

He caught the hint of a shy smile before she ducked her head again.

"Why don't we go see what they've got to eat in the cafeteria?" Miranda suggested to her niece.

"Mommy come, too," Chloe said, reluctant to let go of her mother's hand.

"You go with Aunt Mandy—I'll catch up with you in a few minutes," Mallory said, and pressed her lips to the top of her daughter's head.

"Promise?"

"Promise," Mallory said, and drew a cross over her heart with her finger.

The little girl finally let go of her mother's hand to take the one offered by her aunt.

"I'm glad you called your sister," Connor said.

Mallory nodded. "We're going to stay with her, here

in Battle Mountain, for a few days. We can't go home until the sheriff's department clears the scene, anyway."

"And then what?" he asked her.

She shrugged. "Hopefully I'll figure that out over the next few days."

"How's your husband?" When Turcotte pulled the trigger, the sheriff had responded—and Turcotte hadn't been wearing a vest.

"Still in surgery," she said.

"So…you finally told him you wanted a divorce?"

She nodded. "But I had no idea he had a gun. If I'd known…"

"If he makes it through the surgery, he'll be going to jail for a long time," Connor said, when her words faltered.

"I know." She brushed away the tears that spilled onto her cheeks. "I don't want him to die. He's the father of my child, but…I can't help thinking that she might be better off without a dad rather than have one who's in jail."

Her comment made Connor consider that never knowing his own father might not have been a detriment. It also reinforced his determination to be the best father he could be to Piper and Poppy—and any other kids he and Regan might have together, if he could convince her to give him a second chance.

Regan had planned to play it cool. For Connor's sake as much as her own. She understood that being a deputy wasn't just his job but an integral part of his identity, and she didn't want him to think she was going to get hysterical every time he had a little mishap on the job.

But this wasn't a minor mishap—this was a major event. Her husband had been face-to-face with an armed suspect, working to de-escalate a dangerous situation, and was rewarded with a bullet for his efforts. Someone had actually pointed a gun at him and pulled the trigger.

She couldn't envision the scene. She didn't want to. Every time she thought about Connor in that situation, she felt dizzy and nauseated and more terrified than she could ever remember feeling. But it was his job to put himself in exactly those types of situations and if she loved him—and she did!—she needed to accept that there were inherent risks to wearing a uniform and trust that he would take all necessary precautions to stay safe and come home to her and their daughters at the end of every shift.

Thankfully her parents had driven her to the hospital, so she didn't have to think about anything but Connor. Maybe they'd missed out on a lot when she was growing up, but they were here for her now and she was grateful for their support. She was also grateful that they opted to wait outside while she went in alone to see her husband.

Play it cool.

A reminder that she promptly forgot when she saw him sitting up on the examination table—alive and in one piece with no visible blood to be found. Unable to hold herself back, she flew into his arms.

He caught her close, enveloping her in the warmth and strength of his embrace. But she didn't miss the sharp hiss as he sucked in a breath.

She drew back, just far enough to see the pained expression on his face.

"What is it? What's wrong?"

"I'm a little sore," he admitted.

"The sheriff said that you were wearing a vest. That you weren't hurt."

"The Kevlar absorbed most of the impact," he conceded. "But a bullet still leaves a mark."

She pulled all the way out of his arms now to shove his T-shirt up, gasping when she saw the colorful bruise blooming in angry shades of red and purple against his skin. "Ohmygod."

"Are you going to kiss it better?" he asked.

"How can you make jokes about this?" she demanded, fighting to hold back a fresh onslaught of tears.

"It looks worse than it feels. Well, maybe not," he acknowledged. "But it's just a bruise."

"From a *bullet*," she said. "You could have been killed."

The devastating truth washed over her again, and she collapsed into sobs.

He tried to pull her back into his arms, but she held herself at a distance, explaining, "I don't want to hurt you."

"Having you here, being able to hold you, is the best possible medicine," he told her.

She wasn't sure she believed him, but she stopped resisting, because in his arms was where she wanted to be.

She sniffled. "I can't believe you were *shot*."

"It was pretty damn scary for me, too," he confided to her now. "And I did have a moment… My life didn't flash before my eyes…or maybe it did," he decided. "Because when I was staring at the gun, all I could think of was you.

"And I promised myself that if I made it out of there in one piece, I'd do whatever I had to do to make things right. Because you are my life. My everything."

He cradled her face in his hands, gently wiping the tears from her cheeks. "I love you, Regan. So much."

They were the words she'd wanted him to say, and hearing them now both filled and healed her heart.

"I love you, too," she told him.

He smiled then. "I kind of figured that out from what you said when you were yelling at me the other day."

"I was hurt and angry and—"

"And you had every right to be," he said. "I should have told you the truth from the beginning."

"Or at any other time over the past nine-and-a-half months," she suggested.

"You're right," he acknowledged. "But I was afraid that if I told you the truth, I'd lose you. And I didn't—don't ever—want to lose you."

"You're not going to lose me."

"Does that mean you'll come home?" he asked.

"I'd already decided to do just that when the sheriff called."

"Good," he said. "Because there's nothing I want more than a life with you and our daughters."

"I want that, too," she told him. "And…maybe another baby someday."

He brushed his lips over hers. "It's as if you read my mind."

Epilogue

"**W**hen my mom called to invite us for dinner, I didn't realize it was going to be a family affair," Regan remarked, as Connor pulled into the driveway where several other vehicles were already parked.

"Do you think they know it's our anniversary?" he asked.

"I wasn't sure *you* remembered it was our anniversary," she admitted.

"Of course I remembered. I even booked our suite at The Stagecoach Inn."

"*Our* suite?" she asked, amused.

"Well, I can't help but feel a little proprietary about the room where I first had the pleasure of making love with my beautiful wife," he confessed.

"I have very fond memories of that room, too," she assured him. "And I'm eager to make more, so what do you say we skip this dinner and go straight to the hotel?"

"An undeniably tempting offer," he said. "But unless you want to take Piper and Poppy with us, we have to go inside."

"But we don't have to stay for dessert."

He chuckled as he opened the back door to retrieve the babies' car seats. "We won't stay for dessert," he agreed.

But their plans for a quick meal and quicker exit were thwarted by the discovery that Father Douglas had been invited to share the meal—and preside over a renewal of Connor and Regan's vows.

"We weren't there to share in the celebration of your wedding," Margaret explained. "So we were hoping you would exchange vows again today."

"You might have asked if this was something we wanted to do, rather than springing it on us," Regan noted.

"I want to do it," Connor said, before his mother-in-law had a chance to respond.

"Really?" His wife sounded dubious.

Margaret clapped her hands together excitedly. "Oh, this is wonderful."

"I haven't said *I* want to do it," Regan pointed out.

"I'll let you two discuss," her mother said, and slipped out of the room.

"For what it's worth, I think my parents set this up to show that they've accepted you as part of the family," she said, when they were alone.

"I only ever cared that I was accepted by you," he told her.

"Then you don't want to do the vow renewal?" she asked.

"No, I do want to do it," he said again. "My only regret, when we got married, was that I couldn't be completely honest with you about the reasons for my proposal. So today—" he dropped to one knee on the marble tile "—I'm asking you to marry me again, to take me as your husband and a father to your children, with no secrets between us, knowing that I love you with my whole heart and will continue to do so for all the days of our life together."

"And I actually thought I was starting to regain control of my emotions," Regan said, as her eyes filled with tears.

"Is that a yes or a no?" Connor asked.

"That's a very emphatic yes," she told him. "Because I love you with my whole heart, et cetera."

He lifted a brow. "Did you really just say 'et cetera' in response to my heartfelt declaration?"

"*After* I said that I loved you," she pointed out.

He grinned. "In that case, let's go get hitched so we can get to part two of our honeymoon."

And that's what they did.

* * * * *

MILLS & BOON

Coming next month

SUMMER ESCAPE WITH THE TYCOON
Donna Alward

"This is a great spot," Molly said, leaning back to look at the stars that had popped out overhead. "I mean, I know this is supposed to be some great adventure tour, but I feel as if I'm in the lap of luxury. Wineries and great food and a massage and a soak in a hot tub. It's positively indulgent."

"Enjoy it now. In a few days we'll be roughing it."

The mood had changed a bit, and Molly felt a bit off-balance. She hadn't really been tested so far on this trip, and now she was afraid of looking silly in front of Eric as the more challenging aspects were just ahead. He seemed so…capable. Of anything.

"Just think, though," he said softly. "We'll be out there surrounded by nature, seeing orcas and sea lions and who knows what else? It's pretty amazing."

"I'm trying not to be intimidated."

"But you are?"

She nodded, deciding to confide a little. What would it hurt? That was the whole purpose of the trip, wasn't it? To stretch her boundaries a little? Besides, after this trip was over, she'd never see him again. There was some safety in that.

"I'm good at what I do, but I've lived a pretty sheltered life." Especially since Jack's death, and she was left an only child. "I'm not used to feeling vulnerable. So while kayaking with killer whales sounds amazing and exciting, it's also way out of my comfort zone. I mean…" She gestured down at herself. "I'm this size. And an orca is…"

"Much, much bigger."

"I have this fear that one will swim under my kayak and flip me over."

"We'll stay close to shore. I don't think you have to worry about that."

"Probably not. But…it is what it is." She smiled weakly. "Please don't use that against me."

"I won't." He studied her with a somber expression. "I don't believe in using people's fears against them."

She thought about that for a moment. "Really? Because I'd think that might be a strategy for someone in acquisitions. A negotiating tactic."

He tilted his head as he thought for a minute. "No," he answered. "I might exploit a weakness, but not a fear. And yes, there's a difference."

He removed one arm from the edge of the hot tub and turned to face her, only inches away. Her pulse hammered at her throat as his gaze captured hers. "What you just said? That's a fear." He moved an inch closer. "But the way I'm feeling right now, this close to you? That's a weakness."

Her breath caught. "Are you asking me to exploit it?"

His gaze dropped to her lips, then back up to her eyes. "Oh, it's tempting. Very tempting."

Continue reading
SUMMER ESCAPE WITH THE TYCOON
Donna Alward

Available next month
www.millsandboon.co.uk

COMING SOON!

We really hope you enjoyed reading this book. If you're looking for more romance, be sure to head to the shops when new books are available on

Thursday 30th May

To see which titles are coming soon, please visit

millsandboon.co.uk/nextmonth

LET'S TALK
Romance

For exclusive extracts, competitions
and special offers, find us online: